To,

Still Water

every second every breath

by

A.M. Johnson

BLUE TULIP
PUBLISHING

Still Water
by A.M. Johnson
Published by Blue Tulip Publishing
www.bluetulippublishing.com

This is a work of fiction. Names, places, characters, and events are fictitious in every regard. Any similarities to actual events and persons, living or dead, are purely coincidental. Any trademarks, service marks, product names, or named features are assumed to be the property of their respective owners, and are used only for reference. There is no implied endorsement if any of these terms are used. Except for review purposes, the reproduction of this book in whole or part, electronically or mechanically, constitutes a copyright violation.

STILL WATER
Copyright © 2015 A.M. JOHNSON
ISBN 13: 978-1517019471
ISBN: 1517019478
Cover art by Francessca Romance Reviews

To the underdogs…tell fate she can go to hell.

*For Tracey-Lee,
Every minute…Every second…
I am grateful for you.*

PROLOGUE

Todd

THE CLIPPED NOTES OF THE PIANO keys echoed throughout the high arches of the old church. The last of the guests entered through the large wooden double doors. They filed in like herded sheep, eager for a glimpse. The sweat trickled down my temple, and I felt as if I was suffocating. I pulled at my tie and collar with my index finger hoping no one could see how nervous I was. Nervous wasn't the right word. No... I felt sick... confused. I wasn't sure how I would make it through this. My panic started to rise, as did the bile in my gut, just in time for the quelling silence. The piano began playing the familiar tune as I turned anxiously towards the back of the church again.

She looked utterly phenomenal. The rise and fall of my chest was rapid, and my throat was like sand paper as I tried to swallow. The ivory gown wrapped around her body like a glove, and her thick dark hair fell over one shoulder in silken waves. Her full lips were painted red and begged to be kissed. I was so lucky to witness this, to see her looking so beautiful, so ethereal. I couldn't wait to touch her, to wrap my arms around her and tell her how much I loved her. She beamed. Her smile engulfed all my senses.

My father, who had been like a dad to her, guided her down the long aisle to her future — her happily ever after. Her pace was quiet and elegant, taking her to the place where her life would begin… and where my life would be destroyed.

"She looks… spectacular." I heard the groom murmur as he watched her approach.

I pulled all my suffering together and slapped him on the back in a friendly gesture just like any good groomsman should do. "She's all yours, brother." The pang in my stomach twisted and when he turned to look at me, I saw the trust, love, and joy in his eyes. He was the one that deserved her. He was good for her. I let myself grin. For once my smile felt genuine; she was happy with him, and that's all I ever really wanted for her anyway. In the end, it's all that mattered.

CHAPTER ONE

Todd

Three Years Later

THE HEAT OF THE MID-MORNING SUN burned the bare skin of my chest as I rolled onto my right side: groaning, still half asleep, trying to escape the oppressive rays. The swift movement just intensified the train roaring in my head. My cotton tongue stuck to the roof of my mouth, and my lips felt like leather as I tried to lick them for relief. The sick taste of morning breath, alcohol, and whatever bar fly I brought back here last night coated my taste buds and made me feel nauseous. A small feminine hand snaked its way across my rib cage, and my body went rigid. I never allowed them to stay the whole night. I must have been really wasted last night.

"Mmmm... hey baby." The woman's voice sounded too fucking high pitched for me this early in the morning. "Last night was—"

"Was last night," I interrupted. I quickly moved away from her unwanted touch and sat on the edge of my bed resting my elbows on my knees. I pinched the bridge of my nose to contain the anger, the ever present self-loathing, from boiling over. I was such a screw-up. I was sitting here buck ass naked with a strange woman in my bed. *This shit has got to stop*. I felt the mattress shift as the weight of the woman was removed. She was silent, thank God. I was afraid to look at her, but I knew I had to acknowledge her. Otherwise, she'd never leave. I chanced a glance over my shoulder and cringed. Don't get me wrong. She was a total smoke show. Tall, thin, big ass fake tits I could get lost in, but she wasn't *her*. She was the opposite. Always... always the opposite.

"Don't look at me like that. You don't get to look at me... *ever again*," she screeched as she pulled her skanky dress, which hardly covered that spectacular rack, over her head. I inwardly sighed. Like I gave a shit if I ever saw this chick again. I stood up, found my boxer briefs, and quickly pulled them on noticing the condom wrapper on the floor. My eyes raised to the ceiling in a desperate thank you. At least I wasn't *that* drunk. *Yeah, this shit has got to stop*.

"Look..." I struggled to remember her name. *Rebecca, Reid...*

Her face scrunched up into a very unattractive pout. "Seriously? My name is Rikki... God, you're an asshole." She grabbed her bag from my dresser.

I couldn't help myself, I laughed. "I'm an asshole?" My laughter was full force now. I mean, who the hell does she think she is? She just screwed a complete stranger, and I'm the jerk? Double standard. Her glare was as sharp as a knife. The red blood shot of a rough night crowded her blue eyes. *Blue eyes*. My laughing abruptly stopped. I never banged chicks with blue eyes... those were *her* eyes.

"Get the fuck out!" my voice rasped. She stood there in fear or shock; I didn't really care. I made an effort to calm my breathing. "Please... just get out," I said in a much softer tone as I sat on the bed, dropping my heavy head into my hands.

I couldn't do this to myself anymore. It had been three years since she'd gotten married. Most guys would've moved on by now, but most guys never had the promise of a girl like *her*. He did though, and *she* was his now. She was in such a good place with him. They made each other better, and she deserved a man like him, a man like my friend. I let my body fall back on the bed, the dark navy blue down comforter taking me within its soft depths while I scowled at the ceiling. Rikki had left without another word.

My best friend, the girl I thought I was going to marry, married someone else. I inhaled a deep breath. Generally, if I were being this big of a pussy, I'd go pick a fight with my roommate Seth. He doesn't put up with my shit and would, for sure, pop my stupid ass in the jaw. But last night was *her* birthday, and I'd allowed myself one night of misery no matter the consequence. Now, as I lay in my bed with last night's regret still lingering on my sheets, I would let the memories of her wash over me and let them ruin me one more time.

The classroom was so full. My momma told me not to worry. She said I'd make friends. My hands were sweaty, and my stomach was turning inside out. I noticed the boy sitting next to me was picking his nose. I moved my body away from him so fast. Yuck! My momma said picking your nose was disgusting. I thought so too. Suddenly, my shoulder bumped the person next to me.

"Hey, watch it!" she said as she shoved me.

"Sorry." I turned and looked into eyes that were the prettiest blue I'd ever seen. "Whoa!" I said without thinking.

"Whoa, what?" She looked at me like I was a dummy.

"Your eyes remind me of these really cool glass marbles I have." I smiled.

"My eyes look like marbles?" Her voice sounded hurt.

"Well... yeah. You see, I have these—"

"Just shut up. You're such a—a... big... mean... jerk!"

"I wasn't... I mean... I think they're pretty." I smiled, hoping she wouldn't call me names again.

"You think marbles are pretty?" She turned her head to the side and looked at me like I was a dummy again.

"Sure do!" I made my smile wider. She smiled back.

"Well, thanks... I guess... I'm Elizabeth."

"I'm Todd." My mouth reacted to her smile and pulled into its own giant grin. I had just met the prettiest girl in the whole wide world.

The memory had my mouth turned up into a lopsided smile. Even then, she was just beautiful. Kindergarten... we were so far away from that now. It had been over a year since I'd spoken to Lizzie. She still sent me text messages on special occasions, and, sometimes, she'd send me pictures of her daughter as well. Liz was always trying to keep me tied to her in some way. I'd known Elizabeth Haddington my whole life. She was Elizabeth Bryant now. She had married my old roommate Sawyer. They had a baby together, and she was now living a life with her own family. You would think my dumbass would have gotten over it, but how was I supposed to do that when all I'd ever wanted was her. I had shared everything with her. She lost her parents tragically when she was young and lived with my family and me for hell's sake. We grew up together; we were into all the same things and hung out in a close-knit group of people. Hell, I lost my virginity to this chick. She was everything I ever wanted and more. She was my purpose, even if I wasn't hers. It hadn't felt like three years had passed since I moved to Salt Lake, but thinking about her like this brought it all rushing back.

My chest was so fucking tight. This was it — this was our end. We never even had a chance. My head felt heavy as the blood from my pounding heart rushed through it like a rogue wave.

"I need to know... are you happy?" I closed the gap between us leaving just enough space so that I could attempt to breathe when she twisted the final turn of the knife in my heart.

"Yes, very," her voice was laced with pity. I didn't need Liz's pity. I needed her love, I needed her lips on my mouth, her body perfectly connected with mine, her small hand wrapped up in my palm, her laughter always filling the air, and her smile every

goddamn morning when I woke up. I needed her. Just her. But she was Sawyer's now, and he loved her just as much as me. I had to step back to catch my breath. The space between us was weighted with so much pain and regret... I couldn't stand it.

"I never wanted to hurt you," her voice was tight from holding back her tears. She loved me — just not like I needed, never ever how I needed. I had created this illusion. I had to make it better... I had to let go. I watched as she broke in two when I told her I was leaving for good. The vacant feeling in my heart as I watched her cry for the loss of us was more than I could handle. I closed the distance that was quickly building between us. I was only moving an hour away, but we both knew what was actually happening. There wasn't one part of me that wanted to stay here and watch her be happy without me; I was such a selfish asshole.

I pulled her tiny frame against my body and completely enveloped Elizabeth with my arms, resting my head on the top of hers, and inhaled her sweet gardenia scent one last time. I could feel her cool tears soak through my shirt.

"Oh God, I'm going to miss you so much." She struggled to catch her own breath as sobs shook through her body. She had no idea how much I was going to miss her — this moment had entirely shattered me.

"It's only an hour away. I'll still see you. I'll come watch you guys play with whoever you get to play guitar." I tried to smile, lighten the mood by bringing up our band that was now short a member. I didn't want her to see that she had ruined me. I couldn't do that to her.

"You won't be ten minutes away anymore. Distance, no matter how far, changes everything, and, besides, I can't do the band without you. You know that. I would never replace you."

"You already have," my voice was so quiet I hoped she didn't hear.

"What did you say?" She looked up into my eyes. I prayed the mask I always wore held tight.

"Nothing, baby girl." Nothing of consequence. Nothing that

will change anything. Nothing... I had nothing. *What the hell do I do now?*

This entire mental digression sucked. All these memories were still so fresh, and I needed a reprieve. I stood up and walked into the bathroom to wash off the previous night's mistake. The hot water pounded my tightly wound muscles loose as the steam pulled me back down making it possible for me to relax. Placing both hands against the tiles in front of me, I hung my head underneath the heavy stream of water. I watched the water run over my inked up chest and arms. The small rivers made the artwork look alive. The distinguishable alert my phone made when I'd received a text broke me from my trance. I took a couple of cleansing breaths before I quickly scrubbed my body and hair. As much as I wanted to linger here, I had to face the day at some point.

I wrapped a towel loosely around my waist, grabbed my phone, swiped the unlock screen, and my stomach fell. It's like she knew I was thinking about her. *Shit.* I almost didn't want to open the text. Who was I kidding? There was no way I wasn't opening the damn text. If I thought my day couldn't get any shitter, I was wrong.

Lizzie: *Just thinking of you. We miss you round these parts. Sailor's first birthday was last month. I wish you could have made it.*

Underneath the text was a picture of Elizabeth and her daughter, Sailor. Lizzie looked beautiful — her face was still a bit full from the weight she'd gained during the pregnancy and her dark brown hair was shiny. And Sailor? She was the cutest damn baby I'd ever seen. She had huge blue eyes and dark chocolate curls. *She is going to break someone's heart with those eyes, just like her mother.* I think I noticed a tooth; I chuckled. This picture was just what I needed. I shook my head as I looked at my stupid mug in the mirror. *Who the hell is that guy?*

"I'm such an idiot," I spoke out loud and swore under my

breath. I was missing out on everything all because I chose to bury my damn head in the sand. "Fuck it," I blurted to the image in the mirror as I turned and leaned against the bathroom sink. I dialed the number that had caused me so much panic over the last three years. The phone rang four times; with each ring my heart skipped a beat.

"Todd...?" Lizzie's voice was surprised, and she sounded out of breath. I heard the most amazing little giggle in the background. Sailor. "Todd? Is... is that you?" It felt like a whole minute before I spoke. My brain was misfiring at hearing her voice again — the noise of her home, her life moving forward in the background. How could I bring myself to say the words, to take myself back there again? "Please talk to me," her voice broke and shook my resolve.

"Hey, baby girl." My lips curled into an involuntary smile at my term of endearment for her.

She let out a long sigh. "Hey."

"Um... erm... how ya been, Lizzie Bean?" I wasn't sure what to say. I needed to lighten the dark cloud that had fallen the minute she picked up the phone.

Her soft laugh filtered through the speaker. "It's been over a year. I miss you so much. Sawyer misses you too." And there it was... the reason I stayed away. She wasn't mine anymore. "Gosh Todd, you don't even know my daughter." Liz's voice trembled, and I could tell she was crying. My selfish prick ass was the reason her tears were probably falling hard right now. I needed to stop and grow the hell up.

"I know. I've been a shitty friend."

She chuckled. "Yeah, you have." I heard her sniffle. A small cooing "Mama" came across the line.

"Listen, you sound busy. How about I come up and have dinner soon?" I had to do this. I had to make myself move the hell on.

"Really? That would be great. How about Friday?" The excitement in her voice was tangible.

"Friday doesn't work, baby girl. We're short a bartender. I have to work, but I could come up Sunday. We're closed Sundays."

"Sunday sounds great. Five-thirty okay with you? Sailor goes to bed by eight. I'd like you to spend some time with her."

"Sounds good. See you then, Lizzie Bean." I hoped she couldn't hear how the small plastic phone rattled in my anxious hands.

"See, you." The line went silent.

THE IGNITION OF MY 2009 Toyota 4Runner growled, subduing any apprehension I had from the earlier call to Liz. I loved this piece of shit. I'd had it forever. The silver paint was faded in all the right places, and it had a few old band stickers that were peeling off the back window. This girl had character. I smirked. The best part was it had the perfect amount of space for most of my band equipment. My smile grew as I pulled out of my parking space. *Some things just never get old.* I picked a song from my playlist and started the mental preparation for work. It sucked being short staffed; I needed to hire someone pretty damn quick.

I managed Blue Bar down in Salt Lake. I loved my damn job. I got to play my music with my band once a week and drink for free, but the best part... the owner and I ran a small local record label. Even though I'd been hiding out from my past, the choice I made to move down south was probably the best thing I'd ever done. I was tired of living the small town, farm boy life in good ole West Haven, Utah. Elizabeth getting together with Sawyer just gave me the final shove I needed to get my own life back. At first, it was hard to say goodbye. To be honest, I didn't really want to leave. Elizabeth and my close high school friend, Cam, and I had an awesome band of our own. We were really picking up a huge following. Seth, my now roommate and old friend, had been our drummer. But watching Lizzie live a life without me. No. Fucking. Way. I transferred my credits, moved to Salt Lake, and I had recently graduated with a degree in business.

Seth and I had our own band now, a four-piece with these two dudes we met while out drinking one night. Jack was an amazing bass player, and Graden? Well, that kid could lay it down on the guitar. I sang and also played guitar. We played every Tuesday at Blue. Music always had a way of making everything seem all right, even if it was only temporary.

I pulled into the back lot of the bar and let the song on my iPod play out before I headed inside. My mind was a complete suckfest. How in the world was I going to make it through Sunday dinner at Elizabeth's house? What the hell was I thinking? *Shit.* I needed reinforcements, and I knew exactly who to ask. I pulled my phone from the center console and sent a quick text to my old best friend, and, if I was a betting man, my soon to be sister-in-law.

Me: *I need you.*
Cam: *Don't be sending me dirty texts anymore. Are you drunk?*

I laughed aloud. Cameron Sealy had been my best friend since kindergarten. I had tried to defend Lizzie over an issue with a marker, if I remember correctly. Anyway, the bitch, Cam, was so stubborn. I think I made her cry, so Elizabeth full on hit me. Since then I can't remember a time Cam hasn't been around. In fact, she's around way more than I like now. My brother Colby started dating her a few years ago, and now they're just the perfect damn couple. I rolled my eyes. They fight so badly all the time. It's actually quite comical. Colby always tries to brag about the make-up sex. I shut that shit show of a conversation down real quick. I didn't need to know what Cameron was like in the sack. Don't get me wrong. She is super-hot. Five foot ten, all legs, and long strawberry blonde hair, but I looked at her like a sister. I definitely didn't want to know where her "sweet spots" were. I outwardly cringed at the thought as I typed out my reply.

Me: *Hell no, I'm not drunk! I'm just getting to work.*

Cam: *OK? What do you want? I'm busy. Some of us still go to school. We can't all be fancy graduates.*

I might as well just be blunt.

Me: *I'm going to Liz's for dinner on Sunday. Go with me?*

I waited two whole minutes for a reply.

Me: *Please... I can't do it alone.*

Her next text came immediately

Cam: *I will. I'm so happy right now! I could freaking burst! About time, you moron. What time is dinner?*

I swore. About damn time... Whatever.

Me: *5:30. Bring my stupid ass little brother.*

Cam: *Duh ;) Love ya, Toodles.*

I hated that nickname.

Me: *Don't call me that. See you Sunday, whore.*

Cam: *Nice, real nice. Love you, asshat.*

Cammie and I always had our way; she had me clutching my stomach in laughter at her last text. I was so busy laughing my damn head off I didn't realize I was late. I was stalling, dreading the paperwork I knew was piled high. Frank, my boss, needed help with the label, so I'd taken the first half of the week off. He had signed a new folk band out of Denver. We spent the better part of the week in the studio with them. Their music had a real nice vibe, the best talent we had signed yet. My assistant manager Tiffany was a hard ass; she hated the personnel aspect of the job. She was spitting daggers at me when I'd told her it was her job to hand out the applications. I was sure there were shit loads of applications sitting on my desk right now.

I turned off the car and grabbed my phone. It was now three-thirty. Tiffany was going to bite my head off for being late. I needed to hire someone quick unless I wanted a murder on my hands. Tiff was very temperamental.

My key slid into the back door of the bar. The smell of bleach, pine, and musty cigarettes assaulted my senses as the door opened. Home. I smiled a small sideways grin. The sound system out in the front of the bar was playing loudly, and I recognized the song immediately as *"Waiting Room,"* by the old school band Fugazi. The deep bass beat resonated through the dark hall of the back offices. I set down my stuff on my desk, and, sure as shit, the applications were scattered everywhere. I released an annoyed sigh before I headed out front to see what was in store for me. The fact that Tiffany had music on was a good sign. She was a tiny little thing with long, straight jet-black hair, at least ten piercings in each ear, and covered in tattoos. Yeah, she looked harmless, but I knew better. She'd mess me up before I'd even have the chance to say hello. That little sprite packed a mean punch to the nuts. I knew… personally.

Tiffany's history was why I was nervous coming out of that back hallway. She hated my ass for leaving her to run the joint. As I stepped through the back hallway door, I came to a complete halt. Looking around bewildered for a minute, I gawked at the hot piece behind the bar. The song had picked up, and she was singing and dancing her ass off while dusting the bottles we'd lit up for decoration. *Damn.*

I took a few steps closer to the bar. Her back was facing me, thank God. Otherwise, my deliberate stare probably would've freaked her out. She was totally curvy, petite as hell… sweetest ass I'd ever seen. She was shaking it as she belted out the lyrics. Her hair – Holy shit that hair! – was wild and curly. The copper color shone brilliantly under the can lights of the bar. I was stock still, trapped by just the sight of her. Her hair like a flame licked up and down. It was everywhere. She reminded me of that Scottish Disney chick Seth's little niece always watched. She had on black skinny jeans that hugged every blessed curve of her body. The tight, gray T-shirt she wore had a small surfboard printed on the back in between her shoulder blades. The odd logo in a land-locked state brought me back down from my overly aroused senses.

What the hell was wrong with me? She was just a chick. I haven't had a response to a female like this since… well ever. Lizzie was the only one who could grind all my inner workings to a halt. Until now. It was time for me to pull my shit together.

"Excuse me…" Nothing. I cleared my throat and spoke louder. "Excuse me."

The girl squeaked and about fell over. She knocked over her spray bottle of cleaner and caught herself on the bar with her hands.

"Holy shit, are you okay?" I burned up the concrete to get to her. She could have broken her damn neck. *Whoa… simmer down, Todd*. My inner dialog was pissing me off.

The chick's face hid nothing as she freely drank in all of me with her eyes. Her high cheekbones turned pink. I'd been a swimmer in college, and, since then, my focus was to bulk up a bit more. I'd always been somewhat tall, six foot one with a shit ton of lean muscle. Once I was finished with swimming, I wanted to push my body, see what I could do with it. Besides music, fitness had become my only other hobby. I watched as her eyes took in all the ink. Her mouth popped open in surprise, and I could tell she liked what she saw.

"You… you scared me." Her voice had a deep quality to it, and it was sexy as hell.

"Who the hell are you?" As captivated by this girl as I might have been, I wasn't sure why she was in my bar. My manner was a bit severe, and she stepped back making me immediately regret the tone of my voice.

"I work here." She stood taller before she said, "Who the hell are you?" Her eyes fixed on mine, and I about lost my mind. The large, open, store front windows let in enough natural light that once I got closer her eyes were all I was able to focus on. I had never, and I mean never, seen eyes this color in my life. They were cat yellow with green specks and rimmed with a slight burst of blue. *Was she wearing contacts?* I shook my head slightly and remembered I was supposed to be talking when I noticed she had a smug ass look on her face.

"I'm the fucking boss, sweetheart." I rubbed the back of my neck causing my shirt to ride up and expose a small sliver of my inked up abs. Her eyes immediately darted down. She bit her bottom lip and then quickly brought her eyes back up to mine. It was my turn to be smug. "I'm going to ask you again, why are you in my damn bar?" I took the last step toward the wooden counter. I placed both my hands on the shellacked surface and leaned in waiting for an answer.

"I started working here yesterday. Tiffany hired me." She looked at me like this shit was obvious.

"You got a name?" I couldn't force my eyes away from hers. The green flecks appeared to move when the light hit them just right. They were surreal.

"Lily, my name's Lily." Her irritated scowl dissipated as she held out her hand. "Nice to meet you... *Boss.*" She gave me a megawatt smile that made me weak in the knees. *What the hell was wrong with me?*

"Todd." I took her delicate hand in mine. The dark purple nail polish on her fingernails created a crème like tone on her skin. I had the urge to place my lips on the soft flesh. For just a moment, I thought, I would have died right then for just one taste. Of course, I didn't. I kept it together.

"Todd, nice to meet you." She shook my hand. As I let go of her palm, I gently rubbed my thumb against the satin feel of her skin. It was entirely instinctive; I had no control over the gesture. A soft sound whispered from her lips as she noticed the small touch.

"I'm looking forward to working with you." And I was. If the smile on my face wasn't proof enough, I didn't know what was. This unreal girl... the girl with wildfire for hair and cat eyes was going to be here, in my bar, at least four days a week. Sunday dinner at Liz's didn't seem so bad now. Having this chick here couldn't have happened at a better time. I was a lucky son of a bitch. I started to push away from the bar and noticed a wedding band hanging from a silver chain around her neck. It rested above her full breasts. The gray V-neck amplified her cleavage. I took a deep breath to calm my stimulated hormones. *Is she married?* Of course she'd be married. Why on earth would a girl like her be single? Figures. I was instantly pissed.

"Me too. Tiffany said this place is the best bar in town. I'm lucky she hired me." She smiled that damn smile. I wasn't a lucky son of a bitch. I was in hell. Again.

CHAPTER TWO

Lily

THIS JACKASS WAS STARING AT ME like he either wanted to kill me or screw me. I'm pretty sure I wasn't okay with either option. The heat from his dark brown eyes made my fingers twitch, while the amber burst around his pupils lit his gaze. I nervously twirled at my father's wedding band that I always wore around my neck. His keen eyes followed the movement making me feel as if I was under interrogation. The music I picked to listen to fell silent as I watched this guy's jaw tick angrily beneath his razor sharp jaw line. He had just enough scruff you'd call it a beard. His black *Seaweed* band T-shirt stretched taut across his gym perfect chest. The colorful artwork on his arms flexed as he pushed away from the other side of the bar. The muscles pulled deliciously under the skin. His thick, purposely disheveled, dark blond hair fell slightly over his forehead, desperately in need of a cut. My new boss was way too hot, sexy, stunning... I struggled for the right insight. Alarm bells rang in my brain telling me to stay the hell away. He was asshole personified. I could smell a jerk from less than thirty yards away, and this guy... this guy was trouble.

"Well, I see you met the new hire." Tiffany, the girl that hired me, was smiling like a cat that caught the canary. Tiffany's long black hair was effortlessly straight and polished; her bangs formed an exact line just at the brow line. She had tattoos covering her arms, and I could see the tips of cherry stems peeking out of her low-cut tank that had the Blue Bar logo printed on it. She had smooth angular features and stark hazel eyes. The hard look was only just that, a look. She was, in fact, lovely.

"Yes... I did. Thanks for the heads up." Todd slowly removed me from his death glare.

"Don't give me shit. You left me here for three days. I'll hire who I want." Tiffany, who couldn't be more than five foot-one, poked the bear right in the chest with her teeny finger. I stifled a giggle. They both whipped their heads in my direction causing my smirk to falter... but only a little.

They didn't really scare me. Well, he scared me... but only because right now, the look I couldn't decipher earlier weighed heavy into the *"I want to screw you"* category. *Never going to happen.* Besides, I sort of already hated him. First impressions were a bitch.

"What's so funny, Red?" Todd's deep, gravelly voice permeated the thick air. My posture was prideful at the dare in his tone. *Who the hell does he think he is? Red? What the hell is that?*

"You, if you really want to know." I smirked again and turned my attention to Tiffany. "Is he always this big of a dick?"

Tiffany smiled. "Always."

"What was that about my big—"

"Ugh, Todd! Don't even start talking about your man parts. Jace is bad enough." Tiffany's face pinched into a scowl as she shook her head.

Todd's dense, warm laugh made me smile. At least he could make fun of himself.

"Shit, Tiffany, you're so right. Jace is a douchbag." His head tilted back exposing his throat as he laughed. I watched as his Adam's apple bobbed up and down. He really is an attractive asshole.

"Who's Jace?" I asked.

Todd's full lips pulled into an easygoing smile. "He's another bartender. Worked here forever. He'll show you the ropes. Should be here in about an hour."

"Oh, crap. I need to go home and get ready." I grabbed my purse and keys from under the bar. When I'd come in earlier to fill out paperwork, Tiffany asked if I could start stocking and cleaning while she ran some errands. My shift started at five, and I needed to get my butt home and ready. Sweaty and messy didn't get you tips. I wasn't paying attention as I stood from under the bar and walked straight into the wall that was apparently my new boss.

"Gah! How'd you get back here so fast?" The words tumbled from my mouth.

"Whoa. Watch where you're going, Red." Todd's cut arms enclosed around my waist stopping me from falling flat on my butt. My forearms and the palms of my hands splayed across his solid chest. The scent of peppermint, cedar, and bar soap filled my personal bubble. *Why did he have to smell so good?* I was in Hell, that's why. I pushed away from his embrace only to see a cocky smile. *Yup, total jerk.* "You look a little flush. You gonna make it?" Oh God was he ever the arrogant ass.

"I'm fine. Don't give yourself too much credit… boss." I reached up and spun the silver ring around the chain. My nervous habit.

The humor vanished from his face. "You better not be

late. I have at least twenty applications on my desk that say you're one hundred percent replaceable."

A small huff escaped my lips at his rude words. My chin shot up with indignation as I stormed past.

"Don't worry about him. Like I said, he's always a giant dill weed." Tiffany winked at me, and I couldn't help but smile. She's right. I wasn't going to worry about him. I didn't travel this far to let some narcissistic asshole try to run me down. I had one goal — get a record deal.

THE BAR WAS BUSY, I thought, for a Thursday night. It was just barely eleven, and the place was crowded. The patrons lined the bar, filled the tables, and danced on the small dance floor in front of the stage. The live music was rich and packed the room with such an amazing vibe. The entertainment was a folk band from Denver, and their music was infectious. I couldn't help but nod my head to the beat and hum along.

"Someone's got the music bug." The striking blue eyes of my co-worker twinkled as he appraised my little show.

"Oh, I have it bad. When's open mic again, Jace?" Jace was the complete opposite of Todd. Where Todd was brooding and moody, Jace was light and fun. I liked Jace instantly, and it helped that he was easy on the eyes. Jace was tall and lean. He had muscle, but he seemed softer, like he earned those muscles hauling hay or working outside, and his clean cut air and smile could make any girl stop dead in her tracks. He was thirty years old, just a few years older than my twenty-seven, so I hoped we had lots in common.

Jace pulled his fingers through his sandy brown hair and smiled down at me. "Tuesdays, before Lakeside Prophets goes on."

"Lakeside Prophets?"

"Todd's band... you didn't know?" Jace shook his head and smiled. "They're huge here in the indie circuit. Frank and Todd run the record label Blue Bar Music. Any of this ringing a bell?" He playfully tapped my head.

"Nope, not a chime. I'm not from around here." That wasn't entirely accurate. I knew Frank. Jace looked at me with interest. My mind spun. Todd was in a band? He and Frank ran the label *together*? This could put a kink in my plan. Before I could elaborate, a patron started running off a list of drinks for us to make. I ran through the ingredients for each drink in my head. Jace and I had a good rhythm, and we held our own. My experience back home helped.

I was born and raised in Tampa, Florida, by my hippy dad. My dad was in a rock band in his younger years and toured the country. He met Pam, my mom, here in Utah, and they hit it off one night at a show. They had dinner the next night and nine months later a baby girl. My mom toured with the band and for a while things were great. Until my mom, who couldn't make a good choice to save her life, started sleeping with the drummer. Frank Nadine. Needless to say, the band broke up, friendships were severed, and years of hard work thrown down the drain all over a *"dumb chick,"* as my dad used to say. The thought made my lips pull up into a grin.

"Hey pretty lady; hows'bout yoos get me a Bud?" A short, sloppy-looking frat boy swayed and tried to wink at me. This was hysterical.

"No way, dude. You're cut off." Jace's eyebrows pulled inward.

"Fuck off!" The drunk guy stumbled a bit.

"I know you're not talking to her like that, fuck stick."

Todd's deep baritone rumbled from his chest. My eyes locked with his right before he grabbed the guy and tossed him away from the bar.

I sighed. "Where did Todd come from?"

"Oh, he's always around. He's been around a lot tonight, though. He's been watching you." Jace's eyes narrowed a bit as he watched Todd shove the drunken idiot out of the front doors.

"He's probably making sure I know how to do my job," I said while scrubbing the pint glasses in the bar sink.

Jace's deep laugh seemed to echo in the room. "I don't think so. I think someone's got a hard on for you." He winked.

I balked. "Ew. Please don't ever say that again. I was warned about you."

He snickered. "Oh yeah, how?"

"I was told you were quite inappropriate when it came to talking about man parts." I couldn't help but laugh.

"Damn straight! Dick, penis, wiener, coc—"

"Stop right there!" I squealed. He waggled his eyebrows. "You're disgusting." I was laughing so hard I had to hold my belly to keep from doubling over.

"He is a total sleazeball. Go take a break, Lily." Tiffany smirked and snapped Jace's firm butt with a towel.

"I call sexual harassment," Jace hollered teasingly.

"What? No such thing, you work in a bar." Tiffany's tone was incredulous.

My smile couldn't have been any bigger as I stepped through the swinging door toward the back offices and the small kitchen. Blue Bar was huge inside and offered a full-service bar. It was almost exactly like the club I worked at back home in Tampa, except this place was older and had more charm. The exposed brick, glass shelving, and can lights created a modern feel, but the dark wood was old and somewhat dingy, giving it away that the place had been there for ages. You could still slightly smell the lingering odor of cigarettes from when they used to allow smoking inside. I loved it because it felt like... home.

I walked through to the break room, made a quick cup of coffee, and plopped down onto the sofa. I almost didn't want my skin to touch the fabric. The couch looked well-used. The floral pattern was stained and brown in places. I cringed to think what had happened on this couch. The back wall of the room was covered in pictures of bands, parties, co-workers, and families. Without thinking, I stood and took in all the photos. *I wonder?* My eyes rapidly started scanning the pictures. The photos on the left were obviously older. Wouldn't you know it? My mom and Frank sitting on that same stage out front holding my sister. She must have been six?

"Eve," her name whispered from my lips. She looked so little. My chest felt tight and my breathing was shallow. I started absentmindedly, rubbing my chest while struggling to breathe. The sound of the break room door clicking behind me snapped me out of my memories as I turned just in time to watch Todd as he took a large swig of beer from the bottle he was carrying.

"Drinking on the job?" I looked at him appraisingly, my eyes wide.

"I'm the boss; I'll do what the fuck I want, Red." His boyish grin was at war with his severe tone.

"Lily is my name. Lily Spring."

He chuckled. "Lily Spring? You sound like a stripper."

I was immediately angry. "You sound like a prick." I turned on my heel and tried to move past the jerk.

"Simmer down, sweetheart." His tone was softer, but it did nothing to help my irritation.

"Let's get this straight. My name's Lily..." I said like I was talking to a third grader. "...not sweetheart, princess, sugar bottom, darling, or Red. Got it!" I tried again, unsuccessfully, to get past him. He stepped in front of me. I was toe to toe with him, my furious heaving chest almost touching his. The atmosphere changed, and the crackle in the air between us could almost be heard. The pull was ridiculous, and the silence was deafening. "I need to get back to work." My voice sounded smaller than it should have. He stepped out of the way just enough for me to inch past him toward the door. My breast grazed his arm, and I about died of embarrassment. I was sure my face was at least ten shades of red.

I heard him laugh lightly as the door shut behind me. My annoyance boiled. He was trouble all right.

THE NIGHT SEEMED TO drag after my encounter with Todd in the break room. His intense amber eyes only left me once when he had to throw out another couple of rowdy customers. The way we watched each other in a silent dance of wills left my skin feeling scorched. It was almost two in the morning when the night was finally over; I was beat. As Jace shut and locked the doors, the biting outside air rushed in and cooled my heated skin as the last stragglers finally left. Spring in Utah was a fickle bitch. It could be warm one day and snow the next. A storm was coming in, and the warm weather shorts I had on had been a bad choice. I rolled my eyes. Oh well, there was nothing to do about it now.

The side work checklist was sitting next to the register. I

grabbed it and started working on stocking the beer fridge when Jace came back behind the bar to help.

"Shit, let me get that." He grabbed the crate of bottles from my hands. "How about you start washing those glasses." He threw me that nice guy smile again.

"Thanks."

"So you tended bar in Tampa?" He started back with the questions. All night, I felt like I was being quizzed. I knew he wanted to get to know me, but give a girl a break.

I sighed deeply. "Yup. I lived down south with my dad. He raised me."

"Where's your mom?"

I tried to tamp down my aggravation. I opened myself up for that question.

"She lives here. So does my sister. We have different dads. I'm actually staying with my sister and her family."

"Yeah? That's cool, you get along?" Jace was busy putting away the bottles of beer. He didn't notice the pause. Sure my sister and I got along. Enough. She was super religious and thought all of us lived "crazy reckless" lives. The fact that I depended on her for a place to live made it worse. I moved out here less than three weeks ago, and I already felt like I owed her my life. She was good at holding things over your head.

"Sure." I lowered my head and started scrubbing the glasses again.

"That's cool. You and your mom? You close?" He stood and shut the beer fridge and started filling a red bucket with hot water from the other sink. He opened a packet and dumped the powder into the water. The smell of bleach swirled under my nose.

"No, we haven't spoken in years."

"Really, why?" Jace walked over to the other side of the bar and started cleaning the tabletops. He looked at me now with a frown.

I knew everyone here would eventually figure out my

mom was Frank's ex-wife. They had been divorced for five years. My mom abandoned me, left me to go start another life. I wasn't even sure where she lived. I just knew I didn't give a shit. Maybe I should just put it out there. Let everyone know. *Why not, right?* "You know—"

Before I had a chance to speak, the sound system in the bar blasted on. "*All I Do Is Win*" by *DJ Khaled* pounded out of the speakers. The bass hit me in my chest, and I automatically started swaying my hips just enough to feel the beat as I finished my work. I laughed as Jace started rapping while he wiped down the tabletops.

He stopped rapping when he saw me laughing so hard my head was thrown back. "This is our nightly tradition. We jam out to one song before we finish up. We share turns who gets to pick."

"Whose turn was it tonight?" The thought that anyone here liked rap made me giggle.

"Todd."

Just then Tiffany and Todd busted through the back hall door startling me. I almost dropped a pint glass. I was shocked — at first by the sudden appearance, but then at the spectacle they were making. Tiffany and Todd were dancing like idiots. Todd started singing and throwing his hands in the air like he'd just won something. He was mimicking the lyrics of the song. Even though I didn't want to, I laughed as I watched these three people grind on each other. The stoic, sexy ass from earlier was gone, and now a happy-go-lucky Todd was present. This guy's moods were giving me whiplash.

Todd's eyes found mine, and his full smile about killed me. He had two — yes two — huge dimples on either cheek. A light sheen of sweat covered his forehead as he danced, actually quite nicely, to the beat.

"Red, get your fine ass out here." Todd's voice was sweet. That's another personality trait to add to the ever-growing list that proved Todd was a moody bastard.

"No way." I giggled.

He stopped dancing and furrowed his brow. The look of disappointment that flashed across his dark eyes didn't escape my notice. Still, not happening.

He stalked toward me and headed behind the bar. Jace and Tiffany were too busy dancing like fools to care about me. I ducked my head down and started vigorously washing the glass, figuring if I ignored him he'd go away. I was wrong. I felt his presence before his touch. The crackle from before started whipping up again. He was right behind me, the heat of his body was humid from dancing and it filled the small space between us. I dropped the glass in the sink when his lips touched my ear. *"All I Do Is Win"* the title of the song ringing in my ear. The lyrics rang true. A guy like Todd could never lose.

"Come dance with me." His breath was peppermint again, and, as he closed the distance behind us and trailed his hands down my arms, I realized I was strangling the dishrag. He moved his fingertips into the water and lightly back up my hands before removing the towel from my death grip. I exhaled, effectively breaking the spell I was under. "Come on, Lily. I don't bite." I felt his torso move as he laughed.

I was being stupid. Jace and Tiffany were totally in the moment and having fun. *Why the hell not?*

"Show me what you got," I said as I turned to face him, becoming completely caged between his arms and making an extra effort to stand tall. I was so tiny compared to him. He had to be at least six feet tall. I was just barely five-foot-three. It was intimidating, but I refused to show it. Todd's pupils dilated, the close proximity was affecting him too. I gained confidence from that. "I thought we were dancing?"

"Lead the way." He smirked.

And that's what we did… we danced. We were having a good time, and I wasn't going to feel guilty about letting my guard down and enjoying myself for once. Tiffany and Jace were cracking up watching me shake my ass. Todd came up behind me and moved with me to the bass. Jace catcalled and Tiffany whistled. I dropped down almost to the floor before slowly bringing myself up, teasing Todd with a show.

"Holy shit, bro!" Jace's fist shot up to his mouth as he smiled. "Damn girl, you got moves."

My lips curled into a smile. Music was everything to me: my body reacted to it, my mind created to it, and my hands played to it. I was a musician through and through.

"What I wouldn't do to an ass like that, I could—"

"Don't finish that sentence, Jace." Tiffany grimaced. My laugh died on the air.

I looked behind me and saw Todd had stilled. His jaw strained, and his hands balled into fists.

"Yeah, Jace, you need to learn when to shut your damn mouth." Todd's eyes constricted as he glared at me.

"What the hell did I do?" I didn't appreciate the way Todd was looking at me. Unconsciously, I started twirling my dad's ring.

"Let's get this shit hole cleaned up, shall we?" Tiffany grabbed the red bucket from the tabletop and started wiping down the table and chairs.

"Why don't you head out, Lily? You had a long day. We got this." Jace's smile was small but broke the tension between Todd and me immediately.

"I don't want you working overtime. You were clocked in earlier?" I nodded. "Then get going. Be here tomorrow at five, yeah?" Todd's mouth turned slightly into a frown. Almost like he was hoping I'd say no.

"Yup." I walked behind the bar and grabbed my purse and keys.

"I'll walk you out to your car." I didn't have a chance to protest as I felt the palm of his hand on the small of my back.

The chilled air hit my bare legs, and I groaned. Stupid shorts.

"Maybe wear pants tomorrow? This isn't Florida." He chuckled.

"I know... Wait... how did you know?"

"I know who you are. I figured it out after going over your application. Lily Spring, daughter of Danny Spring, lead singer of the very same band that Frank used to play drums for. Frank flew out to Florida for Danny's funeral last month. It's not a secret." His flippant tone as he spoke about my father's funeral pissed me off. Angry tears threatened to overflow the wall I'd been holding up all night.

"Don't talk about my father like you know something about me." My voice felt stiff. The lump in my throat burned. I didn't cry very often and certainly not in front of this jerk.

"I'm sorry... that was... I was... I didn't mean anything by it." Todd reached toward my cheek in a tender gesture. My legs reacted and took two small steps backward avoiding the touch.

"Forget it. I know it's not a secret. Frank just doesn't know I'm here yet. Let me tell him, okay?"

"I'm sorry. I feel like a dick." *Well, you are!*

"Frank's going to be here tomorrow, right? I'll talk to him then." I turned and unlocked the door to my car, sat in the driver's seat, and started the engine. I quickly turned up the heater and was about to close the door when I noticed Todd's massive frame, his exquisitely inked arm was holding the door open.

"Go away, I'm safe now. It's cold, and I want to shut the

door." I pulled on the handle, but his strong arm was unrelenting. He looked down at me, his coffee-colored eyes soaking through my skin. The energy from before sparked between us. My hair blew across my face as the breeze, announcing the oncoming storm, swirled into my car through the open door. I felt his warm fingers before I saw them. He pushed my untamed copper hair behind my ear.

"Drive safely." He pulled his eyes away from mine before he shut my door, leaving me breathless.

CHAPTER THREE

Lily

THE RAIN HIT THE WINDOWS WITH such force I thought for sure I was back in Florida during a tropical storm. The temperature dropped significantly overnight, and the rain had gradually turned to sleet as the day progressed. I wasn't looking forward to working tonight, and the weather seemed to reflect my mood. I was afraid Frank would be pissed that I didn't come to him directly for the job. Frank and my dad had had such a strained relationship for my entire life; I wasn't sure how he'd react to me.

Frank had come all the way to Tampa for my father's funeral. To say he was distraught would be an injustice to the emotion in general — Frank was destroyed. He couldn't even look at me, let alone speak to me. Regret – it eats you alive and I would know, it was all I had at the moment. My father's ring felt heavy in my hand. The silver had dulled since last month. My chest tightened as I remembered the final goodbye.

The sun was shining and the humid heat pooled and dripped down my back. The black sundress I wore was a bad idea. I didn't even recognize half of the people here. The bass player from my dad's old band was speaking now, leading us in prayer, and I had to stifle a smile. My dad would have hated this prayer. Gabe finally finished his attempt at being spiritual and looked at the coffin with fear in his eyes. My heart split open again. It was like an abrasion on the knee — every time you bent it, it broke open again. Every time someone mentioned how great my dad was, how they were sorry for my loss, how much he would be missed, it ripped the scab, and I bled out over and over again. Gabe came over to where I was standing and put his arm around me.

"You got anything you want to say?"

I shook my head. In my mind, I thought of the things I would have said, "I love you. Why are you gone? What am I supposed to do now? I didn't get to say goodbye. I was being stupid when I said I hated you. I don't hate you. You were perfect. I miss your smell, I miss that stupid Old Spice smell, and I miss your laugh and your smile."

"Danny you were a good man, a great father, and one hell of a singer. Tell the angels to save a spot for me." Gabe's voice choked as he threw a Calla Lily on the coffin. Everyone started to leave, but I couldn't move.

"You coming?" Gabe looked at me with such sadness it was suffocating. I couldn't be with anyone right then.

"No, I'm going to head out soon." I kept my eyes on the casket. Everyone dropped their lilies as they left, making the dark wood of the casket look as if it was surrounded by a pale halo. It was beautiful.

"Okay… just… he knows you loved him no matter how it all ended. He loved you, and you loved him. It is what it is."

"It is what it is." Those words could not be truer. I allowed my tears to fall this one time. I put the necklace on and brought my fingertips to my lips and blew a small kiss up to heaven. My dad would be with the angels all right. Gabe knew. I knew. He died too soon. The good people always do. The bad ones always get to linger. What does that make me?

"SEE YOU TOMORROW, EVE," I hollered to my sister as I bounded up the basement stairs. I was living in the spare room in the basement of my sister's house until I could find a place.

"Please be quiet when you come home. We have to be at church in the morning." Eve's voice sounded annoyed. I stopped before I opened the front door. I was always quiet, what the hell? Instead of leaving I walked toward the kitchen where she was feeding my nephew, Christopher.

"I'm always quiet." I frowned.

"I know, but Christopher hasn't been sleeping well, and I don't want him to cry during church. I hate not getting to listen to Pastor Phillips. I only go to Saturday service for him." She appraised me with tired eyes. "You're going to work dressed like that?"

"Like what?" I looked down at my jeans and black V-neck sweater.

"You don't think that's a little too low cut?" She clicked her tongue and shook her head slightly. Christopher cried out impatiently as she dangled the spoon of what looked like pureed carrots in front of his face. "Oh sorry, baby." She quickly pushed the spoon full of goop into his tiny little mouth. I rolled my eyes. I hate how she treated me like I was the younger sister. I was, after all, three years older than her.

"Eve, geez, it's not that low cut. Maybe you should get out more. When was the last time you went out with Holden, huh? Church doesn't count." I smirked.

Eve's blue eyes squinted resentfully. "Don't Lil. Holden and I are just fine. Don't try and tell me that working at a bar, playing music for pennies, and dressing like a slut makes you an expert on everything." I gasped at the word 'slut.'

"Wow... nice... very Christian of you, sis. Don't worry. I'll be outta here soon." I grabbed my coat from the hook next to the fridge and turned on my heel to leave. I wanted to scream at her. *Who the hell does she think she is? Self-righteous bit — my* thought was cut off as she yelled to me from the kitchen. I was half out the door.

"Lil, I'm sorry. I didn't mean that."

I slammed the door and ran to my car trying to avoid the rain. Eve believed her words. She only felt guilty because she knew she shouldn't mean it.

CHAPTER FOUR

Todd

"Frank, man, you're not pissed she didn't come to you first?" I looked at Frank with disbelieving eyes. Frank was never this forgiving. I'm glad he wasn't mad though. As much as Lily was most likely sent here to torture me for my past wrongs, I couldn't help but want her to stay. There was something about her. God, I sounded like a fucking pussy.

"No, I'm sure she had her reasons. I couldn't even talk to her at the funeral. It was so hard. She was part of my life for so long, Todd. When I knocked up Pam, well… it was like Lily's world ended. She should hate my ass. I destroyed her family. All for what? That dirty bitch almost ruined my life. At least I got Evy out of it." Frank's stare softened. "Lily's a good girl. I want to help her. Evy… she doesn't want any part of my life. Since she joined that damn church, she's all high and mighty. Thinks her shit don't stink. Maybe Lily can help us all heal, you know."

That thought penetrated my thick wall and hung there like a prize waiting to be claimed. He meant his *family* could be restored, but even though that was way too much weight to put on one person, a small part of me thought maybe she could help heal me. A light knock at the door pulled me from my thoughts.

"Uh... hey, Frank." Lily's sexy voice ran all the way down my spine. It pissed me off the effect this chick had on me. Apparently, I needed to get laid. I turned and watched as her eyes shifted between Frank and me. Lily looked incredible. She had on a tight as hell black V-neck sweater that made her hair appear ten times as bright. The copper curls were tamed into a high, thick ponytail. The freckles on her cheeks more evident with her hair pulled back. The freckles on the bridge of her nose were my favorite. If you looked at them just right, they almost looked like a constellation.

"Hey." Frank took a deep breath. "So I hear you work here now." He cocked his left eyebrow. Lily pinned her annoyed gaze on me.

"What?" I asked sarcastically, knowing damn well why she was pissed. I didn't give a shit. This was my bar; I'll do what I want.

"You're such a jerk." She pulled her bag off her shoulder and moved to leave.

"So I hear." My laugh stopped her, and a small growl escaped her lips making me laugh even harder.

"What's going on?" Frank's voice held no humor.

"I wasn't supposed to tell you she was working here. She wanted to."

"Lily get in here and shut the door." Frank's voice had a parental quality. I sat up straighter in my chair feeling like a child. Lily shut the door a bit too hard, and it caused me to jump.

"Have a seat." Frank gestured to the chair next to me. Lily sat stiffly and dropped her bag to the floor.

"Frank, I just wanted to tell you myself. I know it's not a secret who I am to you. But I wanted to get this job on my own. I didn't want you to think I was using—"

"Stop right there, young lady. I don't give a shit what any of these kids think around this damn bar. You're like a daughter to me. I know... I've made giant mistakes. I would've been happy to help you, and you know it."

I watched as Lily schooled her features, holding in the sentiment that obviously needed to boil over. Her chest moved up and down with effort, like she was desperate for air.

"Thank you... thank you for being there. He would have loved that, you know." She rubbed at the ring around her neck. I had the weird urge to pull her small body close to mine. I wanted to feel the deep movement of her chest against mine as she struggled for control. The need to take over, relieve her chaos and watch her let go, was stirring up a storm in my gut, and I didn't like it. I couldn't care like this again. I just couldn't.

"Is there a reason I still need to be in here? I've got shit to do." Standing, I waited for Frank to let me out of this stifling office. I heard Lily's quick, hostile laugh. She thought I was such a prick, but it was better that way.

"Make sure you call that idiot Ray. I need to get the graphics for this album done by next week."

"I'm on it, Frank." I passed Lily on my way to the door. The smell of coconut and sunscreen hit me. Last night in the break room her scent had surrounded me, and I felt lost for the first time in a while. She smelled like the beach, and it was such a contradiction to her fair skin and light features. I almost couldn't take it when we were dancing, as she bent down teasing me with that perfect ass, making it almost impossible to not succumb to the temptation. I wanted everyone to disappear that second so I could show her just what she was playing with. She made me feel out of control, and I hated her for it.

I shook my head and headed for the office door.

"Next time, I'll know better than to trust you. Thanks for that." Her words were bitter.

I opened the door without looking at her. If I let myself see the disappointment in those unearthly eyes, I'd apologize, and I couldn't allow that. Everything I'd ever wanted had been taken from me in some way or another. I couldn't let myself want her. I had to keep it together. Control... it's all I have left.

"No problem, Red." I shut the door behind me. The steps I took away from her hurt more than they should have. I rolled my shoulders back, tilted my head to the left and to the right, stretching the muscles in my neck. *Pull it together, Dixon.* Yeah, I couldn't afford to care again.

"Damn it!" I'd thrown my cell phone down a bit harder than I should have, causing the screen crack. "Shit!" I did a quick once-over of the screen, coming to the realization that I would need a new phone for sure. I didn't have time for this. It was getting close to the rush, and I had to get out on the floor. The sound system was playing *"Believe"* by The Bravery as I walked over to the bar. The crowd was big tonight. It was Friday, the first weekend of spring break, and the place was crawling with hot girls. This was just what I needed to get my head back in the game.

"So? Where the hell is this band we booked for tonight?" Tiffany asked while she shook up a drink in a tumbler.

"Canceled... I don't know what to do." I shrugged my shoulders in defeat.

"We could do an open mic." Tiffany poured the drink into a martini glass. Open mic on a Friday? This was going to suck.

"I guess that's what we'll have to do. I'll get it going."

"Get what going?" Lily asked, her face full of skepticism.

"Open mic. The band for tonight canceled." I tried not to sound pissed. But open mic on a Friday was bar suicide. People wanted to dance, get wasted, and listen to live music...

not go to amateur hour.

"Really?" Lily's voice lifted with excitement. "Cool, I love open mic nights."

"Great, that makes one person in this bar that won't leave." Tiffany laughed.

I chuckled at Tiff's joke. There was no reason to stay pissed, might as well make the best of it. I grabbed some equipment from the back. We had two spare guitars that I'd brought onto the stage, and Jace and I moved the piano forward that had been pushed to the back for the band that never showed. On our regular open mic nights, my band played, so all our equipment was already up here. No drums tonight though. I set up the microphone and signaled for Tiffany to lower the music. I waited for the crowd to quiet down.

"Hey guys, unfortunately, Red Light canceled tonight's show..." The din of disapproval rose throughout the bar. "...I know. Well, we're going to open the stage to you guys. Open mic, yeah?" A few people whistled. "All right then, let's get started and let's be respectful of those preforming. Thanks." I smiled at this hot blonde that was eyeing me from the dance floor. Maybe this night could turn out okay.

CHAPTER FIVE

Lily

I COULDN'T WAIT TO GET ON that stage. I've been dying to sing. I just wish Frank was here. I was told he always left around six, except on Tuesdays — the regular open mic night. Todd was here, though, and it was half his label too. I didn't like the idea of trying to impress him. He was so confusing. One minute he was sweet, the next a total dirt bag. I grabbed a beer and handed it over the bar to a customer as he handed me a five-dollar bill.

"Keep the change." He smiled.

"Thanks." I grinned back. I quickly made change in the till. I watched as the first person started a bad rendition of some Aerosmith song, and I chuckled.

"That's bad," a new, unfamiliar voice grabbed my attention. "Really bad." His shoulders shuddered with laughter, and he shook his head in disbelief. "Hey, can I get a Jameson on the rocks?" The man's voice was smooth and my eyes met his as he pulled at his tie, loosening it from his neck. His large, broad shoulders looked heavenly wrapped tight in a white button down.

The smile he gave me heated my cheeks instantly making it difficult for me to process what he was asking. "Did you hear me, doll?" he asked. He had dark brown, almost black hair, which was neatly tousled. The thing that was throwing me off, besides the fact he had a face that belonged in magazines, was that his very businessman button down was rolled to his elbows exposing sculpted forearms that were covered in tattoos.

"Jameson on the rocks," I repeated while I grabbed the glass and filled it with ice and whiskey. The man's deep blue eyes never left mine as I handed him his drink. His full bore appraisal left me blushing.

"You new here? I haven't seen you before." He took the drink from my hand and sipped the amber liquid. He closed his eyes, and his nostrils flared. Holy damn this guy was hot. "I needed this, thanks. So yeah, you new?" he asked again while handing me his credit card. I placed it with the others that were being held for tabs.

"Yup, day two for me. Are you a regular?" He didn't miss the flirty smile I gave him, and I was awarded with a cute sideways smirk.

"You could say that. *What's your name?*" he shouted the last part. The sound system kicked back on. The first participant on stage had finished.

I leaned in closer and watched as he did as well. A pleasant warmth filled my limbs. "Lily."

"Lily." My name rolled effortlessly off his lips. "I like it."

Before I had a chance to ask his name, Todd's voice broke my bubble.

CHAPTER SIX

Todd

THIS IS NOT FUCKING HAPPENING RIGHT now. My jaw clenched at the sight of my best friend and Lily looking a little too close for my damn comfort.

"What's up, Seth?" I nodded my chin in my roommate's direction. Lily leaned back when she heard my voice. She was flirting with Seth, and her cheeks were pink. I wanted to punch Seth in his damn face.

"Hey, bro." Seth grabbed my hand and pulled me in for a hug. He placed a firm pat on my back as I did the same to him. "What's up with this open mic shit? I came here for Red Light."

"They canceled." I watched Lily as she tried to appear unaffected by the fact I knew Seth. "Lily, I see you met Seth, my roommate?"

"And best friend." He winked at her. *He fucking winked.* We needed to talk. This was not happening again.

"Really? Todd has friends?" She smirked at me.

I leaned over the bar, purposely getting in her personal space. "I've got lots of friends, sweetheart." I held my eyes on hers. The yellow was subdued in the dim light, and the blue and green tones mixed and created the most unusual color. I almost lost my game. Almost.

"I bet you do." She looked back at Seth dismissing me. "Nice to meet you, Seth."

"Likewise." Shithead gave her a cocky grin.

"Can I talk to you for a second?" I tried to keep my voice under control.

"Sure. Talk to you soon, Lily." He grabbed his drink and followed me to the back office.

Once we were in my office, he spoke, "So you got it bad for that chick?"

"What? You could tell?" I sat on my desk as he leaned in the doorjamb.

"You just basically came over and pissed on her, bro. So yeah, I could tell. I was just flirting. I'll back down. No worries. Okay?" Seth looked at me with pleading eyes. All the humor – gone. Seth was there when I lost everything. When my world dissolved. When I left Elizabeth and everything else behind me. Even though Elizabeth deserved Sawyer, and he one hundred percent deserved her, it didn't make it any easier. The thought that I even cared enough about this Lily chick that Seth had noticed... well, it was killing me. Two days and she's got me all mixed up. *This was such bullshit.*

"Thanks man. I don't know. I think she hates me."

"Oh yeah, she hates you all right. Fucking loves to hate you." I didn't miss his double meaning. He punched me in the shoulder, and I laughed.

"Yeah, she does. Let's go get you another drink." I smirked.

"Sounds good."

"How was work?" I asked as we headed back out to the bar.

"Sucks, I hate finance. Working for my dad is killing me, bro. I've got to get that job up on campus. I'm still waiting to hear back." Seth furrowed his brow.

"You'll get it. They'd be stupid not to hire you. You know everything there is to know about music. You'd be a great teacher." I shoved him lightheartedly in the shoulder.

"Thanks, sweetie. Should we hug now or later?" Seth gave me the dumbest shit-eating grin I'd ever seen.

"You're such a tool bag." I smacked him on the back of the head.

"Pot... meet kettle." He laughed.

Our laughter was cut short.

The sound of a guitar playing softly caught my attention as I walked through to the main part of the bar. The slow melodic flow of *"Rivers and Roads"* by The Head and the Heart, one of my favorite songs, drew my appreciations to the stage. My breath hitched as she sang the first few lyrics. Seth bumped into me because I had stopped mid step.

"Dude wh—" His words dropped off as we both listened to the haunting voice. Lily sang the familiar lyrics, lyrics that spoke of loss, family, and distance. The unbelievable sound coursed through my veins. It was the most remarkable thing I'd ever heard.

"Holy shit," Seth spoke close to my ear. "Are you hearing this?"

"Shh." I couldn't take my eyes off her. She sang with such purity it almost hurt to listen. The emotion was profound. In that moment, I could feel everything. It was as if she was making all my hate, pain, loss, and love surface like a rushing faucet. It was to the point that I had to take a deep breath to untie the knot in my chest. This damn girl blew into my bar, into my life, knocking everything over like a fucking tornado. Her voice, her eyes, her smart mouth, all of it. I didn't know if I was coming or going. I just wanted some part of her, and I didn't care how much.

She strummed the last note and the bar was dead silent. She raised her head and her eyes glittered with unshed tears. Lily's eyes found mine and for a split second, before the crowd burst into applause, I lost every bit of control and smiled like I had won the goddamn lottery. Because at that moment, she looked at me like she had won the lottery too.

"Dude! Did you just hear that shit?"

I was still watching Lily as she placed the guitar on the stand. The words of the song swam in my head; her voice silenced everything around me.

"Todd?" Seth's amused tone filtered through my thoughts. "Bro, you guys need to sign that shit like yesterday."

"What?" I was still trying to gather myself. Lily had me so screwed up.

"Lily, your new bartender? That's serious fucking talent, man."

"I know. Frank's got to hear her first, though."

Lily walked to the other end of the bar. A substandard musician started playing a song on the piano while Lily got right back to work helping customers.

"Well, Frank's going to lose his mind, that's all I'm saying." Seth poured the rest of his drink down his throat.

"He's going to do more than lose his mind. Let's get a drink. I want to talk to her."

CHAPTER SEVEN

Lily

SETH TOOK PERCH ON THE STOOL he was in earlier. Todd mixed him a drink, and I couldn't help admire how his large body moved with grace behind the small bar. My teeth drew across my bottom lip in an attempt to hide my smile as I thought of how Todd watched me while I sang. My body was alight with goose bumps. He looked at me like he'd never seen something so remarkable in his entire life. Todd's mask had completely fallen for four whole minutes. In those precious moments, I thought I had glimpsed his soul, and it was the brightest thing I'd ever seen.

I wasn't quite ready to talk to him yet, so I busied myself with customers. This side of Todd was unsettling. I almost preferred the asshole. At least I knew how to deal with that.

"Holy crap, girl, you've got to sing for Frank!" Tiffany's eyes were wide. I laughed at her serious expression as I handed a patron their beer.

"Really?" I giggled.

"That was amazing, Lily." Jace pulled me in for a hug.

Todd pushed away from the bar where he was talking

with Seth; his eyebrows pulled inward, and his mouth made a tight line. The former guise firmly back in place.

"Jace, I need you to go grab some more bottles of Blue Moon from the back," Todd's commanding tone had me on edge again. Jace nodded and released me from his embrace. I thought I heard Tiff snicker under her breath, but the music was loud so I couldn't be sure.

"I'm outta here, bro. Good job tonight, Lily. It was nice to meet you." I noted Seth's manner was now friendly, the previous flirting long forgotten. Which was probably a good thing seeing how I couldn't help but notice that Tiffany watched Seth's every move. I may be new around here, but the relationships everyone shared were starting to show, the surface façade slowly dimming.

"See you later, Tiff." Tiffany looked up from the sink where she was scrubbing pint glasses just in time to catch a stunning smile from Seth. Tiffany's hard exterior melted away as her cheeks turned bright pink. She gave him a quick smile and went back to work. My lips split into a big grin.

"What's funny, Red?" Todd's voice was smooth and too close. While I had watched the exchange between Seth and Tiffany, Todd must have moved closer to where I was standing. The heat from his body filled the space between us. The crowd was dwindling, and, for some reason, I was glad. I didn't feel like working anymore, and I was ready to talk to Todd. I wanted to know if he thought I had a chance to impress Frank. *Frank.* My smile fell. Todd had me feeling like I was on an emotional rollercoaster. I hadn't forgotten how pissed I was at him for how he'd acted earlier. It was like he got off on messing with me.

My prior irritation reappeared. "Nothing." My one-word answer came out hard.

"Can I talk to you for a minute?" I didn't miss his exasperated exhale.

"Talk." I stepped back trying to create room for me to

breathe. Todd was a presence to behold, and having him this close... my anger, my frustration, and my need all ran together. I couldn't make heads or tails out of my feelings when he consumed the space around me so absolutely. It made me crazy that one minute I hated him, and then the next; I wanted him to like me. *What the hell was that about?*

"Let's talk in my office." He grabbed two beers from the beer fridge and motioned for me to follow him.

"It's busy, Todd."

"Jace and Tiff can handle the floor for a minute. Besides, it's dying down." He gave me a small grin that made me feel nervous all over again. I was about to point out the fact that Jace had gone to the back to get the stock Todd had requested, but Jace came through the back door right on time. "Come on, Red."

Why was I hesitating? I wanted to talk to him, and I needed to see if I had a chance at this dream, at the promise I'd made my father before he died.

"Fine." I puffed out a small, irritated burst of air.

I followed Todd toward the back offices wringing my fingers together as I walked ahead of him through the door. I took a deep breath, letting my body rest against the side of his desk. He handed me one of the beers he'd brought back with us. I opened it and drank deeply from the bottle, hoping the alcohol could ease away my tension.

"Whoa. Slow down, Red, you still have about an hour or so left in your shift." Todd's chuckle was infectious. He was actually fun to be around when he wasn't trying so hard to piss me off.

I refused to let him see that he affected me though. "What did you drag me back here for?" I placed the bottle of beer down onto the desk.

"I think you know." It was his turn to take a large gulp of liquid courage. I didn't answer so he continued, "How long have you been singing, Lily?" Todd spoke kindly again, and my name uttered in that tenor made my heart skip a beat. The actual interest in his voice threw me for a loop. He was stirring up feelings I hadn't expected to feel, especially about him.

"Ever since I can remember," I whispered. I couldn't bring my eyes to his. The memories of singing with my father flooded my mind making my chest feel heavy.

"Your voice is..." He inhaled sharply, causing me to look up. He leaned in for a moment and I had to catch my breath. He placed his beer bottle down next to mine and then took a step back. His limitless brown eyes caught my gaze. "...it's so fucking pure and real, Lily. I've never heard anything that could stop me in my tracks like you did tonight. Your voice... I could listen to it all damn day." He took a small step toward me again. I was speechless, his words were breaking me wide open, and it was everything I needed to hear. I could do this.

CHAPTER EIGHT

Todd

Lily's eyes were sea green in the dim light of my office. I had never wanted to kiss a girl more than I did now. She appeared so vulnerable, and the idea that she needed me had me thinking stupid things. Things like what it would be like for her to pick me. What her lips would taste like. I wanted to know how her full bottom lip felt being pulled gently through my teeth. My regard was making her nervous, and she bit into that sexy as hell lip; I almost let the overwhelming lust win.

"You really think that?" she spoke so quietly I almost didn't hear her. Her voice sounded thick like she was about to cry. I cursed under my breath. Her insecurity wrecked me. She needed to know how unbelievable she was.

"Yes. I do. You're amazing." I wasn't sure I was talking about her voice anymore.

She broke from my stare only to look at my mouth. Lily's breathing expanded, and I loved watching her chest rise and fall. I loved watching how my physical presence shook up her world as much as she was shaking up mine. I took the last possible step. Our bodies almost touching, she was forced to sit back on my desk. A light gasp blew from her pink lips making the atmosphere between us feel substantial. The slight exhale of desire that escaped her lips was the game changer.

I parted her legs with my knee; my hands found purchase on her upper thighs. I pulled her lean legs farther apart, roughly bringing her body flush with mine. There was no hesitation, and, with a quick surprised breath, she opened up to me like I was everything she wanted. I wasn't sure what I was doing, but I wasn't going to stop. Lily's eyes locked with mine as I trailed my hands around her hips and up her arms. She draped her arms around my waist giving me permission. I didn't waver. I took her face in my hands and brought my lips just barely to hers. The slight blue hue of her eyes glittered giving me that last bit of encouragement.

Lily's mouth was just as perfect as I thought it would be. Her sexy as fuck, soft lips enveloped mine, and I was gone. I lightly nipped her bottom lip with my teeth, and she moaned. That fucking moan pushed me past the wall of restraint. My hands slid under her ass, and I lifted her body. She complied by wrapping her legs around my waist, her arms linked behind my neck. I turned so I was now sitting on the desk. Lily deepened our kiss giving me full access to her sweet taste. The flavor of berries, beer and something just Lily invaded my senses as her tongue licked my bottom lip. I let out a small groan and lifted my hips to her. My hard arousal met that sweet spot, and I almost lost it. I moved her hips against mine again, and she whimpered.

"Lily," I growled and moved my lips to her jaw. She tilted her head to the side letting my kiss trail down her neck, allowing me to gently bite at the exposed flesh. I brought my mouth back to hers and devoured her small whispered moans. She had me untied. I had no clue where this was going. I didn't know what was happening, but this chick was consuming me, lighting me on fire, and burning down every solid wall I had ever built. I couldn't want something this bad;

I couldn't have another person tear down my world.

Lily's chest was flushed as I pulled away from her lips. My dick twitched against her as I watched her breathing slow. My thumbs traced lazy circles on her cheeks. Her incredible eyes bore into mine, and I knew that look of regret too well. I'd seen it so many times with Liz. Lily was seeing me for what I really was. I had nothing more to give than this. Sure, I could turn her over and fuck her across my desk, watch her body fall apart at my touch, have her sweet scent on my tongue, bury myself in that divine body, not knowing where she started and I ended. I could love every damn second of her, every piece of her. But Lily wasn't like that. She was more than that, and in this moment she saw me for what I was, someone not worth loving… someone not worth keeping.

CHAPTER NINE

Lily

I TRIED DESPERATELY TO QUIET MY breathing. Desire had Todd's usually dark brown eyes burning with an amber flame. He had set me ablaze as well. It was silent, and the electricity between us licked and snapped as we tried to come down off the high of each other. I had never experienced a first kiss like that. The feeling of disappointment washed over me in quick waves when he pulled away. I wanted to lean in and continue where we left off. My brain was trying to tell me to back off; guys like Todd only brought pain and heartbreak to the table. But something inside of me knew better. No man with that much passion could be all bad. I decided to listen to that quiet small voice. I wanted whatever he had to offer. I had a feeling I might regret that decision later, but I was willing to take the chance.

"Todd..." My voice sounded pale in the deep silence. "...I'm not—"

"I know," he interrupted. Darkness invaded his eyes, cooling the spark, making me feel awkward. I slowly moved my body from his, immediately I missed his warmth. My feet touched the ground, and I felt unsteady on my legs. Todd's fresh soapy and cedar scent clung to my skin. I had to gather my wits.

"You know what?" I cringed at how worried my voice sounded.

"This was a mistake. I shouldn't have kissed you." His tone was biting. He stood from the desk abruptly. I felt cold and stupid. I wasn't that girl — I'd never been that girl. I wanted to smack myself. I've known the guy for maybe two days, and for most of it, I thought he was a complete bastard. *Way to go, Lily!* I mentally berated myself. I hated my overly heated hormones right now and more than anything, I hated how easily I let him in.

"A mistake." I nodded my head, still too pissed at myself.

Todd's bitter laugh brought me out of my internal self-scolding. "I knew it," he mumbled angrily. He picked up his beer and swallowed the remaining brew in one gulp. I took a pace backward from where he was standing, his change of mood again spiraling me out of control.

"You knew what, Todd?" My eyebrows pulled inward with irritation. I crossed my arms, suddenly bracing myself for the inevitable pain that Todd was about to dish out.

He had an annoyed smug grin as he spoke. "That you would regret it. That it was a mistake to kiss you. You're just like the rest of them." I felt his hateful glare appraise me.

"The rest of them? What are you talking about?" I was no longer able to confine my fury. My voice rose, and the heat in my chest poured down my body. I balled my fists in frustration.

He slightly shook his head. "I'm fucking tired of it, Lily. I don't need another whore."

My tight fist met his jaw before I even knew what was happening. "How dare you! I'm not a whore!" I rubbed my knuckles — the ache from my bones connecting with his face quickly seeped through my hand. It wasn't just physical pain that had my tears spilling down my cheeks. "Shit! That hurt." I hadn't cried in front of another person in so long. Todd was too busy working his fingers across his shocked face to notice my tears.

My quiet sniff brought his attention back to me, and I watched as his face fell, the mask totally absent.

"Shit, Lily... I'm sorry. I deserved that. I shouldn't have said those things. Are you okay?" He assessed my injured hand with his dark chocolate eyes. The sound of his voice was soothing, and I hated that I felt that way. He moved toward me, and I stumbled backward.

"Don't." I needed to get out of this office. I wiped the salty water away from my cheeks roughly as I turned to leave. My fingers had just touched the door handle when I felt Todd's intense grip on my upper arm.

"Damn it, Lily. Wait, okay. I screwed up. I got into my head, and I assumed..." His chin tilted down with obvious shame. His glance held steady to the floor.

"You assumed what?" I asked curtly.

"That you regretted kissing me. When I pulled away from you, I felt confused. I messed up. I don't really know you, but you have me all mixed up. I can't help that. I haven't felt anything for so long, and, when I kissed you, the numbness started to fade. It scared the fuck out of me." Todd's words penetrated through my anger. He thought *I* had *regretted* it. He pulled me toward him, and I let him. He brought his hands to my face and slanted my head up so I had no other choice but to meet his gaze. I wound my hands around his wrists, not in protest, but because I needed to touch him, to feel him. He was such an idiot. I could have never regretted that kiss. I didn't know a soul on this planet that would have regretted that kiss.

"You shouldn't assume, Todd." I let my eyes drink in his honest features. With the façade gone, he looked so dangerously beautiful. The pad of his right thumb wiped away my remaining tears.

"I'm sorry I made you cry, for making you feel anything less than extraordinary. I'm an asshole." He leaned down and kissed my forehead making my pulse shudder. "But that's the thing, Lily, I'm fucked up. So in the end, this *was* a mistake. I'm your boss. I hardly know you, but I know I'm not the guy you need to waste one more minute on." He dropped his hands from my face and stepped back. I brought the heel of my hand to my chest and pressed down trying to relieve the pressure.

"I don't remember asking your permission, Todd. You can't dictate what I want."

"Lily." It sounded as if he was scolding a child.

"Forget it. You're probably right." I schooled my features and gave him a small fake smile. He was right though. I hardly knew him. I couldn't let one little kiss ruin my plan, my goals. I took a deep breath as I lied to myself. I wasn't fooling anyone — that kiss was more than just a kiss. It was so much more.

"You'll find that I'm usually always right." Todd's lips spread into a brilliant smile, and my mood mirrored his. Without my consent, my smile brightened.

"Friends?" I asked.

Todd's expression dimmed at the word 'friends.' It was unnerving to watch the veneer slip back in place.

"Friends." The smile on his face no longer reached his eyes. "We should head back out there. They're probably cursing our names." His laugh was light and absolutely fake.

I couldn't help but feel weighted down as he walked past me and opened the door. I saw Todd for what he was. He was passionate, angry, and in pain. You'd have to be a moron to not see the wounds he was trying so desperately to hide. Regardless, I liked how he made me feel. He knew how to push all my buttons. He brought me up, tore me down, and moved me sideways with that kiss and with his words.

"Friends." I had to find a way to be all right with that word. Because I had a plan... I had a promise to keep, and I had to do what I came here for. The air filled my lungs and

poured leisurely from my lips. I relished in that small calm moment. My focus was all I had left, because my dignity was still sitting on that desk making out with the boss.

"You coming, Red?" Todd's dimpled smile was inviting.

"Yeah."

Friends.

THE REST OF THE NIGHT went by fast. It was officially closing time, and you would think I would be excited to get the hell out of here, but the night's earlier events had me all knotted up. Todd spent the rest of the shift talking to some slutty looking bottle blonde. She was silicone city, and she was eating up every little charming laugh and wink Todd delivered. It made me sick. I was starting to think *"friends"* wasn't even an option until I heard what Todd was saying to Jace about the girl. I was subtly eavesdropping on the conversation as I wiped down the barstools. Tiff's closing time song choice played lightly so I was still able to hear.

"You going to hit that shit? She was all over you." Jace picked up the crate of bottled beer and started loading the fridge. Todd squinted his eyes, shooting daggers in Jace's direction.

"Don't you ever get sick of that shit, Jace?" Todd bunched the rag he held in his hand and threw it in the sink. "I'm so tired of it."

"You would be, bro, you've basically screwed the majority of the greater Salt Lake area." Jace's laugh had the hairs on the back of my neck standing on end. Was Todd a player? God, I really had no idea who he was. I bit my lip as I internally scolded myself.

I was so busy having a private panic attack over my immature reaction to Todd earlier, that I hadn't noticed he was watching me. Todd's russet eyes had my heart fluttering, making me hate myself even more for allowing him to get me so tangled. I had pride in the fact that most guys couldn't rattle me. Confusion settled in my gut as he trapped me in his hard gaze. I had no idea what he wanted from me. I watched his fantastically sculpted arms tense and the muscle in his jaw tick. I looked away feeling self-conscious at the warmth and color that flooded my cheeks.

STILL WATER
CHAPTER TEN

Todd

THAT FUCKING BLUSH WAS GOING TO destroy me. I've never been this physically attracted to another girl in my entire damn life, not even with Elizabeth. I pulled my eyes away from her in effort to calm the overwhelming need to drag her to my office and just end this now. Jace's self-righteous laughter drew me out of my thoughts.

"Go fuck yourself, man. Like you have any room to talk," I said with irritation at his judgment. Jace was probably a bigger whore than I was. He just hid it. Whereas I — I put that shit right out on display. What was the purpose of hiding it? All those things will come and bite you in the ass eventually.

The hot blonde was lingering by the door. She was waiting for me to bite at the bait she was waving under my nose all night, but I wasn't sure I wanted what she was offering. I was over it. I closed my eyes; Lily's kiss was on repeat in my head, her damn pink lips that tasted like berries. I hadn't ever tasted anything so sweet.

"Hey, that chick won't leave, and we got to lock up." Jace clipped me on the shoulder with his fist. "You sending her packing or what?"

This night was so confusing, and I wasn't sure what to do with all this excessive tension. Part of me wanted to send this chick on her way. I didn't need this shit anymore, but the other half — the half that saw shame in Lily's eyes no matter what she said — that part of me knew better. Still water runs deep, and deep down I was empty. Empty like an abyss. Void of anything permanent. I wasn't worth the commitment. Why should I offer anything more when all of me is never good enough?

"I got this." I smiled up at the blonde and walked to the front door. *Fuck it.*

CHAPTER ELEVEN

Lily

ALL THAT WAS RUNNING THROUGH MY mind on my way home from work was the sight of Todd's back as he left the bar with the skanky blonde. She was so obviously desperate for his attention, it was sad. I watched as she touched his arm, laughed at his jokes, ran her fingers through his hair. A few hours earlier I'd been doing the same thing, and my easy behavior was making me angry. The thing that was pissing me off more than anything was that he chose her over me. I hated myself for caring. I was mad that he'd go home with her, share his bed with her, but not with me. It was disgusting how I was letting all my insecurities boil to the surface. Self-doubt started to pull me under as I turned into my driveway. All the dumb girl questions started flowing like a sieve. Did he not like how I kissed? Was my body not good enough for him? Did he think I was too inexperienced?

My internal monologue was absolutely ridiculous. Todd was a player; I didn't need a guy like him in my life. I would go to work, do my job, sing for Frank, and get the deal I needed to make my album. I quietly walked down the stairs to my basement apartment. My feet were killing me, and all I wanted was a hot shower. There was no way that was going to happen. Eve would have a damn come apart if I woke Christopher. Instead, I got in my worn sleep pants and my dad's gray band T-shirt. Once my head hit the pillow, I couldn't hold back the tears. What the hell was wrong with me that I would be so drawn to this guy who was so obviously and completely emotionally unavailable?

I missed my father so much. If he were still here, still alive, I could talk to him about this. He would be able to give me an answer. If only I had listened to him like I should have.

The hard rain fell onto the roof of my house making it hard to sleep. Derrick broke my heart tonight when I saw him with her. He never really loved me, and my dad knew it. He said he saw Derrick with her the other night at the bar. He had played a show at Marquee and saw my boyfriend with Becca, my so-called best friend. I didn't believe him.

The worst part is I told my father I hated him, and now I didn't know where he was. I wanted to apologize and tell him he was so right. I shifted to my right side. The red glow from my alarm clock taunted me. It was very late. The digital display read 2:30 a.m. Why wasn't my father home? I exhaled an anxious breath while the thunder rumbled loudly and rattled my windowpanes. I rolled to my back. My mind was running a mile a minute. My life here as I knew it was over. My boyfriend was screwing my best friend. My father is pissed at me. I lost my music scholarship.

Worst. Week. Ever.

I stared at the fake palm-frond ceiling fan and finally let myself cry. The sound of Johnny Cash's 'Ring of Fire' startled me. My father's ringtone. My cell phone almost vibrated off the bedside table, but I caught it in time.

"Dad? Where are you?" My voice was wobbly from crying. I hoped he hadn't noticed.

"Lil? Honey, this is Gabe." Gabe's voice sounded like he was in a wind tunnel.

"Gabe? What's up? Where's my dad?" My internal panic was starting to swell. This wasn't right. Why was Gabe calling?

"Lily... honey... there's been an accident."

This reminded me of that night. Me lying in bed, late at night, crying over a boy, missing my father. Except then, my father had still been alive. Well, at least that's what I'd thought.

WORK WAS HORRIBLY BUSY. The band Red Light that had canceled yesterday seemingly rebooked tonight, and the place was stuffed to the gills. The house, so to speak, was full of college kids. Jace, Tiffany, and I could barely keep up. Todd hadn't shown up yet, and we really could have used an extra hand. I tried to pretend that I didn't care he wasn't here. I kept telling myself he was of no significance, but, every time the door opened, I looked up hopeful that he would walk through it. Each time, the disappointment would quickly turn into frustration. I was repulsed with myself. He went home with another girl. My stomach turned at the thought of him with her. The memory of the heat of his hands on my body made it so much worse. Those hands. Where had they been?

I decided that I wasn't going to waste one more minute obsessing over my hot, man-whore of a boss. I had a small, hormonally challenged lapse in judgment. I mean no one could blame me. He was absurdly attractive. Todd's eyes were like hot water on my skin. The peppermint flavor that lingered on his lips and those hands... they felt like home. *Crap.*

"Lily, this band is so great, right!" Jace shouted. His smile beamed as he rocked his body to the music.

"Yeah, they remind me of *Modest Mouse.*" It was next to impossible not to return his smile.

"Hell yeah! I love it." Jace started playing air guitar, and I laughed at his silly display. "What are you doing tomorrow?"

Jace's smile was appealing and open. The complete opposite of Todd. *Stop It!* I had to stop thinking about him.

"I don't know. That's right, bar's closed tomorrow. Probably just veg out." I opened a beer and handed it to a customer. "Thanks," I said as I took his money and placed it in the till. I pulled and tightened my crazy curly ponytail and heard Jace snicker.

"What?" I smiled up at his crooked grin.

"Want to go out? You're new in town, right? Let me show you around." Jace's blue eyes sparkled with excitement and something else I couldn't place.

"On a Sunday?" I didn't know what it was, but something about Jace's easy smile and boyish good looks was off-putting, like he was trying to hide something. The blue fervor in his eyes flickered brighter. It dawned on me that maybe he liked the chase. Was I a challenge? He and Todd seemed very competitive. The other night Todd had pretty much tried to stake his claim on me. Could I go on a date with another co-worker after kissing my emotionally unavailable boss? Should I even consider it? Was Jace a player too? All these questions made my head hurt with anxiety.

"Yeah, Lil, on a Sunday." He laughed and shook his head. "You game?" Jace's muscular biceps contracted as he dried the inside of a pint glass. Holy hell, was I game? Why not? Todd made his decision when he said I shouldn't want him and then went home with that bar fly.

"Sure. Let's do it." My smile was small. I needed a break from my realities for a minute.

Jace's sudden mischievous grin gave me butterflies in my stomach, but not in a good way. He almost looked smug. I started to feel nervous all over again.

"Let's do what?" Todd's deep voice behind me caused chills to run up my spine as heat gathered along my chest and neck.

"Me and Lil have a date tomorrow night." Jace's azure

eyes were challenging. "I'm thinking about taking her to Ledge and then maybe dinner. You like rock climbing, Lil?" he asked, but never looked me in my eyes. He was too busy staring intently at the man behind me. The man, that for some reason, I was afraid to face.

"Um... sure sounds good," I lied. I was terrified of heights. I was feeling overly warm and just wanted to go and hide in the break room and collect my thoughts. Todd placed his hand on my shoulder, and I jumped.

"*Lil,* I wanted to talk about your audition piece for Frank. Follow me." I didn't miss the way he said my name. It seemed Jace had gotten under his skin.

"Sure. You and Tiff got the bar for a minute?" I looked out at the floor; Tiffany was running drinks to one of the far tables. I felt guilty leaving them out here on such a demanding night.

"Yeah, just make it quick. It was nice of you to show up, by the way, Todd. It's been a shit show." Jace's tone was thick with accusation.

"I had some shit to deal with. You guys survived. Let's go, Lily," Todd barked.

"Be back in a sec, Jace." I smiled, trying to keep the peace. I'd like nothing better than to stay up here and run my butt off rather than talk to Todd.

I turned and kept my head down. I didn't want to see the look on Todd's face; the tone of his voice spoke volumes. I hurriedly walked past him through the bar to the back offices. Once the back hall door shut, the loud live band was muted and I could hear my heavy breathing. As I entered Todd's office, the vision of us on his desk made me feel all rosy and, for some reason, guilty. The sound of the door clicking and locking behind me made me turn sharply.

"You're not seriously going out on a date with Jace are you? Not after—"

"Not after what?" I interrupted. I raised my chin and stood a bit taller. The implication in his voice pissed me off.

Especially, after who he went home with last night.

"After I had you straddled around me and my cock pressed up against you on this very desk, *Lil*." My heart skipped a beat, and my breathing felt shallow at his rough words. My cheeks must've been crimson. His dark eyes locked on mine.

"Excuse me?" I was incredulous.

"Oh, you heard me, Red." He stalked toward me causing me to take a step back. My backside hitting the familiar desk. The sensation of the hard wood against my legs made me think of how, just yesterday, my body *had* been wrapped around his on this very spot. I closed my eyes and inhaled trying to gather all my faculties, but Todd's clean scent was everywhere, surrounding me, making me feel things I didn't want to feel.

I opened my eyes and found him staring at my parted lips. I bit my bottom lip out of apprehension and watched as he licked his own. He was so physically overpowering. Everything about Todd drew me in. I wanted to kiss him so badly. Those full lips did crazy things to me, made me want to do things I shouldn't want to do after only knowing him for three days.

"He'll just use you." Todd closed the distance between us and took my face between his hands making me feel breathless. His brown irises faded as his pupils dilated. "That's what Jace does. He likes the thrill of the chase, Red."

"You mean like you did? She didn't make you chase her very long though, did she?" The hateful sound of my voice surprised me. Todd dropped his hands from my face and stepped back like I'd slapped him. "I sure hope you used protection. She seemed a little easy, even for you. Get your kicks with me and then finish off with a stranger. Nice move, boss."

"*You don't know what the hell you're talking about,*" Todd's anger filled every word.

"I don't? Tell me you didn't take her home." I sounded doubtful.

"I didn't take her home."

"Sure you didn't." I rolled my eyes and tried to walk past him. He grabbed my shoulders.

"I didn't take her home, Lily." He exhaled and looked at me directly. All I saw was honesty. "I wanted to and I normally would have, but it felt wrong. Just like you going out with Jace is wrong." He gritted his teeth.

"You don't own me, Todd. For hell's sake, I've known you for like three days." His hands squeezed my shoulders, not enough to cause pain, but enough to know what I'd just said hurt him somehow.

"Damn it, Lily. He takes trophies from the girls he's laid. If I'm no good, that guy is the devil." He took a deep breath. "Trust me."

"That's the thing, Todd. I don't know you enough to trust you, and after last night, the way things went down, I can't deal with this bullshit. I'm my own person, *I have my own plans.*" I pushed his hands off my shoulders and stepped sideways away from his reach. I moved quickly to the door trying to avoid getting stuck in *that* stare. I just couldn't let Todd consume me, because I have no doubt that's what would happen. The attraction between us was unreal, and fires that burn this bright die fast. I unlocked the door and slowly opened it.

"Lily, please, I'm serious. Jace is no good." Todd sounded so genuine right then that I almost turned back around and just let this thing, this crazy thing between us, happen.

"I'm a big girl, boss. I can handle myself." I swiftly left the room as Todd cursed loudly right before the door slammed behind me.

CHAPTER TWELVE

Todd

MY CAR SAT IDLING IN THE DRIVEWAY of Elizabeth and Sawyer's place. It was nearing 5:45 p.m., and I just couldn't bring myself to turn off the ignition and head inside. Not only had it been over a year since I had seen Liz, I was still dealing with the mind fuck that was Lily. I swore out loud and immediately felt like a jackass. I was being such a pussy. I reached over the stick shift to grab the present I'd gotten for Sailor. Elizabeth loved penguins, so I figured I'd buy her little girl a pink penguin. *Chicks dig pink, right?* As I came back to an upright position, I saw Sawyer standing at the hood of the car. *Shit!* I about screamed like a little bitch because he'd startled me. His mouth spread into a shit-eating grin. *Fucker!* I started to laugh hard and honked my horn at him.

I opened the door. "You 'bout gave me a heart attack, brother."

Sawyer's deep laugh twisted in my gut. I missed this guy. "Why are you sitting out here like a stalker?" He moved in for his signature side arm hug. He tapped my back hard as always. I loved this about him. No matter how jealous, defeated, or angry I was that Liz didn't pick me, I never faulted Sawyer. This guy was the best guy I'd ever known. He fought for our country, and he had some rough shit to deal with from his past. We never really got into it, but I could tell he had issues. It made me feel like a jerk; here I was whiny about a girl. My life was good. I had the best parents, a good home, and I threw it all away because I couldn't have *her*. I didn't deserve *her*. He did. My inadequacies were too much for one person.

"It's good to see you, bro." I smiled and punched him in the shoulder.

"We missed you too. Come on, let's head in. I should warn you, though... Sailor is the cutest thing you'll ever see. Be prepared." He chuckled, seeming ridiculously happy. And it was then I knew that I'd wasted too much time. For the first time, I could see what a complete fuckup I was. Elizabeth needed a friend, and I'd walked away. I was done with that shit. *Done.* I took a big breath and exhaled. "Nervous?" Sawyer looked at me with furrowed brows as we stood on the entryway steps. I had to say this. I had to have closure.

"Yeah, man. Listen. I'm over it now. I don't deserve your friendship. Hell, not even Lizzie's. But you guys being together... messed me up. Wait—"

Sawyer was about to interrupt, most likely to apologize. He didn't need to; he shouldn't have to feel sorry for being with Lizzie. "I'm not saying this to guilt you. I'm just letting you know... this shit with me and Liz, it's done. I'm moving on." In that moment, my chest felt lighter. I really was over *her*, and it felt damn good.

"That's good to hear, brother, 'cause I wasn't going anywhere anytime soon." Sawyer's lips turned up into a cocky grin, and I laughed at his smart ass.

The whole house smelled like onions and peppers as we walked inside. Liz had to be making her famous Philly cheese steaks. I mentally high-fived myself. I missed her damn cheese steaks. We walked through the house and in the direction of the kitchen. I came to a complete stop. The smile on Liz's face was breathtaking. Sailor was bouncing on Lizzie's hip and pulling at her mother's hair. *Liz was a mother.* Normally, that smile would've been a kick to the groin, but not today. No. It was just beautiful. Just Liz… my friend.

"You look so happy, Lizzie Bean." I smiled. "Let me see that beautiful girl." As I got closer, I could see Elizabeth's eyes were glittering with tears. My pulse skipped. "You okay, baby girl?"

"I'm—I'm—I'm, so glad you're here," she stuttered and started crying hard, so Sawyer came and took Sailor from her arms. I placed the bag with the present in it on the floor and quickly scooped her into a hug. The tears from Liz's cheeks soaked through my shirt while I held her tight to my chest. Her familiar scent of gardenias surrounded me making me feel at home. I missed this so much. I can't believe I wasted a damn year.

"Shh… it's okay, baby girl. I'm here. I got you." I rubbed her back and squeezed her closer to me. I made myself a promise then, I would never let this much time separate us again. She was my family, and I tossed her aside for my own selfish bullshit. "I missed you so much. Never again, okay? I will never be away from you guys for this long ever again." I kissed the top of her head. She pulled away slightly and looked up into my eyes, her bright blue pools filled with more tears.

"You promise? Todd, it's been hard." She leaned her cheek against my chest again. I felt her inhale a deep breath. "You smell the same. God, I've missed you so much." Her words mumbled against my chest.

"I'll give you two a minute," Sawyer's voice was laced with sadness.

"No way, brother. Give me that fat, little baby girl." I released Liz from my embrace and held my arms out toward

Sawyer. Sailor kicked and giggled as I brought her to my chest. She had huge blue eyes just like her mom, but she looked just like Sawyer. It was so weird. They made a person. A whole human being. And for a split second, I wondered what my kids would look like. *Lily and I could make some cute kids. Shit!* I wasn't expecting that thought to pop into my head. It was dumb to think like that. I hardly knew the girl, and, for all I knew, she was probably getting finger banged as we spoke by the bar whore himself. The thought made me sick to my stomach. Jace's hands on her in any way made me want to break shit. I clenched my jaw.

"What's the matter?" Elizabeth asked, her voice still shaky from our emotional reunion.

"Nothing. This little girl is a doll. You did good, Lizzie Bean... you did good." I felt light for the first time in over three years. This jealousy wasn't going to kill my buzz.

DINNER WAS FANTASTIC, AND I was right — Elizabeth had made her famous cheese steaks. Cam and Colby had canceled coming to dinner. Cam had texted me earlier that day to say she felt I needed to do this on my own. I was pissed at first, she was always there for me when it came to Liz and my stupid ass drama, but in the end, as usual, she was always right.

We were sitting in the living room by the fire. Sailor was fast asleep in her crib holding tight to her new pink stuffed penguin. *Success.* We caught up on the past year. Sawyer's business was doing well. Elizabeth was finishing up her senior year and would graduate in December. It was like I had never left, but at the same time everything was different. Elizabeth couldn't get over my fully tattooed upper body. She loved ink. That was part of the reason I'd gotten so much work done. I thought one day I could be the person she needed. I knew now I was so wrong.

"I just can't believe it. The artwork is so vibrant. I loved seeing Sailor in your arms. There is just something about babies in tattooed arms, I think." She smiled up at Sawyer teasingly. "I think you need sleeves, sir. You have that full back piece, now it's time for your arms." She giggled.

"We'll see, Cricket." Sawyer leaned down and kissed Elizabeth on the cheek. They both smiled so warmly at each other. It was good to see them both happy. They'd been through so much. Once they had been together for a while, it had come to light that Sawyer's dad, Gavin Bryant, whom he hadn't spoken to for years, had murdered a young girl. Sawyer's mother had gone to confront his father one night, and he had killed her. Gavin was twisted, and I knew that he hurt Sawyer more than he'd ever wanted to share. He set a trap for Sawyer, but Elizabeth went instead. Long story short, Elizabeth got shot and almost died. Worst week of my damn life.

Needless to say, seeing them happy now made me feel better, and that's something I hadn't felt in forever it seemed. "Why did you go so dark on the one side and so light on the other?" Elizabeth's eyes met mine. "I mean the one side is so lovely — bright sun, beautiful flowers... it's all so gorgeous, really. That tribal is so intricate, but then your left side is so macabre. I mean bleeding hearts are supposed to be pink, not black." She shook her head.

"That's the point, baby girl. Good versus evil and all that shit." I honestly believed that. I felt for so long that I was worthless, not good enough, and I sort of lost my way. I had light and darkness. I wanted to be that guy — the one who gets the girl, the kids, the dog, and the Goddamn picket fence. But... I knew better. The darker parts of my heart always seemed to win in the end. I couldn't make a good choice if I wanted to, and, because I was so mixed up over Liz for so long, I lost my self-worth. Now that I was free of that heartache, maybe… just maybe, I could find myself again.

CHAPTER THIRTEEN

Lily

I WAS SWEATING BULLETS. THIS WAS the worst idea ever. Jace's hands on my inner thighs had me feeling on edge. He had adjusted the climbing harness at least three times. At this point, I was sure he was just trying to cop a feel. "All right, I'm done. I hate this," I blurted out.

"Already, we've only been at it for like thirty minutes, Lil." Jace's voice held some incredulity.

"Yeah." I started to unbuckle myself.

"Let me—"

"No way, buddy, hands to yourself," I said with a bit more severity than was necessary.

"O… kay." Jace drew out the word like he was talking to a small child. He was such an ass. I didn't know what I was thinking going on a date with him. Dinner was a joke; the whole time all he did was talk about himself. How he was so good at everything he did. *Barf.* He was winking at me so much that I started to think he had something in his eye, but then I realized, nope, he's just a conceited asshole. Not to mention the fact that the entire time I was with him, all I could think about was Todd. Jace couldn't stop talking about Todd either. He told me horrible stories about Todd and how his "reputation" was epic. It made me physically ill listening to all the tales of Todd's sexual prowess.

I quickly got ready to leave and waited for Jace by the front doors. The cold unspring-like weather was getting worse after the sun had set. A cold gust of air hit my bare legs as someone entered the climbing gym. *I needed to stop wearing shorts.*

"Your place or mine?" Jace held the gym door open for me. He had to be kidding.

"I think I'm going to just call it a night." I made a show of yawning. "I'm drained. The first week of work really killed me."

Jace's jaw compressed. "Let's get one drink." he persisted.

"Look, I had a nice time, but I don't—"

"Stop, don't say it," he interrupted. "Let's just call it a night. I'll drop you off, and we can try again another night." Jace's smile didn't touch his eye, and it felt a bit off. I felt guilty though. I didn't want to date Jace, but I didn't want to hurt his feelings either. He was so much nicer when he wasn't trying to get in my pants.

"I don't know. I probably shouldn't date people I work with — unnecessary drama, you know?" I tapped my feet on the concrete. It was getting cold.

"Oh shit! Sorry, Lily. Here get in." The beep of his car unlocking signaled me that the torture of standing in the cold was over. *Praise the heavens.* Once in the car, I had hoped the conversation was over. I was wrong.

"So?"

"I don't know, Jace. Let me sleep on it, okay?" I should've just been straight with him instead of trying to spare his feelings. The guy really did need to be knocked down a notch anyway. I just didn't want to be the one to do it.

"That sounds good." He smiled his fake smile at me again.

The rest of the drive home was filled with awkward silence, and the ride to my house couldn't have taken any longer. Jace jumped out of the car and practically ran to open my door. He took my hand and helped me out of the car.

"You don't have to walk me to the door. Thanks for everything." I quickly moved my feet, one in front of the other, trying to create space. Jace grumbled under his breath as the door to his car slammed shut. I didn't want to give him any false hope by giving him a goodnight kiss. I slowed my pace and watched him drive away. I stopped for a minute at the end of my driveway and looked up at the clear sky and wondered what my dad would be doing right now if he were alive. We'd probably be sitting on the back porch listening to Van Morrison and drinking beer while the cicadas sang in the background. We'd be laughing and talking about what a shitty date that was. I took a deep breath loving how the clean air filled my lungs. It was getting late, and I was ready for bed.

I was about to head inside when Todd's silver 4Runner pulled up to the curb. My heart rate began to sprint. *What was he doing here?* He turned off the truck, and I watched as his hard frame moved toward me.

"What are you doing here?" I asked with irritated confusion. Why did he think he could just show up like this? I meant nothing to him.

"Wanted to make sure you got home okay." His deep voice vibrated through the cold, quiet air.

"Why?" *Was he worried about me?* My voice trembled as he moved closer, our bodies just a small fraction apart. The heat radiated from his body. He looked sexy in the dark gray T-shirt that stretched across his broad chest and fitted jeans. Todd's arms were so stunning. The cut muscle was only amplified by the artwork that scrolled across it. I loved how the ink was brightly colored on one side and dark on the other. I had a feeling there was a deeper meaning behind that choice. *Ugh, I shouldn't want to know anything deeper about Todd.* He was a playboy, and I needed to remember that. Still just the sight of him had me nervous and my stomach twisted in knots.

"Why?" His right eyebrow turned up. "Lily, Jace is a shit. I told you that I was worried."

He seemed different tonight, softer somehow.

"Oh," I mumbled lamely. I didn't know what to say, this man was such a puzzle. He put two fingers under my chin, lifting my face and giving me no other choice but to meet his gaze.

"I don't want you to go out with him again," Todd's voice was an imposing whisper.

"I don't think you have a say in the matter." I sounded unsure. He moved his hand to the side of my cheek, and without thinking, I leaned into the caress. The pull between us was surreal. The electricity in the air was almost visible.

"Oh, I think I do." He leaned down and placed his mouth softly to mine. He kissed my upper lip first, and then lightly pulled at the bottom lip, sending shivers down my spine and heat to my belly. He bound his other arm around my waist and pulled me tight against his body. I craved his hard touch. Our kiss became aggressive, and his tongue mingled with mine. Todd twisted his hand into my hair, pulling my head back making it easier for him to kiss me intensely. He kissed me deeper than I'd ever been kissed before, and a needy moan escaped my mouth. Todd pressed his hips against my body, and I felt his arousal against my stomach.

"Fuck." His coarse word rumbled into my mouth.

"Do you want to come inside?" I asked, sounding more desperate than I thought possible. I hated that he made me feel out of control, but at the same time I was tired of always keeping it together. I wanted a moment of irrationality. Just one moment.

"Is that what you want?" He pinned my eyes. "It's late, you need to go to sleep."

"I don't want to sleep. I want you." I grinned and pushed

my hips into his. He groaned. "Ugh, I forgot. I live with my damn sister. Could we go to your place?"

"Lily, is that—"

"What I want? Yes." What was it with all this hesitation? He wanted me, I could tell. Why else would he be here?

Todd exhaled noisily. The chocolate of his eyes appeared darker; he seemed tired all of a sudden. "All right, I'm driving though."

The minute he conceded I knew I had hurt him, and I didn't know why.

ON THE WAY OVER, TODD TALKED to me... like really talked to me. I found out that Todd had a brother named Colby, who played football for a University up north and was dating Todd's best friend, Cameron. He told me about his family and his friend Liz and her husband, and about how cute their baby was. How he couldn't believe that they had made an actual human being. It was so cute how he was dumbfounded by the simple mechanics of procreation. He had me belly laughing the whole way. I noticed, though, he talked about Liz with a certain reverence. I had a feeling Liz had some part in breaking this boy down. Todd's jaw constricted a bit when he spoke of her, his grip on the steering wheel was tighter than necessary. Yeah, Liz had done a number on him. I was grateful for this small peek into his closed off world. For a second, I thought that maybe he chose to sleep around as a way to forget. Todd wasn't a womanizer, of this I was now sure. He was just broken.

The tension in the car was thick as we pulled up to his condo. I felt as if he'd opened up to me, and now I was going to cheapen it by sleeping with him. But for some reason, I needed him to want me. The attraction between us was so overwhelming. I couldn't get him out of my brain, and then he rejected me. He said he didn't do anything with that stupid blonde, and I believed him. I wanted to believe *in* him. I wanted a piece of who he was. His dismissal cut me more than it should have, and now I had to have some small part of him, no matter the cost.

He dropped his keys into a giant bowl of condoms and candy that sat on the sideboard table in the entryway as we walked into the house. My anxiety picked up a notch, and my heart was beating so hard in my chest I was sure the neighbors could hear it.

"So, where's Seth?" I asked while I took in my surroundings. . It was decorated simply as a bachelor pad would be. The living room we were standing in had large, soft looking gray couches, and the walls had exquisite black and white photos. All the photography appeared to be landscapes of some of the local state parks. The entertainment center had a large television and at least two gaming consoles. *Yep, men lived here.*

"He's out. He's hardly here on the weekend nights. He won't bring chicks here." Todd plopped down onto the sofa. I could have died and been fine with never knowing that tiny bit of info on Seth. "We watching a movie or something?" He smiled up at me. His grin was sweet.

"Or something?" I smiled back suggestively, and his grin fell slightly. I almost thought I imagined it.

"I think we need to slow down. I mean, we hardly know each other, maybe —"

"Why did you drive me over here then?" He was rejecting me again, and it pissed me off how much that hurt.

"Lily… I know, okay, I get it. But I think us…" He swayed his hand back and forth gesturing to himself and then me. "…hooking up, could be a bad idea." He stood from the couch bringing his body just inches from mine. His dark brown eyes pierced through me. "Trust me. Like I've said before, you don't want my baggage."

I was confused and getting angrier. "Then why the fuck did you bring me here?" My voice was louder than I meant it to be. He stepped away from me with a shocked look.

"Damn it, Lily. At first, it was because I got so wrapped up in you. Kissing you is like a drug. I can't fucking think." He shook his head. "Lily, I can't do this shit with you. I'm still getting over some things, and I'll just screw it up like I always do." His hands fisted.

I should've been listening to his warnings, but my stupid ego was too wounded to care. "I don't get it! You'll screw random chicks that throw themselves at you, but you won't get physical with me? What is that about? What... am I not good enough for you, Todd? I'm not Liz or some easy slut so you won't give me the time of day?" Todd's eyes narrowed into slits, he looked like he hated me. I'd taken that small piece of him that he gave me on the ride over and threw it in his face. I was being such a bitch. I couldn't believe how livid I was. What was it about him that made me care this much? My cheeks heated and my pulse beat heavy in my chest. One minute he was hot, all over me, making me feel sexier than I'd ever felt, and then next he was just as cold. This back and forth, this jealous bullshit, it was exhausting.

"Are you serious right now?" He took two massive steps and caged me against his living room wall. "Lily, what do you want from me?" Todd's voice was low. It felt as if he was asking me for forever, but all I needed was right now.

"I want you to want me like you do all those other girls." I couldn't meet his eyes, letting him know how much I needed this – him. He made me feel insecure.

He grabbed my shoulders and kissed me hard. I could tell he was fighting his temper. He pulled roughly at my lips, and I loved every minute of it. The coarse hair from his short, clipped beard burned my lips in the most wonderful way. I savored the peppermint flavor of his lips. The flavor I had begun to crave. Todd's now familiar scent invaded my senses and started me on fire, a slow burn, but worth every bit of pain it was sure to cause after the fact.

CHAPTER FOURTEEN

Todd

"Is this what you want?" I kissed her deeply, tracing my tongue along her bottom lip. My teeth grazed the soft surface of her neck. "Is it, Lily?" My voice was strained, my throat dry. I wouldn't be able to say no to her. I would take her any way I could, even if it killed me later.

"Yes," she whispered. My hand clasped around the back of her neck pulling her close as she bit her lip with anticipation. I needed her to want me more than anything she's ever needed in her life. I opened myself up to her tonight, telling her about Liz, but she still gave me nothing. I wanted to be deep inside her, filling all that emptiness that was obviously drowning her. This girl was damaged. Why else would she seek me out? All I knew about her was she had recently lost her dad. Maybe she felt alone? Maybe she needed to feel something other than the pain she carried, even if it wasn't real. Just like me, reducing herself with meaningless sex.

I needed more than just a one-night stand. I was done sinking. I wanted her to keep me afloat, and that scared the shit out of me. I hated that it hurt me when she chose to come home with me, chose to be like "all of the other girls."

"Why? Why do you want this? Me?" I grasped her face in my hands. I tilted her head up making her gaze lock with mine.

"What?" Her voice was faint and her breath tasted sweet against my lips. She was too far gone with desire to give me a straight answer. She leaned in and our lips crashed together. She took over and guided us to the couch, and I felt her knees hit the cushion. My hands trailed softly down the slope of her neck, and I felt her shiver under my fingertips. She was so fucking ready.

"Tell me, Lily? Do you want me to fuck you?" Her lips touched my neck and the small gasp from her mouth gave me the answer I needed.

"Yes." Lily's otherworldly eyes met mine. "I want you." Her hands traced down my abs, and my dick strained against my jeans. She started to lift my shirt, and I let her. I couldn't remember why I should stop this. I didn't give a shit anymore. If this is what she wanted from me, then I'd give it to her, I'd show her what it was like to *be* with me. If this was all I was good for, then I would give her everything I had.

"Turn around." My voice was rough. She hesitated at first but did as I asked. I kissed her neck as I brought my hands down her sides. She shuddered at the touch. I was trying to enjoy it, the power I had over her, but I didn't want this. I wanted more. My anger flared. I stepped away from her waiting form.

"Todd?" her voice pleaded.

This is all she wants. This is all I'm worth.

"Bend over and place both of your hands on the back of the couch." My voice shook with suppressed fury, but there was no turning back. She did as I asked; her round soft ass sticking up in the air was perfection in all its glory. She stood and bent over as I reached around her small waist and unclasped the button of her shorts. At first, I slowly peeled them off, wanting to savor the moment, but then I remembered she wanted to be fucked, not cherished. I could have done both if she'd given me the chance.

CHAPTER FIFTEEN

Lily

TODD WRENCHED MY SHORTS DOWN COMPLETELY. Naked from the waist down, I felt overly exposed, but then I heard him exhale quietly and felt secure in the fact that he liked what he saw. I heard the buckle of his belt jingle, the sound of his jeans hitting the floor, and the distinct noise of a foil wrapper being torn open. The anticipation had me aching for him; I wanted to turn so I could see his face. I started to turn around when, suddenly, Todd grabbed my hips.

"Don't move, baby. Stay just like this." I felt his finger pull across the sensitive skin of my core. My legs started to tremble as he pushed two fingers inside of me. "You're so ready, *this* is what you wanted." His rhythm picked up, bringing me close to the edge, and, just as I was about to come, I felt his tip at my entrance, his fingers gone. He grabbed my left hip with his hand and pushed hard inside of me without hesitation. The movement was so rough that I cried out. He pulled back and pushed in again with a growl, completely filling me. Todd's strong hands gripped firmly on the soft flesh of my hips. My body adjusted to his size seamlessly, and the pain became pleasure. Todd was relentless, his hands on each hip pulling me back and forth, thrusting into me angrily. It was the most delicious pain I'd ever felt.

"Kneel down, baby." Todd's voice was thick with desire, and it spurred me on. I let my knees fall into the forgiving cushions. "That's it." He pressed the front of my body flush against the back of the couch. My hands were firmly planted on the wall as he kneeled behind me driving himself into my body, my muscles tightening around him. I was so close. My breath was erratic, and my moans felt embarrassingly loud. He reached around and found the spot I needed for my final release. I cried out, and his strokes became furiously hard. My name growled from his lips.

I felt him everywhere. This position had him completely wrapped around my body. He was deep inside me as I pushed against his final strokes. He thrust his hips, enfolding his hand in my hair and pulling me back forcefully as his body went rigid. He kissed my neck dragging his teeth across the surface. His stubble felt perfect against my tender skin. My legs shook as the overwhelming feeling of him engulfed me.

We were both out of breath, my back to his chest — our labored breathing felt synchronized. He pulled away just enough to rest his forehead on the back of my hair. I could feel his hot breath moving in and out of his mouth. I wanted to turn around and kiss his full, flawless lips. I was about to turn around when he spoke.

"It wasn't supposed to be like this, Lily. Our first time shouldn't have been like this. I never wanted to fuck you like a whore." Todd's deep timbre trembled with feeling.

My chest constricted. He was right. I let him attempt to fill the void in my chest by letting him pour his anger inside of me. I let him use me, *"like a whore."*

CHAPTER SIXTEEN

Todd

EMPTINESS WAS THE ONLY EMOTION I felt when I slowly pulled away from our connection, from her. I walked silently to the trashcan to dispose of the condom, too terrified to look Lily in the face. I meant what I said. I never wanted Lily to be just another notch on my bedpost. I didn't really know what I wanted, but this — this was not what I wanted for us. For her or anyone, anymore.

I needed a minute. I wasn't ready to face her, but I was standing in my kitchen buck ass naked. Figuring Seth could have come home at any minute, I decided I probably should pull my shit together. The walk from my kitchen back to her shouldn't have hurt as much as it did, but how else was I supposed to feel when I found her halfway out my front door... leaving?

"What the fuck, Lily?" I couldn't mask the pain in my voice as I watched her trying to sneak out, and it pissed me off. I snatched my jeans and boxer briefs off the floor and swiftly pulled them on, not really giving a shit about much else except stopping her from leaving. We needed to deal with this. "Where the hell are you going?"

She shut the front door, stepping back into the house, but she wouldn't turn to look at me.

"I drove you here, remember? You walking home? I think not, sweetheart." I was doubtful.

"Don't... do not call me that. I feel cheap enough as it is." Her head bowed down, and I felt ill, the taste of pennies coated my tongue.

"Lily... listen..." I took three large steps tearing up the distance between us. Yeah, I was so pissed right now — at myself, at her, at this whole damn messed up situation — but this distance between us was building, and I couldn't fucking breathe. It was too heavy, and there was nothing I could do to stop the weight of it from crushing me. My hands rested on the back of her shoulders. "Please, look at me. I need you to hear me."

Eyes filled with tears met mine, the salty water making the yellow color of her calico irises stand out and shimmer. I inhaled sharply; the sight of her took my breath away. Lily's face was still flushed from our encounter, her copper hair was everywhere, and her tropical scent pulled me in. She didn't resist as I enclosed my arms around her and pulled her to my bare chest. What the hell was happening to me? The overwhelming sickness in my gut twisted even more once I felt her tears start to pour down my heated skin. She silently cried, and I knew then I was the biggest goddamn loser that ever walked this earth.

CHAPTER SEVENTEEN

Lily

TEARS KEPT COMING. I COULDN'T STOP them, and I refused to let him hear me sob. I couldn't show him how this whole night destroyed me, how it took a small chunk of my heart and ripped it into tiny pieces. I hadn't any idea as to why this should have affected me so powerfully. I wasn't in love with Todd. This wasn't some silly insta-love crap I read about in books. This was lust, an irresistible pull that I had no control over. I just kept focusing on the words he'd said like they were a train in my head. My tears fell against his warm skin intensifying that soapy cedar smell that was purely Todd, making it that much harder to pull away.

"Lily, I'm sorry, we shouldn't have—"

I couldn't hear him say it. It would cause the dam of shame to shatter, and I wasn't ready for him to see me break completely. The past few months of my life had been gradually chipping away at the surface of my hard shell. I blamed myself for everything — for my cheating ex, my school issues, my father's death. If I hadn't said I hated him, if I hadn't blamed him for losing my stupid music scholarship, maybe he would still be alive. This *thing* with Todd had the potential to be that final hit on the proverbial nail.

"Stop it, I can't... I just don't want to hear it," I spoke as I pushed hard away from his chest.

"You need to hear what I have to say—"

"Please just stop, I said—"

"Goddamnit, Lily! Just fucking listen..." Todd's voice shook, his face was pale and his eyes were hard. "Please," he said in a much softer tone. My heart was racing and trying to beat its way out of my chest. "What just happened... that was completely messed up. But I don't regret it in the way you think I do. I regret the *how* of it all. I should have taken my time, memorizing every inch and curve of your body. I should have tasted every piece of you, savored your sweet fucking scent, let it cover my lips. Damn it, Lily, you're flawless, and I treated you like some cheap lay. You're more than that."

My world entirely tilted on its axis — his words were scorching across my flesh, turning every bit of fear, every insecure thought, all my doubt, into ashes. My chest was rising and falling at a rapid pace as he framed my face between his palms.

"See, the thing is... I'm sort of out of my league with you. Hell, I've known you less than a week, and you've totally jacked up my game." He smirked down at me. "I like you, Lily... and I'm afraid what happened tonight, just ruined any damn chance I had with you." His rough thumbs caressed my cheeks, lightly wiping away my leftover tears.

I wasn't sure a relationship that started like ours could every really work, but I had been lying to myself. There was no way I just wanted one night, and the minute I felt shame for what I'd chosen to do, was the minute I realized he was more than that to me as well.

"I like you too, Todd... but I don't regret what happened tonight. I can't. I wanted you... I want you, and I can't feel bad about that."

"Yeah?"

"Yeah." My lips pulled into a small smile. I took a deep breath as he leaned toward me, my lips parted, eager to taste him again. Todd's lips were indulgent. This kiss was a whisper, it was like kindling on a fire that was about to burn hot and light up the night's sky with bright oranges and reds. Todd's mouth felt like heaven against mine, our lips moved with languid precision as he pulled us into alignment. Two pieces of a puzzle, snapping into place, the sweet kiss lasted for just a moment, but it was exactly what we needed.

He drew away just enough that I could feel him smile against my lips. "God, Lily, I don't think I could ever get sick of that." Todd was smiling that rare boy-next-door, two-dimpled smirk, and the rest of my apprehension faded.

"Mmm... I should hope not." My hands rested against the surface of his chest. Todd's complete upper body was covered with tattoos. It was one big mural; his right side was covered in vibrant colors — drawings of flowers, animals of all sorts, and the ocean and the sun were all intertwined with a huge colorful tribal. Whereas, on the left side, he was covered in skulls, dying flowers, creatures, wraiths, and a quote that I couldn't really decipher at the angle I was in. These *'dark'* images were entangled within a scrolling labyrinth of knotted tree limbs. The light and the dark met naturally in the center of his chest. The contradicting images blended together creating the most unbelievable piece of walking art I'd ever seen.

"This is so incredible," I said, as my eyes combed across the surface of his sculpted chest and stomach. "What does that say?" I moved away enough to read the script across his rib cage. I watched his skin erupt into small goose bumps under the touch of my fingertips as I traced the lettering.

Todd recited the words, "*'Deep into that darkness peering, long I stood there wondering, fearing, doubting, dreaming dreams no mortal ever dared to dream before.'* It's from —"

"Edgar Alan Poe. I know. Todd this is—"

"Sad," he interrupted, capturing my gaze with his bottomless eyes.

"No, I was going to say beautiful." Todd had been cut wide open by something, someone. Elizabeth really must have done a number on him. "She really hurt you, didn't she?" Todd's easy posture turned rigid.

"I think tonight has been a shit show enough without dredging up all that. Yeah?" Todd's expression begged me to drop it, so I did. The two of us had had enough drama for one evening, besides it was late, and I needed to get home.

"Right." I reached up on my tiptoes and placed a small kiss on his lips. Todd's warm, strong arms encapsulated me again, pulling me in for one last deep kiss. I don't think I'd ever get used to how absolutely crazy his mouth, his lips, and that sexy as hell thing he did with his tongue made me feel. The sensation of his teeth dragging against my bottom lip caused me to moan, sending heat through my entire body centering between my legs. He was addictive.

"Stay," he whispered against my neck. "Let me show you what you're worth." The mix of adrenaline and his words and taste were clouding my judgment. I almost said yes. God, I wanted to say yes, but I had to step on the breaks if we ever wanted to get past today.

I leaned my forehead against his chest and inhaled, committing his smell to memory, wanting to take every piece of him home with me tonight. I wanted to be bathed in all that he was, and I found the courage to say the words I had to say. "I want to, but I think we'd better call it a night, boss." I stepped back and locked my eyes with his as I gave him a flirty smirk.

He chuckled. "I'm glad one of us is thinking with their brain."

My shoulders bobbed with laughter. "Take me home, idiot." I shook my head playfully as I swatted his arm. "You might want to put a shirt on."

"What, you can't handle all this hotness?" He quirked his eyebrow.

I giggled. "Oh my hell, get dressed and take me home before I change my mind about you."

THE MUSIC PLAYED QUIETLY as we turned onto the street where my sister lived. The night's events started running through my brain, and I began to feel uneasy. I absentmindedly spun my father's ring around the silver necklace as I wondered whether or not this *thing* with Todd was really going to happen. I wanted it to; I wanted him more than I thought possible. The butterflies in my stomach were flying full speed as we pulled into the driveway.

"You're always playing with that. Nervous habit?" He nodded his head toward my hands as I fiddled with the large silver ring. Todd's easy smile was a balm to my nerves; the deep tone of his voice soothed me for some reason.

"Yeah, you could say that." I looked down at my lap.

"Don't be nervous... okay?" He reached across the center console and placed his palm against my cheek, and I leaned into the touch. "I think... we're good, yeah?"

"Yes." I smiled. Todd's dimples popped as he smiled back.

"Good. Whose ring is that anyways?"

I tried not to let my face fall; this moment between us was nice, but I couldn't help it. I missed my father so much. "Shit, babe, what did I say?" Todd frowned as worry creased his brows.

"It was my father's. I just miss him." *It's my fault he's dead.*

"I can't even imagine what that would be like, losing a parent. I sometimes wish I could die before anyone in my family does. Is that weird?" He looked at me with serious dark eyes. The thought of losing Todd, or anyone for that matter again, had pressure building in my chest. I had to inhale deeply to release the building anxiety. *Chill Lily.*

I shook my head. "Not weird, no. Morbid maybe." An awkward giggle escaped my lips.

"Hey, shit happens, you know? But life moves on, and you have to just keep floating." Todd gave my thigh a comforting squeeze with his broad palm. "Well, that's what my mom always says."

"She sounds like a smart lady." He took my hand in his and entwined our fingers, the small gesture completely filling the moment. Just an hour ago we were linked in the most intimate way possible, but him here, holding my hand, felt more real, and I have never had real before.

CHAPTER EIGHTEEN

Todd

LILY RAISED OUR JOINED HANDS AND brushed her lips across my knuckles, her mouth was like satin against my coarse skin, and it felt fucking outstanding. I was starting to feel something again, and I wasn't sure if I should be scared or just run with it. I decided then that I had nothing left to lose. I've failed miserably at being happy, at being anything more than just okay. I needed to jump off the platform, find my groove. I felt as if I was back at a swim meet, waiting for the blow of the whistle, for the water to run through my fingers as I pushed myself fast through the impossible current created by those around me swimming also. I could do this. I wanted this win. I needed this win.

"You have tomorrow off?" I asked.

"Yes." Lily's eyes met mine. It was time to say goodbye, but it was like we were stupid teenagers on a first date and neither one of us wanted to be the first to say goodbye.

"See you Tuesday." I leaned across the car again, and she met me in the middle. I searched her face, memorizing the four freckles on her nose, the slightly bigger freckle that sat right in that small divot above her upper lip, and the divine mix of colors that shone bright from her happy eyes before I brought my lips to hers one last time tonight. Her kisses felt infinite. She pulled back, and her smile hit me straight in the chest. Oh yeah, I wanted this win real fucking bad.

LILY LOOKED SO DAMN sexy tonight; her sweater was low cut, and the dark green color made her wild red hair stand out more. She had her hair down, the curls were everywhere, and I loved it. My eyes never left her as I finished setting up the equipment for tonight's show. The bar was packed, it usually was when we played, but tonight it annoyed the shit out of me. I hadn't had a second to talk to Lily. I wanted to know what she was going to sing tonight, and more than anything, I wanted to know how she was feeling about us. *Us*... shit! She had me all jacked up, there was no '*us*,' but if I had a say in anything there sure as hell would be soon enough. She glanced up at me; her porcelain cheeks turned pink and caused me to break out into a lopsided grin.

"Bro, what the hell, man? Are we gonna play or stand here like idiots?" Graden was such an asshole sometimes. He always put me in a pissed off mood.

"Yeah, working on it. You got your shit ready?" I said between gritted teeth. Graden was an amazing guitar player, but if I was honest, I hated his ass. Seth and Graden got into some shit awhile back, not sure what about, probably some piece of ass, but since then he's had the biggest chip on his damn shoulder. One of these days I was going to knock him out if he didn't chill his attitude. "Ready." I tested the microphone by tapping it three times with my finger.

The overhead music turned off. "What's up, motherfuckers? We are the Lakeside Prophets..." I looked behind me and nodded my chin at Seth — his face broke wide with a smile. He loved this shit. The beat of the drum started while Jack plucked away at his bass. Graden's guitar started the high keen of feedback from the amp. It was a perfect synchronization of sound, all that was needed was a rhythm and words, and — that's where I came in. "...let's do this."

Once I started singing it was like I lost time. I spent most of my time trying to be numb, but when I was up here playing my heart out, singing the lyrics that I'd written, it was like an out-of-body experience. I've spent the majority of my life hiding behind a giant wall, but once I started writing music and singing, I could say how I truly felt but said in a way that kept me safe. To everyone else they were just words, but to me... well, they were everything. Tonight I wanted to try and show Lily that I *could* feel, that there was more to who I was, and that I wasn't just some douchebag who would eventually screw her over.

CHAPTER NINETEEN

Lily

I WAS IN COMPLETE AWE.

My words escaped me as I heard Todd's rough voice pull through the speakers, his tenor created a blanket of heat that covered my entire body. I'd never heard such an incredibly sexy voice in my entire existence. At first I thought maybe I was being silly, but as the emotion of each lyric hit me like a freight train, I was overcome with admiration. I was grateful the customers were all watching the show, so I could as well. Jace and Tiffany were busy arguing about something as I leaned against the back of the bar. I couldn't be bothered; all I wanted to do was watch Todd as he sang with his eyes shut, brows furrowed, and heart on his sleeve. My pulse beat heavy behind my chest, the bass of the song was deep, and the lyrics were so sad that I couldn't help the tears that started to well up. Todd's eyes opened just as he started to sing what I assumed was the chorus.

Who are you to bring me here?
Who are you to ask me to stay?
Why can't you see it's killing us,

Loving you this way.

These words, they were his past, and his past was crashing over the wall he had so firmly placed around him. His intense voice trapped me in place. Part of me wanted to stay here and listen to it all, listen to his heartache... But this was too much, he was too much, and everything that was happening between us was all too soon. He was turning me inside out.

Just as I was gathering the courage to leave, the song came to a close and the crowd exploded into praise. Todd smiled bigger than I'd ever seen him smile, his deep dimples making him look five years younger. I reached up and started to twirl my father's ring in-between my fingers. I hadn't even noticed my hands had started trembling until now. This man was bringing me to my knees, and I felt helpless to stop it.

"We thought we'd mix this shit up a bit and play a cover. You guys game?" Todd spoke with a smile in his voice into the microphone. The audience went nuts. "I'll take that as a *"yes"* then..." He chuckled, and my stomach flipped. God, he was so good looking, it really wasn't fair. "...How do you feel about *"Stay"* 30 Seconds to Mars style, yeah?" The crowd hollered in acceptance again, and Todd threw his head back and laughed with such feeling it was impossible to look away. I was sure I would never know all the sides of this fractured man. Graden, at least I thought that was what Tiff said his name was, placed his guitar on the stand and sat down at the piano. The crowd fell silent as the familiar piano riff started to play.

Todd's eyes locked with mine as the exquisitely gritty tone of his voice poured over me. It felt as if he was singing to me, his darkly intense gaze pulled me in. All I could think about was the other night, his mouth against mine, his hot hands pulling hard at my hips, how perfect my name sounded falling from his lips as he came. I ached for him, and without noticing it, I started to move toward the stage. I walked out from behind the bar as if I was stuck in slow motion; the music was loud and infused the air with tangible feeling. Before I knew it, I had abandoned Tiff and Jace behind the bar and was now standing directly in front of Todd. The large crowd of people swayed gently to the melodic song, but it felt as if it was just me and him. It was as if the universe was pushing me down this inevitable path. The path that lead me here, that lead me to finally hold true to my promise, to my dream, and apparently, this passionate, broken boy was going to ride along with me.

Todd's full lips pulled into the most gorgeous smile; his eyes never left mine as he finished the last five lyrics. He wanted me to stay, and I had no doubt that I would. I didn't really even think I had a choice anymore. Jace came up behind me, disturbing the moment I'd just shared with Todd. I felt the heat of his breath against my ear as I watched Todd's smile die and turn into a hard line. The chills that ran down my spine put me on edge.

"It's amazing isn't it?" Jace laughed, but it sounded fake. "How charming he seems. Tonight, he'll be balls deep in some hot groupie. He always is on Tuesdays, never sticks around. I think he took home two girls just the other night..." Jace's lips where nearly imperceptible against my ear. I despised his touch and his words. I was disgusted. "Don't get too caught up in the moment. Guys like him never change." He placed his arm around my waist, settling his hand on my hip; the sensation of falling filled my gut. The raised temperature of the room, the look on Todd's face, his dark brown eyes pinned at the spot where Jace was touching me, it all made me feel sick.

I maneuvered out of his embrace. "Please don't—"

"What? Tell you the truth? He's a user, Lil." Jace's tone was thick with jealousy. The heavy beat of Seth's drums startled me as the next song was starting.

"And you're what, the *good guy*?" My smirk was vicious. Jace must think I'm stupid not to pick up on this game. He wanted me, and he knew that Todd did too. I wasn't a trophy to be had... for either of them. Jace considered me with an angry glare. I couldn't give a crap. "Listen Jace, I should get back to work." I was in the process of heading back to the bar when I felt a large hand wrap around my upper arm.

"I can be the good guy or the bad guy... it's up to you." Squeezing my arm tighter he chuckled. I swallowed down the lump that was building in my throat and brusquely pulled away from his hold.

"Screw you, Jace." I moved fast through the crowd half-expecting him to grab me again. My heart was running full throttle: the music, the voices, the sounds surrounded me making me feel claustrophobic. I felt as if I couldn't trust anyone. Jace unsettled me and made me feel weak, and that was one thing I never wanted to be.

CHAPTER TWENTY

Todd

I WAS GRATEFUL THE SET WAS almost finished; my heart wasn't in it anymore, not after watching Jace's hands on Lily. I almost jumped off the stage and pummeled him. Seth knew what he was doing starting that song so fast. He was always protecting me from myself. It seemed like an eternity, but we finished and set up for open mic. I was eager to find out what the hell dick stick had said to her. She looked at me with such repulsion that I wasn't sure if we were on the same page anymore. What was that saying about planting seeds of doubt and how they grow? Shit if I knew, I just needed to talk to my girl. The thought brought me up short. She wasn't my girl... *yet*.

"Hey, good show tonight, guys." Tiffany's smile was big, her full, red lips spread across her face. The piercings and tattoos didn't hide her beauty, they just added to it. She tried to seem indifferent about her appearance, but I'd known Tiff for a while and, as much as she could be a hard ass, she was a good chick. I scanned the bar for Lily. She wasn't around, but Jace was behind the bar finishing up with a customer.

"Thanks, Tiff... Where's Lily?" Jace's eyes met mine at the mention of her name. A small smirk formed on his lips, and I about lost my shit again.

"She's in back. Whoa, Todd, what's up?" The humor in her voice was gone.

This little game of who's got the bigger dick between Jace and me was about to end. I exhaled sharply, rolled my shoulders back, and cracked my knuckles. I was over his mind games.

"Hey man, let me handle him, all right? You don't want to get fired. Frank's sitting over in the corner booth, bro." Seth palmed my shoulder. "All right?" He gave me a weary smile.

"Yeah." I nodded. "I'll go tell Lily it's time for her to play." I reluctantly walked away from the opportunity to throat punch Jace, but in the end I knew Seth had my back.

The break room door was open, so I didn't hesitate to walk in. Lily was standing staring at the photos on the wall. I expected her to turn around, but she didn't.

"What do you want, Todd?" she asked with frustration. The annoyance in her voice hit me below the belt.

"You still singing tonight? Frank's still out there, but he won't stay long." I hated how much I wanted her to look at me. My need for her started to feel like how I used to need Eliz — I didn't even want to think it. I warily walked toward her, and the closer I got, the tighter my chest pulled. This immense weight bearing down on me with each step. I was terrified of her, of the possibility of yet another rejection, of another failure. This dismissal could be the thing to finally wreck me for good. I thought of the other night, sitting with her in her driveway, and that gave me the courage to do what I wanted.

I scooped the hair away from her neck; her head tilted just enough to grant me permission. I ran the tip of my nose down the slope that followed from below her ear to her shoulder inhaling her sweet smell. My lips feathered against her soft, freckle covered skin, savoring each sacred inch of her.

Lily breathed out a sigh, and my control wavered. My hands wrapped around her arms, and I pulled her tight against my chest.

My lips found her ear. "What did that fucker say to you?" I stated in a whispered growl.

Lily gazed down at the ground. "Nothing, don't worry about it." She tried to pull away, so I turned her to face me. I lifted her chin with my finger.

"What did he say, baby? Because it sure as hell wasn't nothing. The way you looked at me, like I was a piece of dirt, tells me what he said meant something to you." I stared into her eyes, a mixture of blue, green, and yellow — it was a mesmerizing palate. It was so easy to get lost inside their depths.

"Todd, I'm not a trophy to be won. I don't want to be part of some pissing contest." She started to pull away again. This time I took her face in between my palms and brought my lips to hers. She wasn't a trophy or a prize. She was everything, and I wanted her to be mine. She just needed to be reminded. Our lips moved perfectly together, and the soft moan that left her lips was all I needed to hear. I licked her bottom lip, and she pressed against me as both my hands enfolded under her hair at the nape pulling her deeper into the kiss. Lily made me feel good, and I haven't had that in so long. The weight bearing down on me from earlier lifted as I drew away from her supple, pink lips. I rested my forehead against hers and smiled. *I could stay like this with her, all night.*

She giggled against my mouth. "What?" I lifted my head from hers to give her my full attention.

"I could, too." Lily's lips pulled into a megawatt smile that was so big it actually hurt my heart. I was confused though.

"You could too what?" My left eyebrow rose in question.

"Stay like this all night." She held my incredulous stare.

Shit. "I feel like an idiot. I-I didn't mean to say that out loud." I grinned at her reaction to my little slip.

"I'm glad you said it. I needed to hear it." Her smile fell. "Jace made me feel cheap tonight, Todd. You have a... reputation. It's — it's just not fun to hear." She moved her eyes away from mine. I was going to kill that asshole.

"Lily, I can't change my past. The more you get to know me, the more you may start to rethink this whole... whatever this is we have going on between us. But just know that I like you. Can we just start from there?" I prayed her answer would be yes. I needed her answer to be yes. Because being inside her was something I never wanted to forget. I had experienced the incredible feeling of being so deep between her legs; there was no turning back. Lily, in that fleeting moment, had turned her body and trust over to me completely, and that was something I'd never had. She had possessed me that night, and I couldn't see a way forward without her.

She finally met my nervous stare. "All right." Lily's smile was small. She lifted up onto the tip of her toes and kissed me on the cheek. I couldn't help the stupid ass grin on my face. She was destroying me, but it never felt better. "I better get out there before Frank leaves."

"Yeah, you're right. You ready?"

"One hundred percent." She turned away and walked through the door. "I have to be." She said so softly that I didn't think I was supposed to hear it.

I WAS SITTING IN the booth with Frank and Seth. Graden and Jack had left early, and I couldn't say I really cared. Lily stepped on stage, the bright lights made her hair look as if it were on fire. She was a sight on that stage. Frank would be stupid not to sign her. The family tie they had only secured her spot as a new artist at Blue Bar Records. I wasn't really sure what she was worried about. Lily bypassed the guitar and sat at the piano. I tried to hide the surprise on my face, but Seth gave me a look like he couldn't believe it either. She was more talented than anyone could have guessed.

She adjusted the microphone and glanced over at our table. "Hey Seth, can I borrow you for a moment?" She spoke with a smile right into the microphone. Seth looked at me like he was waiting for me to give him the okay. I shrugged.

Seth stood and moved rapidly to the stage. I watched as Lily whispered in his ear. Seth's face broke into a wide ass smile, and I hated him for about two seconds before I realized he was headed for his drum set. I felt dumb for being jealous. Seth would never do that to me. Lily played a quick scale on the piano before she spoke again.

"I'm going to play *"Medicine"* by Broods. Thank you to Seth for knowing this song, you really are a rock star." She beamed at him, and that twinge of jealousy returned. I needed to get it together.

Lily brought the microphone right to her lips. She started humming the first haunting notes of the song before her fingers pressed the keys, beginning the melody. At first, it was just her deep soulful voice and the piano, and then Seth picked up on the beat creating this incredibly sensual arrangement of notes.

"Damn," I whispered as Lily's body moved to the beat, her lips brushing against the microphone, the words from the song hanging in the air creating this dark, evocative moment. Heat radiated through my entire body while watching Lily's hips rock. She was so deep into the music. I didn't think listening to someone sing could get me so damn hard. I shifted in my seat. I was suddenly envious of her microphone.

"Wow, she's amazing." Tiffany took a seat at our booth, breaking me out of my lust-induced state.

"She sure is." Frank had a smile on his face that could only be described as something a proud father would have. "Get her in the studio this week, Todd. You hearing me?"

"Sure, sure. You're leaving?" I asked as Frank stood. "You don't want to congratulate her?" I furrowed my brow.

"I'll let you do that." He smirked, and Tiffany laughed.

"Um, okay?" I wasn't sure what was going on, but I was annoyed. She had been worried about tonight, the least he could do was tell her himself. "I mean, Frank, I think she'd like to hear it from you."

"Look kid, I need to go. I don't want a big emotional scene, and it'll be better coming from you. That way she won't think I'm giving her special treatment." Frank glanced back at the stage as the entire bar erupted into applause.

"Special treatment? What are you talking about, Frank?" Tiff's face crunched into a confused pout. I guess she didn't know about Lily and Frank's relationship. I suddenly wondered if Jace knew.

"Don't worry about it, Tiff. I gotta go, okay? Studio this week. I mean it," he shouted as he walked to the back office.

"What's he talking about?" Tiffany persisted.

"Give it a rest, will you?" I stood quickly from the booth. Seth's arm was draped over Lily's shoulder, and they were both smiling like goofballs as they walked toward us.

"You're a fucking genius!" Seth pulled away from her and smacked her on the ass. What the fuck! I'm going to junk punch him for that later. "She's a musical genius," he continued. "Where's Frank? Awe hell, please tell me he didn't miss this shit? We need to record that, like tomorrow. I'll get my mixer—"

"He didn't miss it," I interrupted Seth's ramblings. Lily's elated mood started to fall when she noticed Frank was gone. "He had to jet, but he loved it. He wants you in the studio this week. Lily that was... un-fucking-believable." I took her hand in mine and pulled her close to me. Sweat glistened on her forehead, her cheeks were flushed, and she looked so damn beautiful. "You did it. We're going to make you an album." I couldn't contain my smile as I bent down and gave her a quick kiss on the cheek.

"For the record, I had no doubt. After hearing you the other night, I knew Frank would be shitting himself to sign you." Seth gave me a smug grin.

Tiff cleared her throat. "Wait a freaking minute, did you just kiss her? He just kissed you. Why do I feel like I never know anything? Can someone please—"

"Tiff, if you make me a drink, I'll give you answers." Seth grabbed Tiffany's wrist and dragged her to the bar. It was probably a good thing, Jace looked like he was drowning and needed help. Not that I gave a shit about him, I was worried about the customers.

"You did good, Red." I smiled at her scowl. I loved that she hated that name.

"Thanks, I should get back to work."

As she turned to head to the bar, I took her hand. "You free tomorrow?"

"You want to get into the studio tomorrow?" She asked disbelievingly. I wanted to see her. I could care less if it was in the studio, here, or at my place; as long as she was there, I was down.

"Can I take you to breakfast first?"

"Like a date?" She scrunched her nose; it was so damn cute.

"Yeah, like a fucking date." I laughed and shook my head. "That sound okay to you, Red?"

She rolled her eyes. "On one condition." She smirked.

"Oh yeah, what's that?" I stepped back and folded my arms across my chest giving her a cocky grin.

"One, stop calling me Red, and two—"

"Hey, you said one condition." I chuckled at her obvious irritation with me. I had her scowling now.

"*Two...*" She said with a defiant tone. "...You record a song with me. I want to sing with you." Her cat eyes casted down with... insecurity?

"I'd love that, Lily." Her eyes darted up to mine, her face breaking into a sincere smile.

"Yeah?" She sounded unsure.

"Of course, I'd be lucky to sing with you." I shook my head and took her hand in mine leading her to the bar.

"I don't know how lucky you'd be, but it would be fun."

I nodded and gave her my best grin.

She didn't realize how damn lucky I was to have *any* part of her.

CHAPTER TWENTY-ONE

Lily

TODD: YOU READY FOR TODAY?

I was still half asleep; Todd's text message was blurry as my eyes adjusted to the light. I laughed out loud once I realized it was only eight in the morning. I quickly tapped out a reply.

Me: *Eager much?*

I sat up and rubbed my eyes. Last night was so busy I could still feel the ache in my feet. Once the excitement of my performance died down and the reality of work set in, the night took a turn for the worst. The crowd had been rowdy, and then Seth and Jace got into it about something and almost came to blows. If it wasn't for Tiff getting in between them, I had a feeling Jace would have ended up in the hospital. Seth was a physical presence. He was at least six-foot-two and all strength. He was broad and so traditionally tall, dark, and handsome, I had no choice but to think he was attractive. I sure as hell could tell Tiffany was all about that man. The look in her eyes when she stepped between him and Jace solidified, at least for me, that she had feelings for Seth. My phone chirped breaking me from my thoughts.

Todd: *Who wouldn't be?*

I chuckled. Todd wasn't what I was used to. I always went the safe, boring route when it came to men. Easy, dependable, and tame is what I thought I always wanted. Derrick proved me wrong. It didn't matter whether or not a guy had been a playboy, college graduate, rich, or came from a stable family. If he was going to screw your best friend in the back stairwell of the bar where you worked, there was nothing you could do to stop it. I shook my head trying to erase the visual I had of my best friend, Becca, taking it up against the wall by my boyfriend. My mood darkened just as my phone chirped again.

Todd: *Be ready in thirty. I'm starving.*

Holy crap, I needed to hustle.

Twenty-five minutes and a quick shower later, I was somewhat presentable. My crazy curly hair was pulled back into my usual thick ponytail. The weather was still chilly so I decided to wear a peach hoodie and jeans. I slipped on my gray chucks and looked at myself in the mirror. If I was being honest with myself, I looked tired. I didn't really have time for make-up, but I didn't think Todd cared about that crap. My lips turned up into a smirk as I thought about how he looked at me last night. He lit me up every time his eyes grazed my skin. How was I going to make it through a whole day of that penetrating stare? I took a deep breath, grabbed my phone, and headed up the stairs.

My nephew was crying loudly from the living room, and I wasn't looking forward to the interrogation Eve would surely give me.

"Hey, buddy. Where's your mom?" I bent down and picked up Christopher from his Pack-'N-Play in an attempt to calm him down. Tears and snot poured down his face like he had been crying for a while.

"*Eve?*" I called out. Nothing. What the hell? I needed to

leave soon. I walked toward her bedroom and heard her crying. As I slowly pushed open the door to her bedroom, I could see Eve's strawberry blonde hair was ruffled and tears stained her face.

"Eve, what's going on?" My sister was as hard as nails; she never cried.

Eve gave me a look like she wasn't sure she wanted to tell me the truth. It was then I realized what she was crying about. "Is it Pam?"

She nodded. "I haven't heard from mom for five years, Lily." She sniffled and rubbed her tissue across her nose. "I mean where the hell does she get off calling me? Who the hell does she think she is?"

Pam was our mother. I wasn't sure if I could call the woman who left me at the age of three to go live another life — live a life with her other daughter and husband — a real mother. She disappeared five years ago with some biker. Simply left Frank, Eve, and me behind. We meant shit to her, and I could give a crap about what she wanted now.

I shrugged my shoulders. "I don't know. You going to be okay?" Eve stood and ran her fingers through her hair, trying hopelessly to tame the wild curls. We got our hair from our mother. She ran the palms of her hands down the front of her shirt in an attempt to pull herself together. Her nostrils flared, and she laughed bitterly.

"No, Lil, I'm not okay. She wants money, can you believe the nerve?" My sister reached out for Christopher.

I wish I could say I could, but I hardly knew the lady. I handed her the baby and quickly checked for stray snot on my clothes. Pam was never a mother to me. At least she got some time with her. I didn't know what to say to comfort her. I was at a loss.

"I—I don't know what to tell you. Did she sound like she was in trouble?" I prayed that Todd would get here soon. It was too early for this drama.

"She's always in trouble, Lily." My sister's tone was scolding. I didn't let it bother me; it wasn't me she was mad at.

"You going to give her the money?" I asked.

She nodded. "I'm going to wire it to her. She's somewhere overseas, I guess. She couldn't or wouldn't give me details... Somewhere in France she said. Said this money could get her back to the states. She sounded awful. And at church we are talking about forgiveness and maybe—"

She was cut off by a loud knock on the door. My heart jumped. Todd.

"That's my ride. Can we talk about this later?" I moved toward the door. I was thankful to not have to finish the conversation.

"Sure, you going somewhere this early?" Eve's appraisal was scrutinizing.

"Yup, breakfast date." I smiled, as she looked at me in disbelief.

"Well, the other night went well then?" She followed behind as I walked to the front door, and I rolled my eyes. I didn't want her to make assumptions about Todd. He was a good guy, but Eve was the type to judge a book by its cover. I didn't feel like hearing her misconceptions later when I got home. She disliked anything that had to do with guitars, tattoos... hell, music in general. She blamed her dad, I think, for everything that went wrong in her life.

"Different guy, sis." I grabbed my bag from the hook by the front door.

She inhaled sharply, "Well."

"Well, what?" I turned on my heel and looked her straight in the eyes. "Well, what? Eve?"

Christopher cried out, and Eve bounced him on her hip. "Nothing... Let's meet him then." Her lips mashed into a hard line.

This was going to be awkward to say the least. I faltered as I opened the door and Todd came into view. I was used to seeing him in T-shirts and worn jeans. Today he looked... different. His hair was artfully tousled, and he must have trimmed his beard back because, today, it was much shorter, putting his sharp jawline on show. The dark black V-neck sweater he had on fit him like a glove and displayed his strong chest and broad shoulders. The dark blue jeans hugged his fit thighs, and I literally gulped as my eyes struggled to take him all in. His quiet chuckle brought me back down to earth.

"Hi." He smiled so big that both dimples popped out, and I swear I heard Eve gasp.

My mouth spread into a huge grin on its own accord. He looked so good.

"Hi." I felt shy, and I had no idea why. I'd had sex with this guy just a few nights ago, but it was like we were starting from scratch, like that night only existed on some other plane, some other universe. This... this was the Todd that was hiding beneath all his pain, and I couldn't wait to meet him.

CHAPTER TWENTY-TWO

Todd

LILY WAS LOOKING AT ME LIKE I was a different person, and I wasn't sure if that was a good thing. I wanted this to work so damn bad. Maybe I over did it? I didn't have time to dwell on it too much because her sister, at least I thought it was her sister, gasped and the little boy she was carrying on her hip squealed. On a second glance, I decided it had to be her sister; her hair was lighter than, but just as wild as, Lily's. Lily smiled as she greeted me, and I decided to put on my game face. I couldn't let my stupid, insecure bullshit, fuck this up for me.

"You ready, baby?" I didn't miss how Lily's sister cleared her throat, begging for attention.

Lily frowned. "Todd, this is my sister, Eve."

I smiled and waved. Eve just stared at me, what the hell? "Nice to meet you, Eve, and who's this little cutie?"

"This is Christopher, my son." She smiled down at him. "Nice to meet you, Todd. She moved past Lily into the doorway and shook my hand. This Christopher kid was cute as hell. He had almost white blond hair that curled in the back and the fattest cheeks I'd ever seen. I pinched his cheek, and he squealed again. I couldn't help but laugh. I liked babies, so sue me.

"That's adorable. You guys should stay here, I can make you breakfast." Eve smiled at me, and I watched as Lily's eyes opened wide in horror.

"Um, that sounds awful actually. Todd, let's get going." She pulled her bag onto her shoulder and pushed past her sister.

Eve laughed uncomfortably. "Well, next time maybe?" she called out from the doorway as Lily pulled me down the front steps.

"Oh. My. God. What was that? You're like a lady magnet. My sister hates everyone, but she sure as hell liked you." I laughed, and she scowled at me as I opened the door of my truck.

I waved again at her sister and climbed into the 4Runner. The keys turned in the ignition as I glanced over at a pouting Lily. She was wearing a peach hoodie, and the color looked stunning on her. She wasn't wearing a stitch of make-up, but somehow her skin appeared to glow, her freckles on full blast. I liked it. No fuck that, I loved it.

"You look beautiful." My palm gripped around her thigh, and I watched as she visibly relaxed. The pout on her full lips gone. Lily looked at me again like she had in the doorway of her house, like I was new and shiny. It made me feel hopeful, and that was something that could ruin me. I leaned over and brushed my lips across hers. I pulled away, and her eyes were bright. It took all my strength not to take her mouth again, but I wanted to do this right. She would be mine; I'd have her like I should have the first time, but no matter what my stupid ass wanted, I needed to take it slow.

"Thank you," she whispered. "You look amazing. You clean up nice." She gave me a sideways smile, and I grinned back in response.

"Thanks. You hungry? Because I'm hungry as hell." I reversed the truck and headed to the diner.

"I could eat." She looked down nervously again at her hands that were wringing together. I reached across the console and took one of her hands in mine, tangling our fingers, and gently squeezed. Her chest rose and then fell slowly in a deep exhale.

"Good, Kim's Café has the best damn scones."

"Scones? You don't strike me as the tea and scones type of guy." She laughed, and her brow crinkled in confusion.

"Tea? What the hell? Please tell me you know what a scone is?" I was about to lose my shit. How could she not know what a scone was?

"Apparently I don't know what a scone is, enlighten me." She giggled at my obvious irritation.

"Holy shit. You really don't know, do you? This is messed up. I might have to turn around and take you back home. Not sure I can hang with you anymore. It's very disappointing." I was almost serious, but then she laughed so deeply my whole body felt warm.

She squeezed my hand, "Shut up, and just drive."

LILY MOANED AS SHE took her first bite of the fried bread and honey butter. It was the sexiest thing I'd ever heard. She closed her eyes and smiled as she slowly swallowed. Everything about this chick made my cock twitch. I readjusted myself, thankfully under the table.

"You like it?" I smiled as she nodded her head.

"It's so freaking incredible. I can't... dear God, this is good." She spoke with her mouth full of food, and I didn't care.

"Told you." I had the smuggest smirk on my face.

"You did, and Sir... you are very correct. I haven't lived really, but now... now I can die a happy woman because I ate a scone." She chuckled.

"Whatever. You about just had an orgasm over there, don't play like I'm crazy."

Lily threw her napkin at me. "Shut up, I did not." She laughed, and I watched as the blush in her cheeks went from pink to rose red.

"You so did. I liked it. I'd like to show you how much I liked it." My grin widened as the color in her cheeks deepened. Hell. Yeah.

"Todd," she whispered. She shook her head and smiled coyly at me, and, damn it, I wanted to leave right then and take her back to my place — to taste her and devour her until I had her crying out my name while her legs shook with pleasure. I wanted to give her everything, all of me. Show her how fucking beautiful she was.

She met my eyes, and it was like she was thinking the same thing. Her breathing was quick, and her hand trembled as it hovered over her father's ring. She cleared her throat and took a sip of water.

"So are we going to the studio today?" She met my hungry stare. I initially wanted to record today, but now I couldn't see past the lust polluting my veins.

"What do you want to do, Lily?" I trapped her in my stare; I wasn't making this easy for her. It was her choice though in the end.

"I want to spend the day with you. I don't care what we do." Her eyes softened as her full lips split into a small smile. "That okay with you?"

"Sounds good to me." I wasn't sure what was going to happen today, but I couldn't wait to see how it ended.

CHAPTER TWENTY-THREE

Lily

TODD WAS STARING AT me like he wanted to eat me alive. I was so overheated that I could barely sit still. I took another sip of water to calm my ragingly aroused hormones. Todd was filling up all the vacant space I'd kept hidden for so long. I wasn't sure I was ready for all this, but I wanted to put the past behind me. I needed to move on.

"Am I making you nervous again?" Todd's easy, flirty smile calmed my anxiety. He had me all over the place. He was chaos, and I wanted nothing more than to lose control with him.

"You want to get out of here?" I don't know how those words escaped my lips, but they had.

Todd's smile turned up a notch, and his deep brown eyes darkened with desire.

"Are you sure?" He was giving me another out, but I didn't want it. This attraction was too intense. We needed this, each other. We needed to get it out of our system. Although, deep down I wasn't sure that once I really had Todd, I'd ever get him out of my system.

"If you are?" I wanted this to be his choice, too. We both needed to be sure if this was really going to work.

"Let's get out of here then."

He paid the check, and we made our way back to Todd's place. I kept sneaking glances at him while he sang "*Fall at Your Feet*" by Saint Raymond as it played through the speakers. Todd's voice was sexy and caused a pleasant burn of anticipation in my belly. He seemed happy, and that made me smile.

"You have such a great voice, I feel like I'm getting my own personal concert," I teased.

His deep laugh made my heart skip a beat. "Well, thank you. I've got nothing on you, though." He turned down the radio as we made a left into his condo's driveway. Insecurity and apprehension had my pulse beating in an irregular pattern. I really didn't know him. I mean he knew nothing about me really. I was so wrong about Derrick; I could be screwing up again. My breakfast started to churn in my gut as I walked through the familiar door. My gaze fell onto the couch, and my cheeks instantly heated. I was so torn between what I physically wanted and what my mind kept telling me, which was slow down. I had a feeling though that my mind was going to lose the argument.

I was so wrapped up in my thoughts that I hadn't noticed Todd watching me.

"You okay, Lily?" He looked at me with such concern; I wanted nothing more than to fully trust him.

"I'm just—"

"What the fuck! It's way too damn early, could you not slam the goddamn door?" Seth appeared from around the corner wearing nothing but boxer briefs. I almost died. Seth's long muscles and bare torso were on full display along with his crazy inked up arms.

"Oh shit. Sorry, didn't know you had company." He gave me a devious grin.

"Go put some clothes on, man. What the hell!" Todd looked as if he was suppressing laughter.

"On it. Don't worry. I have a second interview today, so I'll be out of here in a few. You kids have *plans*?" He emphasized the word plans and raised his eyebrows.

Todd clenched his jaw before he spoke, "Get the hell dressed, dude. No one needs to see your limp dick."

"Hey, don't talk shit about my dick. It's fantastic... well, that's what I hear at least." Seth's laugh was contagious, and we all started to laugh, relieving the awkwardness that had fallen. "I'm outta here. I need to get ready." Seth walked past me and smiled like the Cheshire cat. He was so odd; I couldn't figure that one out... at all.

Todd took my hand in his and led me to his room and shut the door. I suddenly felt claustrophobic.

"What's up, Lily? You look uneasy again. No... you look terrified. We — we can just hang out — chill — and watch a movie. We don't have to do anything." He pulled me close to his body. He placed his two fingers under my chin, demanding my attention in his own familiar way; his eyes searched my face and finally met my gaze. "I want you so badly, but I can wait. I can wait for you as long as you need, because I just know once I've had you, once your mine, I won't be able to turn back. So I want you to be sure, be ready for me, for this..." He used his other hand to point at his chest, "...because I'm sure as fuck ready for you." He bent down and kissed me soft at first, his lips coaxed mine tenderly. I kissed his top lip, licking it slightly. He tasted like he always did, but today it was mixed with honey, and it stoked the fire in me that only he seemed to ignite. A deep groan escaped his lips, and the kiss became rough. In this second, this crazy lust had us all tied up in knots. I wanted to give in — I wanted to let go.

His hands trailed down my arms and a warm shiver erupted across my body. I had to make the choice. I didn't know much about him, but he wouldn't make this choice for me ever again. This was different from the other night. Todd was putting himself out there; he was taking the chance on me, on us. Todd's lips grazed my jaw as he moved down to my neck. I didn't think I could ever get used to how amazing his fingers felt against the flesh of my arms.

"We can stop this. It's your decision," he whispered before he pulled my earlobe between his teeth. I shuddered.

"I want this… I want us to work." I took a deep breath and the heaviness from early lifted. Todd's lips stilled, and he pulled back just enough to give me full eye contact. It was only a second, but his eyes told me everything I needed to know.

"Hell, yes." His grin was cocky, and I loved it.

He pulled me in, colliding his lips with mine. The kiss was violent, rough, hungry… perfect. Once the kiss slowed, I stepped back from him and lifted my hoodie over my head. I let it drop to the ground as I watched Todd drink me in like he was desperately thirsty. I ran my fingers under his sweater and lifted. He complied and lifted it off. Todd's sculpted chest and stomach pulled with the motion. I craved this — him — he was more than I could have ever wanted.

We watched each other for a quiet moment; the air was thick with need. All I could hear was our breathing, and it turned me on beyond anything I thought possible. I felt brave. I unhooked my bra, letting it slide slowly down my shoulders, and then dropped forward carefully letting the bra fall to the floor as I moved to slide my jeans and panties down. I heard Todd's intake of breath as I raised my eyes to meet his. I liked how his eyes swept over my naked form, how his jaw tightened with desire, how his control started to slowly slip. He moved toward me deliberately, as if he was afraid that I wasn't real. Never, not once in my whole life, had I felt this wanted. This was too much, too fast, but this moment with him… it was the chaos I needed.

CHAPTER TWENTY-FOUR

Todd

LILY WAS COMPLETELY BARE TO ME as I lowered her body down onto my bed. The crème color of her skin and the small smattering of freckles across her body had me fucking captivated. I wanted to kiss each one. I couldn't wait for my lips to discover every part of her and taste that flawless skin. Kneeling at the side of the bed, I grabbed her waist and pulled her body toward mine. Lily's gasp at the sudden movement was quickly silenced as my hands moved down the sides of her hips to her thighs. I gently pushed her legs apart. I couldn't stop myself from smiling; she was all mine.

"What?" she asked breathlessly, leaning up to look at me on her elbows.

"You're fucking gorgeous, and I'm going to make this mine. Possess it. Take every bit you have to give, and give you everything I have." I didn't give a shit anymore that I hardly knew this girl — that she had me all mixed up. I was finally getting something I wanted. Finally, I was someone's choice. Leaning forward, my palm ran all the way down her body, starting between her full breasts, down her stomach, and across the curve of her pubic bone. She arched her back and moaned at my touch. I slid two fingers inside her and groaned at how ready she was for me. My arousal was painful, but she was so wet, and I had to know what she tasted like. There was nothing left to hold me back. My need could wait.

I spread her legs further apart and took her into my mouth. She bowed her back again as the sweet taste covered my tongue. Lily whimpered softly at first, but then she began to pull my hair. She cried out my name, begging me, as I licked lazy figure eights across her sensitive flesh. Lily's legs started to tremble, and I increased the pressure. My fingers moved deeply inside her as she came into my mouth. I savored every drop of her. I'd never had anything better, and I knew the minute my lips tasted her... she was going to be my new addiction.

"I want you inside me," she whispered softly. Her cheeks blushed. Lily had me feeling ready to combust. I stood and unbuckled my belt. She sat up and pulled my jeans down. It was my turn to be bare to her. "Todd." Her voice was faint and thick as she looked up at me; I grinned. The color of her eyes appeared to change again — they were a bright green and hooded with lust. I couldn't look away. I watched as she took me in her mouth; my head fell back, and I closed my eyes as her warm mouth took me in almost entirely. I took a deep breath and tried to maintain my control. I looked down at her again, and I almost lost it. I placed her face between my palms and gently pulled her up to my mouth. Our lips collided as I lay her back down on the bed. My lips trailed down her jaw, to her breast, and I took the peak into my mouth, reveled in her moans as my lips kissed her delicious skin. I felt the tip of my dick brush against her, and I couldn't wait to take her. I leaned over and grabbed a condom out of my bedside table and quickly rolled it on.

"You ready?" I grabbed her hips drawing her close, leaning over her, holding my weight with my forearms. I needed to make sure one more time that she really wanted me because I was already hooked, but I needed to know if she was still on board.

"Yes, I need to feel you." She lifted her hips, pressing against me, and I inhaled a sharp breath. I was ready to fucking burst. She took my face in her hands and kissed me deeply as I pushed gradually into her. She gasped, and I swallowed the small sound. I wanted to own every sound, every moment, every second of her. Lily wrapped her legs around my waist, pushing me deeper still. I held myself up with one arm, and I grabbed the headboard behind her with the other. I pulled out just enough to tease her before I thrust myself hard inside of her again. She rocked her hips at the same time, arms above her head; she braced her palms against the wood of the bed causing her body to tense, making it difficult for me to last much longer.

"Hold on, baby." I leaned down and kissed her intensely as I drove myself inside her. I could feel her legs starting to shake. Sweat trickled down my back as I pushed and pulled, hard and then soft. The muscles in my arm flexed as I held tight to the headboard. She started to contract around me, milking my release. I leaned my forehead against hers. Our eyes locked as I continued to press inside her. I ground my hips down into hers, and she shuddered while pulling her teeth across the skin of my shoulder, letting a loud moan escape as we came together. Her name roared from my lips as the aftershock of her spread through me. I stilled and let the feeling of sweet relief pour down my spine.

I took a deep breath and gazed back into her endless eyes. My body relaxed as I gently broke our connection. I leaned down and kissed her with lazy lips, and then I eased down next to her, our overheated bodies tangled in the best way.

"You okay?" I asked. I needed to make sure I hadn't been too aggressive with her.

"I'm perfectly perfect." She smiled as she traced the

artwork on my chest. "You okay? You're not regretting this, are you?" She looked at me, her brows pulled inward with concern.

"I'll never regret this." I kissed her forehead. I could never regret her… this… us, but I couldn't promise myself, or Lily for that matter, that I wouldn't one day regret trusting her. I may have made her mine today here in this bed. She was everything. But I had no control once we were out in the real world. I had no real control over how she would eventually feel about me. I exhaled a shaky breath.

"Good, because I don't think I could ever regret this day." She kissed me sweetly on the cheek.

I hoped that was the truth, because I didn't think I could make it through one more day of regret. I'd had enough of it.

CHAPTER TWENTY-FIVE

Lily

I MEANT EVERY WORD. I'D NEVER regret this day, not the sore feeling between my legs, the burn from his kiss, or the feeling like I was free falling. Todd was exactly what I needed now; he took me higher with each moment I got to spend with him. The wall I'd built wanted desperately to stay crumbled, even if it was just for today. Todd placed my hair gently behind my ears as he watched me intensely. This was such a heavy silence, I could feel the weight of it in my bones, but I wasn't frightened by it — it comforted me. He had the slightest smile on his lips, making the butterflies in my stomach take flight. The mask he wore all the time was gone, I saw who he really was, and for once, I wanted to tell someone every insignificant thing about myself. I wanted to trust him, and I wanted someone to really know me.

"God, baby, you're amazing." Todd's smile made the amber color of his eyes shimmer.

I couldn't stop the giggle that erupted from my lips. "Thank you. You're pretty freaking incredible, too." I placed a quick kiss on his lips.

"Do you ever take this off?" He took my father's ring between his fingers and smiled at me. I hadn't realized it was still on.

"When I go to sleep... I can't believe I forgot to take it off." I turned my eyes to meet his, and I decided to give him a small piece of me. I wanted him to own this part of me too. "Can I tell you something?" My voice was thick, the lump in my throat choking me.

"Yeah, anything." Todd's smile faltered, and I watched as the worry darkened his eyes.

"So... you know my dad died, right?" I took a deep breath and readied myself to continue. Todd nodded and sat up on his elbow in order to give me his complete attention. The small gesture gave me the strength I needed to continue, "Well, I know...I know it's not really my fault, but I feel like it is." Once the words actually left my tongue, there was no holding back the tears. I'd been carrying that around with me for so long. I hadn't spoken about it out loud, and the feeling of having it out in the open was suffocating. Before I had a chance to tamp down the emotion, a sob broke free and I felt like a crazy person.

"Lily." Todd pulled me to his chest and let me cry as his fingertips drew up and down my spine, making me feel so safe. "You know though... right... I mean how could you think it was your fault?" He lightly grasped my chin in his hand. "Tell me."

I drew in all the air I could into my lungs and continued, "The day he died, I was so angry with him. I had this amazing music scholarship to this really awesome private college in Tampa. The school called me that day to tell me I had to forfeit the scholarship because as it stated in the terms, I couldn't have any family members in the business. The scholarship was for graduate students not from *'musical homes.'* I felt like my whole world was crumbling down. I had worked so hard at getting my bachelor's in Music, getting straight A's, never really taking time for me.

"To make things worse, he decided to tell me as I was getting ready for work that day that he had seen my boyfriend Derrick and my best friend Becca at the bar he played a gig at the night prior, and he told me they were all over each other. I was so pissed about losing my dream scholarship, in my mind because of him, that I called him a liar. I told him I hated him." My throat swelled, and the tears started pouring from my eyes.

"Shh, baby, you don't have to tell me." Todd regarded me with such sadness, my heart felt as if it was breaking. *What kind of person did he think I was?* "It's okay, sweetheart, we all say things in anger. We don't really mean them, you didn't really mean it."

"What if I did?" Our eyes met, and his brows dipped with confusion. "What if I'd hated him in that moment, what if I'm being punished? He was such a good dad. He did everything he could for me. My mom left us, and he stepped up to the plate. He did a fantastic job raising me, and I told him I hated him. What kind of person does that?" I tried desperately to control my breathing.

"Someone who can't see beyond her own anger, someone who is human and makes mistakes, and someone who will regret it till the day she dies. Trust me; I've done some things in my life I'm not proud of. Things that I'll take to the grave and be judged for. Lily, it wasn't your fault. Baby, you have to know that." Todd sat up. He took my hand in his and drew me up into a sitting position. It didn't escape me that we were both still totally naked, but it was fitting as I exposed a part of my soul to him; I wouldn't want it any other way. Todd's heated palm wrapped around the back of my neck, cradling my face with his other hand as he said, "Look at me, Lily. I know I never met your dad, but I guarantee you he knew that you worshipped the ground he walked on—" A loud sob burst from my trembling lips. "This is why you want to sing, isn't it?

To make music, to be something in this industry, to prove your love for him?"

I nodded my head. Todd's face was hazy through the salt water that emptied from my eyes. "I made him a promise ages ago that I would make something of myself. He was so sick of singing for crap wages, he always told me to take the gift God gave me in my voice. He said I should take it right to the top because I deserved nothing less." My eyes stared down in shame, how could I deserve anything with how I'd treated him? "Todd, I told him I hated him. I slapped him across the face and called him a liar. I ran out of the house like a raving bitch. That night..." I gulped down the acid that started to burn its way up my throat. "...That night my boyfriend, Becca, and some friends had come to the club where I worked to celebrate a birthday. As I was leaving to come home, I headed out the back stairwell and heard what I thought was someone in distress. I ran down the stairs to see if I could help and... sure enough, Derrick was screwing Becca against the wall. The sight... it... destroyed me." My fists gripped around the navy blue comforter that covered Todd's bed.

"He's an asshole that never deserved you." Todd's jaw compressed, and I almost smiled because he was truly just as irate as I was. He wanted to protect me; I'd never had that before. "Are you smiling?" His lips curled up in a lopsided smirk. "You're smiling, what the hell?" He chuckled.

"I like how angry you got just now. I think if Derrick were here, you would have punched him in the jaw." I laughed and wiped away my remaining tears.

"Fuck yeah, I would have. He's not worthy to breathe the air you do." Todd's grin fell, and I watched as his fists tightened again. I wanted to kiss him so badly right then. I leaned in and placed my lips tenderly to his full bottom lip.

"Thank you." I smiled against his lips.

"For what?" His eyes searched my face for an answer.

"For listening... That night when I got home, I couldn't

sleep. My dad wasn't home, and I knew he was probably out drinking. Whenever he got really upset, he'd go to a bar and drink himself stupid. He normally never drank, only when something really wounded him. I was sick with worry, the weather was bad, it was well-passed closing time for all the bars... and he still wasn't home. Todd, they pulled his car from the bay. He'd driven off the causeway. His blood alcohol was 0.35. I did that to him, to me. I own it. I know it, and I can't breathe every time I think about it. But today..." I sat up straight, trying to gather my wits. I needed Todd to understand the significance of this. Something inside of me recognized that letting him in like this, showing him this small part of me would let him know he could trust me. I knew he needed that. "...today you helped me, because you're the first person I've told. The first person to hear me repent my sin. I knew I could tell you my real thoughts... that you wouldn't judge me, and I'm so freaking grateful."

"Lily, you have nothing to repent for. How could I judge you? Your father made the choice to drink and get behind the wheel. Sure you guys fought, and I think it's honorable that you own your part in that, but his death falls on him. He was an adult, Lil, and he made the choice. You need to know that. It was *his* choice."

For the first time in over a month, I started to believe it. I began to feel free of blame. "It was his choice." The words were faint, but I realized Todd heard them.

Todd brought his mouth to mine with ease. He kissed me so gently and so profoundly I felt as if I was being consumed. We didn't need any more words; we just needed each other. He kissed me like he knew no other way to breathe. I loved his mouth, and I loved how easily his hands brought me to that ultimate climax. I gave him my body again, but this time it was soft, unhurried, and had me aching for release. He was discovering my body in its entirety. My back to his chest, we rested on our sides, his hips driving gently into me, his hot hands on my breasts, and his lips on my neck, his mouth savoring my skin. I felt treasured. I was captured in all that was Todd, and I didn't think I ever wanted to leave this bed.

THE HEAT FROM THE sun was what woke me. I jumped up when I realized I must have fallen asleep. Todd's blinds were opened just enough to let the midday sun pour in across the sheets of his bed. I glanced at the bedside clock — it was just half past noon. I turned to wake Todd, but startled realizing I was alone. My heart dropped for a moment with self-doubt, but I pushed that sentiment down. I needed to feel more secure — more confident. I quickly dressed and pulled my hair back, checking myself in the mirror before I walked out to the living room to see where he had gone. I seemed decent enough.

I opened the door to his bedroom. "Todd?"

"Yeah, out here." I heard clanging of plates.

I followed his voice into the kitchen. I sucked in a breath as I took in the sight of Todd shirtless in just a pair of low-slung jeans. He was obviously going commando, the dark line of hair that led below the seam of his pants and that defined muscular V had me thinking of our morning together in bed; it made my cheeks heat.

"Damn, you're sexy as hell when you blush. I love that you get flustered so easily." Todd handed me a plate, a deep dimpled smile on his face.

"You're ridiculous and vain." Shaking my head with a small smirk, I looked down at the empty plate. "What's this?"

"I made lunch." He looked at me like I was missing the point.

"You did? That's so cute. You cook?" I laughed as he rubbed the back of his neck, obviously uncomfortable with the compliment. "Awe, look who's flustered now, big boy." I bit my bottom lip to suppress my laughter.

"You're asking for it, little girl." He grabbed my wrist and pulled me against his chest.

"Thought you liked it when I begged for it?" My lips pulled into a flirty smile.

Todd's eyes darkened with lust. "Don't tempt me. I'd fuck you across the kitchen table right now if we didn't have to work tonight, but I'm pretty sure you need to be able to stand later."

I gasped. "Todd, you are—"

"Amazing. Sexy as hell. The best thing you'll ever have. Yeah, I know." He smiled bigger than I'd ever seen him smile, the skin around his eyes creased and his dimples were so pronounced I couldn't believe it. Todd's laughter was hearty and had my heart feeling as if it was smiling. He was so beautiful when he was just being him — being silly, he gave off this sense of lightness, and it washed away all the dark spots in my mind.

"You're—"

"An idiot... yeah, I know," he interrupted again. He grabbed the dishtowel from the sink and started to wind it up.

"Don't you dare... Todd, I'm serious." I held the plate up as a shield. He snapped the towel once in my direction, and I squealed. "Todd... don't," I screeched and tried to run from the kitchen, but ran face first into a human wall. Seth. The snap of the towel on my butt pushed my body against Seth even more, and his intensely spicy scent filled my nostrils.

"We having a Lily sandwich today?" Seth's tone was laced with sarcasm, but I slapped his chest for good measure.

"That's never gonna happen. So don't even think it, you perv." I chuckled.

"That's not funny, asshole." Todd's voice held no humor.

"Sorry, man, I was just kidding. Didn't mean anything by it." Seth was apologetic and took a giant step back, almost making me fall to the ground because his weight was no longer there to hold me up.

"Whoa." I stumbled, and Seth grabbed my arm.

"You got it?" Seth snickered.

"Yes. I'm fine, thank you," I said, a bit indignant.

"What'd you make for lunch?" Seth dropped his hold on my arm and walked past me into the kitchen. He was dressed in slacks, a crisp white shirt, and a deep purple tie.

"Just some soup and grilled cheese. You can make your own damn lunch. This is for Lily and me." Todd's voice was back to its usual steady self, and the tension in the room died

I noticed I was still holding my plate in my hand. My fingers absentmindedly gripping it tight.

"Hey, babe, hand me your plate."

I walked into the kitchen and watched Todd dish me up a yummy looking grilled cheese. The bread was a golden brown — just how I liked it — and the cheese spilled from the edges of the crust making my stomach growl. He pulled a bowl from the top cabinet and filled it with tomato soup. I privately smiled. I loved how domestic this tattooed badass was. It was sort of comical.

Seth cleared his throat breaking my attention away from Todd. Seth's tall frame leaned comfortably against the counter. He was smirking and staring at the both of us. "So, how was your morning?"

Todd glared at him through narrowed eyes. "Fantastic. Yours?" Todd placed the soup and sandwich on the kitchen table that was situated in the far corner, next to a set of sliding glass doors that must lead out to the backyard. The kitchen was large for a condo, but the entire place was on the bigger side.

"I got the job." Seth didn't move his eyes from mine. It was strange. I didn't feel like he was doing it to make me feel uncomfortable. It was like he was trying to figure me out.

"What? The teaching gig? That's so awesome, bro!" Todd's

voice smiled.

Seth let his stare drop as he gave Todd a brilliant grin. "I did it, man."

"Hell yeah, you did!" They side hugged each other, and I giggled.

"You guys are adorable, should I give you a minute?" I bit the inside of my cheek in an attempt not to burst out laughing.

"Ha-ha, she's funny. You should keep this little hellcat." Seth walked past me and punched me without real force in the arm. *Hellcat?*

"I plan on it." Todd gave me a kiss on the cheek. I felt awkward, public displays of affection were something I needed to get used to. "Let's eat."

CHAPTER TWENTY-SIX

Todd

SITTING HERE, WATCHING THIS GIRL — this girl who I'd spent the morning having the most mind-blowing sex with — I felt lucky as shit. She had finally opened up to me just enough to have me craving more. I wanted every damn piece of this chick. I always thought I'd end up with Liz, but for the first time, I was glad I hadn't because I would have missed out on this — and this was pretty spectacular. I didn't kid myself thinking I was falling in love or some shit like that. I needed to know this girl better; I needed to own every aspect of her, her body, her mind, and eventually, her heart before I willing gave over mine. I've learned my lesson, and I wasn't placing all my chips in just yet. But if I were a betting man... I'd bet all my chips would be in the pot soon enough. I smiled around the soup spoon.

"You look dumb. What's with that fucking grin, bro?" Seth's cocky tone had me laughing. Lily looked up from her plate and giggled.

"Fuck off, dude." I took an enormous bite of my grilled cheese and smiled like an idiot at Seth. He was trying to embarrass me in front of Lily. Shithead. "So have you told your dad yet... that you got the job?"

Seth's smile fell. "Nah, I will later." He glanced down at his plate. "You guys going to make it into the studio today? I'd love to go."

"I'd like that. I have an idea for what I'd like to work on today if we have time. I'd need to shower before work. So maybe no recording today, but we could practice?" Lily's lips spread into a cute as hell smile.

"Sure, what did you have in mind?" I was eager to get her into the studio.

"I want to do a duet with you. Do you know the song "*King and Lionheart*" by Of Monsters and Men?" Her eyes sparkled with excitement.

"Hell yes, this is going to be amazing!" Seth's palm slapped the table. Lily jumped, and I laughed. Seth's enthusiasm for music never ceased to amaze me.

"Yes, I love that song. That's the song you want to sing with me?" I couldn't help the grin that spread across my damn mug.

"Yes, I think... I think we'd be good together. Don't you?" Her gaze found mine, and I heard the second meaning behind her question.

"I can't think of anything better." Her full lips pulled into a stunning smile, and I felt my chest fill with something I couldn't place. It felt damn good though.

THE RAIN POURED DOWN onto my windshield, blocking the view of my condo's front door. I'd just gotten back from dropping off Lily so she could get ready for work. The radio played loudly as I sat in my driveway trying to comprehend everything that had happened today. This morning ran through my mind – Lily's soft body against mine, and her crazy copper curls everywhere. My body started to respond to the images, and damn if I could help it. I needed to focus on our studio time. Lily's voice was like clear blue water, and I wanted to listen to her every damn day. Our voices together — it was fucking magic. We planned time for tomorrow to practice our duet and a few of her original songs. I was just about to head inside when my phone vibrated.

I opened the locked screen and noticed I'd missed a text from Elizabeth earlier and I had a new text from Lily. I smiled at my phone. Seeing Lizzie's name didn't cause the pain it used to; instead, my chest filled with the warm feeling from earlier as I opened my phone to read Lily's text. Liz's text could wait.

Lily: *Thank you for today.*

I tapped out a quick text back.

Me: *Red, that was all you.*

Lily: *I'm pretty sure you were there, too. It takes two to tango you know. =)*

I laughed.

Me: *I meant the studio. Get your mind out of the gutter*

Lily: *Duh, that's what I meant, perv... Don't call me, Red. See you tonight, boss. xoxo*

I shook my head with a small grin on my face. I'll call her whatever the hell I wanted, and she'd like it.

Me: *You haven't seen perverted yet, baby. See you soon.*

All I could think was how I couldn't wait to taste her again. How I hoped I could have some one-on-one time with her at work. Shit, I was so screwed. Groaning, I shoved the truck door open and ran to the porch. Once inside, I shook the rainwater from my hair like a wet dog.

"You're moping that shit up." Seth's even tone drew my attention to the couch. He was eating a bowl of cereal, most likely Reese's Peanut Butter Cup Puffs. That guy was such a kid sometimes.

"Snack time?"

"Fuck yes, this man's gotta eat." Seth's mouth turned into a crooked shit-eating grin right before he shoveled in a bite from his bowl. I laughed out loud.

"You're so damn weird," I said through heavy laughter that had my stomach muscles aching. I kicked my shoes off onto the tile entryway. "I need to hurry and get ready for work. You coming down tonight?" I asked as I walked to my bedroom door.

"Possibly..." Seth's eyes didn't meet mine. Blue was his go to spot to pick up chicks, but lately he'd been mixing up his stomping grounds. He never brought chicks home though, never dated, never showed more interest than one night, really. I thought I had trust issues with women; he's issues were deeper than I could probably comprehend. As good at the game as we both were, I was so tired of it.

I already knew the answer, but I wanted to ask. I wanted to hope for his sake, that maybe just once, he'd say yes. "You think you'll actually pick up a chick and want to keep her around?"

"I'm going to go ahead and say not likely." His dark blue eyes narrowed before he stood brusquely. "I'll see you though, probably round eleven. You better get ready; you don't want to be late." He wouldn't look at me. He just stared at the quiet television. I took that as my dismissal.

"See you then, man." I opened the door to my room.

"Hey, Todd?" Seth's voice was tight like he was trying to hold back some sort of emotion. For a split second, I worried that I'd pissed him off. Seth was like a brother to me. He was there for me in my darkest hour even though he himself fought demons. Raised by just his father, abandoned by his mother, dirt poor for most his life — yeah, he had issues.

"Yeah?"

"That Lily chick... she seems... cool. You going to be all right? You think you got this one handled?" Seth's eyes met mine, and I nodded.

"I hope so. She's pretty amazing so far." I held his stare and smiled.

"I'm not gonna lie. You look really stupid when you smile like that." His lips twitched with suppressed laughter.

"You're an asshole, bro." I almost wanted to pop him in the jaw, but I didn't want to be late for work.

CHAPTER TWENTY-SEVEN

Lily

THE BAR WAS DEAD, LIKE POST-APOCALYPTIC dead. There were maybe six people all together, and Jace was lingering at a table with four platinum blondes. Jace poured on his natural charm thickly. The girls giggled and ate up every word he was spewing. *Barf.* At this point, I almost wished a pack of zombies would break through the front window. At least then this horror show I was watching unfold would end.

"I hate that guy sometimes," Tiffany spoke quietly next to me. Even though Band of Horses played overhead, the room felt pretty quiet.

"Sometimes?" I lifted my left eyebrow in question.

"Hey, I'm not the one who went on a date with him." Tiff poked me in the arm with her tiny index finger.

"Ow, that hurt!" I chuckled. "You're strong for being so tiny, and, for the record, I didn't know better at the time."

"Right?" It was her turn to giggle. "Oh my God, I wonder if Todd will let me go home early. It's so dead?" She pushed off the back of the bar.

"I bet he'd let you."

"I bet he would if *you* asked." She placed her hand on her hip and looked at me with a skeptical smirk.

"What does that mean?" I asked with just enough incredulity in my tone I almost laughed.

"It means that if we're going to be best friends, which I thought we were..." She put her hand to her heart as if injured. "...I wouldn't be the last to know that my *best friend* was the daughter of Frank's ex-wife *and* was screwing the hot boss man. I need to know these things, Lil. I *need* to know." Her big hazel eyes opened wide when I gasped at her words. "You are! You little slut, I'm right. I love this. I must have every juicy detail. Please, I haven't had a date in months. I need to live vicariously through you."

She gave me such a serious look I couldn't stay mad at her for her *'little slut'* comment. I wasn't ready to talk about Todd though. It was all so new, and I wasn't even sure what *we* were yet. Honestly, this morning was the best morning of my life — this day was everything. Todd hadn't fixed the broken pieces I handed him today. No, he pulverized them, turned them to dust as if those pieces had never needed to be part of me any longer. I could tell that once Todd let someone in — gave all of who he was — it would be game over. I just hoped I could find the way there with him. He was a rollercoaster, and my feelings for him were building like a storm on a hot day on the Florida coast. The heavy passion we carried would be hard to bear alone. I wanted to be part of his life, living it with him, seeing where this crazy ride could take us.

A slow smile broke across my lips.

"Okay, what? Why are you smiling like that, Lil?" Tiffany's eyes were full of amusement, the laugh lines next to her eyes creased.

"I think I really like him." My gaze dropped, talking about my feelings out loud made me feel silly.

"Yeah?" Tiffany giggled.

"Yeah. Today was amazing. We went to the studio and sang together. It was there, sharing that experience with him... It sort of made me fall in crush with him."

"In crush with him?" Tiff's laughter was full bodied now. The tiny frame of her shoulders shook with humor. "Awe, that's so cute."

"What's cute?" Jace's voice penetrated the air and ruined my good mood.

I didn't want to be out here any longer. "Hey, I'm going to take a break for a minute. Want me to ask Todd if you can go home early?"

"That would be great." Tiffany beamed up at me.

"Asking the boss for favors already? Things must have gone well for you today." Jace's tone was accusatory.

"Excuse me?" I didn't miss what he was implying.

"I'm just saying... you must be pretty talented. Todd's never been one to dole out record deals to just anyone. Your mouth must be gifted. I'm bummed I missed out, but I didn't have record deals to give, did I?" His tone was mocking.

Before I could even process the insult, a deep voice boomed from across the bar top.

"Please tell me you didn't just fucking say what I think you did?"

I turned and saw Seth standing taller than I'd ever seen him stand; his jaw pulsed and his hands began to close into fists.

"Don't come in here trying to talk shit, Seth. This girl comes into this bar, blows through two guys already, and just happens to know Frank *personally* too. Come on...?"

"I didn't blow through anything, you asshole. I went on one date with you and that was it! Don't try and make it sound like I'm some sort of slut." My head pounded with a furious heartbeat.

"Hey, I'm not the one who went out on a date and just a few days later is getting fucked by the boss."

Tiffany gasped and shoved Jace as livid tears started to fill my eyes.

"What the hell, Tiffany! Don't freaking touch me." Jace grabbed Tiff's small arm with force and shoved her to the side to get closer to me, causing her tiny frame to slam into the wood of the counter. She cried out in pain.

Seth's lithe frame came across the bar and grabbed Jace's shirt with one hand and the back of his head with the other bringing Jace's head down in one swift powerful motion onto the surface of the bar. The sound Jace's skull made when it met the wood counter top made my heart stop. His body fell to the floor into the fetal position. One of the girls from the table shrieked in fear, and the other said she was going to call the cops.

Jace cursed loudly, and I took a deep breath. At least he wasn't unconscious. He looked at me with such disgust, as blood trickled from his forehead, and his eyes seemed unfocused.

"Go get Todd, Lily! Tiff go with her. This motherfucker's gonna—"

"Seth, don't. Just leave it." Tiffany looked at Seth imploringly.

"Babe, he touched you. He said that shit to Todd's girl. I can't let… just go." The muscles in his arms flexed.

Tiffany and I ran to the back to get Todd.

What the hell had just happened?

CHAPTER TWENTY-EIGHT

Todd

LILY AND TIFF PUSHED THROUGH MY office door and started rattling off about what was going on out front.

"Wait, he said what to you?" I cursed under my breath as I stood and my shoulders tensed. If Seth didn't kill him for touching Tiff — he had a soft spot for that little sprite — I'd definitely mess him up for saying that shit to Lily.

"Todd, just go help. Someone called 911." Tiffany looked as if her whole world was falling apart. Jace must have really scared her.

"You guys stay back here. I got this handled. Stay," I ordered again when they both looked as if they were about to argue. Lily nodded and wrapped her arm around Tiff. The last thing I heard before all hell broke loose was Lily consoling Tiffany. The sound of breaking glass had me running to the front of the bar.

The bar was empty; the customers must have hightailed it out of here. I wouldn't blame them; the place was trashed, and glass was everywhere. Jace and Seth looked like they were in a cage match; both were shirtless and covered in blood. Jace was obviously worse for wear. He swayed as if he were about to fall.

"Seth, that's enough. The cops are coming." The sound of police sirens started to build.

Seth dropped his defensive stance and wiped sweat from his forehead. "You're lucky, motherfucker."

Jace's smile turned wicked. "You win, boss. I was hoping to get a piece of that hot little body..." I was on the edge of losing it; my fists ached to connect to his jaw. "...but you got there first, didn't you. That mouth... Well damn, I almost had it wrapped around my—"

Seth's fist smacked violently into Jace's skull, knocking the asshole out cold just as the cops busted through the front door.

Shit!

THIS NIGHT COULDN'T GET any worse. Seth was arrested for assault and battery; Jace was in the hospital with a concussion; I had to close the bar early, and I would have to keep it closed tomorrow as well to repair the damage those two idiots had caused. Frank flipped his lid at first when I called and told him what had originally happened. I explained to him what Jace had done. He officially fired him and said Seth was allowed free drinks for a month. I sent Tiffany with money from my savings to bail Seth out, and now Lily and I were sitting on my couch awaiting their arrival. She was pretty messed up over the whole ordeal.

"I feel responsible," she spoke, breaking me from my thoughts.

"Don't. He shouldn't have said that to you. He shouldn't have hurt Tiffany. He deserved what he got." I cringed remembering how I had once slapped Liz out of anger. I was so drunk that night; it was the first time I had seen her with Sawyer. I couldn't see past the betrayal I'd felt, all I saw was his body embraced around what I thought was mine. My fucking heart was broken that night — smashed into fragments. I'd put everything into her, into that one hope, and to see it fall away from me... It fucking broke me. When she told me she was with him, I lost all my sensibility and acted impulsively. Nothing I could do or say justified my actions. I was a piece of shit for hitting her. I would regret that day till the day I died. I'd never ever thought I'd be a guy that could hit a woman, but I had. My chest started to ache with the memory. *Who the hell was I to judge Jace?*

"What's the matter?" Lily's worry made my guilt turn in my stomach. Elizabeth and Sawyer had forgiven me, but I'd never forgive myself for that lapse in control.

"Nothing." I stood from the couch and Lily's concerned gaze. I grabbed my phone to check the time.

"Don't lie to me, Todd. What's up?" Lily asked in a soft voice.

I didn't want to get into tonight. "Listen, I made a big mistake once, okay? Nothing you need to worry about. This night, it's just messing with my head, baby." I sat back down on the couch, leaned in, and kissed her gently on the lips.

She pulled away. "Tell me." Lily's eyes penetrated mine. I was terrified to lose the chance with her. We were barely starting. "I'm here... with you. I've told you my biggest sin. What's yours?"

Her face held no judgment as I told her about the night I hit Liz. I wasn't sure how much I should tell her about my relationship with Elizabeth. I loved her so much and for so long, I didn't think Lily would understand. I wanted her to like Lizzie, not look at her as a threat.

"So you were jealous?" she asked.

"It was more than that, Lily. I used to love Elizabeth..." Lily sucked in a ragged breath. "Used to, babe. She was all I ever knew. I grew up with her, remember how I told you?" She nodded. "She was who I thought I'd end up with, but I didn't. I messed up a lot back then, and I don't want to lie to you, it's not fair to you. But yeah, I was in love with her."

It was quiet. The room felt hot, the space between us seemed to widen, and I thought I could physically feel her emotionally pulling away from me. Lily's eyes cast down, and I watched as her chest moved in and out deeply. "Look at me." I lightly pulled her chin up; her eyes hesitantly met mine. "I loved her once, yes, that's true, that's how I am. When I fucking love someone, it's fierce and real. I lost myself in that girl, but I've moved on." I took her face between my hands. "I need you to hear me. I moved on, Lily. I'm ready. I'm ready, and I can already feel myself getting lost in you, in your fucking eyes every time I look at you. In your voice, in who you are. I can already tell this is going to hurt, but I want it. I want the risk. I haven't wanted that in so long, but I fucking want it with you. So trust me."

Lily's eyes filled with tears I placed my lips on the corner of her mouth, kissing her easily. My lips eased up her jaw to her ear. "Trust me," I whispered.

She exhaled deeply before she spoke. I pulled away so I could look into her eyes, the eyes I couldn't stop thinking about. "I trust you." She smiled quietly.

"Yeah?"

"Yes. I'm glad you opened up to me. I'm still processing everything. It's a lot to take in. I get that you once loved her and that you will always love her as a friend. I understand why you were so hurt that night you made that huge mistake in hitting her. I think it's sad that you haven't forgiven yourself, but believe me… I understand that, too. I'm just scared, Todd. I just think everything is going so fast. We need time. I don't want us to burn out."

"I know, and I agree, time's a good thing. And I'll prove to you that Liz is a done deal for me. She texted me earlier today inviting me over for dinner. My brother, my best friend Cam, and Liz's husband Sawyer will be there. Come with me?"

"To meet your friends?" She appraised me with a nervous smile.

"Yes, come with me. It'll be fun. This Sunday, you in?" My heart was thumping hard inside my ribcage. It was as if this answer could make or break us.

"I'm in."

I let my lips find hers. She tasted so sweet right then, I licked her bottom lip and the now familiar berry flavor had me needing more.

"Nice to know you were concerned about your best friend being in jail?" Seth's jovial tone made me laugh against Lily's mouth. Always the cock blocker.

CHAPTER TWENTY-NINE

Lily

THE CRUNCHING SOUND OF the thick brown paper that covered the pint glasses I was unpacking was the only noise to break up the heavy silence that had taken residence at Blue Bar. The damage to the back bar display proved to be much worse than what we'd thought, causing Frank to keep the bar closed for the rest of the week. The glass shelving and decorative custom liquor bottle lighting had been destroyed. Jace had been released from the hospital and was subsequently fired by Frank. I was grateful though to not have to ever see his face again.

Seth acted like he was fine with everything, even though his face had been cut up from the brawl. To make matters worse, Seth had to help pay for the damages, so he was now going to have to work at his new teaching job and still work on some of his father's accounts. According to Todd, Seth was being a *"total bitch"* about it. His words not mine. I chuckled as I tried to finish up unloading the box of glasses.

"What's so funny?" Frank's voice grumbled with irritation.

"This whole thing, if you think about it." I was just trying to be positive.

Franks lips turned down into a frown. The deep wrinkles from sun damage, smoking, and age gave his face such a hard look, but I knew better. Frank Nadine was a good man. He may have betrayed my father once, but I think love is such a crazy thing. It's like war and religion, people do senseless things to have it. Who was I to begrudge what he thought he needed? Besides, he's suffered enough from his choice. My mother treated him like crap, slept around, and then left him. He'd paid his dues.

"I don't think it's funny at all. Bills, Lil, bills. Plus, your studio time went down the drain, more bills, you see my meaning?" He sat brusquely on the bar stool, the black collared shirt he wore was faded, just like his spirit. I might not have known Frank well, but I could tell when a man had led a rough life. "This is the longest the bar has been closed, ever, and it pisses me off. For hell's sake, it's Saturday! I gotta pay for all new shelving —"

"I thought Todd's friend Sawyer was giving you a discount?" I asked confused.

"Well yeah, but can't a man just be pissed? Shit, Lily!" Frank stood quickly and with a small huff. "I'll be in my office. Let me know when Todd gets back, will ya?" Frank turned on his heels and stomped off to the back offices. My head was swimming with guilt. Of course Frank would be hurting. This place is all he had left. I felt foolish for my earlier laughter. I wished Todd were here, he'd have known what to do to make Frank feel better.

Instead, I was here alone for most of the day. Tiffany had the day off, and Todd was out picking up supplies for Sawyer. I hadn't met Sawyer, but Todd spoke so highly of him, and it was really cool he was putting off finishing a job today to install the new shelving. Apparently, he was going to work tomorrow, on a Sunday no less, to complete the project he was supposed to do today. I almost thought Sunday dinner over at Elizabeth's house was going to be canceled, but Todd reassured me Sawyer and Colby would get the job completed in time for dinner. I didn't want to admit it to myself, but part of me hoped it would have been canceled because meeting Elizabeth had me all sorts of anxious. Every time I thought of it, I could feel my stomach turn.

I cursed under my breath. I was being stupid. Elizabeth was married to this Sawyer guy, who, based on the way Todd and Seth talked about him, was apparently a walking God. According to Todd, Sawyer was this ex-Navy badass, who was not only really nice, but treated Liz like a queen, which was how she deserved to be treated. Again he spoke of her with that reverence that had me feeling insecure. My main fear was how I was ever going to live up to her, to Todd's expectations? I mean, if Liz deserved this superhero, what did that say about me? I shook my head and exhaled coarsely. I had to be okay with just me because *just me* was all I had to offer.

My hand pushed my curls back from my face as I bent over to grab the next box of pint glasses. I was struggling to lift it when the front door opened. I turned abruptly to see who it was and almost dropped the box. The weight of the heavy glasses inside shifted, throwing me off balance. My eyes locked with the most vibrant set of green eyes I'd ever seen.

"Holy shit, you got that, ma'am?" The man's voice was deep but had such a soothing quality to it. He walked with rapid grace across the bar, his tall broad frame moved, it seemed, with little effort.

It took me a moment to collect myself, but I was able to just about set the heavy box on the bar top. "I'm fine, really I–"

"Let me get that for you." The man grabbed the box with his large, powerful looking arms and eased the box to the counter. With a small, genuine smile he turned back in my direction. From the description Todd gave me, this had to be Sawyer.

"Sawyer?" I asked, my smile turning up on its own. He was ridiculously handsome — my earlier assessment of superhero could not have been more accurate. The dark red, long-sleeved Henley pulled tightly across his massive chest.

His smile widened and a small dimple popped. "Yeah." He held his hand out and I took it. "Nice to meet you…?" his voice dropped off in a question.

"Lily… sorry Lily… just Lily." What the hell was wrong with me? My smile felt awkward, and his smile widened. I hadn't missed the fact we were still absentmindedly shaking hands.

"Todd's girl? Well Lily, it's really nice to meet you." He squeezed my hand gently before releasing it.

Todd's girl? Todd told him about me? The stress I'd felt building in my shoulders earlier dissipated. I felt my lips pull into an involuntary smile. "Yeah, I'm Todd's girl. It's great to meet you, Sawyer. I've heard such good things." *I was Todd's girl.* Todd said it himself, he had moved on. I needed to trust that, trust him, and trust myself that I could make a good choice.

"Don't believe everything you hear." Sawyer laughed in earnest, and the earlier dimple deepened.

I smirked. "What? You can't leap tall buildings in a single bound? Move as fast as a speeding bullet?"

Sawyer's laugh reverberated in the room. "No, but my daughter… she's my Kryptonite."

That's right they had a daughter.

"Who… Sailor? That little girl is perfection, brother." Todd's voice radiated with his smile. I hadn't heard him come in. I watched as he walked across the bar and grinned. That sexy as sin man was mine, maybe just for the moment, but he was mine. *I was Todd's girl.* I kept saying it over and over in my head. I had never wanted to belong to anyone more.

THE EASY TONES OF acoustic guitars filled Todd's truck as the hard spring downpour beat against the metal roof. I wondered when this damn weather would let up. Todd quietly hummed to the music. I recognized the song that was playing, *"Better than Love"* by Griffin House. We were on our way to Sawyer and Elizabeth's place, and the panic started building as we turned onto a farm road. The clean scent of rain clung in the air; taking a long breath, I inhaled the soothing smell. *I was going to be fine,* I told myself silently. I started to hum along with Todd. Music was always something that could calm my nerves. I wondered then if Todd had chosen this album as a way to soothe me. He was so much like me, speaking to people through music was sometimes the only way I could be true with my feelings.

Todd's lips pulled into a brilliant smile as we both harmonized with each other. Singing with him, our voices blending with precision, the sound was infinite. I wanted to be connected to this man for as long as possible in every way. Todd had me wanting to try again; I wanted to take all this guilt I'd been living with and pour it into notes — let it hang in the air, let the anger, fear, and sadness of death go into the wind, and let it be blown away for good. My heart was slowly opening again, and for once, I wanted it to.

The truck came to a stop. I hadn't noticed we were there already. The earlier feeling of fear was still there, but it had turned into more of a need for acceptance. I wanted to be with Todd… I needed his friends to like me, to take me in as theirs. Sawyer had been super sweet to me yesterday at Blue, so I had hoped today would go well with his better half.

Todd reached across the stick shift and pushed a loose curl behind my ear. "You look so scared right now." The tone of his voice was filled with humor.

"I feel like I could puke at any minute... seriously." I took his hand in mine and toyed nervously with his fingers.

His deep laugh made me smile. "Shit, babe, don't puke in here. I'll never get the smell out." Todd's face almost looked serious.

"You're an ass." I instantly dropped his hand and punched him in the shoulder, which served to only make him laugh harder.

"I'm kidding, I'm only kidding." He spoke through his amusement. I was trying to pretend not to think this was funny, but seeing Todd so open and carefree, it was pulling on my heartstrings.

"Your laugh... it's extremely attractive. I really love it."

Todd's chocolate eyes found mine, and his smile was soft. "You think so, huh?" He pulled his thumb across my bottom lip as I nodded. The heat from his hand seeped into my skin as he wrapped his palm around the back of my neck. The electric charge that consumed the air whenever we were together picked up its pulse, and I felt him in every pore, in every part of who I was. I unconsciously leaned forward and brought my lips to his mouth, pulling my teeth across his full bottom lip. A slow growl escaped his hungry lips, his hand was firm as he gripped the back of my head, pulling me closer, his fingers tangled in my curls. The outside world didn't exist to me when we were like this, tasting, pulling, and pushing each other to the brink. "Fuck, you drive me crazy." Todd's voice was rough as he spoke against my lips. He lightly nipped my top lip and then kissed me softly once, twice, and one last slow time before he whispered, "I need to stop, or we'll never make it inside."

"You promise?" I unwound my hands from his hair and held his face in my palms. He tilted his head in order to look at me. We stared at each other in a heavy silence until the air started to burn with need, and I could feel my body ignite again.

"Lily..." He closed his eyes and exhaled. After a second, his intense brown eyes opened. "I'm... you've got me all crazy for you right now. I want to take you right here in this driveway, I want to tell you how much I crave your smell and how it lingers on my skin once you've left. I want to hear that sound that only you make when you come. I need to feel you lose control while you're wrapped around me, but at the same time, I need to hear your voice and your fucking laugh. You... this is not what I was expecting."

My heart was sprinting in my chest, and my fingers trembled against his cheeks.

"Damn, Lily, all I can think about every moment of every day is you. You and that sweet voice... and that even sweeter smile. I'm fucking addicted." Todd's dimples were on display as he smiled at me with more hope than I'd ever witnessed. I suddenly felt whole.

"Really?" I couldn't think of anything else to say. I just hoped that the happy tears that were falling were confirmation of my feelings for him.

"Hell yeah, baby." He gently kissed my cheek as his lips tasted my tears.

"I'm not sure when it happened, Todd, but I want to belong to you. I want to be the one you wish for. Is that... is that weird?" I tilted my head down; I couldn't meet his eyes. I couldn't believe I'd just spoken those words aloud.

I felt the familiar pressure of two fingertips under my chin, urging me to look at him. "Lily, did you not hear a damn word I just said?" Todd's gaze searched mine. "All I've ever wanted was to belong to someone. Hell, I'm in deep." I noticed the vulnerability in his voice, and all I could think about was how I wanted to make him feel loved, feel a part of a whole. I felt the shift in my heartbeat. He was starting to own pieces of me, and I wanted him to — I wanted him to have all of me.

I leaned in and placed a quick kiss on his lips before I said, "I heard you babe, and trust me... I'm in deep too."

Todd kissed me again, but this time his lips were possessive. He was taking me in as his. It felt so primal, the way our mouths linked us as one. I could have sat out here with him, like this for hours, but we didn't have hours. Instead, we had a house full of people that scared the crap out of me. But in order to belong to him totally, I needed to belong to them and I was ready.

THANKFULLY, TODD LET ME wear his raincoat over my head; otherwise, I'd be meeting Queen Elizabeth looking like a drowned rat. I tried to ignore all the tension in my limbs as Todd rapped his knuckles on the door. I took one last breath just as the door swung open.

"Hurry, get inside before you wash away. Ugh, this weather, it's the worst." Her voice was light, and her smile was immense as her giant blue eyes swallowed me whole. She was gorgeous. All the amazing things Todd told me in the car, all the security I felt, drained from my veins as if I was sliced opened with the sharpest knife in the drawer. "You must be, Lily? Sawyer told me he met you yesterday; I was so jealous."

An uncomfortable laugh escaped my lips as we walked through the threshold of the house. What on earth did she have to be jealous about? The thought caused another nervous giggle to erupt. I nodded. "Yes, it's nice to meet you, too." I felt Todd step behind me. He pulled me into him, my back pressed against the length of his body, as his strong, warm arms enclosed around me, and I instantly regretted my doubt. This one gesture bandaged the wounds of finally seeing *her* in the flesh. He wanted me to belong to him. I needed to trust that. I needed to believe in myself.

Elizabeth's laugh caught me off guard, pulling me out of my internal war. "You must be so nervous coming home to meet the family. Don't worry, I can already tell that we're going to get along. Anyone who can put up with this idiot is a friend of mine."

My lips pulled up at the sides, my smile no longer a fragile replica of the real thing. "Family, I like that. You're right, though..." I decided in that moment to be true to me, true to Todd, "...I was terrified. I'm just glad to have someone to talk shit with. Todd... well... do I really need to say more?" My laugh tickled all the way down my body as I felt Todd's sturdy arms turning me into his chest.

"Hey, screw that, Red. I'll just have to keep you away from this one." He lifted his chin in Liz's direction before he smiled down at me. "I'm awesome, don't you forget it." Before I knew what he was doing, he placed his lips on mine. For a split second, I was self-conscious by the show of affection, but then I realized he was showing me that I was bound to him. The kiss was sweet, his lips tenderly coaxing me, and for about thirty seconds, he had me totally wrapped up in the moment. Todd's thumb gently stroked my cheek as he pulled back from my mouth, and for a few more seconds it was just us as I watched his eyes alight with amber flecks of fire.

A movement in my peripheral vision brought me back down to earth. An easy measured grin spread across Elizabeth's face. She bit her lip trying to suppress her smile. She looked so genuinely pleased for Todd in that instant that I couldn't dislike her. She loved Todd and wanted him to be happy. That little smile on her face told me everything I needed to know. She wasn't a threat; he quietly claimed me, and she looked as if it was Christmas morning.

Todd gave me one more peck on the cheek. "You ready to meet everyone else?" His smirk was cocky. That kiss was more than just a kiss, and he knew it. I nodded.

"Lizzie Bean, where the hell is my baby girl?" Todd took my hand in his, lacing our fingers. Liz's eyes didn't miss the action, and her smile spread wider; her blue eyes gleamed as she motioned for us to follow her.

"This way. Sailor has been so spoiled today. Cam never puts her down when she's here." Elizabeth brought us through the living room, the wood fireplace crackled, and the earth tones throughout the house made me feel at ease. This was such a home; it made me nostalgic for a future that maybe one day would match this one. Growing up I always had such love from my father; he did everything he could to make our house ours, *'our little piece of heaven,'* he called it. I had to swallow down the emotion growing in my throat. Todd squeezed my hand as we walked into the kitchen.

"You okay, baby?" His voice quiet but full of concern.

I really was. He was making this day so much easier; if only my stupid brain would stop taking me back, back to where I couldn't ever go again. "I'm better than okay, I'm really fine, just a little home sick."

Todd's eyebrows dipped. "You sure? Because—"

"Oh my God, look who decided to grace us with his presence." A tall, leggy strawberry blonde stood next to the kitchen counter, bouncing a fat little baby with dark curls and eyes that could only belong to Liz on her hip.

"Shut the hell up and give me that damn baby." Todd let go of my hand and grabbed Sailor from who I assumed was Cam.

She reluctantly handed Todd the little cherub. "Don't think you can just come over here and start barking orders again." Her angry tone was at war with the welcoming smile she held.

Todd hugged her like a brother who hadn't seen his sister in years, and the small portions of my heart that belonged to him multiplied seeing him like this — the front gone. The small town boy, the good friend, the boy next door was more than I'd hoped for. Underneath the tough exterior, Todd was a sweetheart. Sailor cooed and grabbed his nose; the light laughter and easy smile that fell across his face had me falling hard. "It's good to see you, truly. You…" Cam pointed at me, and my pulse skipped. "…must be Lily? I don't know how you put up with this asshat, but, hell, it's sure nice to find someone who can." She reached out as if to shake my hand, but pulled me into an embrace. I felt awkward. I wasn't really a "hugger," but just as she pulled away, she whispered, "Hang in there, he's worth it."

I immediately knew Cam was my favorite person here. She patted me on the back lightly just as she took the last step away. She perched herself on the counter and popped a carrot from the tray of veggies that sat on the kitchen counter in her mouth. "Todd, you've had that baby forever already. Five more minutes, and that's it. You hear me." Cam snickered.

The relationship between Cam and Todd made it so easy to laugh. "It's nice to meet you guys, really, and it's nice to see this side of Todd."

"Oh, you mean you were getting sick of the moody bastard? Why?" Cam snorted at her own joke, and Todd shot her a glare.

"Fuck, why am I the only guy here? Where the hell is my brother? Sawyer?"

"Dude, don't swear in front of the baby." Cam giggled.

"It's not funny, Cam. Yesterday Sawyer hit his toe on the coffee table, and I swear she repeated every word." Elizabeth's smile was infectious.

"Uh oh." I laughed.

"Right?" Elizabeth's eyes sparkled with humor.

"Oh my God, she can barely say Mama let alone the 'F' word." Cam rolled her eyes.

Todd's deep laugh resonated through the room, grabbing our attention. The girls looked at him with proud smiles as he peppered Sailor's cheeks and neck with kisses causing her to giggle wholeheartedly. The rough scruff of his beard must have tickled her cheeks. The light color of Sailor's skin next to Todd's tattooed arms was such an interesting contrast. He was so incredibly sexy. The dark gray shirt he wore fit him just right — the short sleeves hugged his biceps, and, with the way he held this little girl with such admiration, I was hooked.

"He's so cute with her." I shook my head as I watched Todd quickly wrap around Sailor's finger.

"He really is. Who knew?" Elizabeth joked.

Todd glanced at me, and I gave him a wicked grin. "Are you ever going to share?" I asked as I reached to take Sailor from his arms. She was heavier than she looked. She was solid, but soft at the same time; her pudgy fingers swatted at my father's necklace.

"Are they still at the job site then?" Todd asked as he started on the veggie tray as well.

"I guess. I haven't heard from Sawyer. They should have been back by now, but he always calls me before he leaves." Elizabeth busied herself with dinner prep. Whatever she was making smelled great. "Colby hasn't texted either has he?"

"He did about thirty minutes ago, said they were almost finished." Cam hopped down from the counter. She pulled her phone from her pocket. "I'll send him a quick text and tell them to hurry their asses up." Cam tapped out a quick text. It felt as if hardly a minute went by and her phone beeped. Cam's face drained of color as she read the text. Her eyes swept the room and landed on Liz, as she rapidly tapped at her phone's keypad.

Liz's back was turned as she stirred the boiling contents on the stove. My pulse started to rush; I could sense something was horribly wrong. I turned my attention to Todd, who was now staring at Cam with unease. They shared a look, and my chest constricted. With Sailor in my arms, I watched everything that happened next as if it were slow motion.

Elizabeth wiped her hands on the towel that hung from the oven door, "Well? Are they on their—"

Liz turned just in time to see Cam hand Todd the phone. Todd read the text and cursed under his breath. The anxiety in the room was profound.

"Lizzie…" Cam's eyes were filled with tears.

"What, Cam? What's going on?" Elizabeth's hands shook, the rosiness from her cheeks gone as she swallowed hard.

My heart felt as if it was about to rip through my chest.

Cam started to cry as she attempted to speak but couldn't.

Todd took three large strides and brought Liz to his chest. I could tell her body was trembling with fear — fear of what no one wanted to say. "Lizzie… Sawyer is on his way to the hospital." Elizabeth cried out, her sobs buried into Todd's chest, her legs buckled, causing Todd to tighten his grip. "He fell off some scaffolding, hit his head. It's bad, baby girl. He's un—"

Todd's speech was strained; he took a deep breath trying to keep himself in check. "He's unconscious. Colby's in the ambulance with him, and they're almost at the hospital." Elizabeth's body shuddered as sobs wracked through her. Todd rubbed his palm up and down her back in an attempt to soothe her.

She pushed away from him with force. "Take me to him…take me to him, now. Please, please God… Just take me to him, Todd." She wiped frantically at her cheeks, but started to break down into uncontrolled tears.

"Let's go, baby girl. Cam grab her bag." Todd's voice was flat. He looked over at me, and it was then I saw the red rim around his glassy brown eyes. "Can you watch Sailor, sweetheart?"

I nodded; I'd do whatever he needed me to. He needed to be there for his friends. "Of course, if that's okay?"

"I could stay if you wanted to go with Todd, Lily?" Cam suggested.

"She needs you, Cam. Come on, let's go. Lily's got this." He gave me a small smile.

"Be careful," I whispered.

He nodded at me as he took Liz's hand in his, and they

left quickly through the front door. The rain seemed heavier than it had earlier. I prayed that he would drive carefully. The sound of the rain mixed with the anxious feeling in my chest for Sawyer, and for Liz, was substantial and excruciating. I knew exactly what could be waiting for her at the hospital. I just hoped, for everyone's sake, her news wouldn't be as bad as mine had been on that one, horrible, rainy day.

CHAPTER THIRTY

Todd

THE SOUND OF LIZ BREAKING IN two wasn't something I was prepared for. I almost had to carry her into the hospital. By the time we got there, Sawyer had already been brought upstairs to the intensive care unit. According to Colby, Sawyer fell about twenty-five feet off of the scaffolding he and Colby were working on. They were finishing up a custom staircase banister. Colby couldn't tell us exactly what happened; he was too damn upset to get any real answers to Liz. She lost it when the doctor came out to bring her to the consultation room. At least they let her take Cam.

I was pacing the waiting room as I waited for Elizabeth or Cam to come out of the ICU doors. Every time the doors opened, my stomach churned. The wait was killing me.

The doors opened again, and two nurses who were joking amongst themselves walked out. I growled. "For hell's sake, what the fuck is taking so long?"

"I told you, he's in a bad way, man." Colby sat with his elbows on his knees, his head hung low. "I couldn't help him. I feel like I should have done more."

"What the hell happened?" I asked without blame.

"We were cleaning up... gathering shit. I turned around for just a second, and he fell. He may have caught his foot on one of the cords, who knows. All I know is one second he's fine, and the next I hear him holler, and then, nothing... nothing at all." Colby's eyes glazed over, and he rubbed his temples.

The electric doors swung open again. Cameron's soft cries didn't bode well for the good news I wished for. She walked quickly to where Colby and I were waiting.

"Only two visitors at a time, so one of you can go next." She plopped down into the seat next to my brother. Colby grabbed her hand in his.

"Well? What did the doctor say, Cammie?" He asked with the sound of terror in his voice. I was worried for Colby. This wasn't his fault, but my kid brother always tried to take on more than he should.

"He has a traumatic brain injury..." Cam's voice choked off, and she started to cry again. She swiped the tears from her eyes and took a deep breath. I didn't think I could take this anymore, but then I remembered Liz, and how this was her husband, the love of her life. I needed to be strong for her. "The swelling in his brain is causing pressure, I guess. They rattled off big words, Colby. I have no clue. All I know is that the doctor said he didn't need surgery yet, and the scan showed a small fracture on his skull. They purposely sedated him, and they've got this machine breathing for him. They said the first twenty-four hours are the most important. The doc said they'd be doing more tests tomorrow. They said the way he fell, he didn't hit head first, or the damage could have..." Cam's voice trailed off. We didn't need to hear those words.

"How's Lizzie?" It was a dumb question, but I didn't know what else to ask.

"She's freaking out. You should go back, see her... see Sawyer. She'd like that." Cam laid her head on Colby's shoulder.

"You okay if I go back first, bro?" I asked.

"Please, I need to be with Cammie anyway. Shit man, I can't see him like that. I just can't." My little brother looked as if he was about to fall apart.

"Maybe we should head back. Todd, tell Liz we'll head back and stay with Sailor, okay? Your lady is probably freaking out." Cam had a small watery smile.

"Yeah, thanks, tell her I'll be there soon to come get her?"

"Sure thing."

Cam and Colby said their goodbyes to me. We hugged longer than normal, but hell, I guess you never can take shit for granted. Small pieces of Lily started to flash across my brain — her face and the little freckles that made that constellation on her nose. How was it possible that I was missing her already? How could this girl be so far under my skin after knowing her for less than a month? After a day like today, I didn't care. I didn't need a rational answer. Life hands you fucking shit most of the time. So now, when I finally got something worth keeping, I sure as hell wasn't going to let time dictate a damn thing. Hell, we had no idea how much time we had left.

I pulled out my phone.

> **Me:** *Just going in to see him and Liz. Cam and Colby are on their way back. See you soon, baby.*

She responded quickly.

> **Lily:** *Is he going to be ok? You holding up?*

She was worried about me. It was wrong for me to feel happy about that right now, but I did.

> **Me:** *We don't know specifics yet. I'm fine…*

I hesitated before I tapped out the next text.

> **Me:** *Just missing you. Leaving in like thirty minutes.*

I needed to be honest with her and myself if this was going to work.

> **Lily:** *Missing you, too. Be safe.*

Me: *I will.*

SAWYER'S ROOM WAS FILLED with the low hum of the ventilator, the quiet beeping of the vitals machine, and the dripping of the medicine in the IV's. Liz sat next to the bed in a stiff looking chair with her head rested on Sawyer's chest. She was sleeping now — she looked so tired, and her tear-stained cheeks were pale as the sound of sleep exhaled from her lips. I'd been back here for a while. At first, all she did was cry. I soothed her the best I could, but seeing such a strong man like Sawyer reduced to this — it was gut wrenching. The tubes were everywhere. I never thought it was possible for him to ever be in this state, but I told Liz he was a fighter, that I was sure he'd been injured worse than this before, that he was a fucking Navy SEAL. The words I spewed seemed to help, I just hoped what I said was true. She had calmed down enough to tell me she'd spoken to his friends in California, and that they were sending him prayers.

It was not until she had finally fallen asleep that I finally broke down. Elizabeth looked lost. It was like we were ten all over again, and she was crying in my basement about how she'd never see her parents again, how she'd always have the horrible images of their death in her head. I hated that my best friend had to see her husband laid out in front of her, unable to breathe on his own. I was fucking pissed at the universe for hurting Sawyer. Hadn't these people been through enough? What if Sailor never got to know her father? All these questions caused my throat to painfully constrict as I tried to swallow. I hated that these damn tears were building in my eyes. I needed to get the hell out of here.

I swallowed down the emotion and kissed Liz on the cheek. I was grateful I didn't wake her. I leaned down and

whispered into Sawyer's ear.
"Don't fucking quit, brother."

CHAPTER THIRTY-ONE

Lily

SAILOR WAS SLEEPING SOUNDLY IN HER crib by the time Colby and Cam got back from the hospital. I'd only met Sawyer the one time, but I was devastated for Elizabeth, for Todd, for everyone. Losing someone you loved was something I wasn't a stranger to; it was like having your sternum slowly cracked open, one small break, day by day — it was agonizing. Colby told me Todd would be back soon. He looked so much like his older brother, but there was enough difference to make them each unique. Colby's eyes were so much lighter than Todd's; you could tell he hadn't ever suffered real heartbreak, but tonight his light eyes were rimmed in red as he mourned for his friends. I was grateful he and Cam let me be alone. They sat quietly in the kitchen. The murmur of their voices, the heat from the fireplace, the sound of the rain against the roof, and the exhaustion of the day had my head pounding. I rested my body on the couch and closed my eyes, hoping Todd would get here safe and soon.

"Hey, honey bell, you're looking so beautiful today." My *father's calloused fingertips traced the slope of my nose. "Time to*

wake up." *He quietly chuckled. The smell of Old Spice sifted through my nose, and a small sleepy smile spread across my cheeks.*

"Hey." *My voice was still thick with sleep.*

"Hey, you don't want to be late for your audition, honey."

A small, irritated noise pinched through my pursed lips. Why did my dad always make me feel like a child? It was time to get my own place, and soon. I needed to do well today — to prove to him I could do this. Arcadia College of Music only let in ten graduate students a year. I would be one of them if it killed me.

"Dad, I'm not five anymore. You can't just walk in my room... it's weird. What if I wasn't decent... what if —?"

"Just get up, and quit your bitching..." *My father's smile widened.* "I just want to see my daughter succeed. I'm excited, so deal with it, honey bell." *My dad's smirk was pronounced; the deep laugh lines creased, making me unable to be angry about his invasion of privacy. He just wanted the best for me. I should be grateful he still lets me live at home. Yes, it was my dream, but he was always there to help me flourish.*

I felt guilty but laughed at the proud goofy grin my father had splayed across his face.

"All right, all right. Out! I need to get dressed." *I laughed; it was crazy how excited my dad got when I actually took his advice.*

"You want me to drive you?" *He looked so hopeful, how could I say no.*

"That would be nice, Dad. Thanks." *He leaned over and hugged me.*

He cleared his throat, and I noticed his eyes were bleary as he pulled away.

"Shit hon, I'm so proud of you."

My breathing became shallow as I tried to hold in my own feelings. "Love you, too, old man. "

THE SOUND OF TODD'S deep voice seeped through my dreams. The heat of his hand on my face and the soapy scent I'd grown accustomed to surrounded me. "Why are you crying?"

My lids fluttered open, and dark chocolate eyes searched my face with worry. The tears poured freely down my face. The dream, the memory of my father, was still so hard to endure. This night was forcing it all to the surface. Todd feathered a kiss to my forehead as he pulled his thumbs across my cheekbones, wiping away the evidence of my dream. I couldn't find words; the fear of breaking down clogged my throat.

"Bad dream?" He asked, as his fingertips pushed the stray hairs from my face. I nodded.

"Yes... no. It was a memory... I just miss my dad so much sometimes. Tonight, it's screwing with me." I was surprised that I let the tears fall now, that I hadn't tried to get a hold of myself.

"I know what you mean. This night... I just need a minute to fucking breath, to escape this shit." He gently kissed my mouth; the feeling of his lips pulled me further away from the past. "I'm sorry about your dad." The sentiment brushed against my waiting lips.

"I'm sorry about your friend. Will he be okay?"

"I hope so." Todd lingered for a second, his breathing picked up and his nose grazed mine. When our lips met this time, it felt desperate, endless. We needed to lose ourselves.

I wrapped my fingers in his dark blond hair and pulled him in, eager for more. Our lips melded together like they were meant for each other — the soft pull of his mouth against my bottom lip, the sting of his beard against my chin, his tongue tasting mine. My body responded to him like an instrument responds to the skilled musician. Todd played my strings just right, and I thrived under his touch, I shone brighter than I ever had before. This was heartache; this night was full of destruction, but this one moment between us, this kiss, played out in harmonious notes. This was music at its finest, even if the room was silent. The sound of his love resonated through my bones as his body pressed against mine. The weight of him was a heady thing.

"I need to be with you." The gravelly tone of his voice caused my pulse to quicken.

"Where is everyone?" Todd's lips trailed down my neck, and his hips pushed down against mine allowing a small moan to escape my lips.

"Asleep… come here." He shifted his body from mine and stood to take my hand, lifting me from the couch. I hurriedly followed him down a set of stairs to the basement. I was still disoriented from sleep. Todd led me to a small room; it appeared to be a guestroom.

"Here?" I almost didn't recognize my voice. The desire to be with him was urgent, but I wasn't sure if this was the right place for this.

"Lily… I realized something tonight." Todd shut the door behind us. "This life is so fucking short, and I'm so tired — tired of not doing the right thing. You're my right thing, and I don't want to waste one more minute trying to deny that." He cradled my face in his hands; he searched my eyes for just a half a second before he brought his lips together with mine. The way he took possession of me with that kiss, he devoured every last bit of my fear, anxiety, and mistrust. I felt lightheaded, my legs almost unable to stand, at the impact of his words and the feeling of his chest rising and falling under my palms. He had me thinking things I shouldn't. I didn't want to think the words I was thinking. The three little words that were begging to fall from my traitorous lips. The three words that would surely ruin everything.

"Lily." He needed me, and I wanted to be needed. Todd's hands lifted my shirt over my head. The skin of his hands dusted down the curve of my hip. "Is this okay?"

"Yes." I sought for more words, but all I could think to say was the one thing I couldn't.

Our lips met again furiously. Our bodies were dying to be connected, screaming for each other, and my heart cried out to align with his, the feeling of it, the pressure building... it was intoxicating.

We shed our clothes and our pain, both laying on the floor a forgotten thing of the past. The warmth of his solid body united with mine, and the sight of Todd so vulnerable... was beyond beautiful. I felt him press against me as I laid myself open for him. Skin to skin, no barriers this time.

"Are we okay... to not use a...? I mean... are you—"

My hands shook as I ran my fingers through his hair. I nodded and answered him with a whispered, "Yes." I knew what he was asking me. I wanted nothing more than to show him that I trusted him with all of me. I was falling in love with this man.

He leaned down and kissed me passionately. My legs shuddered as I felt him slowly push into me — nothing separating us. It was him, just him, and I could hardly bear it. He was too much, all of this was so fast, so crazy, but I wanted every damn second of it. The rhythm was gradual. He pressed so fully into my body with each stroke that I couldn't understand how I'd gone so long without knowing this, knowing how it felt to be whole, to be so full of another person. I wasn't sure I would be able to tolerate the ache of his absence. He was a part of me now.

"Sit up." The words were a gentle, quiet plea. He situated himself so that I was now bound around him absolutely. We were heart to heart, chest to chest, mouths together, linked and moving in a rhythm that was seamless.

"Damn." His voice was strained as he thrust himself fully inside me. My body clasped around him with each pulse, our bodies slick with a slight sheen of perspiration. I was so close, but I wasn't ready yet. I wanted to savor every inch of him. He groaned, and I pushed against him, his strong hands grasped my hips, slowing my pace to his.

"I need you to move slower. Feeling you like this… I don't ever want it to stop." Todd's eyes locked with mine. "I need to feel you come, baby, wrapped all the fuck around me."

His fingers dug into the flesh of my hips, and his powerful arms pulled my body just the way I needed it to move. The force, the sweet assault, had my nails digging across his back as I cried out in pleasure. Todd's teeth nipped at my neck as his hands held me in place, the unrelenting pressure sent spasms through my body. I felt him still as the low rumble in his throat built. He released my hips just to pull me hard against him again, his lips crashed into mine, and my fingers twisted in his hair. His release was powerful, and his growl tore through the dark quiet. He swore as I rolled my hips against him, causing him to shiver. He gripped my hair at the nape, forcefully exposing my neck.

The softness of his lips against my throat was the perfect contradiction to how rough he took me in that moment. Watching him lose control, how the muscles in his jaw ticked and how his eyes blazed… there was nothing like it. I rocked my body one last time, and he groaned loudly before he took my mouth to his.

Our lips were lazy and our bodies drained as we kissed each other down off the edge.

CHAPTER THIRTY-TWO

Todd

ELIZABETH'S RINGTONE BROKE THE EASY SILENCE of the early morning. Lily's flame-colored hair surrounded me, and the plush feel of her breasts lying against my naked chest, the way her body draped across mine... I never wanted to wake up again any other way. I reached easily to the bedside table to grab my phone quickly. I didn't want her to wake up just yet.

"Hello." My voice was light.

"He's awake. He woke up." Elizabeth's hopeful tone made me smile. Sawyer would never leave her, never. He was a fighter.

"Really, baby girl? That's so great." I exhaled a large breath as the weight of the past twenty-four hours lifted. Lily shifted slightly, and I lowered my voice. "Is he doing okay?"

"I think so. The doctors said they lowered his medication to see if he could wake on his own. He did. Oh my God, Todd, he was fighting that ventilator and everything. They just took him for another scan to see how much the swelling went down." Her voice broke, and I could tell she was trying to hold back tears. "The doctor said he was so lucky."

"Luck had nothing to do with it. He's a tough son of a bitch," I whispered.

"Why are you whispering?" Elizabeth asked in a whisper as well, making me laugh quietly.

"Lily is still asleep."

"Oh… oh. Well, I should… um," she stammered.

"It's fine. We all stayed at your place. Cam and Colby have Sailor upstairs with them."

"I know, I've spoken with them. They're on their way here. I don't think they knew you were there, Todd." She laughed. "But I should let you get some rest. Go be with your girl. But Todd…? Can you make it up here today? Soy's still in really bad shape, and I think having everyone here will help him. He needs his family." Lizzie's words were tight; she was still trying to keep it together.

I ran my fingers through Lily's hair. She was still sleeping soundly. "Yeah, I'll be up to the hospital in a little while."

"Talk to you soon. And Todd…?"

"Yeah?" I asked.

"Love you." It sounded as if the tears had won and were falling.

"Love you too, baby girl." I ended the call and let my phone fall to the ground. Sawyer was awake. I took another huge breath, allowing the feeling of loss to evaporate with the exhale.

I continued to watch Lily sleep. I let my fingertips run along the curve of her body — her silky skin was smooth under my touch. This girl was made for me, and I couldn't stop thinking about how fucking good it felt to have her come against me with nothing between us, how I had poured myself inside her. I'd never done that before, never been with a girl without protection. There was no barrier, and I couldn't help how goddamn amazing I felt right now. She let me in — let me mark her as mine. I sounded like a damn caveman, but it was surreal. I didn't think I'd ever want that, but I do.

This chick was killing me slowly; I loved how different I felt with her. She made it so I never doubted myself. She lifted me up, and she made me feel like I was worth keeping. I was fucking falling in love with her. I shook my head and let that thought really sink in before I rolled my body just a bit so I could enclose my arms around her tiny frame. She was the first real thing I'd ever had. My relationship with Liz had been something completely different, and the other girls... well, they were just placeholders.

THE WATER FROM THE shower had just run cold when I heard Lily open the door.

"Sorry I slept so late," she muttered.

"Don't worry about it, it was a long night." I opened the shower curtain and reveled in the blush that crept across Lily's cheeks. I regretted not waking her up with my mouth between her legs.

"It was. Have you heard any news?"

"Sawyer's awake. I'm heading to the hospital soon."

Lily's eyes met mine, and her sweet smile made my chest tight. Shit, I was in deep.

"Really, holy crap, that's awesome."

"Yup." I grabbed the towel off the rack and started drying myself off. Lily bit the corner of her mouth, and it took all my rational thought not to pin her against the wall. "You hungry, baby?" I said as I pulled the towel around my waist.

"You probably need to get going, and I'm dying for a shower. You think you could drop me home on the way to the hospital. We could meet up later." Lily walked over to where I was standing and wrapped her arms around me; the palms of her hands flat against my back, her head tilted just enough to meet my eyes full stop. Without thinking I kissed her. It just happened — like how my heart beat without any conscious effort of my own. It was just the most natural thing I ever needed to do.

"You don't want to come up to the hospital with me?" I asked, as my lips pulled from hers. *God I want those lips on my body.* I craved her like she was my last dying breath.

"You need to be with your friends, and I need to do some things today anyway. We could have dinner later," she suggested.

"Yeah, maybe want to try for some studio time? It's Monday, and we need to get back into the studio, babe. The bar opens again tomorrow, so let's get that track laid out?" Lily and I singing together was something I was eager to do again.

"All right, that sounds awesome, actually." She stretched up on the tips of her toes and kissed my cheek. "Now get dressed, because I need to get home and brush my frigging teeth."

An hour and a half later I was sitting next to Seth in the hospital waiting room. Cam and Colby left about thirty minutes after I arrived. Colby looked wrecked, and Cam looked just as bad. The ICU only let two visitors back at a time, and getting them to let Sailor in was a damn joke. What the hell? She was his kid; she needed to see her daddy. I wanted to punch the stupid male nurse sitting at the desk for giving Lizzie shit, but I didn't feel like going to jail, so I didn't. Sailor and Liz were Sawyer's two visitors, so Seth and I were stuck out in hospital purgatory.

"I'm still fucking pissed you didn't call me last night with this shit, man? What the hell?" Seth stood and started to pace. "I mean, what if... what if—"

"I know bro. I'm sorry, my head wasn't right last night."

"You think? A quick text would have been nice. That's all I'm saying. I could have sat with Liz. She was alone, man." Seth's angry eyes appraised me.

"She wasn't alone, she was here with Soy. I'm sorry, okay?

Dick move on my part."

"Dick move," he grumbled and started pacing again. He looked like a caged animal. Seth couldn't deal when his friends were hurting. "This place is making me crazy. I'm going downstairs for coffee. Want one?"

"Sure, thanks."

Just as he turned the corner, Elizabeth came through the automatic doors that led back to the ICU with Sailor in her arms. She gave me a small smile; she looked exhausted. The dark circles under her blue eyes gave her face a sunken appearance.

"Let me take her. Sit down, Lizzie Bean, you look like shit." Taking the baby from her arms was the least I could do to help her.

"Geez, thanks." She plopped down into the chair.

"I just mean you should let me go back and see him. You need to go home, get showered, and change your clothes." Sailor squirmed in my arms so I threw her lightly in the air and caught her. I did this a few times and each time she giggled harder. "I mean he's awake, right?"

"Yeah, the tests came back good. The swelling is down, but he's in so much pain. But they said the way he fell; it was just the right way to do it. Seeing him lying there, watching him struggle to do what he normally does on his own, watching that frustration flash across his eyes... It's so hard. He's so strong, and to see him like this... I just want him back home with me. He has some tremors in his right hand, and they need to do more tests to see what that's about." She ran her fingers through her hair; the rough movement had her looking overly disheveled.

"He'll be back in shape in no time. That's how he is Liz, he's a fucking machine."

"Todd, language!"

"Sorry." I frowned. Sailor giggled as I bounced her on my hip.

"Oh, I almost forgot. You'll never guess who his nurse is today." Liz gave me a sympathetic look.

"Who?"

"Emma. Emma—"

"Dawson?"

"Ah uh. I haven't seen her in forever." Liz nodded her head.

Holy shit, I hadn't seen her since the night of Lizzie's wedding. I was in such bad shape that night. I don't really even remember much about it; all I could recall from that night was that I was out of my mind drunk, and Emma and I had apparently slept together. I had no idea how, or even why that even happened. I mean, I dated that chick for a bit, but she was so uptight about sex, about saving herself for marriage; she was way too moral for the fucking likes of me. So, it was surprising she took me back to her place that night. The sad thing was, I didn't even remember it. All I remember was driving in her car and then waking up next to her as she was crying. I felt like the biggest piece of garbage. I mean, the girl I thought I loved had just married another man, and there I was, drunk as shit, waking up next to a crying girl. Low point.

"Emma Dawson? I haven't seen her since your wedding. She's a nurse?" I asked without real interest. Sailor slapped my nose; I pretended to bite her fingers as she smacked my nose some more. I loved this fat little baby girl.

"Yeah, she told me she graduated last year. Changed her major; I guess. I had heard she was struggling awhile back.Apparently she's a single parent, but I guess this nursing degree has helped her get on her feet." Liz smiled, and I just stared at her blankly.

"Single parent? She's got a kid? When did that happen?" I couldn't believe Emma-fucking-Dawson had gotten knocked up. Man, I missed a lot when I moved away.

"Her daughter, I think she said her name was Molly, is two years old. I guess the father's not involved, which is too bad. She told me today that she had her that November after Sawyer and I were married."

My head started to spin, and the acid in my stomach began to churn. Emma had a two-year-old daughter? The morning after Liz's wedding ran like a movie in my mind.

My head was pounding, where the hell was I? I sat up, the alcohol still burning my throat. I was still wasted. I scrubbed my palm down my face, the feeling of cotton in my mouth. Why was this damn chick crying?

"You okay, sweetheart?" My words slurred. Shit, I was still so drunk.

"No Todd, I'm not okay... I'm one hundred levels below okay. I'm so screwed." The girl started to cry harder.

"What's... what—?"

"Just stop, I made a huge mistake. What am I going to do?" She stood from the bed, and I could feel her staring at me.

I lifted my head; the light made my headache split nails in my temples. Emma Dawson. Emma Dawson? I took in her appearance — the sexed up hair, the black lace panties, and small tank. I looked down at my naked body covered in a sheet. Holy shit, I banged Emma Dawson. I think?

"Did we?" I pointed to her, then myself.

"Yes, Todd, we had sex. Oh my gosh, what was I thinking?" She sounded irritated. I felt bad. The fact I couldn't remember shit meant that I probably sucked, and she didn't get hers. Wow... Emma Dawson. Wait, did she just say, 'What was I thinking?'

"The fuck? That's rude." I stood and found my pants on the floor. I stumbled as I tried to get dressed.

"You were a mess. I felt so sorry for you, Todd. You were crying and—" Crying? This chick was crazy. *I listened as she rambled on; my inebriated brain had a hard time keeping up. "I brought you here to try and sober you up. Like we used to, remember? You'd come over, tell me all your crap about Lizzie, I'd listen, and you'd fall asleep. Like old times, I thought. But you were so sad, and I've always cared about you, but you just never saw past*

her." Emma angrily grabbed her jeans and shoved her legs through each pant leg. "I broke down. You kissed me, and, heaven help me, I had a slip in judgment. I let my love for you cloud my brain, and I did the one thing I never thought I'd do. I let you use me." Emma started sobbing.

The bile in my stomach started to rise. She loved me? I used her? She let me. How could I let this happen? "I'm... I'm—"

"Don't freaking say you're sorry. It broke, Todd! It freaking broke. Now what am I supposed to do? I hope for both our sakes nothing happens, because I can't do this with you."

I broke her? I was so confused, and the taste of pennies pooled in my mouth. "I think I'm going to be sick."

This whole time I thought she meant I broke her heart. When she said she couldn't do this with me, I thought she meant a fucking relationship, which I didn't want anyway so I didn't ask questions.

"Todd, you look pale. Are you sick?" Elizabeth stood and took her daughter from my arms.

Did she mean the condom broke? When she said she "*Couldn't do this with me.*" Did she mean be a parent? The numbers and dates ran through my brain, making me feel dizzy.

The ICU doors swung open, and the female's voice rang in my ears. "Lizzie, Sawyer is back, he's asking—"

The loud clang of her clipboard dropping to the floor was all the confirmation I needed, as her face turned white as a sheet and her trembling hands hung limply at her sides. "Todd?" My name fell from her shaky lips, and I knew only two things in that moment. I was a father, and my daughter's name was Molly.

THE TEARS THAT FILLED her eyes and spilled down her cheek

cut me open, and the loss of feeling in my limbs tingled like pins and needles as if I were becoming paralyzed. The surrounding noise faded, and the clean, white walls of the hospital waiting room started to blur. My breathing felt superficial, but I could feel the anger start to scorch its way through my veins. This damn girl stood here weeping, and the only sentiment coursing through me was rage.

"T-Todd, I... I—" Emma stammered.

Liz's voice was faint in the background. She was asking me something, but the throbbing in my temples blocked it out. My jaw ached from how hard it had been clenched. Emma looked at me, and she saw the hurt and the betrayal plain as day on my face.

Taking in the stale hospital air, I attempted to speak through my haze of anger. "How could you?" My throat contracted. I didn't cry. I was a fucking man, but for some reason, I felt pain trying to leak its way through my eyes. "How could you not tell me? I'm... I'm... a father?" My breathing was deep and measured as I tried to gain control of the shit storm in my head.

Elizabeth gasped. "Todd, what? Emma?" Lizzie's voice quivered as she realized what I was saying.

Emma took five steps toward me only leaving a small space between us. Everything in me repelled, and my hand twitched. "Back away from me, please." The words were calm, but I was anything but.

"Todd, listen... please." Emma reached for me, and I took a step back.

"Don't." My heart was hammering. I needed to get out of here, but the need for answers swarmed inside my sick gut. My head progressively started to let my surroundings fall into place. Elizabeth was standing next to Seth, two cups of coffee in his hand, and his mouth was in a firm line as he took in the scene before him.

"I c-can't do this here. Please let me –"

"Explain! Are you kidding me? On what plane of existence is it okay to keep a father away from his child?" My hand clutched around her upper arm pulling her closer to me. "By all means, explain it to me."

"Todd, bro, calm down," Seth's voice was a whisper. "This isn't the place, man."

"Todd, please…" Emma's soft cry carved me open. Lessening my grip on her arm, my glare met hers, and guilt emptied from her brown eyes. "I'm about to go on break. Please, just wait here. Let me take Elizabeth back to her husband, and then I'll tell you everything. Just… just wait here. I need… just don't disappear again." She quickly wiped the tears from her eyes as I dropped my hold on her arm.

Elizabeth gave me a pointed look gluing me in place before she walked back with Emma. She was making sure I wouldn't run, because that's what I had done wasn't it? I ran, I *"disappeared."* The heaviness of my legs caused me to stumble as I moved to the chair and sat down. Seth stood before me and handed me my cup of coffee.

"Looks like you need this even more than I do." Seth's sarcastic bullshit was not what I needed right now.

"Don't even start with your shit. This isn't a fucking joke." My voice was louder than it should have been for an ICU waiting room.

"I'm not making a joke. I heard what you said. You're in some shit then?" he asked as he sat in the black plastic chair next to me.

I couldn't speak, so I just nodded my head. My heart was in my damn throat. The weight of this revelation, the fact I had a daughter… It was as if I was sinking fast into deep water, and the feeling of suffocation started to work its way into my lungs.

"May I make a suggestion?" Seth's tenor implied I didn't have a choice.

"By all means, please… please tell me how to feel.

Because right now, all I want to do is scream, Seth. I want to know how the fuck Emma thought it was okay to not tell me I had a kid." The words were a hissed whisper. My molars mashed together, but it didn't ease the ache in my chest, not by a long shot.

"You need to calm... the... hell... down," he spoke slowly. "You want to see your kid? Then chill. This chick holds all the damn keys, man. Don't let another girl ruin your life — don't let her control you like that. You take what's yours, but do the right thing. Remember it's not all about you anymore. It's about that child, too. Trust me when I say this, your kid needs both of you." Seth stood and gave me a firm clip on the shoulder with his fist just as Emma came through the automatic doors. "You got this?"

I nodded.

"I'll head to the studio. Want me to text Lily and have her meet me there?"

Lily. The name sounded twisted. How the hell could I even begin to explain this to her? She was my one right thing, and no matter what, no matter how hard I tried, I was bound to mess it up.

"Yeah, let her know I'll be late. I'm not even—"

"Stop, don't let this shit ruin you. I can't watch you go down that road again. You got this or not, bro?"

The breath that pulled into my lungs allowed me to say yes, allowed me to say the lie. In reality, I didn't have this... I didn't have anything.

THE RAIN HAD LET UP, so Emma and I were sitting outside in the hospital courtyard. The silence was killing me, but I wasn't sure what to say; the anger I felt just wanted to boil over. My eyes were fixed on a small speck of dirt that clung to Emma's scrub pants. It was so small, but it was the one detail that kept me in check. This small distraction created a little bit of reality for me to cling to.

"She looks just like you." Emma's voice cracked causing my bubble of peace to burst. I could hear the air leaving my lungs. Those five words were like a punch to the gut. "When I look at her every day, I'm reminded of you. Of how much I loved you. Of how much you loved Liz. You were so blind. What would you have done? Would you have married me? Lived a miserable life until you resented me and Molly for taking away your freedom, your spirit? I couldn't do that to you. You were already so lost... it never would have worked with us." She wiped at her eyes. She was hurting, but so was I.

"I would have liked the fucking *choice*." The last word erupted from my lips. My hand ran through my hair as my jaw pulled tighter than it ever had before.

"The choice, Todd? The choice? What should have I chosen? I'm all ears." She sat up straight, and her hard stare met mine.

"Me... Emma, you should have chosen me. That's all I've ever wanted... to be someone's choice. You of all people should've known that." The words were hard to say, but they were true. Emma and I had a rocky past, but she had always been there for me. Emma's eyes softened, and a sob spilled from her trembling lips. I felt like a dick, but, damn it, I was still so pissed. "Hell Em, I'd be a great father... I'm *going* to be a great father, and I could have loved you. We could've made it work. I never thought you wanted anything with me. You always chose your faith over me every damn time." Emma had belonged to a super strict non-denominational church; they didn't mess around when it came to following their commandments. She used to push me away anytime I tried to get close to her. *What else was I supposed to think?*

"I loved you, Todd, and I wanted to have a real relationship with you, but I couldn't live like you did. I have my faith, yes. I shouldn't have to change who I am for anyone, and neither should you. So I made the choice, yes, the choice to give you your freedom, to not be tied to me, to a commitment you couldn't keep. I loved you so much I let you... I let you go." Her tears came harder.

I stood from the bench and kneeled in front her, my hands embraced her face. "You let me miss everything. You made a choice for me, and you chose wrong," I spoke softly. "You should've let me be there, let me hold her little body the day she was born. I could've watched her walk her first steps, heard her first words, but you took that from me. Fuck Em, I could've loved you so much." I placed my forehead against hers, my tears pooled and spilled as my fury turned to regret. I saw the life missed, and it was my fault. Back then, my life was so screwed up, and Emma was only trying to make the choice she thought was best for her and her daughter. Seth was right. It wasn't about me anymore.

"Todd... our daughter, the older she gets, the more I wished I had chosen differently. Doing this alone and still... still loving you... it's the hardest thing I've ever done." Emma broke down, and her shoulders shook with sobs. *She still loved me?* The words were drumming in my ears as I pulled her body against mine, while her tears soaked the collar of my shirt. I smoothed my hand down the back of her head; her familiar hay colored hair was just as soft as I remembered.

"Shh, listen... listen to me. We can make this work, Em, we can." Emma felt comfortable in my arms. She was the mother of my daughter. She was the one who picked me up every time I got my heart broken by Liz. She was there the night I thought my life was over. The debt owed to her on my part was greater than any wrong choice she could have made.

"We can?" Emma pulled away from me just enough to let our brown eyes meet.

"Yeah, we can." The pad of my right thumb wiped away the salty water from her cheek as my left hand settled at the nape of her neck. This moment felt too intimate, it felt wrong. In that moment, Lily's smile, her laugh, that one little freckle that sat above her upper lip, her crème skin running under my fingertips, my mouth tasting hers, and that sweet smell of coconut ran through my mind.

Emma's lips parted, the small separation between us was all that kept me from my future. But which future would be mine? I couldn't make that decision right now. Emma Dawson loved me. My heart pounded hard within its confines, but I was falling in love with Lily. I leaned in and placed my lips to Emma's cheek. The salty water brushed across my mouth. Emma exhaled a small breath. Standing, I took her hand in mine. The look of disappointment flashed across her features.

"Can I see her?" All that mattered right now was Molly — the rest of it could wait. My priorities had now been changed.

"Sure, I have some pictures on my phone." Emma stood and took her phone out of her front pocket.

I wasn't prepared for the heartache I was about to sustain. This little girl was everything; I didn't know I could love someone so unconditionally with just one look, but it took my breath away as I looked into the biggest brown eyes I'd ever seen. There was no denying those were my eyes — the light amber flecks around the irises shone. Molly's thick dark blonde hair fell down in soft curls, and her cheeks were so full. The brick in my throat started to hurt when I noticed the dimples. Molly was my daughter. I had the most beautiful baby girl in the world, and I'd missed every minute of her life. Every. Precious. Fucking. Second. A promise was made to myself in that instant — not one more moment would be missed. Not. One.

CHAPTER THIRTY-THREE

Lily

"Hey Lily, can you sing that last part again?" Seth asked as he fiddled with the soundboard.

"Let's break for a bit. I sort of want to wait for Todd anyway." It was an hour past the time Seth had said Todd would be here, and I was starting to worry. The ever-familiar anxiety I felt when people were running late was starting to rear its ugly head. "Maybe I should text him?"

Seth mumbled, and for a minute I thought he'd said something about needy chicks. What?

"Um, did you just call me needy?" I was not amused.

Seth chuckled. "Yeah, sorry. You weren't supposed to hear that."

"I am not needy. He's an hour late, Seth. What if something is wrong? What if—"

"He's dead in a ditch? Highly unlikely, Hellcat."

The breath I was holding blew out in a huff. Seth wasn't aware of how his words were like a knife to the heart. "Shit, what did I say?" He watched me with guilty eyes.

"Don't worry about it." My father's ring twirled between

my fingertips, and Seth's eyes slid down to the motion of my hand.

"What's with that ring, anyway?" Seth pulled a stool over to where I was and sat down. "Well? You married?"

I laughed without humor. I wouldn't be with Todd if I was married. "No, it was my father's."

"Was?"

My attention was drawn to him, to the tone of his voice. He sounded so sad. "Was... he got drunk one night. The man that never drank got drunk and drove off a bridge into the Gulf of Mexico. So yeah, I'm indeed needy when it comes to my loved ones running late."

Seth's crystal clear eyes cast down. "Shit." His hand rubbed at the back of his neck. He cleared his throat. "You're *loved ones*?" His tone was skeptical as he looked up. "Todd? He's in that category now, is he?"

"Absolutely." Our eyes locked as he finally met my stare.

He nodded. "I'm sorry about your dad. You and your mom—"

"Thanks. My mom... haven't seen her since I was three, but you don't need to know all this, sorry. I just... get anxious. I care about Todd, and I can't help that–"

"No, I'm an idiot. I shouldn't have said that." Seth placed his hand on my knee in a friendly gesture; his thumb rubbed small circles trying to ease my worry. "Look, I'm really sorry. Can you pretend like I am not a giant, insensitive dick? Please?" His lips tipped up at the corners.

"Sure thing, just don't tell Todd I called him a *'loved one.'* I have a feeling he'd run to the hills."

Seth smacked my knee with a smirk. "Nah, that kid loves to be loved. He's a fucking sicko."

My laugh sounded muted in the sound proof room. "I think I'm going to text him."

"No need, I'm right here." Todd's deep timbre filled my chest, and I could finally breathe, he was infiltrating every part of my heart.

"Hey you." I greeted him as he gave me a small peck on the cheek. The gesture felt off, cold. You pecked your friend or your mom on the cheek, not your girlfriend.

"Hey." He handed me the bag he was carrying, and I placed it on the table next to me. "I grabbed some takeout, hope that's okay? I'm not really hungry, so I just grabbed you a sandwich." The smile on his face didn't reach his eyes, and the alarm bells in my brain started to go off. *Something was up.*

"Did you grab me anything?" Seth asked.

"Shit, I forgot you were even going to be here. Honestly, I'm not feeling it right now." Todd wouldn't look at me, the panic started to shape in my chest.

"It's okay, we got some of Lily's voice work done. Tomorrow's another day. I should head. I'm meeting up with some people anyway. Good job today, chick. Remember what I said, this shithead right here… total sicko." Seth grinned at me, and it made me smile through my panic. Maybe seeing Sawyer today had put Todd in a funk, and maybe Seth was right… maybe I should tell him how I feel.

"Nice. Get the hell out of here, dude." Todd threw a drumstick at Seth.

"See you guys later. Oh, and keep it down. Hearing you guys bump uglies, as much as it turns me on, it's weird the next day." Seth's low laughter lingered as the studio door shut behind him.

"Oh my God, he can hear us?" I was mortified.

"He's just messing with you — and me." Todd's smile was now genuine as he searched my face with eager eyes.

"You swear?" My embarrassment subsided.

"I swear." He placed his hand against my cheek, and I leaned into the touch. "Hey you." The palm of his other hand rested against the back of my neck as his mouth claimed mine. The kiss was soft and took away any bit of insecurity I had. The tip of his tongue licked at the seam of my lips, seeking entrance, and he tasted me with such adoration; I felt revered.

"Mmm, I needed this." He hummed against my lips.

"Me too. You okay? Sawyer? Is that why you were so late? He's still doing okay, right?" The glimmer in Todd's eyes from our kiss faded. He exhaled nosily.

"No, he's fine. I just had some stuff to work out. Long ass day, baby, don't worry. I promise we'll talk about it later. I just want to be with you right now."

"Anything I can help with?" My lips met his; I was bound and determined to get that spark back in his eyes.

"This is helping," he said between kisses.

"Good." My arms linked around his neck, as he pulled me up from the stool. Todd's able hands ran down my back. He grasped at the backs of my thighs and lifted me suddenly. I squealed and laughed, my legs enclosed around his waist and he carried me as if I weighed nothing. The hard surface of the wall met my back as Todd kissed me forcefully, pinning me in place. My nails pulled down his back, and he shuddered.

Our breathing was heavy. This was how I showed him that I cared about him, how I showed him every piece of me was his.

"You make me feel out of control," Todd's full lips whispered against the skin of my neck, and a shiver ran down my spine making me grin.

"I'm glad." I bit my lip in an attempt to hide my smirk.

He chuckled. "You're glad you make me crazy, that you've basically stolen my heart?"

Todd didn't miss my intake of breath. "I have?"

He nodded, his lips curled into a small sideways smile before he took my mouth with an easy precision. With smooth strokes our tongues met, our lips paced, and his teeth grazed my upper lip. "I love this fucking freckle." He smiled.

"I love *you*." The words slipped out, and Todd became still. I was horrified that I'd let those words fall out of my stupid mouth.

"Lily... I—"

"I didn't mean to say that." I shook my head.

Todd's brow furrowed. "Then why did you say it?" He spoke as if he was wounded. He started to ease me to the ground.

"Wait. I mean... I mean I do, I care about you. Shit... or maybe I'm falling in love, I don't know. This is so new for me." Todd's strong arms pulled me back up into my previous position. "All I know is that when I'm with you, and even when I'm not, your there. I feel it in everything that is whole inside of me. You own every second... every breath."

Todd pressed me against the wall; his eyes never left mine as he kissed me. He worked my skirt further up my thighs and my panties down, as the heat between my legs grew with his intense stare. My hands eagerly loosened his belt, just barely pushing his pants down before he rocked his hips and thrust himself inside of me. A twinge of pain pulsed through me until I was able to adjust to the connection. He waited, letting his thumbs trace my jaw, before he started to move gradually. I felt the cool wall against my back, the fullness between my legs, and I watched the passion in his eyes flare with each stroke of his body within mine. I wanted to hear him say the words — Todd was showing me he cared about me, but I needed to hear it.

"Say it," I spoke, but the sound was just a breath. He rolled into me with a delicious force. "I need to hear you say it." His fingers fisted in my hair as he clasped the back of my head. With my arms around his neck and his eyes fixed on mine, Todd pulsed against me, and I cried out, the low rumble in his throat resonated through my body. The surface of my skin felt electric, my climax still making me sensitive.

"You need to hear it?" Todd's tone was seductive, as he plunged into me again, causing me to moan and my body to tense. "I'm falling for you, Lily. Every time you leave, the minute you walk away, I want you back. When you said I owned every second, every breath, I wanted more... more of you, every inch." Todd held me against him, taking another sweet kiss. The way he brought me in drew us together again, causing a small needy sound to fall from my lips; I pulled away from his kiss to catch my breath.

"You've got me so fucking far gone, I can't tell where I begin anymore. And I don't care. Being with you like this, getting lost inside you, feeling you fall apart..." I raked my bottom lip through my teeth. I was surrounded by Todd as he punished me with a flawlessly slow rhythm. "...it's all I need."

He growled against my lips, and his fingers dug into the flesh of my backside as his release poured through his body. He held me firmly against him for a moment more before he eased me down to the floor. My skirt billowed down, the hem just scarcely missing the floor.

My legs felt like Jell-O, but Todd's hands gripped my arms as I wobbled. "Whoa." I giggled at the proud smirk that spread across Todd's face. "Don't look so pleased with yourself." His carefree laugh caused butterflies to go wild in my stomach. I shook my head and grinned. "Have I told you how much I love your laugh?" My arms draped around Todd's waist, my cheek rested in the center of his chest.

The tip of Todd's nose ghosted across the top of my head. He inhaled, breathing me in. "This right here... you and me together... I love it. I love everything about you."

I felt him smile against my hair and heard his heartbeat quicken with his words. I smiled brightly as I spoke, "Every inch, baby. Every. Inch."

CHAPTER THIRTY-FOUR

Todd

STANDING HERE WATCHING LILY WORK BEHIND the bar, my guilt started to build like a brick wall. The past few days weighed heavy on my shoulders. My feelings for Lily were so fucking real. All I wanted was to be with her, but what I wanted didn't really matter anymore. I wasn't lying when I told her I cared about her, I did. She's the first girl to actually want me for just me. Lily caught my gaze, her brow creased and I smiled, trying to make my face look less terrified. She tilted her head to the right with a small unsure smile on her face. I nodded my chin in her direction as I pushed off the wall I was leaning against.

Several times this week I had the urge to tell her about Molly and Emma, but how did you tell the girl you just started a relationship with, the girl you were falling for, that you had a kid? I had to tell her tonight. We spent most of the week in the studio. My band didn't play this past Tuesday because Graden was out of town for business, so I devoted most of my time with Lily to getting her album laid out. Watching her work in the recording studio, seeing in person how her mind worked as she wrote lyrics, was a privilege. I watched as she held the guitar pic in her mouth, and loved how her hair fell on her face as she scribbled down the words for the song she was composing. Every minute with her was like a stolen secret... a prize. I couldn't help but think our time was limited.

It was close to closing time, and I was grateful tomorrow was Sunday. Lily had agreed to stay with me tonight so we could go see Liz and Sawyer in the morning at the hospital. Sawyer was doing much better and had been transferred out of the ICU and was now on a lower acuity floor. This past week was a real shit show on all accounts, but at least he was doing better. I had texted with Emma, and I was meeting Molly tomorrow night. A giant part of me hoped that Lily would come with me, but I doubted the odds were in my favor. The thought of meeting my little girl was so overwhelming, how was I supposed to do this? I still hadn't even told my brother. That conversation with my family would have to happen soon.

The bar patrons started to pool to the front as I turned on the lights indicating closing time. Lily and Tiff were laughing and talking quietly behind the bar. I took a deep breath as the last customer left and walked to where the girls were starting their closing side work.

"We've got to hire some more people, Todd. This shit sucks." Tiffany grimaced as she appraised all the glasses that sat at the tables scattered around the bar.

"It does. I'll get the glasses, Tiff, if you can wipe down the tables and the store front windows?" Lily smiled a knowing smile at me. Tiffany hated washing glasses.

"What the hell are you going to do?" Tiffany cocked her perfectly sculpted black eyebrow at me.

"I'll stock the heavy shit. But you're right. I'll look through those applications this weekend and schedule some interviews for Frank for this Tuesday. Sound good, princess?" I laughed as Tiffany frowned at my term of endearment; she hated it when I called her that.

"You're a dick." She huffed out a sharp exhale as she pushed past me to start the nightly cleaning.

Lily chuckled softly at the exchange as she picked a song for the night's cleaning party. *"Hero,"* by Family of the Year, started to play. The song calmed my nerves, and it was as if Lily could feel my anxiety as she wrapped her arms around my waist.

"What's up, baby?" She rested her chin on my chest as her gaze searched my face. "You've been so weird all week. Are you finally going to tell me what's on your mind?"

"You still staying tonight? I've missed you all week." I leaned down and kissed her forehead, my arms found their way around her little waist.

"You're such a jerk. Stop avoiding the question." She playfully slapped my shoulder, and I grinned for just a second. But then the image of Molly popped behind my eyes, and my smile fell. "See, what's that about, Todd? What's up?"

"Can we talk at my place?" My pulse started to pound as Lily's eyes darkened with discontent.

"Sure." She started to pull away, but I pulled her in closer.

"I swear we'll talk tonight. I wanted to speak to you sooner, but you hurried home after work every night. You avoiding me, lady?" My attempt to break the heavy mood worked. She smacked me again this time on my chest.

"No, I've been trying to record, work, and help my sister as much as I can. I need to get my own place. Can I have a raise, boss? I'm perfectly ready to sleep my way to the top." She winked at me, and a loud laugh burst from my gut.

"Holy shit, you're terrible at seduction, sweetheart. Good thing I already know what you're working with." I leaned down to kiss her, and the palm of her hand met my nose as she pushed my face away.

"Don't even." She giggled.

"Could you two stop flirting and maybe do some work?

Some of us have empty beds to go home to, you know?" Tiffany stood at one of the tables, a hand on her hip and a scowl on her face.

"Awe, shit, Tiff, want to come home with us?" I joked.

Tiffany's mouth looked as if she tasted something bitter, and her eyebrows dipped low on her brow. "I'm going to pretend like you didn't just say that." She turned and started vigorously wiping down the table.

"Um, me too." Lily shook her head at me, but the smirk on her lip belied her words. I laughed harder than I had all week, and my stomach ached from it, but the fun and games would be over soon, and I wondered if my bed would be empty tonight as well.

CHAPTER THIRTY-FIVE

Lily

THE TIP OF TODD'S FINGER TRACED odd shapes and patterns on my belly. The morning sun would be rising soon, and he still hadn't brought up what was bothering him. Whatever was going on it was affecting us, and I wanted it out on the table. One minute I felt him slipping away, and then the next he was clinging to me for dear life. I was used to the fact that Todd was moody, but tonight, he made love to me like he was desperate, like this was the last time we'd be together — like he was saying goodbye. It didn't help that I had to spend most of my time with my sister. The money she gave our mother had her budget short, so I helped as much as I could on the mornings she couldn't afford daycare. I'd only seen Todd in the studio and at work, and by the time the bar closed, I was so tired from lack of sleep I just wanted to go home.

Tonight was the first night we'd had just to ourselves since the beginning of the week. We needed this time together. We both hid our feelings behind our actions, and without his physical love, I felt lost. Todd's lips pressed against my neck, and his nose tickled at the sensitive skin below my ear. I hummed in appreciation.

"The way you respond to me, the little sounds you make... damn baby, it's everything." He nipped at my earlobe, and I shivered.

As much as I wanted him, needed that connection with him, we needed to be honest with each other or this would never last. We'd burn out like I had thought we would when we started this thing. The thought made me sick to my stomach. "Be real with me, Todd, what's going on?"

His body stiffened next to me, and I heard him inhale sharply. I sat up and pulled the sheet with me covering my body. He rolled over on his back, his one arm across his eyes and the other laid palm down on his chest. The fear in my heart started to flutter like a trapped bird against my ribcage as I watched his chest rise and fall faster with each second that went by. "God Todd, what is it? You're scaring me." My voice sounded weak in the quiet room.

He took a deep breath. "When I was at the hospital I ran into an old girlfriend..." My mouth felt like sandpaper as he continued, "I hadn't seen her since the night of Lizzie's wedding. She wasn't really even a girlfriend. I mean we dated a while ago, but—"

"Just spit it out." I couldn't contain the panic, and my words rushed out severely. Todd's history wasn't exactly a secret — his list of women was something I didn't have specifics on necessarily, but I was sure it was lengthy.

He sat up abruptly. "What the hell, Lily?" Todd appraised me with angry eyes.

"So some chick you screwed saw you at the hospital. Great, what happened? You want out, is that it?" My anger was irrational, my jealous green monster was on full display, and I hated myself for it. I dropped my eyes and started to curl the sheet into and out of knots with my hands nervously.

"Hell no! Lily, look at me." Todd tried to place his fingers under my chin, but I turned away from him, my emotions were too high. The bomb was about to drop, and my lungs were gripped tight in a vise. I couldn't believe I let myself fall for someone again, someone who would just leave me for another girl. Why was this happening to me again? "Lily, please, fucking look at me." The sadness in his voice momentarily cooled my temper.

Our eyes met, and the amber brown color that I'd grown to love had dimmed. They were now glassy and rimmed in red. Was he crying? "Please just say what it is you need to say." *If you are going to destroy me, please just do it quickly.*

"Emma, her name is Emma..." The ache in my throat was acute; I was helpless to stop the quiet sob that passed from my shaky lips, trying so hard to hold back the tears that were trying to fall. I almost broke when he placed my face between his palms. "Please listen, it's not what you think."

"Sure it isn't." The words were watery.

He wiped away the tears that were streaming down my face. "Lily, you need to listen, okay? I ran into someone I used to date, and yeah, you're right... she's someone I've screwed. One time. On the night Lizzie got married. The night my fucking heart was bleeding out on the damn floor. The night I was so drunk I didn't notice the condom broke. The goddamn night I made a child."

The room fell silent, and the air felt thin as everything started to spin. "Wh-what?" I didn't trust my own ears.

"I have a two-year-old daughter I never knew about. Her name is Molly. I saw Emma at the hospital, and it all came out. She never told me, didn't think I would've wanted to be a dad. I'm not what she envisioned for her daughter, you know?" Todd's face fell in defeat before me, and I felt my anger flare, but for a different reason.

"She didn't tell you that you had a kid? What the hell kind of woman does that?" I enfolded my hands around his wrists pulling him away from my face.

"I was pissed at first, too, Lily, but she had her reasons.

Back then, who would've wanted me as a husband or a father? I don't blame her." He tilted his chin down with shame, making my heart stop. Todd was too good of a guy. He blamed himself, and I wouldn't let him this time.

"No way." I place my hands on his face, tipping his head back, forcing him to give me eye contact. "You *do not* feel guilt for this. She should've told you, baby. She should have given you the freaking choice.

CHAPTER THIRTY-SIX

Todd

THE SINCERE SOUND OF LILY'S VOICE when she called me *baby* rattled the cage around my heart. The heat of her palms against my cheeks was like a balm. The way her eyes shimmered, making them look like emeralds in the dim light, took my breath away. But... the way she looked at me, like I was breaking apart, had the fucking tears that I shouldn't be crying falling from my eyes. Here I was telling her that my stupid ass mistakes of the past were here to possibly ruin our future, and she was sticking up for me, trying to make me feel better. This girl was everything I'd ever wanted, and I was about to tell her I needed space to figure shit out. I didn't want her to settle for me, my life was about to get so complicated, and she needed to be with someone who wouldn't always mess shit up.

"You're right, she should have, but she didn't, and what's the point in fighting. She's willing to let me be a part of Molly's life now."

A small puff of exasperation blew from her lips. "Willing to let you? Todd, that's your little girl. You have rights."

"I'm meeting her tomorrow." The weight in my chest shifted as Lily's hands dropped from my face.

"Will she be there? Emma?" Lily wrapped the sheet tight around her body like a shield.

"Yes." I didn't let my eyes leave hers. Lily's hold on the sheet tensed, her unease rolled off her in waves. I wasn't ready to let her go, I wasn't ready for the *space*, but my head was so mixed up. Emma still loved me; I could be a father to Molly, maybe make things work with Emma? My history of reckless choices spun through my mind, and I started to feel nauseated, the taste of metal pooled in my mouth. The thought of not having Lily with me tomorrow was making me feel so damn panicked that I decided to say screw it and just go with my gut.

"I'd like it if you'd come with me." Once the words left my mouth I started to feel better, the twinge in my stomach subsided. Lily let her grip on the sheet slack, her face no longer pale.

"Yeah?" She exhaled, her shoulders relaxed and she smiled.

"If you're sure you want to, I would understand if you wanted to end this." I pointed to my chest.

"Why would I end this?" Her brow furrowed.

"Why wouldn't you? This is a lot to take on for just starting out in a relationship." My teeth were clenched; my molars throbbed with the force.

"Todd?" She moved toward me letting the sheet fall, exposing her breasts, her flawless skin out in the open. The freckles that covered her body were a stunning assortment, and I haven't discovered every shape, every spot yet. Dread eased its way around my throat; the thought that I wouldn't know every spec of this woman was a dark cloud that hung over my head. "This is what caring about each other means. Let me be here for you."

"What if I can't let you? What if I don't want this for you?"

My jaw pulsed, the stain of my past failures pumped rapidly through my veins as I awaited her answer.

"That's not your choice, it's mine. Don't take away my choice, or then you're just like her."

The truth of what she was saying seeped through that brick wall I was trying to build. I had to let her make her own decisions. My heart wanted Lily, but my loyalty lay with my daughter, and I would do just about anything to have her in my life.

Lily wrapped her arms around my neck, and, as her chilled skin pressed against my chest, all the apprehension melted away. "Don't pull away from this. I felt you trying to all week. I felt you say goodbye tonight in every touch. Don't give up on us." She placed her lips to mine with a hurried kiss. "Let me be here for you," she repeated. A spark ignited across my skin as she trailed her fingers down my chest, the pale color of her hands against the colorful artwork inked into my skin was the perfect contradiction.

My body responded to her touch, but I couldn't let what I needed to say be clouded by my desire to be with her. "I'll try, Lily, that's all I can give you right now. You know I care about you, but my baby girl, Molly... she's my number one now and I need to be a dad to her."

"That's the best thing you've said all night." Lily surprised me by quickly placing her soft lips to mine. She pulled her hand through my hair taking the kiss up a notch, just enough to get me going, just enough to make it impossible for me to stop myself from having her. I couldn't give her more — the more that she deserved — not right now. Right now... all I had was uncertainty. I'd promise to let her be there for me, and I would, but right now, all I could do was make her feel... feel just how much she meant to me.

The fluorescent light in Sawyer's hospital room was taking my headache to a whole new level of shit. Sailor, Lily, and Elizabeth had just headed down to the cafeteria to grab some snacks for the baby. Sawyer was going home tomorrow; his recovery wasn't over, and he still had a small tremor in his right hand. The doctors assured him with physical therapy he would get the full function of his hand back in no time. Sawyer sat on the edge of his bed in his dark blue sweat pants and a gray T-shirt with NAVY across the front. His hair was messy, but he still looked like a fucking brick wall. He was staring at his hands as he rubbed his left thumb into the palm of his right hand.

"Does it hurt?" I wasn't sure if I should ask. He was quiet, and I figured he was the *'suffer in silence'* type.

Sawyer slowly pulled his attention from his hands. "I'm sorry, what did you say?"

His mind was obviously elsewhere, "Your hand, does it hurt?"

"No man, that's the funny thing. I wish it did… I wish I could feel the pain of it, because then I'd know how to deal with it. Pain is something I can handle, it lets me know I'm still alive, still breathing, still have a chance. This numbness is fucking driving me crazy. How the hell can I be fine one minute, and then not even be able to hold a damn pencil the next?" He brusquely pushed the tray table that sat next to his bed with his left hand, the pencil he was working with earlier fell to the ground — the sound oddly poignant. A small object like a pencil was bringing down this great man.

"Soy, physical therapy will help. The doctors say you'll be all good, bro. Don't let this shit bring you down, you're too strong for that, right?" I met his hard stare.

He nodded. "Thanks."

"All right then." My tone was placating, and Sawyer laughed. My lips pulled into a smirk. "What?"

"You're so sweet to me." Sawyer's shoulders shook with laughter as I looked for something to throw at him.

"Shut the fuck up, man. You were being a little bitch. I was just making sure you remember who you are." I couldn't help but laugh.

Sawyer took a deep breath, his smile still in place, and looked down at his right hand. "I got this," he whispered.

"You got this. I feel like a proud parent right now."

Sawyer appraised me quietly for a second before he spoke. "Speaking of being a parent—"

"Awe she told you, fucking Liz."

"Watch it, brother, that's my wife." His jaw tensed slightly, and I backed down. Sawyer was right, of course, Liz would tell him.

"I know, I just haven't told my family yet. I'm so screwed up over all this; I'm not sure what to do." The palm of my hand scrubbed down my face as I leaned back in the chair I was sitting in.

"What do you mean you don't know what to do? You be a man and own that shit. That's your kid, right?"

"Yes, Emma isn't one to sleep around, and the dates match up. I saw Molly's picture, and she looks just like me. So yeah... she's mine."

"You're a father." Sawyer's smile lit his eyes, and for some reason, this gave me hope. If he had faith in me, then maybe I could do this.

"I'm a father... I mean, I made a kid. I'm not a father until I step up to the plate, which I'm going to do, full on... I get to meet her today." I rubbed a piece of string from the ripped denim of my jeans between my fingers anxiously.

"Todd, being a father... it's more than I could have ever imagined. My little girl, she's my whole goddamn world. I have no doubt that once you see her, once you hold your own flesh and blood in your arms, once you see yourself in her eyes, you'll know exactly what to do. You'll be a goner." He shook his head and grinned. "Todd's a daddy... don't screw this up, brother."

"I won't." As the words left my mouth, the truth of the statement filled my chest with security, and I could breathe just a bit better than before.

"Your lady know?" Sawyer regarded me with sympathetic eyes.

"She does, and she's handling it all really well considering this thing... this relationship is so new. I'm just waiting for the ball to drop, I guess." A sharp pain pulsed behind my eyes. The day's stress was finally getting to me, and my headache was getting worse. Pinching the bridge of my nose between my thumb and forefinger, I continued, "I don't know, maybe it'll all work out."

"Just don't mess it up." He chuckled. "You have a tendency of doing things ass-backward, and Lily seems like a good girl. It'll work out. I like her, by the way. I didn't get a chance to tell you before I decided to take a twenty-five foot nose dive, but, yeah man, she's cool and pretty easy on the eyes."

"Keep your eyes to yourself." The sound of my voice was laced with jealousy. Sawyer's low chuckle made me grin.

"My eyes are firmly in place, brother, but it's good to see you really like her. I'm happy for you."

The feelings I had for Lily went far past anything I was equipped to deal with. When Elizabeth married Sawyer, I told myself I'd never again let someone in, never again let myself be duped into loving another girl, but I was saturated in everything that was Lily. She was everywhere: traces of her taste lingered on my lips, the feel of her skin on my fingertips, her hair on my pillowcase, and her image burned behind my eyes. There was no doubt that I could love Lily with everything that I am, and as hard as I tried to deny it to myself, this girl had taken root in my heart and, fuck, if I didn't love every second of it.

"Yeah... she's pretty damn sweet."

Sawyer smiled the biggest smile I'd seen on the dude all week. "You got this, brother."

CHAPTER THIRTY-SEVEN

Lily

"It was nice of you guys to come visit. Come for dinner this week? Maybe Sunday?" Elizabeth juggled Sailor between her arms while trying to take a bite from an apple. We'd been at the hospital for the majority of the day. The lack of sleep from the previous night was starting to take its toll, my limbs felt substantial, and all I could think of was how great a hot bath and a nap would feel right about now.

"I think so, Lizzie Bean. I might take Molly to meet my parents though, so I'll let you know. I'm hoping Emma will be okay with that." Todd kissed Elizabeth on the cheek. "You guys probably need the rest anyway, but I'll let you know. It was good to see you. Hang in there man." Todd gave Sawyer a quick hug; both men clipped each other on the backs, and I stifled a smile at the show of testosterone.

"It was good to see you again, Lily." Sawyer drew me in with his powerful arms, his sweet woodsy smell filled the space, and I felt entirely consumed by his form. It should've felt awkward to be so completely embraced by a man I hardly knew, but this was just his way. Sawyer was a giant sweetheart, and you couldn't help but feel like you'd known him forever.

As I pulled away from his hug, Todd smiled down at me and took my hand in his, interlacing our fingers. He inclined his head to mine and placed a quick kiss to my lips. "You ready to go, baby?"

I nodded. "See you guys soon."

THE GOODBYES WERE HAPPY; it was such a different feeling from how it was the last time I was here at the hospital. We were headed back to my house so I could shower and get ready to meet Molly — meet Todd's future. As much as it should've scared me, the way I felt for Todd trumped any fear I had. I said I would be there for him, and I would.

The spring air smelled rich, the scent of the cottonwood trees pulled through the truck's open windows, the wind ratted my hair, the heat of the sun soaked into my closed eyelids, and the slow motion of the moving vehicle rocked me into a sleepy state. It was peaceful. Todd was humming to a song by Band of Horses and in that moment everything felt as it should, as if this was just another day, another moment in time with him. I felt blessed. The rest of the day could wait — everything was right as rain.

"Hey babe, you awake? Your phone is vibrating like crazy." Todd wrapped his hand around my thigh.

"Yeah, sorry, I didn't feel it."

Eve's name flashed across my phone's lock screen. I had three missed calls from her and one text.

Eve: *Where are you?*

I swore, something must be wrong.

"Everything okay?" Todd asked, his brows furrowed.

"I don't know."

I tapped out a quick text.

Me: *I'm with Todd. Was up at the hospital visiting a friend. What's up?"*

Eve's text was immediate.

Eve: *Mom is here.*

My heart stopped, my stomach flipped, and the bile burned my throat.

"Pull over, Todd. Now! I'm going to be sick."

The truck swerved and came to an abrupt stop. I dropped my phone to the floor as I opened the door, hardly making it out in time before I emptied my stomach onto the side of the road. The bitter taste made me gag and dry heave again.

The sound of crunching gravel alerted me to Todd's presence. "Oh God, Todd, please don't… I've just been sick."

"*I know*, are you okay? What the hell, baby? What's the matter?" The alarm in Todd's voice helped me rein it in. I leaned against the truck passenger seat; my grip on the interior door handle was weak. Todd leaned passed me, and I heard him shuffling through the center console. He pulled back and handed me a napkin from a fast food place and his bottle of water from the hospital.

"Thanks." I wiped my mouth and took a long sip of water. The cool liquid poured smoothly down my throat easing the acid in my gut.

"What's going on?" Todd's fingers brushed the hair from my face and pulled it behind my ear.

"My sister said my mom is home. Like home… home, like at her house."

Todd's eyes grew wide. "You shouldn't go there then. Come back to my place. I'll go grab your shit, and you can stay with me. Fuck babe, don't worry, you don't have to see her." Todd pulled me to his chest, and I summoned all my inner strength not to cry. I felt stupid for my overreaction; he shouldn't have to worry about me today. Today he gets to meet his Molly.

The cedar fragrance of Todd's skin permeated through his shirt and comforted me more than I thought possible; it gave me the fortitude to do what I needed to do. I eased away from his embrace. "No, I should go home. You need to see your daughter, and I need to see my mother. Seems as if fate has its own freaking plans for us today." I laughed without humor.

Todd's face fell just enough that I noticed. "You don't owe her anything. She left you when you were only three. She's not your mother... she was an incubator." Todd's eyes turned dark, and the line of his jaw grew sharp.

"You need to go see your little girl, Todd." I tried to smile, tried to show him I could do this, tried to convince myself that her leaving me — never once looking back, and never once caring whether I was dead or alive — hadn't bothered me. After all, she was just a person — a person who I thought didn't hold the power to destroy me anymore. I was wrong.

"I could call Emma. Reschedule. Let me–"

"No way. You need to see her. Really, I'll be fine." I sucked in a large breath. "I'm sorry I scared you. I just wasn't prepared. The reaction I had was over the top, and I'm sorry." My cheeks heated with embarrassment, and I dropped my head down.

"Hey." Todd grasped my chin in between his thumb and forefinger, his intense brown eyes found mine. "Don't be sorry... never be sorry for how you feel about her. That woman left you, made you think you were worthless. That's not okay with me. You don't get to be sorry for her actions. It makes me crazy that she's got you this upset. I really don't think you should go home. Stay with me. Come home with me."

"No." Every nerve ending in my body rebelled at the word. "I can't... I need to face her, just like you need to go face your future. I can do this... let me do this." My voice shook, the swelling in my throat made it hard to speak.

He gave me a curt nod.

"I'm just sorry I can't go with you today, be there for you like I wanted to."

"I'll be okay. It's you I'm worried about." Todd placed a chaste kiss on my cheek. "Let's get off the side of the road before we get hit by a semi-truck." Todd gripped my hips with his hand and lifted me into his truck. I'd never get used to how easily Todd could pick me up. The door shut and I started to feel ill again, so I forced myself to take deep breaths in and out, to get myself under control before he opened the driver's side door. I couldn't shake the notion that I was letting him down.

I unlocked my phone and typed out a short text to Eve.
Me: *On my way.*

Ten minutes later Todd's truck was idling in my sister's driveway. An unfamiliar black car was parked in front of us.

"Let me at least come in with you," he pleaded.

I gave him a small nervous smile. "You're running late as it is. I'm fine…" He frowned and looked at me with skeptical eyes. "Really. You have more important things to worry about than me, than this."

The crease in his brow deepened. "You're important to me, Lily. So this shit show you are about to walk in on has me on edge."

"Exactly, that's why you need to go home, get showered, and go see Molly. Text me when you're on your way home, and I'll meet you at your place. Sound good?"

"Yeah, sounds good." The tone of his voice implied that it didn't sound good at all. I reached across the console and kissed him on his cheek; my mouth tasted like death, and I regretted not having gum because I needed nothing more than to kiss him right now, to feel his ownership, to feel his love for me.

Todd rested his nose in the crook of my neck, the sensation of his breath against my skin caused goose bumps to form down my arms and back. "I want to kiss you so bad right now. I figured you wouldn't want me to, but I just thought you should know." His lips pressed against the spot below my ear, and I heard him inhale. He spoke, his lips brushing against my skin. "You call me immediately if anything goes wrong. You need me... I'm here."

I leaned my cheek against his and smiled. We were always desperate to be linked in some way, but his touch... this touch was enough.

"Just text me when you're done, sweetheart." My fingers pulled the latch on the door, and I gave him a kiss on the cheek before I jumped out. The dread that flashed through Todd's eyes as I shut the door almost made my mask fall. He couldn't see me freak out again, I wouldn't let him. Todd didn't pull away until I was inside the house. I watched through the sidelight window as he drove away. I heard Christopher giggle and a loud, throaty laugh that belonged to an older woman echoed through the house; the sound was so unfamiliar. What did I have to be afraid of? She was a stranger, a nobody, a figment of my imagination.

"Lil, is that you?" Eve's voice called from the kitchen.

I hung my purse on the hook by the door. "Yeah, it's me."

"Lily?"

A medium sized woman with bright red curls stared at me. *That could be me in twenty years... that could be me.* A wash of sadness coursed through my body at the thought of my father having to look at me every day, having to see her in me. It must have killed him slowly.

CHAPTER THIRTY-EIGHT

Todd

THE GPS ON MY PHONE INDICATED I had reached my destination as the wheels of my truck came to a stop in front of an older home. Emma's house was on the small side; the red brick and white trim fit the old architecture of the area. She lived in the historic district of Ogden. I'd always loved the houses here, it felt quaint, and I was glad Molly had such a nice place to live. The engine in my 4Runner cut off as I turned the keys with shaky hands. I rubbed my palms down my pants to try and ease my nerves. My head was so jacked up right now. Lily was probably in the thick of it with her family, my worry for her didn't help my growing panic. I was about to meet my child, the little girl I didn't know I had, the little girl I was a stranger too. The irony of two daughters meeting their absentee parents on the same day was not lost on me. However, I wasn't going to miss one more damn day.

The walk up the drive was short; I closed my eyes and took one last inhale before I rang the doorbell. I heard a high-pitched squeal, rapid footsteps, and Emma's voice as it rang through the door.

"Give me a second, honey. Let mommy see who it is first, okay?" Emma's laugh was light as the heavy wood door opened. The smile on her face radiated, her thick hair was pulled into a messy knot on the top of her head, her black-rimmed glasses she only wore when she was home sat on her nose, and all the memories of her surfaced in one big wave making it hard to catch my breath. "Well hello. Come on in. She's expecting you."

"She is? Does she know who I am?" I asked nervously as I stepped through the threshold of the house. I thought I should have said *"hi"* or *"how's it going,"* but I wasn't sure how a guy was supposed to act the first time he met his kid.

Emma's smile fell as she whispered, "For today I just said mommy was having a friend over. This is scary for me, too, Todd. I'm glad you're here, but I'm terrified. Everything I've built for us could fall apart. Just... just—"

She didn't get to finish because a blur of blonde came running headfirst around the corner of the foyer. The mass of curls came to a dead stop when she saw me. She was wearing a yellow dress with white polka dots, and her cheeks were flushed from running. My pulse started to pound through my entire body, my throat constricted, and my breathing became shallow and rapid as I tried to comprehend the amount of love that filled my heart. My notrils flared as I attempted to hold back my emotion, and my hands started to tremble as I watched her shyly approach.

"I Lolly." Her little voice broke me — my legs buckled, and I dropped to my knees. The weight of so much loss, of so much gained... I couldn't bare it. "He cry, ma-ma?" The salt water spilled down my cheeks, and my heart split open as Molly looked at me with worry.

I wiped the tears from my eyes. "Lolly?"

"She had a hard time with the letter 'M' for a while, still does from time to time." Emma's speech was strained.

The corners of my lips turned up in a grin. "Well, Lolly,

I'm just happy to meet you, baby girl." Her big brown eyes met mine, and she smiled, a dimple formed in her full cheek. She was me; she was my blood, my bones… my soul. I looked up at Emma, the tears streamed down her face, and she gave me a sad smile.

"I two." She held up one finger, and I barked out a laugh.

"Wow. You're such a big girl."

She nodded and took two more steps; she placed her tiny hand on my arm. The touch sparked through veins and another few tears escaped my eyes. Molly's fingers traced the artwork on my arm. "Dis pweety." The smell of lavender and baby powder saturated the air. Molly's scent encircled me, the immediate feeling of home swept over my body. This was exactly where I should have been, and it was where I belonged.

"Thank you." The urge to push her hair behind her ear overtook me, and I lightly tugged on a loose curl. "I think you're the prettiest girl I've ever met, even prettier than your mom." Molly's smile widened, both of her dimples formed inside her cheeks, as she moved hastily toward me. Her small arms wrapped around my neck, and at first I was shocked still, until I heard Emma chuckle behind me.

"She's very lovey." Emma gave me a knowing look.

My arms pulled her snug against my chest; she was so little I was afraid I'd break her. I easily lifted her up and stood. She sat on my hip and was cradled safely in the crease of my arm. She ran the palms of her hands across my short beard and scrunched her nose up, her eyebrows dipped with a disapproving look.

"Guck." Molly wiggled her fingers in an attempt to rid the rough feeling of my facial hair from her hands. She was the cutest damn thing, and I couldn't restrain myself from laughing.

"Guess she doesn't dig the beard." I grinned.

"I guess not. Should we have dinner then?" Emma asked

as her fingertips swiped at the tears under her eyes.

"Lead the way." I motioned Emma forward with my free arm. Emma laid her hand on my shoulder and squeezed. The look she gave me told me I had done well.

"Follow me." She smiled brightly.

Molly pushed at my chest. "Down."

She practically jumped from my arms, and I was expecting her to take off running like a toddler would, but instead she took my large hand in hers. The whole world fell silent the instant I felt my daughter's hand in mine. This connection was greater than anything I'd ever experienced. For a moment, I felt like I had been this fraudulent human, just getting by. I was a shell of who I could have been, but in her I saw my true potential. I would be a better man for her, for my family. In her, I finally found the real meaning of unconditional love. In that exact moment, when her little fingers attempted to lace with mine, it was as if this was the first time my heart truly started beating.

CHAPTER THIRTY-NINE

Lily

"PAM?" THE SOUND OF HER NAME on my lips felt wrong. My so-called mother ran her fingers through her hair and actually smiled at me. The large grin pissed me off, and my next words came out in an angry rush. "Why are you here?"

"Well!" Her hand darted to her chest as if injured. Her southern drawl was unmistakable even in just the one word. She spoke with such astonishment as if I had no right to be rude, as if I had no right to hate her. "I'm here to see my daughter and grandson. I didn't realize you were staying with Evy until I got here."

Pam's statement confirmed to me she never thought of me as her daughter — the hammer inside my sternum split me open, the cracks almost visible, and the pain I tried urgently to hide started to seep into my system. The fury started to well in my eyes, the burn of the salt water was almost too much to handle. Why hadn't I just gone with Todd? I didn't need this crap. In the end though, I never considered her a parent. When you leave your little girl behind, you lose that privilege. For her, it seemed, I was never something she held in high regard.

I was just a burden from her past.

"I won't be here long. Just grabbing my things." I cleared the stone from my throat. It sliced its way down, making it almost impossible to keep myself whole.

"Lil?" Eve. The sound of her footsteps grew louder as she walked across the family room. My body was stiff; I hadn't moved from my position by the front door. "Hey, I just finished dinner, you staying?" She held Christopher in her arms, her eyes widened and silently pleaded for me to stay.

"Probably not, I'm staying with Todd tonight." The resonance of my voice fell flat.

Eve's shoulders drooped, and she met my eyes with disproval. "Please." She mouthed the word inaudibly; the private exchange had my guilt levels at an all-time high. I shouldn't leave her to fend for herself either. Eve hadn't seen her mother in five years, and she was probably feeling just as lost as I was.

Pam already looked bored with the conversation, as she picked at her nails without real interest. This small minute, while I watched her total indifference to me, solidified my decision. Pam, my *mother*, wasn't worth it. Not one more portion of my heart would wish for her to want me ever again. I was nothing to her. I exhaled sharply. "Nah, Eve, I think I'm going to head out..." An almost imperceptible flash of sadness crossed Eve's eyes. "...we booked the studio super early so—"

"Oh! " Eve's voice was loud and made me jump. "Speaking of music, you got mail today, from some music school. It's over there on the coffee table." Music school? She must be confused. "Anyway Lily, I really wish you could stay. I'm sure mom would love to catch up." As soon as she said it, Eve realized she had said the wrong thing and regret was written across her face. "I mean... I just mean—"

"Evy, its fine. I don't need to play catch up. I know where I stand with this one." Pam blew out a puff of annoyed air and shook her head.

For a split second, I thought I was going crazy. Did she blame this on me? My temper flared. "*Are you freaking kidding me right now?*"

"Lily. Calm down." Eve was horrified.

"No way… how the hell do you get off talking to me like I'm some piece of crap? You… *you* abandoned me when I was three-years-old. You left *me*." The hostility boiled in my blood. My whole life I always felt just inadequate enough to hate myself — if my own mother didn't want me, then what good was I. Over the years, I'd healed from the wounds left behind by my run-away mother, but today it was like she was cutting me open all over again.

"Abandoned you?" Pam laughed without humor. "Danny, mister perfect, threw me out, wouldn't let me see you."

The throbbing in my chest grew when she spoke of my father. The pressure built and my head felt fuzzy. "Don't even speak his name. *You* cheated on him, *you* screwed him over. He lived alone, dedicated himself to *me*… you were just too selfish to care. You had a new family, your *daughter* Eve, so you didn't give two shits about us. Don't try to pin this on him. You had every chance to see me, to get to know me, but you didn't, damn it." My hands were curled into tight little fists, and my breathing was ragged as I tried to calm my rage.

"Please, calm down, okay? The baby. Geez, Lil." Christopher started to whine as Eve's tears trickled down her cheeks. The stricken look on her face brought me back down to reality. Pam had gotten to me.

"I could have fought your father, made you come here every other Christmas. I could have cut you in two, but what was the point really? You would have ended up hating me anyway. Ask Evy. I'm not cut out for this. I'm no parent of the goddamn year." The strain in her voice was evident. "I never wanted to be a mother, but I've done the best I could."

The light in the room made her eyes glitter as the tears started to brim to the surface. I should have felt empathy, but I didn't. This woman was never there for me, and I didn't plan on ever being there for her. Even though she left me behind, Eve hadn't fared better. She was in and out of Eve's life too. She was a wrecking ball, and I had no desire to let her destroy the small peace I had built. The loss of my father taught me one thing. Life is too damn short to waste on people who don't love you.

"If that was your best, then I'm glad I never witnessed your worst." I pushed past Pam and my sister. I grabbed my mail and my car keys off the coffee table.

"Lily, please. Let's fix this? Let's try to do what's right, let's forgive." I heard the seriousness in Eve's tone, but I just couldn't let Pam ruin one more second of my life.

"Eve, I love you and I love what you're trying to do for you and your family, but I have forgiven. I've forgiven myself for ever letting her hurt me, for ever thinking less of myself because I wasn't good enough for her. I've moved on, and I'm done worrying about it." It was true. The overpowering sense of relief washed through me with the declaration. This confrontation was the final thing I needed to let go.

"Shit Evy, I don't need her forgiveness." Pam gave me a blank look before she turned and walked to the kitchen. The remark should have bothered me, but it didn't. My mouth turned up at the corners. She didn't control me any longer.

WHEN I'D FINALLY LEFT my sister's house, I'd driven around for quite a while. I had driven for so long; I wasn't sure where I was going anymore. I was now in a town called Bountiful, well according to the signs on the off-ramp that's where I was, and was parked next to what was probably one of the most beautiful churches I'd ever seen. The stunning white-spired building was situated on the bench of the mountain, looking over the entire valley. The cool evening air bit at my bare shoulders; my long coral maxi dress blew in the breeze as I leaned against my crappy blue Corolla looking out over the vast expanse of land. I could see where the land met the Great Salt Lake, how the entire city sparkled in the darkening sky. From up high on this mountainside, it was as if I finally saw the world for what it really was — and it was magnificent.

My phone vibrated, pulling my attention from the view. It was just a text from Eve saying she was sorry. I let out a sigh. I'd hoped it was Todd. I'd sent him a text telling him I was on my way to his place, but that had been an hour ago. I imagined he was just busy with his little girl, but it was getting late, and I figured he'd be home by now. With all my might, I tried to push down the insecurity. He needed this time with Molly. I used to feel as if I had little to offer, as if I had no value, but after tonight, after seeing Pam, finally telling her she didn't matter, it was like I'd been blind this entire time. I would be able to finally see myself in the mirror as a real person, not this smudge, this blur, this ugly small thing.

The temperature felt a bit too cool, so I decided to pack it up and head back to Todd's hoping he would text me soon. My bag of clothes and toiletries sat on the passenger side of my car while my fingers turned the keys in the ignition automatically. Immediately my thoughts wandered. I started to worry if staying with Todd for the next few days until Pam left was the right thing to do. He needed to get his life together, and I didn't want to be a distraction. Just as I started to change my mind, my phone vibrated again.

Todd: *You okay? I'm sorry, baby. I'm on my way home now.*

A giddy grin plastered itself on my face.

Me: *It's ok. You were with your daughter. I'm fine. Hope it went well for* you.

The next text was immediate.

> **Todd:** *This has been the best day of my life. I feel like a shit though for missing your text. Molly was playing with*

my phone.

I chuckled.

Me: *Don't worry about it. See you soon.*

Todd: *Can't wait.*

The lights in Todd's apartment were on, and Seth's black Audi was the only vehicle in the driveway. Grabbing my bags, I stepped from my car and headed toward the house. Loud music blared from behind the front door so I had to knock several times before I heard Seth swear and turn down the music. The door flew open. Seth's murderous expression became soft as soon as he realized it was me.

"Hellcat, what's up?" Seth's grin pulled nicely to the side, his dark hair was wet, and the spicy fragrance that he wore smelled stronger than usual. He had on a soft looking, tight, black T-shirt and gray sweats. "Sorry, I was in the shower. Just got home. Where's Todd?"

He leaned his body closer to me, each hand braced on either side of the doorjamb. The way the light hit his high cheekbones made him look absurdly attractive. I laughed. "How are you single?"

"What?" Seth's brow creased, and his nose crinkled.

"You heard me." I joked as I pushed past him to enter the house.

"Um, okay, sure come on in," he mumbled to himself.

"You know I can hear you?" My smile widened as he scowled at me. He observed me quietly as I placed my bags near the couch and plopped myself unceremoniously onto the plush cushions.

"Me being single… is my business. Why the hell are you here? Where's Todd?" Seth's irritation was only making me more amused; he was so easily ruffled.

"Todd's on his way back from seeing Molly."

"That doesn't explain why you're here? Having unsolicited visits from females in the evening makes me feel all unhappy and shit." Seth dropped down next to me on the sofa, his heavily tattooed arms stretched on either side of him on the back of the couch.

"You're in a pleasant mood. You need to get laid." I snorted at my own joke.

Seth's smile was cat like. "Trust me, I get what I want when I want…" Seth let his sentence drop off and the humor left his eyes. He leaned forward, his elbows on his knees, and pinched the bridge of his nose. It felt like several seconds ticked by before he spoke again, "Nah, just a shitty day."

"Tell me about it," I muttered.

"Bad day, too?" Seth's previous annoyance had faded as he gave me his full attention. This guy's moods were worse than Todd's, I gathered.

Something about Seth made me want to tell him all my stupid little secrets, and I wanted to confide in him. He saw through me anyway, his crystalline eyes appraised me, and I felt the courage to open up to him. "You really want know?"

"Lay it out for me." Seth smiled that award winning smile again as he leaned back into the couch and turned just enough so he was facing me.

"My mother, Pam… well, I haven't seen her since I was three, right? She showed up at my sister's house today, and she's planning to stay there for the next few days. She acted like I was nothing of consequence." The muscle in Seth's jaw pulsed. "She referred to Eve, that's my sister, as her daughter, not me… no, not me. She basically was completely indifferent, and then when I called her on her B.S., she tried to blame my father. God, she sucks. I wish I still hated her."

Seth swallowed hard before he spoke. "You don't hate her?" He asked the question with innocent abandon. This topic was something that cut to his core, the way he searched my face with such sincerity. I could tell this was the real Seth, and in this tiny second, I was seeing him for who he truly was.

"No… I don't," I whispered the words, the moment felt too personal to speak much louder.

"How?" His jaw tensed again.

"I can't hate her anymore. I can't hold on to all that hate. It ate me alive for so long, stopped me from believing in myself. Once I let go, like really let go… today when I told her how I felt, it was freeing. I'm free Seth, and it feels freaking wonderful." My cheeks spread into a smile as I watched him grin.

"Way to go, Hellcat." Seth grabbed my knee and squeezed before he stood from the couch. "I'm hungry as hell, want some pizza?" The front he always portrayed was firmly back in place.

"Sounds great. Let me go put my things away. I'll be staying for a few days. Sorry, lots of unsolicited female time headed your way." A giggle bubbled passed my lips at his playful eye roll. Seth was someone I'd probably never get the honor to really know. I had a feeling he didn't let many people in, if anyone at all, but this glimpse of the man behind the mask made me feel special. And as cheesy as it sounded, it felt like I'd made a friend.

Traces of Todd's wood and soap scent flooded my senses and made me miss him. Hoping he'd get home quickly, I started going through my things so I could freshen up. The envelope I'd shoved into my bag earlier stabbed me under the fingernail, and I swore out loud. A cursory glance at my nail was all it took to see that I hadn't gotten a paper cut. I pulled the letter out, and the familiar logo on the front made my heart skip a beat. It was from Arcadia College of Music. My panic to leave my sister's house was the only feasible explanation I gave myself for not seeing this earlier. My thoughts started to fly as I hastily opened the letter.

Dear Ms. Spring,

Your sister, Mrs. Eve Far, recently informed me that your father has passed away. I am terribly sorry for your loss. I feel it is imperative that we reinstate your music scholarship for the Musical Theory and Voice Composition Master's Program. I was able to work it that you could have the full amount of previously discussed funds based on the fact that you no longer have a family member that is an active participant in the music industry. I know that may sound insensitive, but I was hoping you would give attending our college some consideration.

I am truly sorry for your loss.

Deepest Sympathy,
Dean Theodore Hawthorne.

Tears dripped onto the surface of the crème colored paper; the ink smearing just slightly. I hadn't noticed I was crying. *Eve had done this for me?* The connection I never thought I had with my sister snapped into place. She was trying to give me my dream, and now the future I always wanted was staring me in the face. Arcadia College of Music was the goal my father had put in place for me. After he had died, I set out to try and make him proud. The promise I made to myself, to get signed, to use my voice like my father wanted, it was all I thought about when I first got here. I thought getting signed by Blue Bar Music was my ultimate objective, but that was before I knew I could have my real dream, my father's dream.

Strong arms snaked around my waist, as firm, yet soft, lips kissed my neck. "Hey you, I missed you today." Todd's warm honey tone created a hurricane of confusion in my head. I held my one true dream in my hands while the man I was falling in love with held me in his arms.

CHAPTER FORTY

Todd

"WHAT'S THE MATTER?" AS LILY PULLED from my embraced, I noticed her cheeks were wet with tears. The letter she held in her hand quivered.

"Nothing, just a long day. This letter from home just sort of brought everything rushing back." She folded the letter in a hurry and placed it back in its envelope. She turned in my arms and let her mouth connect with mine. I'd never get sick of Lily's lips and how they moved effortlessly with mine. She got my body riled up in seconds.

She pulled my bottom lip softly with her mouth as I eased our lips apart from each other. "What's going on? What happened with your mom?"

Lily sighed and sat on the edge of the bed. The words poured from her mouth as she told me about how it all went down with her mother. Lily's eyes were rimmed with red; I hated the fucking defeat in her shoulders and on her face. After I'd heard everything she had to say, I wanted to punch something. Pam was such a bitch, and I couldn't stand that I'd let Lily go through that alone.

"I'm sorry I wasn't there for you. I feel like a douchbag for not seeing your text." I kneeled down in front her, and my palm rested against her cheek. She leaned into the touch like she always did and closed her eyes. "I let you down today."

The surreal green and yellow flecks in Lily's eyes glimmered with unshed tears as they opened and found mine. "You did not let me down, but… I think maybe we—"

"Guys, pizza's here," Seth yelled from the living room.

"Yeah, just a sec. What were you going to say, baby?" Lily stood and drew me up from my kneeling position, threading her fingers in mine.

"Nothing…" But it hadn't felt like nothing. "I was just saying that you didn't let me down, you were doing something good for yourself and your daughter, and that's all that matters. How'd that go, by the way? How does it feel to be a daddy?" The smile on her face gave me a sense of pride as she gazed at me with awe.

"Let's go get some food in you, and I'll tell you and Seth all about it. Yeah?"

"Yeah." This time Lily's smile was fake, my concern for what she had begun to say and didn't get to finish started to eat at my gut. "I'm so happy for you, sweetheart." She reached up and pecked me on my cheek, the gesture just barely consoling the fear that was twisting itself around my spine. I figured she'd confide in me about whatever was bothering her in her own time.

As Lily finished up dinner, her mood improved. I could tell she was genuinely excited for me to have met Molly. Lily listened to every word I said as if they were the most important words ever spoken.

"She's so smart. I loved how she had to show me every single toy she owned. I think at one point I lost count on how many fairy princess dolls she had." My laugh echoed in my chest; thinking about today gave me a feeling of fullness, of purpose.

Lily's laugh matched mine. "Sounds like you're going to have your hands full."

"Yeah, Lolly's very stubborn. I guess she gets that from me, too."

Lily's face lit up. "Lolly?"

"Yeah bro, what's that about?" Seth's brows turned down in confusion.

"Molly can't say her 'm' sound well, so it's sort of like a nickname." A nickname I thought was cute as hell. Another dumb grin pulled across my face, and Seth gave me a look as if I was from another planet.

"That's so adorable." Lily took my hand in hers. "You're going to be a great father."

"Let's hope so." Seth was always such a sarcastic bastard, but, in all reality, that was the one thought that weighed in my mind all day. I had to be a great father because that little girl deserved nothing less.

IT WAS LATE NOW, and the steam from the shower spilled from the bathroom into my bedroom. "You going to join me?" Lily's smirk was inviting. She lifted her dress over her head; her slim back was facing me. She was so sexy. Lily had agreed to come with me this Wednesday to pick Molly up for lunch and to meet my parents this Sunday. I wanted Lily woven into my life as much as possible. She was someone important to me, and I wanted my family to meet both my girls.

"Be right in."

I pulled my wallet and cell phone from my pocket and saw a missed text from Emma.

Emma: *Thank you for today.*

The text came with a picture of Molly and me playing on the floor with blocks. Joy pulsed deeply into my heart. The memory of today, of tonight, would stay with me forever.

Emma had dark circles under her eyes. Even though she had aged since I saw her last, she was still beautiful. She walked out of Molly's bedroom leaving the door open just a crack, and I sensed the nervous tension as it rolled off her shoulders.

"She's waiting for you." Emma's bottom lip trembled, and her amber eyes closed. The rise and fall of her chest became rapid.

"Emma, I can do this." The bond between Emma and I was tangible. My hands rested on her shoulders. "I can do this."

Her eyes opened. "Todd... I can't let her get hurt. You have to be there for us."

I wasn't sure I wanted an 'us' with Emma. "I'll always be here for her. Molly is my family now, and I'm not going anywhere. If you had given me the chance, I could have proven that to you two years ago." I let my hands fall from her shoulders.

Two silent tears lazily snaked down Emma's cheeks. "I made a mistake, and I'll regret that for the rest of my life. I took away those precious two years. But you know what the sad thing is...? I'll regret never knowing if you could have loved me."

"Emma," her name was a tight whisper, her pain wrapped around my throat. I was well acquainted with this kind of pain. My arms enfolded around her hips as I pulled her body close to mine. "I could see myself here with you, with Molly. Sunday Morning pancakes, bedtime bath routines..." I brought my right hand up and wiped the tear from her cheek with the pad of my thumb and smiled. "Emma, I could be happy with you."

"But." Emma's eyes never left mine.

"But I'm falling in love with someone else." I exhaled; it felt good to say it out loud. Saying it to her made it concrete, and it was as if I never really even needed to decide. Lily was what I wanted. Emma's bottom lip began to shake again, and I placed my thumb against it trying to ease the hurt she would feel after I said what needed to be said.

She cried lightly as I kissed her forehead. "Emma." My hands held and tilted her head gently so she would look at me again. "I would always wonder if I stayed with you now... would it be for Molly, or for you? I never loved you like that. I should have, but we could never get our timing right. You had one thing right though... I was blind back then, and I'm sorry I never saw you because, fuck, I could've been so lucky to have you. We could've made each other so happy. But you made your choice the day you decided to leave me in the dark about my daughter. I forgive you for that, but my life is different now, I'm different now."

"What's her name?" The tears gathered in the corner of her eyes.

"Lily."

"I'm glad for you, Todd. I really am." She turned slightly as my hands dropped from her face. "Thank you for being honest. Just make me one promise?"

"What?"

"Always be here for Molly, okay? No matter what."

"No matter what." I smiled and squeezed her shoulder.

"Go tuck your daughter in." She wiped the tears from her cheeks and grinned. Emma's strength was never just an appearance. It was one of the things I'd always liked about her and hoped she could instill in our daughter.

Molly lay down on her pillow; her blonde hair was everywhere as she snuggled down into her bed. Emma was letting me tell Molly a "story" about who I was. I wasn't sure how much she could understand at her age, but I figured I'd give it a go. Besides I didn't want my baby girl calling me Todd. I was her father, her daddy.

The tiny sized bed made me chuckle as I sat with my legs criss-crossed underneath me.

"Lolly, can I tell you a story?"

She nodded and grabbed her purple sock monkey. I traced my finger down her nose and she giggled. "So once upon a time... no, wait that's dumb... scratch that... actually I wanted to tell you something really important, is that okay? It's not really a story because it's true." *Molly's eyes blinked slowly as she yawned.* "I wanted to tell you that... I'm your daddy. You see me and your momma… well, we… liked each other a whole bunch, and we were so lucky because…" The confined feeling in my throat made the next part hard to say, "…well, because we made you. God wanted us to have a Molly, and we got you."

Molly's eyes opened wide, and she smiled. She probably had no clue what I was saying, but I continued, "Lolly, you're the best thing to ever happen to me, and I'm so sorry I wasn't here at first, but now that I know I'm your daddy… nothing can keep me away from you." I leaned down and kissed her nose. "You want to know what else? Being your daddy means I love you so much. You know how much?"

She nodded animatedly, "To m-m-m-moon." She squinted in concentration as she struggled to say the word.

"To the moon and back." I laughed. "Does your momma tell you that she loves you like that, too?"

"Yup." She giggled and burrowed her face into her pillow.

"So now you have two people who love you all the way to the moon and back and then some, sweetheart." I pulled the covers up to her shoulders and gave her a peck on the cheek. "Night, baby girl."

I stood and walked to the door, and just as I turned the light off I heard Molly's small voice. "Night, Daddy."

Those two words broke open my entire world and filled it with a love I could hardly hold.

The sound of Lily singing brought me out of my thoughts, her voice echoed off the tile giving it a haunting tone. I stripped down and threw my clothes in the hamper. The silhouette of Lily's curves behind the shower curtain pulled me in.

Lily was my choice, and I wanted everything to fall into place. We were almost there, and if I reached out and seized what I wanted for once, maybe — just maybe — it could all be golden.

CHAPTER FORTY-ONE

Lily

HARD, MUTED RAIN FELL AGAINST THE studio roof, the bass drum vibrated through my body as my voice slightly wavered with feeling as I belted out the final lyrics of the song I wrote for my father. The mood was somber, everything fell silent with the final beat, and I inhaled trying to catch my breath, attempting to stop the panic from rising. Each day that had passed since I received the letter from Arcadia added another iron weight onto my shoulders. The need I had for Todd grew, but after meeting Molly this past Wednesday, I feared I was taking him away from what he really wanted. After all, having grown up with just my dad, I was an expert on what it was like to grow up in a family minus one parent. Todd had never spoken about Emma before, he told me she was just a one night stand, but the more the pieces fell into place, the more it became apparent he might have loved her if it wasn't for Liz. He could have had a life with her, a life he deserved with his daughter. Who was I to take that from him? My chest tensed at the thought of leaving — my soul wanted this, wanted Todd — but I wasn't sure I could make it through another loss. My father's death was still fresh, and Derrick and Becca's betrayal still haunted me. I wasn't ready for another person to leave me.

Todd had brought Molly to his apartment for lunch on Wednesday before work. I hadn't gone with him to pick her up, but I'd had to go with him to drop her off on our way to the bar. My hands had been full of nervous energy as I lowered the stereo in the truck. I watched as Todd embraced Emma, his strong, wide form ate up her skinny frame. She was drop dead gorgeous. Emma was on the tallish side with long, golden blonde hair, and, with her model-like features, I could see why Todd would have liked her. The three of them looked perfect together, smiling and laughing. I swear all they needed was a freaking dog, and it would be the all-American family. Watching them from the front seat of Todd's truck was the first time since meeting him that I'd felt inadequate, and it was also the first time I felt selfish for loving someone. I was the reason he wasn't going inside with his family, with his baby girl. We had had such a nice time at the apartment just us three, but seeing them together made me feel small, and any hope I had started to wane.

"What's your favorite ice cream, sweetie?" I bent down placing my hands on my knees as I looked into the most expressive brown eyes I'd ever seen. This little angel was all Todd, and I couldn't help but fall in love with the girl that could get Todd to smile like he hadn't a care in the world, like he had everything he ever wanted in her, like his life was truly complete.

She shrugged her tiny shoulders, her blonde curls bobbed with the motion.

"You like chocolate?" I giggled as her eyes bulged, and she violently nodded her head. "Yes, chocolate it is."

I stood from my kneeling position and walked to the freezer, the chocolate and strawberry ice cream we had purchased earlier sat on the shelf in waiting. Grabbing the ice cream and three bowls from the cabinet, I began to scoop it into each bowl. I was nearly finished as I felt a small hand tug at the hem of my skirt.

"Sis Lil?" It was so cute how Molly couldn't say her 'M' sound very well yet. All through lunch she had called me 'Sis Lil' instead of Miss Lilly. It was very endearing.

"What's up, sweetheart?" Molly hugged my legs, and my pulse skipped a beat. This lovely little girl was taking root, and the warm feeling of acceptance washed over me.

She smiled up at me and pointed over to Todd, who leaned against the doorway with a pleased and sexy grin that stretched ear to ear. Molly held tight to my leg, and I couldn't help but smile back at Todd. This quiet moment between the three of us felt good. We didn't need words; this was special, and I was extremely lucky to be a part of them.

That day had been everything I'd hoped it could have been. Todd shined brighter than any star or any sun when he was with Molly, and watching him interact with her melted my heart. He was going to be such an exceptional father, and I felt guilty now for hoping I would be there to witness it. To witness the milestones, the daddy-daughter moments that would make him the happiest man alive. My eyes started to fill with liquid, and I dipped my chin, looking down at the floor of the studio in an attempt to hide my private freak out.

"You doing okay, baby?" Todd's strong hands rubbed my shoulders from behind, his skilled fingers worked at the knots that had drawn together from the stress of this week. I nodded. "That song is so damn sad. I wish I could've known your father." A sob spilled hastily from my lips. "Shit, I didn't mean to make you cry, I'm—"

"It's all right." I sniffed. "The song just gives me all the feels." I turned taking in his worried brown eyes and wrapped my arms around his waist. The soft fabric of his shirt rested against my cheek as I let myself fall into Todd, fall into the man I wasn't sure I could live without.

He chuckled. "The feels, babe?"

"Yeah, it makes me feel all sad, and happy, and just... all

of them. Each and every emotion consumes me. It's suffocating at times." Todd's arms pulled me tight against his firm body, and though the constriction should make it harder for me to breathe, being this close to him, having him totally surrounding me, it was the easiest I breathed all week.

He kissed the top of my head before he spoke, "You ready to go meet the family?"

My eyes opened wide. I had forgotten about that. The Todd and Emma situation was messing with my mind, not to mention Blue Bar was busy as hell and having to train two new employees sucked. I was grateful for this Sunday, this time to be just me. "Maybe I should just skip this time, Todd."

"What? Why?" He pulled away from me enough to gauge my expression? Hurt shadowed his dark irises.

"Awe, Hellcat, don't be scared. The Dixons don't bite." Seth gave me a rueful smirk as he stepped away from his drum kit.

"I know, I just think... I mean... this is the first time they're going to meet Molly. Todd, you told me your mom cried for an hour after you told her she was a grandma. I think this is more of a fam—"

"I want you there... I need you there. Please don't bail on me." Todd's eyes pleaded.

I shook my head; this was a bad idea. "I'm not bailing on you, but... are you sure they won't care I'm there."

"I told you, baby, my mom is excited to meet you both. Plus, Lizzie and Soy will be there with Sailor. It's not just family." Even though Elizabeth and Sawyer weren't blood, they were still Todd's family, and I didn't want to be the odd person out on such a special occasion as meeting a grandchild.

"Yeah, thanks for the invite asshole," Seth joked.

"Shut the hell up, bro. You go to your dad's every Sunday, and you know it." Todd laughed. "They're going to love you. How could they not?" He gave me a lingering kiss on the lips.

"And... that's my queue to leave." Seth grabbed his backpack. "See you guys later?"

"I promise, Seth, my sister told me Pam leaves tomorrow. You'll be rid of me soon enough." I giggled at Seth's annoyed glare. "What?"

"I told you, Lil, you stay as long as you want." Seth's hard features relaxed. "Mi casa es su casa."

"Uh, it's my house, too, asshat. She's my girlfriend and can stay as long as she wants." Todd pulled me under his arm possessively.

"Calm down, caveman. That's what I just said. See you later, Lily." Seth lifted his chin in a nod as he left the studio.

THE SKIN OF MY hands felt numb as I rubbed my palms obsessively over the fabric of my skirt and down my thighs. We pulled up to Todd's parents' house. Molly was humming to herself as Todd placed the truck in park.

"This is it." He looked over at me nervously.

The house had a worn look to it; the stormy gray sky made the massive trees that surrounded the house a vibrant green. The yellow colored brick was trimmed with muted brown shutters and a brown, shingled roof. A large rusted wagon sat in the front lawn as decoration. You could see the huge barn just slightly behind and to the right of the house. Todd's family home sat on at least two acres of land. The rain had stopped and vapor seeped up from the paved drive.

"Well, what do you think?" Todd's face split to one side in a sideways smirk.

"It's nice."

"Nice?" He barked out in laughter. "Just wait till you smell the cow shi—"

"Todd! Molly's in the car... Remember, Daddy." I laughed

as his brow dipped, obviously internally scolding himself.

"I suck at this." He frowned.

"You're a great dad." He started to protest. "Stop, I'm serious. She lights up around you. Isn't that right, Lolly? Your daddy's the best."

"Yup." She giggled.

"Thanks." His smile was small as he leaned over and kissed me on the cheek. "I'll grab her if you wouldn't mind getting her diaper bag."

"Sure thing." My anxiety coiled through my ribcage like a vine as Todd shut the door behind him. This was it. I was meeting his mother and father.

We hadn't even made it up the stairs to the house before the front door swung open. A beautiful older woman with flaxen hair bounded down the stairs. Her full lips spread into a giant grin as she took in the sight of Molly in Todd's arms.

"Is this… is this… my grandbaby?" The emotion poured from her lips, and her russet eyes spilled over with tears.

"Ma, please don't cry." Todd's voice was heavy from held back emotion and his eyes shined with unshed tears. "You'll scare her."

"I won't scare this cute baby girl, will I?"

I wasn't sure what to do, so I just quietly observed Todd as he introduced Molly to his mother, and I watched Todd pull his mom into a hug with one arm and hold Molly in his other with an overpowering sense of pride in his stature. Todd's world had been turned upside-down, but he didn't let it shake him. He grabbed the world by its axis and turned it just where he wanted it. He owned his life, and I loved him for it.

"Oh gawl, I'm so sorry, my manners." Todd's mom rubbed at the running mascara. "I'm Karen, you must be, Lily?"

"Yes." I smiled at her meekly.

"Well, it's just wonderful to meet you, hon. Come on inside guys before it rains again." She gave Todd a private smile and led us into the house. The aroma of apples and cinnamon hung in the air, and my stomach growled. The house was simply decorated with a country style. Family photos lined the walls.

"It smells good, Ma, you making apple pie?" Todd asked as he laced his fingers through mine. He gave me a kiss on the cheek and squeezed my hand easing my wired nerves.

Karen watched us and grinned as her hand rested against her chest like she was trying to steady her breathing. "I made all your favorites: beef stew, buttermilk biscuits and, yes, apple pie."

"Hell yes."

"Todd, language." Elizabeth's voice was soft as we walked into the large open kitchen. Cameron, Colby, Liz, and Sawyer sat at the table snacking on what looked like a cheese and veggie plate. Elizabeth was the first to see Molly, and her smile couldn't have been any wider. Sawyer looked much better than that day in the hospital. He lifted his chin at Todd in a silent hello as Sailor pulled at the collar of her daddy's shirt. Todd had mentioned his recovery was going well.

Everyone's eyes landed on Molly as we fully entered the room. Cam's hand shot to her mouth, and Colby's lips split into a slow motion smile as he took in his niece. An older, handsome gentleman with tanned skin that wrinkled around his eyes smiled at us from the stove. There was no doubt that he was Todd's dad. Todd had his mother's eyes, but he looked just like his dad.

He gasped as he looked at Molly. "My heavens, son, she's you."

"Yup, but with different plumbing." Todd laughed.

"That's gross." Colby scrunched his nose.

"And inappropriate." Karen clicked her tongue.

"When have I ever been appropriate, Mom?" Todd's eyes sparkled with amusement.

"Good point, son. Now can I meet these beautiful ladies?"

Mr. Dixon offered me his hand.

"Oh yeah. Dad, this is my girlfriend, Lily."

"Hi." The room fell still as Todd's father's hand met mine. The familiar feeling of rough skin and the smell of old spice encircled me. My father's scent was everywhere; with each rise and fall of my chest the smell grew in strength, and I was on the verge of having a mental breakdown in front of all these people, these strangers.

"Nice to meet you. You okay, sweetheart?"

I shook my head slowly; I wasn't able to find the words. Todd's father wore the same cologne as my dad, and the memories started to inundate my brain. I felt so foolish standing there like a mute.

"Here Ma. Lolly can you go with Grandma for just a second, sweet pea?" Todd spoke in a soothing tone, his voice was the only thing to snap me out of my downward spiral.

"I'm fine... I'm sorry, I'm just... hungry. We skipped lunch, and I just had a wave of nausea. Really, I'm fine. I'm sorry to worry you, Mr. Dixon."

"Call me, Alistair." He took my hand again, but this time he embraced my hand with both of his. "Let's get you some food. Everything will be ready soon if you want to go have a snack with the others." He smiled kindly.

"Thanks."

Before we sat down to eat dinner, everyone had a chance to meet Molly. She ate up the attention and flourished in the spotlight. Todd had been worried she would be scared of everyone because it had been just her and Emma for so long. Molly wasn't used to a big family, and he worried too many people would make her act shy and his family wouldn't get to see the active, whirling dervish that was all things Lolly.

Dinner was delicious, and the conversation was varied. It seemed as if Karen and Alistair were the parents to everyone. They basically raised Elizabeth, and Cam came from a divorced home. Cameron's mother, I found out, moved to

Arizona for a new job opportunity, and her dad worked all the time, so he wasn't really around much. For all intents and purposes, Todd's mother and father were like stand-in parents for everyone, and the respect I had for them grew exponentially.

I offered to help Karen with the dishes and was scrubbing away at the soup bowls when I felt Todd's lips graze my ear. A shiver ran down my spine, and I almost dropped the bowl.

"Careful, these bowls were my grandma's." He trailed his hands leisurely down my arms causing my stomach to constrict with need; Todd's touch got me going from zero to sixty in three seconds.

"You keep touching me like that, and I'll definitely drop the bowl."

His chuckle resonated deep in his throat as he skimmed the tip of his nose down the line of my neck. "Damn baby, you smell so fucking good," he whispered against my skin, and I was sure he could feel my pulse with his lips.

Heat flushed across my chest, and I pressed my body against his. His fingertips brushed across my stomach, tracing lightly under the top of my skirt. I turned my body to face his and leaned my cheek into his waiting palm. Todd drank me in with hooded eyes. We had this dance down. His lips found purchase on mine, and he kissed me deeply. His tongue tasted me, my teeth drew across his bottom lip, while my hands moved across his broad chest to his shoulders, finally clasping behind his neck. Todd's left hand grasped my backside pulling me against him, his arousal pressed against my stomach, and he groaned.

"Get a damn room, what the hell?" Colby admonished in a low voice. "If Mom walked in here right now, she'd freak, and you know it."

My cheeks were crimson for a whole new reason. I was mortified. "Oh God, I'm—"

"Don't apologize to this shithead. He's just being a

douchebag."

"Shut the hell up. Remember that time Mom caught you and Emma making out in the basement while you were dating, that was classic." Colby snickered, and my stomach dropped.

"You're an asshole. Don't worry about anything this idiot says. I'm gonna splash some cold water on my face, I'll be right back?"

"Sure." I composed my features enough to ease Todd's mind.

"Don't be a dick, Colby, or I swear to God..."

Colby laughed. "I'm just messing with you, bro."

"Cut that shit out. I'll be right back, and then we'll head home, yeah?"

"Yeah." I nodded and grinned at the dimple that formed as Todd smiled brightly at me.

Todd left the kitchen. The noise of everyone chatting and laughing in the living room echoed throughout the house making me feel somewhat at ease again, until I saw Colby staring at me with raised eyebrows. "What?"

"Home? You guys living together now?" He appraised me suspiciously.

"No, I'm just staying with him until my sister's guest leaves."

"Oh good, 'cause I was gonna say, you guys hardly know each other." His eyes locked with mine. I didn't like the way he looked at me like an errant child, so I turned and busied myself with the dishes as he spoke, "I mean Todd's life just got hella complicated. I'm sure that's been messing with you, not to mention how close he is with Emma. Shit, that would make me crazy. Here let me help you, Lil."

"I'm not the jealous type." I handed him the bowl to dry.

"Oh sorry, I wasn't meaning that. I just mean... this is serious. That little girl is everything, you know, and I can tell you guys really care about each other. But I've watched Todd give of himself, give his all once before, and to say it ended badly would be an understatement. I guess what I'm trying to say is… this is a lot to deal with, and I think for Todd's sake he needs to deal with this on his own."

Colby turned to put the bowl away in the cabinet. My heart hammered in my chest, and everything I'd worried about surfaced. How I didn't fit in here. How I wasn't one of them. How Todd needed to be with his family. How he needed to do this on his own. I didn't want to believe it — I couldn't stand to hear it. "Todd's a good man. He'll do the right thing, Colby. I know it." The lump in my throat distorted the sound of my voice.

"I know he will. I just want him to make his choice. I'm not trying to be a jerk, I'm just watching out for my brother, my blood. Lily, you seem real good for him. This is the happiest I've seen him in years. But I'm just saying I hope you let him come to his decisions on his own. He doesn't need to get hurt again. You guys are just starting out. I'd hate if—"

"I understand," I interrupted and placed my towel on the counter. Todd needed space, he needed his daughter, and I was just a distraction. As much as I'd grown to love Todd in this short while, I couldn't let him make the wrong choice. I couldn't let Molly grow up in a one-parent household; she needed her mother and father. Colby was right, Todd and Emma were close, and I hindered them from trying to make it work. I loved Todd enough to let him go, to let him live the life he deserved. "Thanks for the advice."

CHAPTER FORTY-TWO

Todd

"What advice." Lily looked pale, and Colby's face was lined with remorse. "What the hell did I miss?"

"Nothing Todd, do you mind if I use the restroom while you get our stuff ready to go?" Lily's eyes were blank, and her body was stiff. I suddenly had the urge to punch my fucking brother.

"No problem, baby." I watched Lily move uncomfortably from the kitchen. "What the hell did you say to her?" My hands bunched into fists.

Colby blanched. "Nothing man, I just told her she needs to step back and let you make your own choices." My jaw clenched, and I grabbed the collar of his shirt. "Dude, chill out, I was just looking out for you. I don't want some chick messing with your head again."

"I fucking care about this girl. I want her in my life." The fabric of his shirt strained as it twisted in my fist. "You need to mind your own goddamn business."

"You've known her little over a month, and I see how she controls you, man. I watched this shit go down with Lizzie,"

Colby's voice wavered. He exhaled harshly, and I released him from my grip. "I love you, and I can't watch you destroy yourself over another girl. All I was saying to her, and she didn't let me finish, was that she better be all in or all out, 'cause you deserve all in Todd, nothing less."

My little brother never had much tact, but his dumb ass heart was in the right place. "Colb, you gotta let me handle my own shit. I've changed. I've grown up. I have a little girl that means more to me than anything. Don't worry, I got this."

"You better, that's all I'm saying. I don't want you to disappear again, alright?"

"I'm not going anywhere." No matter what, I wouldn't lose myself again.

LILY WAS SO GOOD with Molly. When they met for the first time, I was nervous all of this would really set in, and it would prove to be too much for her. But when I saw my daughter cling to Lily's leg on Wednesday in the kitchen, ice cream dripping down Molly's face, I could see how bright my future could be. There were times today I actually believed that my life was headed in the right direction. There were moments when Lily wasn't paying attention, and I watched as she naturally mothered Molly. Like how she played with Sailor and Molly on the floor, her smile bright as she braided their doll's hair, and how she wiped Molly's mouth during dinner and gave her Eskimo kisses every time Molly giggled. This woman had claimed my heart entirely over this past week. I was sure if I had to I could do this alone, but Lily's acceptance of Molly into her life so fully, had me wanting more, had me thinking crazy thoughts like what our children would look like.

But now, as the truck moved easily down the freeway,

my earlier feelings of security were starting to fade. Lily had been quiet the whole way home, her silence expanded after we dropped off Molly. She didn't say one word. The night had been perfect until Colby opened his stupid mouth. I wasn't sure what Lily was thinking, but I could tell she was shutting down, and I wasn't having it. The small attempts I tried at getting her to open up were shot down with words like *'I'm fine'* and *'I'm just tired.'* The truck tires splashed the puddle in the pothole in front of my driveway. Before I even had the keys out of the ignition, Lily was out of the truck, door shut, and was walking up the front path. Seth's car wasn't here, and that was probably for the best because it felt as if things were about to get ugly.

I shut the front door while Lily dropped her bag on the sideboard. She stood there, stock still, her eyes casted down, and my breath caught. The tension was so thick I couldn't seem to make my lungs take in any valuable oxygen. My words were failing me. I had to fix the damage Colby had inflicted, and this was the only way I was capable. Lily's hair was pulled back in a bun, the long black and white striped skirt she had on just barely skimmed the floor, the black V-neck she wore fit her curves effortlessly. Everything in me cried out to touch her, to feel her skin, to taste her lips. It felt as if my time with her was fleeting. She was like sand, and I was going to watch her slip through my fingers. I lifted my foot to take the step I needed to be closer to her.

She held up her hand to stop me. "Don't."

"Don't what?" I didn't listen to the protest as I tried to draw her into a hug. She pressed against my chest attempting to push me away. My fingers enclosed around her arms gently and held her in place. The green in her eyes was vivid as she met my stare. "Don't what? Do this?" My mouth collided with hers; she resisted at first, but that only made me more anxious for her to submit. My lips eagerly moved against her still mouth, my tongue licked at the seam, and, like always, she finally let me in. The earlier tension subsided, and I moved my hands to her lower back, pulling her against me. I needed her to feel me. "Don't let what my brother said ruin our night. This is you, baby, see what you do to me?" She groaned as I pressed hard against her. I took her hand in mine and led her to the bedroom.

The door shut loudly behind us as I fitted her against me again. Our lips met once more, but this time it was much softer. She felt like satin and tasted like berries. Lily moaned into my mouth, her hands skated down my chest and pulled at the buckle of my jeans. I stopped her hand; I didn't want this time with her over too quickly. "Wait a second."

"I can't wait one more second, Todd," she said in a shaky voice and then pulled her shirt over her head. The pink color of her nipples showed through the navy blue lace of her bra. She looked incredible. Once she removed her bra, the peach color of her skin was only interrupted with the dusting of freckles. The curve of her hip taunted me, begged me to grab her and take her against the wall — to bury myself, take what I needed… what I wanted. My breathing became uneven as I knelt in front of her and effortlessly pulled her skirt and panties down. The tip of my nose brushed low across her stomach, my lips tasting her as my hands eased her legs apart.

"What are you doing?" she asked breathlessly.

"Taking what I want." I stood and removed my shirt. Lily's impatient hands undid my buckle, my clothes now on the floor. I grabbed Lily's ass and lifted her as she instinctively wrapped her legs around my waist. That was the thing with us, everything was second nature — we didn't hesitate, and we didn't fumble. With her it was always flawless motion. Lily's back hit the wall, and her breast pushed against my chest as she lowered herself down just enough to tease me, to make me groan.

"Take what you want, Todd." Lily's eyes were lit with desire as I thrust myself inside her, her body pulling me in deep. Our lips moved fiercely as I took her against the wall. Lily lifted her hips urging me on.

"Hold onto my shoulders." She complied as I carried her to the bed, not breaking our connection as I sat on the edge of the mattress. She started to roll her hips, taking control as my hands gripped her waist while roughly rocking into her. Lily ground her hips down, her thighs tightened their grip around me as she came, her body pulled me over the edge, and I came hard with her. Our moans were muted as we devoured each other, our mouths moved smoothly together and our breathing slowed.

"Damn." I was breathless. I rested my forehead against hers. Lily could be soft and tender one minute and rough and raw the next, but no matter what she did, she owned it, and I fucking loved every piece of her. I was ready to tell her how I really felt. "Lily, I lo—"

"I'm leaving, Todd." Lily pulled away from me, and it was then I noticed the tears, the tears that stained her cheeks and poured from her eyes.

"What? Right now?" I was confused. Had I been too rough? "I didn't hurt you did I?"

"No." She stood and started getting dressed. I grabbed my boxer briefs and pulled them on.

"Then why are you leaving?" My stomach started to ache as her crying became uncontrolled. She rummaged around my room gathering all of her things, and I started to panic.

"We shouldn't have… I didn't want to do that." She was gasping for air as she spoke.

"What baby, talk to me, say something that makes sense." I stood behind her as she filled her bag. I turned her and forced her to look at me. "Please Lily, I'm starting to feel sick. What's the matter? Is it…?" She attempted to pull away from my hold. The imaginary rope that bound us together was frayed and ready to snap "…*Just… goddamn it, just talk to me.*" I swallowed down the metallic taste in my mouth.

"I'm moving back home, Todd." My pulse rushed with dread, and I tried to govern my breathing. "I made the decision tonight at your parents. I got a letter last weekend from the music college I was supposed to go to, the one my father always wanted me to attend, remember?" I nodded, my alarm building. I was losing her. "They're letting me back in, they're reinstating my scholarship. It was his dream... it was my dream."

"So this was a goodbye? You thought you would just fuck me and then leave?" My agony was turning to anger. This wasn't Lily; she wouldn't do this to me.

"No, oh God... Todd I... I didn't mean for that to happen, I never wanted to—"

"Hurt me." I finished the sentence for her. It was a statement that I was too familiar with.

Lily wiped the tears from her eyes. "*Shit!* Todd, I don't want to leave... but this is best for both of us. You have a daughter now... you have a child to raise. Getting into this school was everything he ever wanted."

"What do you want, Lily?" I didn't hold out hope that it was me.

"I want the dream, Todd."

Those five words chewed up my fucking heart and spit it out.

"If that's what you want, I can't keep you from it... I won't keep you from it. You do what you need to, Lily. I need to start taking care of myself." The desolation was like a thin layer of ice on my skin. My hands dropped from her shoulders, and the small distance was enough to pull me under.

She nodded and grabbed the last of her things. Every item she placed in her bag was like a stab to a vital organ, and I was bleeding out. I fucking loved this girl, and she was walking away.

CHAPTER FORTY-THREE

Lily

THE LIE LEFT A BITTER TASTE in my mouth. I didn't want the dream — I wanted him, but in the end it didn't matter what I wanted. He needed to raise his little girl; he needed to start taking care of himself. Todd wouldn't look at me as I left his room. I inhaled one last breath of him before I opened the front door. I tried to memorize the feel of his body against mine, the way he always claimed me as his, the sound of his laughter, and the way he said my name with such devotion. The cool night air burned, and I started to feel anxious with the distance building between us. I couldn't let myself forget.

Just before the door shut, I heard a loud crack like glass breaking.

"FUCK!" Todd yelled the word at the top of his lungs, it was drawn out, and the pain in his voice cut me. Every fiber of my being wanted me to go back and tell him I love him. Tell him I choose him, but that was selfish… and he deserved so much more.

My world was spiraling out of control, and I was gasping for air as the images of Todd's broken expression and the hurt that blackened his eyes swept through my mind. My hands shook violently as I turned the key and started my car. My tears were blurring my vision as I backed out of the driveway making it difficult to see. The loud sound of a car horn made me jump and slam on my brakes. Seth's black Audi was behind me, the bright light of his headlights glared in my rearview mirror causing my headache to throb behind my temples. The night's events churned in my belly as I watched Seth step out from his running vehicle.

He tapped his knuckles on my window. He was the last person I wanted to talk to; he was going to hate me. He knocked harder and bent down to look through the window. Seth's eyes narrowed as he took in my appearance. There was no avoiding it, so I rolled down my window.

"What the fuck's going on?" Seth's tone was severe. He'd never spoken to me like that, and it made it hard to gather my already emotional state into some coherent semblance of order. "Why the tears? What's happened?" His hands grasped the door as he leaned quickly through the window and grabbed the keys out of the ignition. "You're not going anywhere like this. You trying to kill yourself? Breathe, Lily, just breathe." I hadn't realized I was still hysterically crying, my breathing was shuddered, and the water fell like a river from my eyes. Seth placed his right hand on my cheek, and his thumb moved softly across my skin. "Shh… breathe, sweetheart, just breathe. D-did Todd…" Seth's jaw ticked. "…did Todd do something to hurt—?"

"No." I inhaled deeply. "No, I'm… I've got to leave. It's the only way." The admission squeezed my chest making it difficult to continue.

"Leave where? You're not making sense, Hellcat. What's the only way?" Seth dropped his hand from my face, and the heat from his skin dissipated, the cold dead feeling that threatened to consume me moved quickly over my body, and I had no other choice but to succumb to it. It was the only way I was going to survive this. Survive Todd. Survive ever knowing someone so infinitely right for me. I had to let myself fall into the still water — let it drown me, let it fill all the spaces he resided; otherwise, I'd never let go, and letting go was my only option. Todd had his life to live, and I'd made my choice. There was no going back.

"I'm moving back to Florida. They reinstated my music scholarship." My voice held no inflection.

"Are you serious?" Seth leaned back from the window. "I thought you wanted to make a record? What about Todd? Awe, shit!" His gaze moved from me to the front door of their condo and back to me in slow motion. "You're going to break him, you know that right? Why? Why are you doing this?" I moved my eyes from his and stared at the small crack in my windshield ignoring his question. "Is this about Molly? Emma?"

I whipped my head in his direction, and I snapped. "Give me my keys. I need to go."

"That's it, isn't it? I can't believe you'd do that to him. I should've known, though. You bitches always leave." Seth dropped my keys in my lap and pushed away from the car.

"You don't know what the hell you're talking about, asshole." Anger heated my cheeks. I didn't need this right now. I was doing what was right… what was right for Todd.

"I don't?" He raised his eyebrows and stretched his arms out from his body. "Explain it to me then. 'Cause from where I'm standing, I can smell the fear pouring off of you, and I hoped you were stronger than that. He's worth more than that."

"I know," I shouted. "He should have it all. He should get

his chance at happiness, and Molly should have a father and a mother that will love her and be there for her. They should all have a chance at life, and I — I just don't equate into that scenario."

"That's fucking bullshit." Seth walked closer to my car. "You're running, Lily. You're making the wrong choice."

"I'm making the right decision for him. Besides this is what I want. This school… this was my father's dream for me. I need to do this, please Seth… just move your car. I need to go." I was tired, the weight of the night threatened to crush me, and all I wanted was to go home and sleep. I didn't even care that Pam was there.

Seth shook his head. "Fucking women. Always doing stupid shit." He took a deep breath, his hard blue eyes held mine. "You okay to drive?"

I nodded curtly.

He looked back at the house and his shoulders fell. "This is going to be a damn nightmare," he muttered before he turned his gaze on me again. He lifted his chin. "See ya round, Lil."

Seth's frame disappeared into his car; the headlights moved as he backed out, letting me do the same. It was as if rubber strands were connecting my heart to Todd — the further the separation, the tighter they pulled. It felt wrong to think, but all I wanted was for these bonds to snap, to break away, because if they didn't, I wasn't sure if I could resist the pull.

CHAPTER FORTY-FOUR

Todd

THE LASTS WORDS I SAID TO her kept ringing in my ears. I needed to take care of myself, but I needed her too. I wanted her to be part of Molly's future and my future. My fury started to heighten as I stared at the shards of glass spread across the carpet, and the knuckles on my right hand started to swell. I was battling the urge to rip every damn thing in this house to shreds.

My reflection was scattered throughout the shattered fragments — it was like a fucking sick metaphor. Lily had picked up my broken pieces and fit them with hers, and I'd let her do it, I'd let her in, and I'd let her wreck me. She owned my heart, and I had no idea how I would surface again. Leaning down I picked up a section of the mirror. My appearance was unrecognizable. The wet and bloodshot eyes weren't mine. They couldn't be mine. I couldn't be back here again. She destroyed everything we'd built, and now I was lying in the rubble of what used to be me — I was now a ruin, a shell.

The anger started to boil again, and I squeezed the sharp glass in my palm just enough to break the skin, just enough to feel the pain; anything was better than the ache. The fucking gaping hole in my chest, where my heart had been, burned around the edges.

The blood trickled down my hand and thickened before it was able to drip free from the surface. I let the shard dig deeper until my hand unconsciously dropped the glass, the stinging pain intensified as the air hit the wound, and the brownish red liquid stained my skin.

"Oh my God, Todd. What the fuck?" Seth sounded frightened as he ran over to me. "Are you a God. Damn. Idiot? No chick... *no chick* is worth your life."

"I'm not trying to die, Seth. I'm trying to feel anything other than her. She's everywhere, man, everywhere." My voice cracked, and, for the first time since she walked out that door, I let it all in. I let the tide fill me up, and I couldn't hold back the torrent that was pushing at my supports. I let myself fall to my knees. As I leaned back, my spine roughly hit the foot of the bed. There was no stopping the emotion that emptied from my eyes.

"Give me your hand." Seth's tone was clipped as he stood before me. I kept my head down; I couldn't look him in the eyes. I was broken again, and I couldn't let him see this. "Get the fuck outta here." I grabbed the towel from his hand. The rough texture of the fabric pulled at the cut, and I hissed.

"I'm not going anywhere till you calm the hell down," Seth scowled. "I just saw her outside. She told me she's going back to Florida. She left, bro. It's not the end of the world."

"I'm telling you to get the *hell* out of this room, Seth... *now*." He was starting to piss me off. He didn't understand how I felt. He'd never had a relationship.

"Quit being a dick. You know damn well you'll be fucking Emma or some easy slut in less than a week."

The speed in which I moved almost made me fall over, but not before my fist connected with Seth's jaw. My already swollen knuckles split with the force. "Shit!" The pain radiated up my arm. "Shut your damn mouth. You have no clue what the hell you're spewing to me right now." Seth rubbed his jaw and smirked. "Don't look at me like that. I'm warning you... leave me the hell alone." My raised voice only made his grin wider. "What's so funny, asshole? The fact you just disrespected not only the girl I fucking love, but also the mother of my child."

"Nothing's funny, I'm just trying to give you your fight back. So you love her then?"

We both stared at each other for a moment. I nodded. "Yeah."

"Then fight for her. Don't be a fucking cry baby. Go get her." Seth looked down at the blood on my hand. "Otherwise, the next time you need to feel something, go bury yourself in some chick. Don't cut yourself open, you've been cut open enough." Seth's glare relaxed.

"She chose her dream, Seth, she doesn't want me, and she doesn't want us. But I've got Molly; I need to do right by her, by Emma. I can't go down that path again — the one night stands. I'm done with all that. I lost my shit just now, and I'm sorry you had to see all this." The excruciating ache in my hand started to make me feel queasy.

He shook his head. "If that's what you want to believe... whatever man, let's just clean this shit up. I swear to God you're the biggest pussy I know." Seth smirked and punched me in the shoulder. I wasn't in a joking mood, but I chose to keep my shit together long enough to appease him, long enough to clean up the destruction in front of me, but the minute he left, the minute the door shut behind him, I'd let myself fall apart. I'd let myself inhale the small portion of her that still remained on my sheets, remember what her body did to mine, what she sounded like when she sang, the fiery way she'd take my crap and throw it back at me. I'd let it all crash down, and I'd let myself sink into everything that was Lily. No matter how much it was going to kill me, I'd let myself die this slow death, let her drain from my system. It was the only way to move forward.

CHAPTER FORTY-FIVE

Lily

PAM'S VOICE ECHOED DOWN THE AIR vents in my basement bedroom. It was only eight in the morning, and my head pounded from being up all night crying. I sat up in bed — the yellow walls were overly bright today as the sun sifted through the window wells. My only hope for today was that I wouldn't have to see Pam. Quietly I stepped out of my bed, and my bare feet hit the plush brown and tan speckled carpet. The cold, damp air of the basement sent chills up and down my flesh. I moved to the bathroom quickly and was startled by my image in the mirror. My hair was a mess, and my face looked like a punching bag. The mascara smeared around my eyes and down my cheeks, my eyelids were puffy and red, and my lips were swollen. I couldn't look at myself for too long, or I would lose it again.

A shower was just what I needed. The hot water scalded my pale skin, but the slight twinge of discomfort was worth it. The heat pulled away the night's agony as the water washed the last trace of him from my body. Todd no longer lingered on my flesh, his scent had been scrubbed away, but no matter how hard I tried, I'd never forget his lips and how they felt as he kissed mine. The ache between my legs from how hard he took me last night was already fading, and I couldn't bare it. A wave of nausea swept over me, and my lips trembled as I tried to breathe through my rising panic. Why had I showered? I started to sob violently. Why had I let myself wash him away? I turned the water off and held on tight to the metal support bar on the wall of the shower while I mentally berated myself. He was gone. How had I let myself fall in love so quickly? How was this even possible?

"Lily? When did you come home?" Eve's voice hollered through the closed bathroom door pulling me out of my dejected state. "Lily, are you okay? Why are you crying?"

I wiped the tears from my eyes, opened the shower curtain, and wrapped myself in a large towel. "I'll be out in a sec, Eve." I checked my appearance and, even though my eyes were still puffy, I looked much better.

I opened the door and Eve gasped. "Holy crap, Lily, what's the matter? Pam left like five minutes ago, is this about her? I'm so sorry. I should never have let her stay here. I feel horrible. I mean... she's my mom, and I guess I—"

"It's fine, Eve, this isn't about her, I could care less about her. And you're right, you guys have a relationship, I didn't and I'm okay with that. I wouldn't want her as a mother probably as much as she never wanted me as a daughter."

"Lily," she reproved.

"It's true, Eve. But like I said, this isn't about that. I broke up with Todd."

She gasped. "Why?"

"I'm going back to school." I smiled a small smile. "Thanks for believing in my vision, thanks for giving me back my chance to prove to my dad I could do it. You didn't have to do that, but you did. I'll never forget this."

Eve smiled and wrapped her arms around my towel-clad body. "I'm so proud of you. You should know I sent the request for admittance before you got serious with that guy." She pulled back from the hug. "I feel bad now. You don't have to go, you know? I'm glad you want to still do something great with your talent, not waste it away on some dive bar record label. But don't you guys care about each other? He seemed so nice. He was so cute with Chris." She smiled, but she didn't know how her words cut me. Blue Bar wasn't a dive. Todd had built that place up beyond any hope Frank could have had.

"I do care about him, but this is my life. I need to make a choice just for me, just this once." I was able to smile through the lie. It was getting easier to tell every time.

Eve's lips split into a giant grin. "I did good, then?"

"You did good, *Evy*. Thank you." She hugged me again and squeezed. Even though I felt like shit, I was still able to laugh at her enthusiasm. If anything, at least I was finally getting to know my sister, and getting that relationship was something I never thought I'd have.

"When do you leave?"

"I want to leave tomorrow. I'm going to pack up everything today, go and talk to Frank, then head out early in the morning. It's a long drive back." I wasn't looking forward to three days alone on the road.

"You should have Holden look over your car today when he gets home from work."

Eve was always putting so much on his plate. "I don't need your husband to check out my car, Eve. He's got enough to do around here. It's fine really."

"Okay, well, will you have dinner with us tonight? I'm going to miss you. Even though we fight, it's been—"

"Nice. It's been really nice." My sister's lips pulled into a shaky grin, her eyes glassy from suppressed tears. "Do me a favor, don't be so hard on your dad. Frank's a good guy. You should give him a chance like you did for Pam. Trust me, he deserves that."

"I will, Lily, it's been great having you here, and I'm so

glad we're all starting to mend everything. It's been too long. It's time to start forgiving." She dabbed at her eyes. "Oh dear, look, I'm going to mess up my make-up. Oh, and you should probably get dressed." She laughed. "See you in a minute?"

"I'll be up in a few."

The snap of the door brought me back to reality. I went through the motions of getting ready for the day, spreading my lotion on my skin, dressing in jeans and my old green Sunny Day Real Estate T-shirt, mascara, gloss... It was all very mechanical. The sack of laundry I had from the past week at Todd's needed to be washed before I left. I grabbed the bag of clothes and headed to the laundry room. The mundane tasks were enough to keep me sane; I just needed to make it to the end of the day and then tomorrow I would rinse, wash, repeat, and, hopefully one day, I wouldn't feel so alone, I wouldn't see his face, I wouldn't need his touch.

I dumped the bag of laundry into the washer when something caught my eye. "It couldn't be?" I whispered. My fingers curled around the familiar worn fabric of Todd's favorite band T-shirt. I brought the soft, navy blue cloth to my nose and inhaled. The rich cedar smell and everything that was Todd filled my lungs. The stone in my throat ached as I tried to quell the devastating sadness that flooded my veins. The torture was acute as I pulled my shirt off and replaced it with his. This was the only way I could feel him now... this was all I had left.

THE SOFT FABRIC OF Todd's shirt offered little comfort as I pulled up to the Blue Bar. The silver 4Runner I was used to seeing every day wasn't here yet, and I offered a small thank you to whoever was watching out for Todd today. I was sure seeing me was the last thing he needed. It wasn't easy breaking someone, seeing them dissolve before your eyes, watching the one person you were finally letting yourself love be split open by your own hand. But he needed to be a father, and I wasn't going to sit by and watch him fumble around me. He needed to focus on himself and Molly. At least that's what I kept telling myself; it was the only way I'd get on that highway tomorrow.

Tiffany and Frank's cars were here, and, just for the moment, I allowed myself to smile. It would be nice to say goodbye to Tiff. I hadn't really gotten a chance to know her. My time was always spent with Todd in the short time I was here, but she was the first female I'd ever really gotten along with well enough to actually have some sort of friendship. The discomfort in my chest was sharp; she'd probably hate what I was doing, but I was doing what was right, she'd figure it out. The back door of the bar creaked as I pushed it open. Walking into the dark hall, smelling the greasy pine, mixed with cigarette smell that had become familiar, was bittersweet. This was the last time I'd be here, the last time I'd get to remember how it felt to sing on that small stage, and the last time I'd have to remember how beautiful *he* looked upon it.

Frank's office door was open and the sound system was playing quietly. Tiff's office was dark, so I assumed she was up front. Frank looked up from his paperwork and grimaced. "Come to break my heart too, sweetheart?" The leather texture of his skin created deep circles under his eyes.

"What's that supposed to mean?" The significance of his words was clear to me; I just couldn't allow myself to admit out loud.

"Todd called in sick. He's never, not once in three damn years, called in sick, and I guess you're giving me your final notice. When are you leaving, Lily?" Frank stood abruptly from his chair and moved with a hurried stride to me.

I stepped back automatically. "In the morning."

He reached out and placed his hand on my shoulder.

"You just got here. You and Todd, I thought… that kid cares about you more than you think." I hadn't deluded myself into thinking Todd didn't care about me, but I was cutting him loose before he was too far in to find his way back out. "Once you start running away from the people you love, Lil, it's a dark road… believe me."

"I'm not running." I pulled away from his touch; his advice wasn't needed, and of all people, I was aware what running could do. Pam was the runner, not me.

"You're running, doll." He held his hand up to stop me from arguing. "But, you do what you gotta do for you. Todd's a strong man. Looks like he's got more to worry about now than lady problems." He shook his head. "Tiff's got your final check. After Todd told me what went down, I knew it was a matter of time before you strolled through my office door." Frank sighed and watched me with tired eyes. "Where're you staying?"

"Gabe's going to let me stay with him until I get on my feet." I was grateful that my father's old friend was willing to take me in. Gabe had been like a second father to me, so I wasn't surprised, but that didn't make me any less thankful.

"Well, take care at your fancy school, hon." Frank's smile was broad, the crow's feet by his eyes pulled tightly. He drew me into a bear hug, and the feeling I was trying so desperately to hold in almost burst through the cement wall I'd built around my heart. *Almost.*

"Thanks, I'm going to go say bye to Tiffany. Take care, Frank. Thanks for everything." My words felt heavy as I pulled away from his arms, they were like weights trying to keep me in place, but I was strong enough to keep moving past them, to continue ahead.

The reality of my choice to leave grew as I walked into the main portion of the bar, walked away from what was now my past. The bright sunlight from the huge front windows spilled through the room, making it look even dingier. Tiffany was setting up the till in the register when she looked up at me and smiled. "You leaving, lady?" Her bright red lips spread in a brilliant smile. Tiffany's straight black hair was pulled up into a high ponytail exposing her neck tattoos.

"You heard." A small laugh escaped my lips. "Word travels fast."

"Well, Frank has a giant mouth." She reached under the counter and pulled out an envelope. "Here's your check."

The white envelope was stiff in my hand. "Thanks."

"Well, I'm shit at goodbyes, so… see you around." She shoved my shoulder, and I grinned.

"See you around." My smile fell. "Take care of him, will you?" The briny liquid gathered along my bottom eyelid. I internally scolded myself for letting my wall have a chink in its armor.

"Lily… don't do this. Stay. I've never seen him this happy, never. Todd is such a brat, but I love that guy like a brother, and I'm thinking you're pretty sweet on the guy, too, since you're wearing his shirt." Her words were like a punch in the gut. I looked down at the shirt, the faded band name almost no longer legible, as the wetness dropped from my cheeks darkening the navy to black. "I'm trying really hard to put myself in your shoes… I get it… trust me… no one wants to play second fiddle to another woman. That concept is something I struggle with on the daily, my friend, but you're *his* woman, not her."

"It's not about that. It's about him and his daughter." The dam was starting to break. I clumsily wiped away my tears.

"I'm sorry, this isn't my place. I'm not going to lie, though. When I have to pick up the pieces around here because he's so messed up over you, I may fly down to Florida and kick your ass." She gave me a wicked grin.

A stuttered laugh echoed in my chest. "I look forward to it." I shoved her back in the shoulder. "Take care of him?"

She nodded.

Saying goodbye to Blue Bar was harder than I thought. Again, the feeling of being tethered, that binding force that kept trying to pull me back, surfaced. I was able to keep the tears away as I drove back to my sister's house, but I wasn't prepared to see Pam's car in the driveway when I pulled up. This day couldn't get any more dramatic if it tried. I suddenly wished I hadn't thought those words and tempt the fates to utterly annihilate me. If I were religious, I'd cross myself or something. The front door swung open, and Pam walked down the front steps just as I stepped out of my car.

"Fuck my life," I mumbled under my breath. Surprisingly enough, the anger I'd thought I feel at seeing her wasn't there. This past twenty-four hours had made me numb, and I was appreciative for that one small thing.

Pam's bright copper curls were wild today and wreaked havoc in the breeze. "Pam." I bowed my head briefly in her direction.

"Lily, wait." She gently grabbed my wrist as I tried to walk past her. My fight was gone, and my indifference wavered. I wasn't a runner.

"What? Today is not the—"

"I know, Eve told me." Pam's voice was not as brash as it was the other day, and in the sunlight you could see how the world had eaten her up and spit her out. The tone of her skin was a blotchy mix of freckles and age spots. She appeared so much older than she really was, and the fact that the lids of her eyes drooped, didn't help.

"I wanted to say sorry for how I was the other day. I'm not perfect, Lily, and I'm a piece of shit, if you want to know the truth. And I didn't mean to hurt you. I'm just fucked up, plain and simple." Her chin dipped down, and she fidgeted with the hem of her shirt. "There's no real mystery to it." Her confession took me for a loop. She was admitting she had failed me? "I made so many wrong decisions, Lily. Trust me when I say they were decisions I'd never be able to come back from. So I fell deeper and ran further. I evade, that's how I survive."

"So what am I supposed to do with all this? Say it's okay, grant you forgiveness?" Because I wasn't doling out clemency today.

"No Lily, I'm actually trying to give you advice. I've never treated you like a daughter, and I don't plan on trying to be *mommy of the year*, but I can do one thing for you."

"Oh yeah, what's that?" My smile was smug.

"I can stop you from turning into me."

My intake of breath seared as it whistled down my throat.

"Lily, Frank had always been my choice. But I felt bad because I hooked up with your father first. I sacrificed my feelings for others, and it made me a bitter bitch." She released my wrist. I had forgotten she was even holding it any longer.

"That makes no sense. You got Frank and Eve in the end." My brow furrowed in confusion.

"I was so angry all the time — the resentment had taken over, and I didn't see the light at the end of the tunnel any more. Once I had what I wanted, it was twisted and wrong. I abandoned you, and I broke Danny. I was destruction. No matter what choice I'd made, I ruined something or someone. Can't you see that?" Tears started to trickle from her eyes.

"No matter what I chose, someone got hurt, so I left. I lived my life the best way I could, but all that hurt, Lily, it never leaves, and I can't help but think you're about to pull the keystone. You're about to make a choice that will set you up for the rest of your life, and I'm not sure it's for the better. You have feelings for that boy? Then stick around. Everything will work its way out. But if you leave… Well, you're looking at your life, honey."

I didn't want to believe her; she didn't know the whole story. She didn't know about Emma and Molly. "Thank you for your advice, but I'm not leaving because of him. I'm leaving to go to school like my father would have wanted."

"What do *you* want, Lily?" She thumbed away the liquid from under her eyes.

"I want to pack my shit, get in my car, go to school, and make something of myself. I'm not you, Pam, I'm not."

"I know, honey, that's my point." She smiled. "I'm just trying to help instead of hinder for once."

She was trying, I had to give her that much. "Thank you." The words were genuine, not a snarky comeback. "I'm doing the right thing, you don't need to worry, but the fact that you were… worried… gives me a little hope for you." I smiled, but it didn't completely reach my eyes.

She laughed. "There's no hope for me. But there is for you. Drive safely, that's a long drive." There was no goodbye hug, no sad parting tears… that wasn't our way, but I felt a small bit of resolution in watching her walk away. This time she wasn't running from me, she was trying to get me to stay.

CHAPTER FORTY-SIX

Todd

SEVEN DAYS. IT HAD BEEN SEVEN, fucking days since Lily cut me open. Seven days since she left me to hemorrhage, and I still could hardly breathe. So many times I wanted to text her, tell her to stay, tell her she could go to school here, tell her we could figure this out, but she said she didn't want me, and I had to find a way to deal with that. Emma had texted me earlier and invited me to dinner at her place. The thought of seeing Molly was the only piece of happiness I could find in this mess. The sun had just set and my room was pitch black, not even the moonlight seeped through my closed blinds. The wounds on my hands had already started to heal, it was time to get my ass out of this house. I sat up when my bedroom door whipped open.

"Get the hell out of bed. I'm over it. It's all very sad and depressing, but you need—"

"I know, I need to function. I get it, bro. I was about to get in the shower."

"I was going to say, *you need to work*. Rent won't pay itself, and I'm broke as shit after all my court fees." Seth shook his head. "Jace. I hate that son of a bitch. I'd have rather rotted in a cell than pay him to drop the charges."

"I get it, I'm up. You're broke? Did you ask your dad for help?" I pulled back the sheets and stretched my sore limbs. It actually felt sort of good to be up.

"You know I don't ask my dad for money, man. I used some of my trust fund though." Seth gave me a dark look.

He was right, he didn't, but I figured this was an exception. "This is different."

"Thanks, but you need to worry about this shit storm *you* got going on."

"I know. I'm going to Emma's place to see my little girl." I pushed past Seth and headed to the bathroom. "You going to join me?" The sarcasm was thick.

He laughed. "I see you're getting your humor back... good sign."

The air exhaled noisily from my chest. "I've got to pull my shit together for Molly."

"Sounds like a plan. Have you spoken—?"

"No, she hasn't contacted me, and I can't... I can't hear her voice, it'll just..."

"I got it... go wash the stink off. You're pretty ripe." Seth smiled and left the room with a chuckle. I wasn't able to laugh back. I wanted nothing more than to talk to Lily,to hear her voice, to feel her breath on my neck and fingertips against my skin. My jaw pulsed until it became painful. The love I felt was too much, too much for such a short time. I wasn't stupid, this wasn't normal, but these feelings were real none-the-fucking-less. I just had to figure out a way to endure it.

MOLLY'S GIGGLE WAS LIKE a salve for all the wounds I'd sustained this past week. She was sitting on my lap as I tickled her. She was supposed to be getting ready for bed and the look Emma was giving me had me full on belly laughing.

"All right, baby girl, you're mom said it's time for bed." I spun Molly in my arms, and she held on tight to my neck as I stood and started for her bedroom. "You want me to sing you a song, Lolly?"

"Yes, pewees." She burrowed her nose into my neck the sweet smell of lavender assaulted me. This was the new thing I craved, the new memories I was going to make. My chest constricted as bright copper curls flashed through my mind. I closed my eyes and took in a long breath.

"You all right, Todd?" Emma's quiet voice broke the coil that was building.

"Yeah. Sorry." I moved quickly, getting Molly in her pajamas. She snuggled into her bed, and I situated the stuffed animals like she had the last time I was here. "You ready for a song?"

She bobbed her head and smiled. I started to hum at first, trying to find the right tone. The lyrics from "*Fix You*" by Cold play fell smoothly from my lips. The meaning behind the words were sad but hopeful, and I wanted hope for Molly. I needed to believe that I would always be here for her, no matter how hard I was hurting right now. She was my world, my sweet baby girl, and I had to be a whole person for her, I just had to. My fingers dusted over her small face, her soft skin was the most perfect thing I'd ever felt as I tried to soothe my daughter to sleep. Molly inclined toward the touch, and my mouth turned up at the edges.

Once the song was over, I bent down and kissed her on the cheek. "Night, my sweet girl."

"Night, Daddy."

Emma sniffled as I pulled Molly's door shut. "Todd... that was... so beautiful." Her eyes glistened. She raised her hand to my face, her fingertips brushed at the hair that was hanging low on my forehead. "I'm sorry I ever doubted you. You're such a good man."

"I'm trying, Emma." My smile was small. Emma lifted onto her tiptoes, her lips met the corner of my mouth and lingered. She turned her head infinitesimally, her mouth now flush with mine. My hand instinctively lifted to her face as her lips moved gently against me. This kiss was like a slow poison — the physical touch I required, the love I needed to feel. "Lily," I whispered against her lips.

Emma stepped back abruptly. The motion brought me back to reality. The shame started to suffocate me immediately. "W-what." Her hand shook as she brought her fingers to her mouth. "Oh my gosh, I shouldn't have kissed you. I'm sorry, you looked so... and I just care about you... I mean... I forgot about her." She looked down at her feet.

"I'm sorry, Emma. I'm—"

Her head shot up. "Wait... you kissed me back, Todd."

"Lily left me, Em. I'm all mixed up right now. I'm sorry, I'm such a shit. I shouldn't have—"

"She left you?" Emma looked at me with compassion.

"It's a long story, but I'm just fucked up over it." I winced. "Sorry, I shouldn't swear."

"You kissed me back because you wished it was her." It was a statement, not a question.

I didn't want to hurt Emma, but I couldn't be with her like that. She wasn't the one who made everything right for me. "I need some time to get my head straight, but I'm here for Mol, okay? I wasn't lying when I told you I'd be here for her no matter what."

"I'm sorry I kissed you." She gave me a repentant smile. Emma was a good person; she just wanted the wrong guy.

"I'm sorry, too." I wrapped my palm around the back of her head as I gently pulled her to my chest. "You're a good girl, and I'm so glad, so damn appreciative, that Molly has you to look up to."

Emma enfolded her arms around my waist as she spoke,

"We can do this."

I wasn't in love with Emma, but right now, in this moment, we were both just two broken people, two friends, two people who never seemed to get what they wanted, but just maybe in each other we could find some semblance of happiness. We had one hell of connection after all, and her sweet little eyes were closed as she slept in the next room. "We can."

I WAS ABOUT A MILE away from Emma's house when my phone dinged. My stomach dropped when I saw it was just Colby.

Colby: *Seth said you're in town. Can you stop by?*

I wanted to kill him for what he said to Lily. I thought it best if I didn't see him in person.

Me: *I don't think you want to see me right now.*

His text was immediate.

Colby: *I know she left. Seth told me. I feel like shit.*

Me: *You should feel like shit...*

Colby: *Just stop by.*

I ignored his text and continued to drive south. My phone alerted again. This time it was Cameron.

Cam: *Please. Your brother is an asshole and feels like a dick. Let him apologize.*

Maybe I'd just stop by, punch him in his face, and then leave. I smiled, that sounded perfect.

Me: *On my way.*

Cam: *Thank You.*

She wouldn't be thanking me in about ten minutes. I was going to lay that little shit out. I made a U-turn, and the engine roared as I pushed down on the accelerator.

Colby and Cam lived up by the University in a small, one bedroom apartment. The apartment complex was always crawling with Frat boys, basically party central. I hated coming here, and, right now, all I wanted to do was put my fist through Colby's jaw. The alarm for my truck chirped twice as I pressed down on the remote lock. They lived on the first floor, so Cam must have looked out her window when I pulled up because she met me at the front door. She hurriedly stepped out from the apartment and shut the door. My adrenaline was thrumming searching for release.

"Whoa, Todd. I know you're upset, and I know how you guys get with each other, but listen... he feels super bad." Cam's eyes widened as she took in my appearance.

My jaw was tight, my shoulders rolled back, and my nostrils flared. "Cammie, get the hell out of my way." She pressed her palms flat against my chest.

"Todd, he didn't... I've never seen you this pissed... you need to breathe." Cam pushed on my chest again, and my muscles flexed. Nope, there was no way I was backing down. I was beyond fucking pissed. All my rage, all my hurt, all this damn loss was flooding my circuits. I was misfiring, and it was because of him, because what he said spooked *her*... Lily, I allowed myself to think the name. The thought of her name, the sound of it, was like shrapnel in my head.

"Get. Out. Of. My. Way." I easily pushed forward, Cam's huff lost on me. Cold fury washed over my body as I stepped through the threshold of their apartment. Colby was just coming from the kitchen when he saw me.

"Hey, we need—"

I didn't let him finish. The force in which my fist hit Colby's face caused the bone to crack noisily and blood to spurt from his nose. My left fist met his stomach, and he fell to his knees gasping for air. My breathing was labored as I tackled him to the ground. We wrestled on the ground, and I was able to get him into a headlock. Colby punched me in the side, and I grunted, losing my grip on his throat for a split second. My hand slipped in something wet and we both fell over onto the ground.

Cam's piercing cry broke me from my testosterone charged state. "Stop! Stop. Please, Todd." She started to cry. "You're not angry at him, you're angry at her. *She* left you. Colby made a mistake, but in the end…" Cam inhaled trying to catch her breath. "…she left you. So be angry at *her*, be sad, go home and hide in your damn room, but don't come into our house… my God, Todd, look what you did." Cam's eyes spilled over with tears.

I took in my surroundings — the numbness faded, my lips throbbed, my fist ached. The floor was covered in blood, and my brother was sprawled on his back holding his nose. Colby's eye was swollen shut, his left eyebrow was split open, and his nose was most definitely broken. *Fuck.* I'd lost my damn mind. "Colby, I'm so sorry."

"Don't Todd, I'd have done the same shit."

"Colby! Don't condone this crap." Cam was incredulous.

"Cammie, I love you, baby, I do… but this is what we do, this is how Todd and I roll." He attempted to smile and winced. "If this shit went down with me and you, babe, sure as shit I'd be beating down this idiot's door. I said some things I shouldn't have. I let Lily believe one thing when I was really just trying…" Colby groaned as he attempted to sit up. I took his hand in mine and helped him up into a sitting position. "I messed up, man. You're my brother. Like I said, I was just trying to gauge where that chick was at, and, apparently, she wasn't all in." Colby's eyes locked with mine. "I'm truly sorry that she wasn't."

Cam kneeled down and started assessing Colby's injuries. My head dropped into my hands. Lily wasn't all-in. She wasn't. If she cared about me like she said she had, she would have made this work. But she never really said she loved me, did she? The one time she uttered the words, it had been a mistake. She didn't mean it. It was a short-lived, passionate, lust-filled illusion I must have created in my head.

"When are you going to start looking out for just you, man? You don't need this shit. You got a kid now. Focus on that." Colby grabbed my hand and pulled me into a side hug.

The ground felt unstable as I stood up on shaky legs. Colby pulled himself up as he gripped my forearm, and Cam helped by supporting his shoulder. "You broke my damn nose." Colby chuckled.

"This isn't funny." Cam's lips made a hard line.

It wasn't funny, none of it was. How was I supposed to go on from this point? I couldn't see a solution. Once again, I'd fallen for a girl who wanted something more than me, and I was left in the wake to fend for myself. This time though, Colby was right, I needed to focus. I'd go through the mechanics of each day, create a happy world for my daughter, work at the bar, make music, produce records, and make other people's dreams come true. But at night, when I was no longer on display, I'd let the certainty of my life engulf me. I'd let the loneliness sink in. I was back at square one. I was damaged, I was worthless, and I wasn't worth keeping.

CHAPTER FORTY-SEVEN

Lily

THE HOT, HUMID FLORIDA SUMMER AIR soaked me down to the bone and had my hair almost as big as a house. The thunderclouds rolled in over the bay, heavy with the scheduled midday rain. The smell of damp decay and salt water sifted through with the wind as I sat next to my father's grave. These past three months had been the hardest of my life. Being without him... without Todd, was harder than I'd ever thought possible. He had entwined his roots in my heart, and each day they grew thicker; instead of the pain subsiding, it got worse.

"When's it going to end, Dad? This can't be right. How can this one man hold so much power over me?" The thunder clapped and startled me; the sea breeze moved the storm closer still. Since I'd been home, I'd come here every day after classes. Being here with my father, even though he wasn't exactly present, helped, and at this point, I needed all the help I could get. Arcadia College of Music wasn't what I'd been hoping it could be. I didn't want to teach, I needed to perform, to be on a stage, to compose, and to let this agony release the hold it had on my body through lyrics and sound.

The sun fell behind the clouds, blotting out the light. My father's headstone stared back at me. Missing my father was something that was just a part of me now, and I had wished I'd been able to compartmentalize my feelings for Todd the same way. But his grip on me was so much stronger than I ever knew. A large drop of water fell from the sky in slow motion and splashed against my cheek as I looked up into the clouds. I blew a kiss to my father's grave and grabbed my bag in a dash to my car. The rain was a downpour before I made it inside. The air conditioner was on full blast as my old, run down Corolla started, the oppressive heat from earlier now put on hold during the torrential rain. My skin prickled with goose bumps.

Turning down the A/C, I checked my phone for the time and noticed I had a missed call from Gabe. I switched my phone to silent and backed out of the parking spot. I'd talk to him when I got home; I wasn't really in a good place right now to chat. Besides, the drive home only took about five minutes, so it seemed silly to call. The rain seemed to ease within the short ride from the cemetery to Gabe's place. Mother Nature was so confusing.

Gabe's house was small and falling apart. The white vinyl siding had a slight green hue to it from the large oak trees that it sat under. The Spanish moss that hung from the branches waved in the wind as my car rolled to a stop in the dirt drive.

Being already drenched didn't prevent me from running full speed to the house; the lightning cracked with force and had me running scared. I hated lightning. Breathing fast, I slammed the front door behind me.

"Gabe?" I called out.

"Yeah, Lil, in here," Gabe shouted from the kitchen.

Dropping my bags in front of my bedroom door, I slipped my wet shoes and socks off and headed to the kitchen. "Hey, you called me?"

Gabe smiled. "Got caught again?" His hands gestured at my drowned rat-like appearance.

"Every damn day. You would think I would learn." I laughed.

"You'd think." He smirked as he poured himself a glass of sweet iced tea.

"So... you called." I grabbed a glass from the cabinet and poured myself some tea as well.

"You got some mail." He gave me a pointed look.

"All right." I swallowed a gulp of tea; the sugary yet bitter liquid was my favorite. The slight taste of lemons made me think of hot summer days with my father as a child.

"From Utah."

I spit the tea from my lips.

"Shit, Lil." Gabe frowned, as he wiped the mess from his shirt with a nearby dishtowel.

My hands started to shake and a shiver ran down my neck. "Who... who's it from."

Gabe continued to clean himself up as he spoke, not really paying attention to my current panic attack. "Just said Blue Bar Music, Lil. It's on the coffee table."

I moved hastily out of the kitchen and into the living room. The yellow package sat serenely on the table, while my nerves were in overdrive. My heart was in my throat, and my breathing was frantic. My steps were measured as I moved closer to the table, and, once I was able to reach down and pick it up, I hesitated. I knew the minute I touched the smooth yellow envelope that everything would be real — the distance, the time spent with him. I had a feeling as to what was waiting for me inside, and I wasn't sure I would be able to survive this final blow.

My fingers traced the side of the package, and I could have sworn I felt electricity pulse up my arm. I curled my fingers, resisting the inevitability; once I opened that letter, my entire world would be thoroughly devastated.

"Well, what is it?" Gabe spoke from behind me, breaking the trance.

"Not sure," I was unable to speak any louder than a whisper.

"You gonna open it?" he asked. Gabe had no idea of what happened in Utah. He didn't know about Todd, my music, none of it. Speaking about it made it real, and I'd rather pretend it hadn't happened than mourn the loss of what could have been the love of my life.

"I'll be in my room. Let me know when you're ready to go to The Tavern for dinner." I picked up the parcel — the weight of it was light, but the damage it held inside I'm sure was monumental.

I sat with my legs folded underneath me on my bed. My fingers ripped the package open carefully, and I dumped the contents in front of me. A tattered looking letter and a CD fell out, and my breath stopped. Without a doubt, the CD was Todd and I in the studio, and the thought of hearing him sing, hearing his voice again, brought out the sob I was trying to hold back. The white paper of the letter trembled as I picked it up. The letter was wrinkled as if it had been balled up at some point. The handwriting was unmistakably his, and I closed my eyes and brought the paper to my nose praying I could have some physical piece of him again. The faint smell of ink was all that I could decipher, and my disappointment fell from my eyes in waves as I read.

Lily,

I wasn't going to send the studio sessions. I wasn't going to even write this letter, but I miss you like hell. At times, I feel like you've died, and I'm missing a ghost, but then I remember you're alive, and it was you that decided to leave. I wanted to be angry, but I can't be mad at you for not caring about me like I cared about you. Mixing these songs together and listening to your voice over and over, it was torture, Lily, pure fucking torture. But it had to be done. Something like this, something as great as your talent, shouldn't lay incomplete on the cutting room floor. I hope you find what you're looking for. I'd thought I had found my one true thing and, although listening to your voice splits me in two, at least I have that, at least some part of what we had was real. I want you to be happy, baby, and if that's what you're feeling now, living the dream you always wanted, then I'm happy for you.

Much Love,
Todd

Tears ran down my face as I moved quickly to the stereo with the CD in my hand. I couldn't get the music on fast enough. Todd was wrong; I wasn't happy. I was miserable, I was drowning every second of every day, and if this music, if hearing his voice could aleviate any of the constant pressure on my chest, I'd listen to this on repeat every freaking minute. The light sound of his guitar played through the speakers. My fingers turned the volume knob up, and then I lay flat on my back on my bed. My white ceiling was cast in odd shaped shadows as the storm moved the tree limbs outside. Our cover of *"King and Lion Heart"* by Of Monsters and Men eased its way over the sound system and soaked my atmosphere with all that was beautiful about Todd. The way he played guitar was different than anyone else I'd ever listened to... every chord was effortless.

Todd's deep melodic voice spilled from the speakers, making my heart stutter. The scratchy and sexy quality of his tone was distinctly him. The lids of my eyes fluttered closed, and I pictured the studio in my head, the pull of his muscle as he strummed the strings of his guitar, the tendons in his neck and how they strained when he was really getting into the song, and I remembered the perfect way his hair fell over his forehead. I smiled. The pain in my chest was almost unbearable, but I smiled because I had a piece of him again, something real. He gave me a gift today, whether that was intentional or not, I'd take it.

CHAPTER FORTY-EIGHT

Todd

"You're killing me, bro." Graden threw his guitar pick across the room. "You need to snap out of this. You sound like shit, man. It's been what; three months... you need to get laid."

"Shut the hell up." I wasn't hearing this from him right now. Today had been a crap day — some days are better than others, but I hadn't seen Molly or Emma in over a week since they were on vacation in Idaho visiting her family. They would be back tonight, and I couldn't wait. Work and band practice wasn't enough to keep me occupied, to keep my thoughts from falling back to her.

"I'm serious; we haven't played right since that bitch left. You need to get—" Graden was interrupted by the drumstick that hit him square in the back of his head. If Seth hadn't intervened, my fist would have been planted in his damn jaw.

"I'm done with this." Seth stood briskly from behind his drum kit. He grabbed his shirt and pulled it over his newly inked up chest. The kid was fully covered now all the way down onto his hands and up to his neck. He looked like a badass. "I'm out."

"What do you mean, you're out?" Jack, our bass player, asked indignantly.

"It means... I'm fucking out. Todd, man, Graden is an asshole, and your head is up your ass. This is shit, and we haven't played a show in months. I'm out."

"See you then, asshole. Drummers are easy to find." Graden sneered at Seth, and I about lost my control.

Seth just laughed. "You're right, they are."

"But singers are hard to come by, especially ones who run a damn label. I'm out too, bro." I smiled at Seth. This felt right for some reason. This band hadn't been what it once was, not for a long while, and it felt good to cut the ties. I had too much going on with Molly and Emma and the label to be worried about singing in a band.

"Are you serious?" Jack gave me a disbelieving glare.

"I'm serious. My life... it's too complicated right now, and I need a break." I set my guitar on its stand.

"Whatever." Graden grabbed his guitar and put it away in its case. He gave Seth a dirty look. "You're a dick. Throw something at me again, and I'll—"

"Cool it, Graden." Jack grabbed his things. "Let's just go. See you around guys. Call me when shit gets less heavy, man." He bowed his head in goodbye. Graden didn't say a word as they left through the studio's back door.

"What a douchebag." Seth grinned, and it made me laugh.

"I can't believe you just broke up the band, Yoko." My lips split into a cocky grin as Seth chuckled at my bad joke.

"It was time, man. Those guys were getting sloppy anyway."

"They really were." I started to pack away some of the equipment.

"And you do sound like shit," Seth said without humor.

I lifted my head and glowered at Seth. "You got something to say?"

"What are you doing, man?" Seth's keen eyes searched my

face.

"I'm cleaning up, what the fuck does it look like I'm doing? I've gotta meet up with Emma in an hour." My words evaded the real question, but Seth wasn't so easily derailed.

"You getting together with Emma?" Seth's brow dipped, and he looked as if he swallowed something bitter. "'Cause that's the most stupid thing you could ever do."

His advice was unwanted and unwarranted. He didn't have a clue as to what my pain was like. Each day that ticked off the calendar, each day without her… without Lily, was another bullet to the chest. I had to find some reprieve, I had to try and get my life back.

"Emma cares about me." My voice didn't even sound believable to me.

"You fucked her yet?" he said with acid in his voice.

My hands balled into fists. "Excuse me?"

"Have you bagged her yet? Are you sleeping with her… tell me, Todd… have you even thought about it? Once?" He narrowed his eyes.

"That's not your business." I rolled my shoulders back and cracked my knuckles ready for a fight. "Don't talk about the mother of my little girl like that."

"Okay, fine then, what about Lily? Have you thought about her? Have you thought about how she could be in deep with another guy right now? How her lips could be wrapped around his—"

I shoved him hard, and he stumbled backward. "What the fuck! Why would you say that?"

"Now think about Emma like that, think about her screwing some guy, think about her laid out with another man, how does that feel? The same?" He looked at me skeptically.

My jaw compressed, my molars ached under the strain. "No man, it doesn't." The thought of Lily with another guy made me crazy, made me want to crack skulls, but Emma with another man, it didn't bother me in the same way. Emma was special, and I wanted to protect her, but I didn't want her like I wanted Lily.

"Quit lying to yourself." Seth shoved me in my chest. "Wake the hell up. Don't lead Emma on. You're not that big of a dick, are you? You think Emma doesn't know where you'd rather be. Don't you think the minute you let yourself be with her you would regret it and ruin the chance of having a friendship with the mother of your child? You think... for one second... that you could even feel half the physical need I watched and heard Lily pull from you? You're out of your damn mind." He shook his head.

My tongue was thick and my mouth was dry, making it hard to swallow the lies I'd been feeding myself for these past three months. I'd told myself I needed to move on, that I could be happy with Emma if I tried. I lied, and as I buried every thought of Lily down, each memory a knife to the chest, I brought Emma deeper into my selfish need to be loved. I *wasn't* that big of a dick, and I'd put an end to it tonight.

"You love her?"

"It doesn't matter if I love her, Seth, she doesn't—"

"Go there. Ask her to her face. Take your sorry ass down to Florida and get your woman. She loves you, man. She left for you, and you can't see that because you've been burned. And, fuck dude, if you keep protecting yourself, you're going to miss out on something that's rare."

Seth never spoke like this; he'd never had a relationship, and he'd never trusted women.

"You are rattling off some serious romantic bullshit right now for a guy who's never been with a girl for more than one night." I laughed without humor.

"That's the messed up part, Todd. I'm as screwed up as they come, but I can see what's right in front of you, and you can't. She left because she thought she was giving you a family. She didn't want the dream, Todd, she wanted you.

She's just a really good liar, another thing you guys have in common." He turned to leave.

The pulse beat hard behind my temples. Could he be right? Was I that blind? "You think I should go down there?"

"Yes, asshole, that's what I'm saying. You need me to pack your bags for you too? Jesus!" He glared at me with annoyance.

"Maybe I will." The thought of getting on a plane, of seeing Lily again… it was as if the damn sky was opening up, and all that light made it easier to see.

"Thank, God. I'm so sick of your moody ass." Seth turned and walked out the back door without another word.

EVERYTHING SETH HAD SAID plagued me all afternoon until I finally bought a plane ticket to Florida for the next day. The flight left at six a.m. The hunger I had for Lily never went away. The need she'd fired up in me never blew out. The way she was with Molly, the love I saw in her eyes when she looked into mine, I'd let all that lay dormant so I could believe the propaganda I'd created in order to be without her. But I was finished playing dead. Lily was mine, and I was a part of her. I loved watching her fall into me as I claimed each bit of who she was. When I got on that plane tomorrow, there was no other option — she was coming back with me. She was coming home.

The night air was dry and cool as I stepped up onto Emma's front porch and knocked on the wood surface of the door. My thoughts of Lily made me optimistic and my smile was genuine when Emma swung open the door. Her smile radiated.

"Hey you, don't you look happy." She leaned in and kissed me on the cheek.

I placed a chaste kiss on her cheek. "I'm happy you guys are back."

"Daddy." Molly's squeal made me chuckle as she tackled my legs, making it hard for me to walk.

"Sweet girl, I missed you so much." Molly leaped into my arms, and I squeezed her into a tight hug. She squeaked. "Did you have fun, Lolly?"

"I did." I shifted Molly to my hip, and we walked into the family room.

"I'm so glad, but I'm happy you're home now." I nuzzled my nose into her neck, and she giggled as the hairs from my beard tickled her face. My fingers tickled the backs of her legs and she squirmed.

"Stop dat, Daddy." She snickered uncontrollably.

Her hair was in pigtails, and she had on a jean skirt, pink shirt, and pink cowboy boots. These were details I'd forgotten to notice in my past visits here. The time spent with Molly had been cast in a shadow, and I hadn't realized it until now. I felt so light tonight, and the difference was obvious in how I responded to her. "God, I love you so much." I kissed her cheek, once, twice, and a few more times until I had her in a fit of giggles again.

"She missed you. It was a long week. She talked about you nonstop. She's getting really good with her words." Emma looked at our daughter with pride. "You going to stay for bedtime?"

Molly wiggled in my arms, so I let her down. "Come play." She tugged on my hand.

"Take her out back, please, and let her run around. We can talk after she's in bed." Emma reached down and tightened one of Molly's pigtails.

"I can't stay for bedtime tonight. I have to catch an early flight tomorrow."

"Oh yeah? Where to? Getting another band to sign?" Molly pulled on her mother's hand now. "One second,

Mommy and Daddy are talking. Can you go get your play shorts on? You know, like I showed you, honey. Like a big girl?"

"Yes! Big girl." Molly ran off to her bedroom.

"Sorry, you were saying." Emma walked into the attached kitchen and opened the fridge. Her body leaned down, pulling items from the refrigerator for dinner.

"I'm going to Florida." The sound of my voice was flat.

Her back was stiff as she stood and shut the refrigerator door.

"I need to tell you something, Todd." Emma's body moved mechanically as she turned and looked at me with worried eyes.

"I'm going to see her, Em. I need to see her. I wanted things with us to work… but—"

"I'm seeing someone." Emma's face paled with her confession. "I was going to tell you, but you've been so distant. I couldn't wait around for you anymore. You could never want me like her; I know that now, so I've moved on."

The gut reaction I had was anger, but not because Emma was seeing another man, but because another man was going to be in Molly's life. "What about Molly?"

The carrots, lettuce, and peppers spilled from Emma's arms onto the kitchen counter. "What about her?" She gave me a confused look.

"You don't think this will confuse her?" I asked with an edge.

"No more than Lily confuses her." She put her hands on her hips. "I don't want to argue about this. I'm dating someone. I'm happy for once, and tonight, when I opened that front door and you smiled at me like you had all the hope in the world, well, that was the first time you really lit up since before she left. Molly will be fine if we're happy. Lily isn't trying to replace me, and Mark won't try to replace you."

"Mark… he sounds like a tool."

Emma laughed. "Jealous?" She quirked her eyebrow.

"No, I'm just—"

"Being irrational, argumentative, unreasonable... just being you." She grinned.

My laugh echoed in the small kitchen. "Yeah, I guess I'm a little territorial."

She pulled the cutting board down from the shelf and gave me an amused glare. "A little?" She shook her head and laughed quietly.

"Okay, a lot. I just want Molly to know who I am, to have no doubt I'm her father. I helped make her... she's my baby girl."

"She knows all of that. Just make sure she doesn't forget. Remember... no matter what, Todd."

"No matter what." My eyes met Emma's. The promise that bound us together was something I held close to my heart. I kissed her on the cheek. "Always." I squeezed her shoulder, and she smiled at me.

"Outside, pewees." Molly pulled on my pant leg.

"Did you hear that?" I grinned at Emma.

"Uh oh, I think I did. It's...it's—"

"The tickle monster," I said with a growl as I scooped up a shrieking little girl and threw her over my shoulder in a fireman hold. Molly kicked and screamed, the heel of her shoe hitting me in the face. Emma laughed enthusiastically. Today had turned into a good day. Tomorrow... I wasn't sure what was in store for me, but at least I knew it wasn't the same as yesterday or the day before that. Because at least I had faith that something could change, at least I wasn't sinking down into the lie any longer.

CHAPTER FORTY-NINE

Lily

IT WAS THE FIRST TIME I'D been on a stage since I left Blue Bar. Last night Gabe and I had dinner and a few drinks at The Tavern. After listening to nothing but Todd and I singing together for two hours, alcohol seemed like a good option, but it must have been fate. The flyer for open mic night was plastered all over the bar, and I wanted to seize that opportunity more than anything. The opportunity to sing again, to let my fingers run along the strings of my guitar — my soul begged for the chance to be free.

I'd left Gabe at home watching television with the promise I wouldn't be out late. He didn't like me going out alone, but he had an early morning planned so I wouldn't let him tag along. The bar had maybe ten patrons since it was a weeknight, and I'd already played one of my own songs, but I wasn't ready to be done, and I doubted anyone cared if I continued to play. I started to strum the notes to my favorite version of *"Wrecking Ball"* by Boyce Avenue. The world around me became quiet, and it felt as if it was just me in the room. I let the blackness of the past few months fill my lungs, and the lyrics rushed past my lips. They soared throughout the dingy bar, and the therapeutic feeling of release fell over me, and for those few minutes, I felt peace. The last note hit the air, and the room erupted into applause. I couldn't bring myself to look up at the small crowd. My moment was over, and my reality started to seep its way back into my veins.

I pulled my guitar strap off my shoulder and kneeled down to put it away. The clips of my guitar case, as usual, had trouble snapping shut. I sighed as I struggled with the clasps, but once I finally got it to clamp shut I smiled in triumph. As I lifted my head, my eyes locked with a pair of brown eyes — the eyes that knew me better than anyone, and they were the same eyes that haunted me every day. The deep russet color was darker than usual in the dim light of the bar. My heartbeat matched the rise and fall of his chest, rapid and hard. I was sure he could hear it. My lips parted in a quiet gasp as he took the last few steps toward the stage, toward me.

"Don't cry, baby." His voice was the comfort I'd craved for so long, a miracle drug that started to close my wounds instantly. The coarse pad of his thumb brushed away the tears I hadn't even realized were falling.

He was here. The butterflies in my stomach frenzied, causing me to feel light headed. I inhaled a shaky breath gathering my courage to speak; I was able to utter one word before I was sure I would wake up. "Todd?"

CHAPTER FIFTY

Todd

THE ADDRESS ON THE PAPER MATCHED the numbers hanging from the run down porch. The GPS in the rental car said I was at my destination, but Lily's car wasn't here. The only vehicle was a chromed out Harley that sat under the carport. What if she had given a fake address to Frank? The acid in my already anxious gut started to boil. She could have lied, and then I'd never find her again. The thought was something I wasn't prepared to deal with so I figured I'd see if this really was the place where she was staying.

The driveway was muddy from the earlier storm, and the overbearing heat hadn't dissipated at all as the sun went down. Once I landed, I went straight to the hotel, showered, and gathered all my willpower to get into the car and drive over here. The storm had delayed me, and now I was cursing myself for not just coming over here straight away. It was late, and I didn't want to piss off this guy Gabe she was staying with. Frank had told me he was an old friend of his and had been a member of Lily's father's band. My breathing was even as my finger pressed the doorbell. The years of putting on a façade were helping me right now. On the outside, I might look calm, but on the inside... I was full of wreckage and debris, and the only *thing keeping me together was this one tiny prayer that I could see Lily again.*

My posture straightened as I heard the heavy footfall and the deadbolt turn in the door. An older man with a black motorcycle shirt and black jeans stared at me from behind the screened door. "Can I help you?"

My chest pulled tight as I tried to take in a lung full of air. "I'm looking for Lily... Lily Spring. This was the address I was given."

"It's ten o'clock, son. You don't think it's too late to be ringing doorbells?" His thick country accent hung in the humid air.

He started to close the door and I panicked. "Wait, please, I need to see her. Does... does she live here?" My mask was beginning to fall, and my voice vibrated.

"Who wants to know?" The man gave me a disapproving look, and the fire of hope started to kindle brightly in my chest. This must be Gabe.

"My name's Todd... you must be Gabe. She told Frank she was staying with you, and I—"

"Frank. You one of her friends from Utah?" he interrupted

"Yes, sir. We... she was my girlfriend... before she left."

"Boyfriend? She didn't tell me about no boyfriend. What did you say your name was?" He put his hand on the door again as if ready to shut it in my face. Hell, if I had to, I'd give this man my kidney if he would just let me see her.

"Todd. We worked together at the Blue Bar and—"

"Blue Bar Music," he mumbled to himself as if putting two and two together. "She's not here, son. She's down at The Tavern playing open mic night... I'll tell her you came by." He started to close the door.

"The Tavern?" I almost shouted.

"That's what I said." Just as he was closing the door, I thought I heard him chuckle.

Hearing Lily's voice live stripped me down to ashes. The lyrics seared through me, and the pain that inundated the sound was enough proof she was just as lost as I had been. The flame of her hair was incandescent as the spotlight shone down onto the stage. The lowly lit bar added to the effect, and it felt as if it was just her and me — everyone else in the room were phantoms. Lily singing was something I'd never forget; it was a permanent part of who I was now. For just a moment I was brought back to the first time I'd heard her sing, that first week at Blue Bar. It felt so long ago, but in reality it was less than six months. She was who I wanted then, and she was who I wanted now. Nothing was going to ever change that... not time... not distance. She was who I wanted in my life... forever. Call me crazy, but that's how I was, who I am. I loved hard and fast, and I wasn't going to apologize for it.

My steps gradually brought me closer to the stage. My movements were paced so that I wouldn't spook her as I watched her pack up her guitar. Lily lifted her gaze, and her otherworldly eyes pinned me down. The tears almost immediately started to fall, and the yellow-green hue of her irises sparkled. She never looked more beautiful than she did in this very moment. I struggled to catch my breath as my feet brought me to where my heart belonged.

"Don't cry, baby." The touch of her skin against my palm sent a current up my arm as the wet tears pooled against my thumb.

"Todd?" She searched my features as if I was a figment of her imagination. "W-what are you doing here." Her upper lip quivered, and I wanted to kiss away the fear I could see surfacing in her eyes.

"I couldn't do it—"

"You couldn't do what?" She dropped my stare.

I brought my other hand to her face and placed two fingers under her chin urging her eyes to stay with mine. She inhaled a jagged breath. "I couldn't live the lie, Lil. I couldn't let one more day go by without you in it." I took her face between my hands and brought my mouth to hers. Lily's lips parted, and the sweet taste of berries and everything that I remembered about her reunited with my senses. I was home again. She was eye-level with me as she kneeled on the stage, her arms wound around my neck, and my hands skated down her back pulling our bodies together. My tongue traced the curve of her bottom lip, and she sighed into my mouth.

We were each other's half, we were meant to be like this. The love that ran through my veins, the love she poured into me with this kiss, started to heal all my cuts, all my bruises. I could have kissed her like this all night, but the loud catcall reminded me we were in a bar. Lily gasped and pulled away from my embrace.

"Oh my God." She jumped to her feet, grabbed her guitar, and scrambled for the back door of the bar.

What the hell? "Lily *wait*." I followed behind her, the heavy metal door almost hitting me in the face. The wet air made each breath a chore; my pulse sped as I called her name again. "Lily. Please."

She stopped — her back toward me, and her head hanging in defeat. "You shouldn't have come here," she said almost inaudibly.

Her words threatened to cut me open again, but that kiss told me everything I needed to know. "You don't get to tell me what to do."

The edge in my voice broke through her barrier, and she spun around and glared at me. "What?" She dropped her guitar case, and her fingers rolled up into tiny fists. "You have a family! Todd, you have to go home, you shouldn't be here." She shoved me furiously in the chest; her cheeks were red and damp from her tears.

My hands clutched around her upper arms, and I drew her in close to my body. She tried to fight my grip, and, as much as I didn't want to hurt her, she needed to listen. I shook her gently. "Damn it, Lily, just fucking stop. Stop, baby." Lily's eyes were glassy. She exhaled harshly, and her defiant stance slackened under my fingertips. "You can't make my choices for me. I'm my own, goddamn man and I want to be with you."

"What about Emma and Molly? They're your family, Todd. You need—"

"You're my family, too." Dropping my hold on her, my fingers trailed up her arms and curled around the back of her head. My thumbs rested lightly against her jaw as she regarded me with trepidation. "Lily, I don't want Emma like that. Can't you see that?"

"And Molly?" She started to cry harder, her voice wavered.

"I don't need to be with Emma to be a good father. We can all be there for her." I smiled at the thought of us — Lily, Molly, and me — together.

"What if I screw up?" The vulnerability in her voice shook me to the core.

"You will, and so will I. It's a part of life. You're not your mother, Lily. You're not Pam."

She allowed a sob to shake through her body, and her forehead fell against my chest. "Todd, let's be real. We've just barely started really getting to know each other. What if—"

"I know I fucking love you, and that's all that matters." I was tired of skirting around the issue, and I was taking what was mine. Lily's head shot up, her eyes wide as she took in my stare. "Lily, in the end, none of that shit means anything. How long am I supposed to wait to tell you that I am in love with you? What's a socially acceptable amount of time for you? Because from where I'm standing, I couldn't give a shit what the world thinks. Lily, you're exactly what I've always wanted. Nothing… nobody… is going to change that." Our mouths came together with a violent need. Her breath, her skin, her taste, and her heart were linked to mine in that moment. Our lips moved in perfect rhythm, and her nails pulled across my back as she tried to pull me closer to her.

CHAPTER FIFTY-ONE

Lily

"I MISSED YOU SO MUCH, BABY," his words whispered against my lips.

He leaned his forehead against mine; his eyes were filled with love. All the lies, the insecurities, the walls I created to stop myself from loving him came tumbling down. I should have never left. I should have never parted from this man. My soul felt whole when he was in my life, so much so, my heart could burst, and I didn't want him to ever doubt himself again.

"I love you so much." I tilted my chin up so he could see into my eyes clearly as I let everything I wanted to say, everything I should have said ages ago, escape the small box I had kept the words hidden in to protect myself, to keep myself from shattering. "I ran. I was scared. I couldn't let your daughter grow up in a one-parent household, and I thought I was a distraction from you getting to be with Molly... and with Emma."

"A distraction?" Todd frowned.

"I saw you with Emma and Molly, and you looked so right together. Then Colby confirmed my fears when he told me to step back and let you make your choice. So I ran. I ran to give you your life. I ran from my feelings, and every day I was gone, a part of me died. So, I made myself feel nothing. But the love... the love I have for you never left. It gutted its way through my heart, and I wasn't sure I was going to be able to survive it much longer."

Todd brought his lips to my cheek and kissed away the salty liquid. "You're so fucking stubborn." He gave me a boyish grin. "Lily, you can't make my choices for me. Being without you these past three months was... it was a living hell. All I ever wanted was to be someone's somebody, and when you left, I thought it was happening again. I thought I was being discarded. But then I realized I let you go, I didn't fight to show you that you were wrong, and I'm so fucking sorry. But—"

"Don't, this isn't—"

"Let me finish?" I bit my lip and let him continue. "But I don't want to be with just anyone. I tried to feel for Emma — she told me she cared about me, but she wasn't you. I love you, Lily. You are where I begin and end."

His words encompassed me in a slow embrace. I let my mouth connect with his again, his lips demanding that I let him in, and I complied. The peppermint flavor of his tongue mixed with his familiar scent brought me where I'd longed to be. The kiss became intense; his hands grasped at my backside lifting me up slightly. He broke from my mouth and took a deep breath. "Come home with me, Lily." The brown of his eyes darkened with desire. "You belong with me... you belong on a stage, not in a classroom. Come home with me, baby."

Everything about what he said was true. Music was my life, and Todd was my heart.

My lips brushed along the spot just below his ear as I whispered, "Yes."

"Yeah?" he pulled away just enough to search my face. His face split into a brilliant smile, his dimple showed proudly as he soaked in the word.

I nodded and said it again. "Yes."

"Hell yeah." He smacked me on the butt, and I jumped.

"You're ridiculous." My grin was wide as I bit my lip in order not to laugh.

"Yeah, but you fucking love it." He took my hand in his our fingers laced together.

I did. There were so many things in my life that had gone wrong, so many obstacles I had to face, but loving him was never one of them. The love I had for him tried so many times to break through to me, but I had shoved it down and attempted to hide from it. Not anymore, I wasn't going to deny myself the look Todd was giving me right now. I was no longer going to deny his touch and how it brought me home, the chance to watch him be a father, or the love we both shared for each other. This man had taken root, and I couldn't wait to be overtaken by everything that we could be… together.

"Stay with me tonight? We can figure out everything else tomorrow. I don't want to be without you tonight." The cocky grin Todd wore had fallen — the mask gone — leaving him exposed.

"I don't want to be without you again, either." I squeezed his hand in mine.

"Let's get out of here then."

CHAPTER FIFTY-TWO

Todd

LILY MOANED AS MY LIPS PULLED at the sensitive flesh, her hips bucked and I grasped them to keep her still. She swore and gripped my hair in her hands. "Please, Todd..." I increased the pressure, and her entire body started to quake. I smiled against her as she came intensely. I let her breathing slow and watched as she licked her lips, her cheeks were pink, and her skin glistened. She looked at me with hooded eyes, the blue flecks burst with need.

We had been lost inside each other for the past twelve hours. It was our way, and I didn't hesitate to take her again, to fill her with all I had. I let myself slide gradually into her again, taking pleasure in each inch of her body. She pulled me deeper still — every movement, every second, every fucking breath this woman gave me, she let me possess her, love her, take every little bit, and mark it as mine. Lily arched her back allowing my hands to guide her body, letting me work myself into her. My hips rocked faster as I climbed higher to the edge. Lily began to constrict around me, and my muscles strained as I released, my control gone. My body collapsed, and I fell to her side, my head rested on her breast, her tropical smell that I missed so much was stronger from the heat that our bodies had created.

"I love you so much." I could hear the smile in her voice as she spoke; her fingers ran through my hair causing me to shudder.

I pulled up onto my forearm so I could see Lily's face. My index finger trailed down the slope of her nose, down her chin, and between her breasts. I watched in awe as her flesh puckered in goose bumps behind the finger. My hand stopped at her belly and rested against the soft skin. "You were made for me. Nobody, baby, nobody owns me like you do. You've given me everything tonight. You let me take back what I'd lost. In you, Lily… inside you is where I reside, don't ever forget that."

A tear trickled down her cheek. She bit her plump bottom lip before she blew out a breath. "You're my king, Todd. You rule this heart more than you'll ever know." Her bright eyes locked with mine as I brought my mouth to hers. Lily had given me her loyalty and her love. The two things I thought I would never have. I wasn't sure where we went from here, but I knew in each other we could find the way. Our love could heal us slowly and make us feel valuable again. We belonged to each other — Lily was my one true thing, and I was hers.

EPILOGUE

Todd

Two months later

SAILOR AND MOLLY WIGGLED THEIR TINY bodies to the music. Lily's laughter interrupted her singing as she brought her hand up to her mouth to hide her smile.

"Keep going. This is so cute," Cam called out to me as I strummed the chords to *"If You're Happy And You Know It"*.

Lily continued to sing through her giggles. Her laughter was like a damn lightning bolt to my chest. She made me so happy. We were down in Elizabeth and Sawyer's basement playing with the kids until dinner was ready. Today was going to be special — to everyone else this was just another Sunday dinner at the Bryant's, but I knew what was coming.

Molly clapped her hands as the song finished. Just as I put the guitar down, she ran over to me and jumped into my arms. "Hey, baby girl, was that fun?" She was out of breath, and her cheeks were flushed. I gave her a quick peck on the nose.

"Dat was, Daddy." She rubbed her palms across my beard like she always did; her nose crinkled, and she giggled.

"I think it's growing on her, baby." Lily lifted up on her toes and kissed me on the lips lingering long enough to get my heart racing.

Molly put her arms out for Lily just as Elizabeth called downstairs for dinner. "Here, honey, let me take her." Molly easily slid into Lily's arms. Cam grabbed Sailor, and we all headed upstairs.

Cam handed Sailor to Lizzie, and the girls moved in front of me toward the kitchen. My anxiety rose as my brother fell behind with a questioning look.

"You ready?" Colby asked, his brow dipped as he looked at me with uneasy eyes.

"No, but this is how we planned it, right." I stared at him warily.

"You boys coming to dinner, or are you having girl talk." Seth's snarky laugh was irritating.

"Don't be a dick. You know today is the big day." Colby shoved Seth in the shoulder.

Seth just laughed again and headed into the kitchen. I took a deep breath. "Go ahead. I'll be in in a second." I gave my brother a tight smile.

"Don't be freaked, this is a good thing." He patted me on the shoulder and left me alone to gather my thoughts.

I heard the laughter spill from the kitchen. My friends, my family, the girl I loved, my Molly, we were all about to see another change, another move forward, and I was so overwhelmed with expectation for all that could be. I inhaled deeply and shook my head warding off the last bit of worry. Strong hands clasped my shoulders from behind.

"You headed in, brother?" Sawyer's low voice startled me.

"Yeah, let's eat, man."

We were halfway finished with dinner when Colby gave me a pointed look. I gave him a small nod, letting him know I was ready. Colby stood and cleared his throat nervously while everyone in the room fell silent.

"I'd like to say something if that's okay?" Colby looked over at Sawyer, who nodded for him to continue. Sawyer's lips twitched, suppressing a smile. He was too perceptive. "Cammie, we've been through so much together these past few years. We fight with passion, but we love with just as much fire." Cam's eyes started to shine with unshed tears. Lily reached over and squeezed my hand as she bounced Molly on her knee. "After watching Todd go after what he wanted, watching him and Lily take back what was theirs, it got me thinking. Babe, I don't ever want to fight with another person." The room erupted in soft laughter. Cam bit her cheek, and my smile grew. My baby brother deserved so much, and Cam was like a sister to me, only now it would finally be official. Colby looked at me giving me my cue. "Cammie, will you do me the honor of becoming my sister… finally." She laughed, but her laughter was cut short when Colby kneeled down on both knees. He whispered in her ear, and she blushed.

"Marry me, baby? Make an honest man out of me. Be mine for all time?" He reached into his pocket and pulled out the ring I'd helped him purchase last week. It was a modest ring, but Cam would love it. She wasn't flashy, and, by how her eyes widened, I think we did well.

"Of course, I will." Colby stood and scooped his fiancée into his arms, and I couldn't be prouder of my little brother than I was now. He was taking what was his and deserved nothing less.

Everyone took their turn congratulating the happy couple before they left. Colby and Cam ducked out early to celebrate their engagement. I was cleaning up the last of the dinner dishes when Seth came into the kitchen. "I'm going head, man. See you and Lily later?"

"We've gotta drop Molly off, then we'll be heading home. You going to your dad's?"

He let his gaze fall to his feet. "No, he's gone on business. I'm going over to see Tiff. I told her I'd maybe let her give me some new ink. Let her practice. She was offered a job at that new tattoo shop, *Magnolia's*."

"Tiff?" Seth didn't have friends that were women. Lily and Liz were as close as it came, and they were off limits sexually speaking. But Tiffany, she was single, and, as far as Seth was concerned, probably fresh meat. "No way, don't shit where I eat, man."

Seth raised his chin and locked his steel blue eyes on mine. His posture tensed. "Go to hell. I'd never fuck, Tiffany."

I gave him a disbelieving look. "No?"

He gave me a sideways smirk. "She's not my type." Anything with tits and two legs was Seth's type. "Just helping out a friend, Todd, remember... I'm very helpful." He smacked my shoulder and smiled widely.

"Yeah, yeah, just don't—"

"Trust me, I won't... see ya later." He turned to leave and almost ran into Lily. "Hey, Hellcat, keep an eye on that one. He's a nosey bastard."

"Um, okay." She giggled and gave me a questioning look. I shrugged my shoulders. "He's so weird, but I kind of love him."

I wiped my hands on the dishtowel as Lily snaked her arms around my waist. "Oh yeah, why's that? Should I be jealous?" My lips gently kissed the top of her head.

"He snapped you out of it and gave you that final shove out the door. Without him, we might not have ever had our chance." She looked up at me with sentiment. She was partially right.

"Seth did give me a swift kick in the ass, but I would have eventually done what was right. I'm telling you, Lily, I was dying a slow, cold death without you." I gave her a self-assured grin.

She swatted at my chest. "I'm serious."

"So am I." I let my hands fall to her ass, and I pulled her firmly against me. "You and I apart, it doesn't make any sense.

We would've found each other again, because this…" I placed my lips to hers. "…and this…" I moved my hand to her face. "…This is all I ever wanted, and it was only a matter of time before I figured that out on my own." She lifted up on her toes and kissed me with sincere lips.

There wasn't a doubt in my mind that she would one day be my wife, that we would one day make a child of our own, give Molly a little brother or sister. I could see our path lined out before us, and I was ready… ready for her… ready for us.

ABOUT THE AUTHOR

AMANDA MARIE JOHNSON was born and raised in Valrico, Florida. She's now surrounded by mountains with her husband and three children in Ogden, Utah. She attended Weber State University and graduated with her A.S.N. She is a full-time registered nurse.

Reading and writing have always been something she is passionate about. She loves to write about the human experience, love, and happily-ever-afters.

ACKNOWLEDGEMENTS

THANK YOU SO MUCH FOR READING this little story. Todd and Lily are so close to my heart. I wanted this story to feel real, and, like Still Life, I infused a large portion of who I am within these characters. I hope as you read you find a little piece of you as well.

I'd like to thank my miraculous husband. Evan, *you're my king and you rule this heart more than you'll ever know.* Thank you for the late nights, the sleep-ins, and keeping our children fed and mostly clean. I'm nothing without you.

To my munchkins. Griffin, Meghan, and Kellen, you guys are my light and love. Thank you for being just down right awesome.

To my Instagram AJ's Crew... I can't even find words to explain how blessed I am to have you in my life. Thank you for constantly talking me down off that ledge, for your immense support, for loving these men like they were your own. For making edits like crazy and overall just being rock star females in general. #cyclesisters4Life @bookobsessedgirl (Anna) @book_ish_life(Lisa) @sucker_for_books (Jellie) @mg_herrera (Maria) @midnightowl80 (Narine)

@btus_biggest_fann (Lacey) @73jem (Jo) and @mt.reads (Michelle). Only ever you gals... only ever you.

To my beta team...You ladies are more than just readers... you're my life line! Cynthia A. Rodriguez, Beth LeMilliere, Maria Macdonald, Anna Alonso, KE Osborn, Giovanna Cruz, Sarah Symonds, Lisa Wilson, Michelle Trzecinski, Heather Bennett and Sasha Safdiah you ladies are my world. You make and break me each day. Your support and pure love for reading make you the best beta team a girl can have. You guys are my friends, but aren't afraid to tell me "Hey, this is shit." Yes... you have made me cry... but that's your job, keeping it real, and I love every one of you for it.

Maria and Beth, you guys are my British soul sisters. Cynthia, I am so damn lucky you gave me that review, and we became friends. I aspire to be a writer as glorious as you. Anna, I love that you and I are basically the same person; you get me. You are such a good friend, and I am honored to know you. Michelle, thanks for always being there for me. It means the world. Your loyalty and love are felt deeply! Sasha, you know all my dirty secrets... and I love it! I can't imagine not knowing you; my life would be lacking color that's for sure. Lisa, you are such a good friend and such a blessing, and I'm never going to be able to not use emoji's from this point forward because of you. May Gandy be with you. Kim, thank you for keeping me on point, and I can only hope to accomplish as much as you have. You're a rock star, never forget that. Sarah, get in the damn cave. I'm grateful every day that you took a chance on me. Giovanna... thank you for passionately loving my guys. You are the female version of Todd, and one day I will big squish hug you. Heather, I know betas are supposed to be readers and not cheerleaders, but who cares, you are the captain girl!

Tiffany Ly, my first love. Thank you for giving me the world.

To all my Instagram family, I wish I could name you all.

Thank you for your endless support; reposts, edits videos — just loving my stories and giving me a chance. I will always try to personally thank you for all you do for me. You guys are the best!

Thank you to all of family and friends for putting up with my incessant phone use, my lack of real world dialogue in general, and for supporting me no matter what. Morgan Karpus, you especially had my back during Still Water. Thank you for your feedback and weekly dates.

Kathleen Payne… You seriously have made me a better author, and I can't find enough words to express how truly thankful I am for you, for our friendship. Besides… I'd use too many commas, and you told me to keep this shit short.

Amy Senethavilay, thank you for keeping my characters true and genuine, for seeing my vision so clearly, and for making my story better. Thank you so much for your gentle hand and "red ink." I'm better for it…

Kaylene Osborn, thank you for being a real friend and keeping me sane. You are like a second mother to me, and I love ya chick.

Emma Mack, you are my glitter goddess. I can't wait for you to be on American soil.

Martha Cothron aka Diva Does 4 Good you are my life coach.

HUGE thank you to Nathan Van Dyken and everyone at Blue Tulip.

Last but not least… Tracey-Lee, this book is dedicated to you. You're my shining light, girl. You're with me every night in the cave; you feel these characters like I do, and I'm a better writer for it. Oz better be prepared for the tears I will shed when I see your lovely face for reals. You're beyond incredible.

Okay, I was told to keep this short….
THANK YOU
You know if you're in my life that I am grateful for you.

Still Surviving
PROLOGUE

Seth

THE COLD SEEPED THROUGH MY BONES, the street light was brightly shining through the sheets of rain. The tears, I couldn't handle them anymore. This life was full of shit, full of disgusting promises, promises I couldn't keep. She looked up at me with bright hazel doe eyes, her shiny black hair, now soaked lay limp against her cheeks and shoulders, her dark green shirt clung to her breasts, fuck she was beautiful, she was everything and I was…nothing…I was darkness…sickness…I couldn't corrupt her like the others. She was too good for my brand of love, my black heart. I watched the chill creep into her flesh, the goose bumps splayed across her arm as the heat left her body. We were so close. I should reach out and warm her, comfort her, tell her what she wants to hear, but I'm her shadow and this can never be.

The deep pink of her lips paled as they trembled I couldn't watch her suffer much longer. The clear jade of her eyes became hazy as they filled with more tears, "Why?" She asked. The voice so familiar to me, the voice of fear, of rejection, of the never ending inevitability of failure.

She shivered and I couldn't let her dangle on that ledge any longer. The rain beat against my back as I rested my forehead against hers, my hands grasped at the back of her head, cradling her even closer, my heart was heavily beating inside my ribcage, my veins full of the poison of love, this fucking girl had infected me and I had to let her go. I was her shadow, meant to follow, always stalking behind, never truly there in the present, always a half a step behind, it was safe to admire from afar.

"I'm not who you think I am." My whisper sounded false to me. She knew me, better than anyone would ever know me, but this had to stop here, she'd never understand who I was deep down, my flame...my light blew out a long time ago.

"What the hell are you talking about?" She pulled away from me, forcing my hands to frame her face. The look she gave said it all, said I was crazy for ending this, for not letting it even start, for not letting her in. She didn't have the faintest idea of what I could do to her. My faith was broken.

I let my eyes meet hers letting the inevitable connection happen. I owed her that much.

The rain started to fall harder, but I didn't care, I was caught up in all that was her, for once I wanted something, I wanted this, and I wanted her. My eyes were drawn to her mouth, those wicked fucking lips were surely made to torture. I was ready for her punishment. I brought my lips slowly to hers, a small faint breath exhaled from her parted lips, the cool air keeping her sweet breath suspended. Just before our lips met, she sighed, I could almost taste her, but that small sound brought me to my senses. I pulled away and she started to cry harder.

"You fucking break me, and I can't...I can't do this with you...I need to go." My voice sounded foreign like I wasn't really controlling it, robotic, cold, this was who I was, this was all I knew.

ALSO FROM BLUE TULIP PUBLISHING

BY MEGAN BAILEY
There Are No Vampires in this Book

BY J.M. CHALKER
Bound

BY ELISE FABER
Phoenix Rising
Dark Phoenix
From Ashes

BY STEPHANIE FOURNET
Butterfly Ginger

BY JENNIFER RAE GRAVELY
Drown
Rivers

BY E.L. IRWIN
Out of the Blue

BY J.F. JENKINS
The Dark Hour

BY AM JOHNSON
Still Life
Still Water

BY KRISTEN LUCIANI
Nothing Ventured

BY KELLY MARTIN
Betraying Ever After

The Beast of Ravenston

BY NADINE MILLARD
An Unlikely Duchess
Seeking Scandal
The Mysterious Miss Channing

BY LINDA OAKS
Chasing Rainbows

BY C.C. RAVANERA
Dreamweavers

BY GINA SEVANI
Beautifully Damaged

BY ANGELA SCHROEDER
The Second Life of Magnolia Mae
Jade

BY K.S. SMITH & MEGAN C. SMITH
Hourglass
Hourglass Squared
Hourglass Cubed

BY MEGAN C. SMITH
Expired Regrets
Secret Regrets

BY CARRIE THOMAS
Hooked

BY RACHEL VAN DYKEN
Upon a Midnight Dream
Whispered Music

The Wolf's Pursuit
When Ash Falls
The Ugly Duckling Debutante
The Seduction of Sebastian St. James
An Unlikely Alliance
The Redemption of Lord Rawlings
The Devil Duke Takes a Bride
Savage Winter
Every Girl Does It
Divine Uprising

BY KRISTIN VAYDEN
To Refuse a Rake
Surviving Scotland
Living London
Redeeming the Deception of Grace
Knight of the Highlander
The Only Reason for the London Season
What the Duke Wants
To Tempt an Earl
The Forsaken Love of a Lord
A Tempting Ruin

BY JOE WALKER
Blood Bonds

BY KELLIE WALLACE
Her Sweetest Downfall

BY C. MERCEDES WILSON
Hawthorne Cole
Secret Dreamst

BY K.D. WOOD
Unwilling

Unloved

BOX SET — MULTIPLE AUTHORS
Forbidden
Hurt

www.bluetulippublishing.com

Made in the USA
Charleston, SC
04 April 2016